THE PSION OF DARKNESS

THE STARSEA CYCLE BOOK SEVEN

KYLE WEST

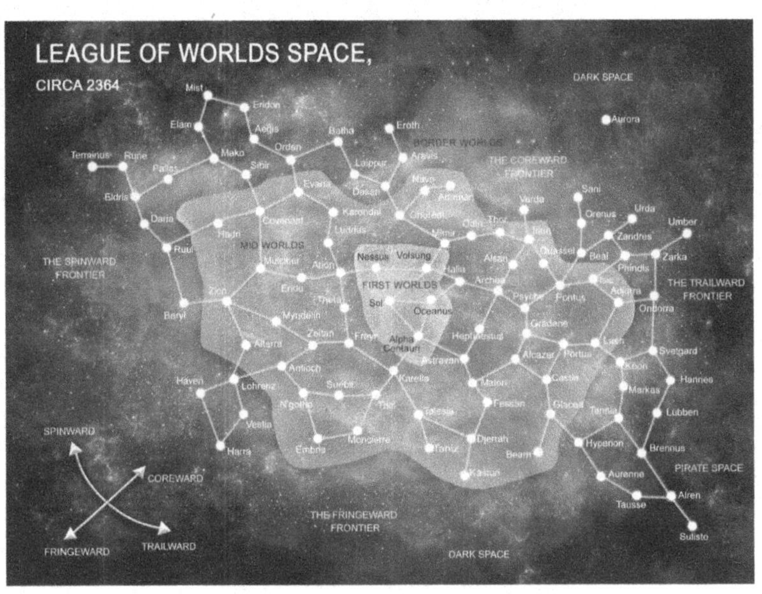

LEAGUE OF WORLDS SPACE,
CIRCA 2364
DARK SPACE
Aurora
Mist
Eridon
Elam
Aegis
Batha
Eroth
BORDER WORLDS
Terminus
Rune
Orden
Arsis
THE COREWARD
FRONTIER
Pallas
Mako
Sibir
Laippur
Sani
Eldris
Evaria
Dasan
Niavo
Varda
Orenus
Urda
Daria
Covenant
Kacondal
Astennar
Umber
Hajn
Ludrus
Ghotall
Zandres
Ruul
MID WORLDS
Dalls
Thor
Zarka
Mulciber
Ation
Nimir
Isin
Phindis
Beal
Nessus
Volsung
Quassel
Eridu
Italia
THE TRAILWARD
FRONTIER
Zion
FIRST WORLDS
Alcan
Adiarra
Theia
Archias
Ondorra
Baryl
Sol
Oceanus
Psyche
Pontus
Myndelin
Gradene
Zeltan
Freyn
Alpha
Centauri
Heph.aestus
Loch
Altarra
Astravan
Alcazar
Porttia
Svetgard
Haven
Amloch
Karella
Okeon
Hannes
Lohrenz
Sumbit
Maioris
Castra
Markas
N'golho
Thir
Fessan
Glaceil
Tannia
Lubben
Vestia
Talassa
Djerrah
Hyperion
Brennus
Harra
Embria
Mongetre
Taniz
Beam
PIRATE SPACE
Aurenne
Airen
Kastun
Tausse
THE FRINGEWARD
FRONTIER
Sulisto
DARK SPACE
SPINWARD
COREWARD
FRINGEWARD
TRAILWARD
THE SPINWARD
FRONTIER

LUCIAN WALKED between the high sandstone columns toward the light in the distance. A hot, dry wind swirled from the opening, carrying with it layers of dust that hadn't been disturbed in decades, if not centuries or longer. From beyond that exit, Lucian heard the low, muffled drone of a thousand or more voices. Wherever the space-time portal had taken them, it was somewhere with many people.

He pulled to a stop about twenty paces from the exit. "Be ready. For anything."

Serah stopped next to him. "As long as we don't have another lava basilisk to deal with, I can deal."

"A lava basilisk is *highly* unlikely," Fergus said.

Serah sighed. "Why must you take everything I say *so* literally?"

Fergus remained silent as the group looked out the temple's open archway leading outside. The bright light was material- izing into dusty mountains in the distance, along with a few red-stoned towers. There was little else Lucian could see, at least from where he stood. It was a city in the desert. The only desert city Lucian knew was Kalm in the desert of Psyche. They couldn't be there, though, because the odds of *two* Orbs being on the same world were insurmountable. Besides, those mountains in the distance were far too low to be the Mountains of Madness.

There was only one conclusion that made sense: they were on an entirely new world, a world that had seen colonization by humanity.

Mira stepped up beside him. "Son, we don't have to go out there. Couldn't you just . . . do that warping thing of yours to get us out of here? No sense risking ourselves over nothing. We got what we came for."

His mother did have a point, but any time he had felt for the Orb of Dynamism, he had sensed it spinward across the Worlds. There was no telling just how *far* spinward, but their next goal, Mako, was in the Spinward Border Worlds. If they were lucky, they might not have far to travel at all.

"Let's see where we are first. If we're trying to go to Mako, this planet might be closer than anywhere I know. If it's dangerous, I can always create a portal to get us out of here."

Mira didn't seem convinced. "I guess."

"Breathable atmosphere," Fergus said, taking a deep whiff for good measure. "Would've killed us by now if it wasn't." He coughed from the dust.

"You sound like *you're* about to die," Serah said.

"Normal gravity, too," he went on, ignoring Serah. "Those two things alone don't narrow it down much."

Serah opened her slate. "Hey, we can settle this right here, right now. The GalNet will tell us *exactly* where we are!"

"Make sure it's receiving only," Fergus said. "We don't want to broadcast our position."

"I'm not an idiot. Besides, I have privacy software installed."

"That's not a guarantee."

Her eyes narrowed on the screen. "Huh. I can't even *connect* to the GalNet here. Does that narrow it more? You know things, Fergus."

"Somewhere remote. That's all I can say. But from the sound of that crowd, it certainly doesn't *sound* remote . . ."

Lucian was already stepping toward the wide-open threshold. There was no point in conjecturing when they could figure things out by just walking outside. He was utterly confident in himself, knowing full well that nothing out there could hurt him. He held six Orbs now. Even with that, he had to remind himself to be careful. All it took was one bullet, one moment of carelessness, to lose it all.

"Just stand by me," he said. "I can get us out of here easily enough. If it comes to that."

No one protested as he passed the threshold. Nothing could have prepared him for what he saw.

He stood at the top of a stairway carved from the side of a red mountain, with a crowd of thousands cheering below. Beyond those crowds rose a golden city, filled with towers, bridges, temples, and minarets, situated in a valley surrounded by gilded mountains shining under the light of the hot, desert sun. A few spaceships hovered in the sky, all facing him as if to do him homage. It was as if he was a hero or something.

Such a reception was the last thing he expected, and made absolutely no sense. How had they known he'd come out like this? And why were they cheering him?

The others stood beside him, taking in the sight as the wind swept at their mages' cloaks. Lucian grasped his Focus to steady his nerves. He was just now noticing the dozens of priests surrounding them, all old men with long beards and robes of varying colors. Before he knew what was happening, they were approaching with bowls of fragrant oil, perhaps myrrh, judging by the woody scent tinging the air. Before Lucian could protest, they were flicking his face with the stuff while murmuring sacraments in low voices.

"Hey," he said, wiping his face. "Cut it out!"

Thankfully, the oil didn't seem to be harmful. The strange ritual was over after a few seconds, after which the priests took up their former positions at the top of the stairs, leaving Lucian more confused than ever.

One priest, however, remained behind. He was an elderly man with a ring of gray hair, who wore immaculate white robes that reflected the light of the sun above. He beamed a wide smile, as if Lucian were a long-lost son. Lucian was just about to ask him what the rotting hell was going on when the man raised his leathery arms, as if in benediction.

"Praise be to the One! The Sealed Doors of the Temple of Light have opened. In accordance with prophecy, the Last Messiah has come!"

The man's jowls were aquiver with zeal. All Lucian could do was to blink in surprise. "Last Messiah?"

"Yes," the old priest said, with great enthusiasm. "You are the fulfillment of our prayers. You have come, just as the High Prophet said you would! The Sealed Doors have opened, and the Temple of Light has gone dark."

Lucian looked at the crowds. As if in answer to his doubts, the crowd roared its approval.

"I don't understand. I'm supposed to be this . . . Last Messiah?"

"Yes," the priest said. "As foretold by the High Prophet Sharo Khalin: *When the Sealed Doors of the Temple of Light open, the Last Messiah will come and he will be a sign of the One's Favor. When the Temple of Light goes dark, the Last Messiah will lead the One's Crusade against the darkness. For only with the Miracle, the Last Messiah will save the One's Chosen.*" The priest blinked with great emotion. "For more than five standard decades, we have waited for the fulfillment of these sacred words. From the founding days of Holy Zion, the High Prophet said they would come true during his lifetime. Never did he waver! Never was he shaken. Many doubted, but now, he is vindicated! The One is vindicated. Last Messiah, be welcome to Holy Zion! The Priests of the One, along with the Holy City and the High Prophet himself, stand ready to serve!"

At this, the elderly man gave a regal bow, and following his example, so did the dozens of other priests, their colored robes flowing in the desert wind. Following their masters' example, a great many people in the city below did likewise, though most only cheered louder.

Lucian immediately saw that it would be impossible to clear up the misconception. During the priest's long rambling, he revealed a key piece of information. They were on Zion, the seat of power of the Oneist Faith. More commonly, they were known as Believers. Their High Prophet, Sharo Khalin, was a force feared in the Worlds as much as the Pirate Empress Zheng Yang.

There was no way Lucian could tell the truth about what he was. The Oneists of Zion hated the mages, blaming them for most, if not all, of the Worlds' ills.

That left him no choice but to pretend he *was* this Last Messiah, at least until he learned more. And who knew? If the High Prophet had predicted his coming, maybe there *was* something to this prophecy. All Lucian cared about was finding a spaceship fast enough to get them to Mako in a reasonable amount of time. He didn't know how many Gates it was from Zion, but it was certainly closer than from Volsung.

"Your devotion is . . . noted," Lucian said to the priest. "Just one question. How do you know *I'm* the Last Messiah and not one of my friends here?"

The man frowned, seeming to be unsure. "Well, you *were* the first to step out. Are you saying that you *aren't* the Last Messiah?"

"No, I am. I was only curious." Before the priest could say anything more, Lucian pressed on. "This High Prophet. Where is he, exactly?"

"You will meet him soon. As good as his word, the veil of light surrounding the temple has dissipated. Upon recognizing this holy sign, everyone in the city gathered to witness the fulfillment of Sharo Khalin's prophecy. Knowing the High Prophet's words to be true, the One's Priests prepared the procession that will take you to him. He is in the Grand Cathedral of Holy Zion."

"You mentioned a *veil of light*?"

The man frowned, as if Lucian shouldn't be ignorant of this sign. "Why, the veil of light! Ever since the early days of Zion, a great column of radiance rose from the peak of Mount Zion, right there behind you. Upon the extinguishing of that light, the Sealed Doors opened. As uttered by the mouth of Sharo Khalin himself, it is the sign of the Last Messiah. The sign of the Last Days. We have prepared everything for the Crusade. You have come armed with the Gift, more powerfully than any prophet of the One Faith before."

Rather than ask more questions, Lucian risked a small Psionic-Binding dualstream to parse the man's thoughts. Combined with the man's information, he quickly pieced things together. He was not only a savior, but he was *supposed* to have magical powers. That was what this priest meant by "the Gift." This confused Lucian, because to the Believers, there was no enemy greater than a mage. But, he also learned that there were some among the One's Priesthood who had access to magic. They just called it "the Gift." Lucian learned all this, and more, during the short duration of the stream. He didn't understand how it fit into their theology, whether they hid it from their followers, or what they even did about frayed priests. Perhaps all those questions would be answered later.

What Lucian *was* sure of was that this *veil of light* was connected with his acquisition of the Orb of Dynamism. Securing the Orb must have caused the veil to disappear. This veil was similar to the auras that had surrounded the other oracles, veils created by the magic of the Orb itself. The veils protected the Orbs against incursions and the ravages of time. Each time Lucian had secured an Orb, the magic protecting the oracle vanished. He was sure it was no different here. The temple behind him, along with the mountain that held it, must have been a remarkable sight up until a few hours ago.

But there was still the question of how Sharo Khalin had predicted Lucian's arrival in the first place. Of course, only one answer made sense. Despite the High Prophet's vitriol against mages, it was probable he was one himself. With the Aspect of Psionics, he could have prophesied Lucian's arrival, although a prophecy of such accuracy would mean Khalin was a *powerful* mage.

Of course, Lucian could never learn for sure unless he met him, which wasn't something he exactly wanted to do.

He opened a Psionic link to Fergus. *What do you think? Should we just get out of here?*

Well, I would think twice about that. Zion is just four Gates from Mako. Volsung is seven. A journey from Volsung would take twice as long. We won't get any closer than this. These people are deferring to you. Maybe getting a ship wouldn't be too difficult. Seems it's the least they can do for their Messiah.

Lucian understood his meaning. He turned back to the

priest. "The High Prophet is in this Great Cathedral, right?"

The priest smiled pleasantly. "Yes. Come. All has been prepared. You, of course, will lead the procession, along with your retainers. The High Prophet awaits at the end."

"I'm no retainer," Mira said. "I'm his *mother*."

The priest seemed surprised at this, as if someone as holy as the Last Messiah couldn't have a parent. To his mind, Lucian might have sprung from the Ether itself.

"So, what do you mean by *procession*?" Serah asked. "Is that a parade or something? Will there be fireworks? Music? Dancers?"

Only Lucian was worthy of a response from the priest, something that miffed Serah from the way she aggressively blew a strand of hair out of her eye.

Lucian opened a link to her. *Sorry. I have to play the part.*

Of course, your Holiness. Just don't expect me to lick your boots.

Seems they wear sandals around here.

Nothing good ever came of sandals.

Is that a Psyche proverb or something?

It's a Serah proverb. Look alive, Chosen. Or else all of us are dead.

Already, the priests were leading Lucian down the stairs, and the others had no choice but to follow.

2

THE AIR WAS hot and dry, the sun burning the back of Lucian's neck. After everything that had happened, he was simply tired. The truth was, he was still reeling from his battle with that strange Shadow. He didn't know how to make sense of it.

But he had to set that aside to face Sharo Khalin of the Oneist Faith, and maybe even wrest a spaceship from him. The sooner they were off this desert hunk of rock, the better.

He was only half-present as he took his place on the automated, open-air carriage at the bottom of the steps. It was just large enough to carry him and his companions. As soon as they boarded, it slowly rolled away from the steps of the Temple of Light to the roar of the crowds. An energy shield powered on with a hum, which would be powerful enough to deflect all but the heaviest forms of weaponry.

As they rolled down the broad promenade, lined with date palms and overshadowed by tall, stone buildings, the crowds jostled, waved, and cheered, held back only by a line of crimson-robed priests bearing battery-powered shockspears and shield packs. From their lean strength, stoic expressions, and uniformly bald heads, Lucian supposed them to be some sort of soldier class. Maybe even warrior monks.

In the street's shade, it was cooler, but Lucian held his Focus, ready to stream in case this was an elaborate trap. Trumpets blasted and drums beat while streamers and white rose petals spiraled from above. Some of the buds even settled on Lucian's shoulders and head. Lucian wondered how they had slipped past the energy shield, until he remembered that an energy shield only triggered when an object struck it quickly enough.

Looking behind, there were more carriages. The first few carried the white-robed priests that had received them, while the next carriages contained priests of an assortment of colors: green, blue, and yellow seemed to be the most prominent. Behind them marched even more of the crimson-robed warriors, all bearing shockspears. There were even large, lumbering beasts, with stony skin and long snouts that looked like a compressed version of an elephant.

Lucian leaned over to Fergus, who stood on his right, figuring he would know more about the Oneists than anyone else. "Do you know anything about this prophecy?"

Fergus's face remained stoic as he shook his head. "I don't know much about the Believers' ways, outside the basics. For the last fifty years, they've established themselves on Zion. From here, they've formed a sort of base, taking root and spreading their religion to the wider Worlds. They've had some success at it, from what I gather. Their beliefs are mostly an amalgamation of the old Abrahamic faiths, which fell into obscurity following the Climate Wars of the late 21st century. Same God, just a simpler system of precepts that can appeal to a larger swath of people." He looked around at the surrounding buildings and crowds. "Their god is called *the One*. You can think of it as meaning *the one and only*. And this place can be none other than the City of Zion, capital of the planet of the same name."

"I figured that much. I realize we're closer to Mako here than anywhere else, but I don't like it. There was this Believer I met on the way to Volsung. She let me know exactly how the Believers feel about mages. This is probably the most dangerous place in the Worlds for us to be."

"So, no streaming?" Serah asked from his left side.

"Not until we find a working ship. I also read the thoughts of that white-robed priest. Some of these Oneists can stream. It's a part of their religion somehow, like a secret society. We should be on guard."

"Seriously?" Mira asked. "They're the ones who persecute mages the most!"

Thankfully, the environment was so loud that there was no possibility of them being overheard. If there had been any electronics on board capable of listening to them, Fergus would have alerted Lucian immediately.

"Never expect most religions to make any sense," Fergus said.

"Shucks," Serah said. "Well, hopefully, they don't notice my skin. This cloak is good at covering me up." She nodded toward the streets. "And it looks like I'm in good company."

Lucian saw what she meant. Most of the women were covered from head to toe in dark, plain clothing, leaving only their faces and hands bare. Only Serah's hands had obvious coloration. Whatever the case, Lucian wasn't concerned about it. If anyone gave her grief about it, they'd be hearing from him.

Lucian was relieved when they entered the last stretch, an avenue that ended in a long, wide stairway of red stone, rising toward a massive cathedral in the neo-Gothic style. The edifice had lofty, rectangular towers that reached for the bright blue sky, each of them ringing victoriously with bells. The thick crowds ended at the base of the stairs, and a line of white-robed priests, as well as crimson-robed warrior monks bearing shockspears, lined the ascent. At the top stood a single man in resplendent white robes. He almost seemed to glow to Lucian, though that might have been the effect of the bright sun shining from above.

The carriage rolled to a stop, its side door opening. The crowd thundered as Lucian stepped off and took to the stairs followed by the others. The crimson-robed warriors, each with battle-hardened faces, did not break their concentration as Lucian went up. Lucian climbed quickly to reach the High Prophet, who surveyed them like an eagle eying his domain.

When Lucian reached the summit, a dry breeze blew, surprisingly cool from the mountains. The High Prophet stood alone on the great porch before the Great Cathedral. He was of short stature, with a bald head and heavily wrinkled skin, and dark brown eyes that seemed to peer deeply into his own. That gaze might have shaken him once, but Lucian had come far, and had no trouble meeting the man's eyes.

If Lucian remembered his history lessons, the High Prophet of the Oneist Faith had come to power shortly after the Mage War, when the hatred of mages had burned at its hottest. Sharo Khalin had been stoking that fire for over five decades, and it was under his leadership that the Believers had turned into such a powerful political bloc. And now, they were independent of the League, and willing to fight for their autonomy. And with the Swarmers invading from the Trailward Stars, there was absolutely nothing the League could do about the High Prophet's bid for power.

Looking at him face to face, Lucian was certain Sharo Khalin was not only a mage, but a formidable one. There was an undeniable aura of ethereal power about him, of the kind

Lucian had only felt around Transcend White, Ansaldra, Vera, and even Xara Mallis. That in itself was quite surprising. Learning that he was a mage was one thing, but one of unusual strength? Lucian would have to tread carefully.

He had to remember he could always get everyone out of here with a quick Space-Time stream. Even if Lucian were technically more powerful than Khalin, the High Prophet was no doubt crafty. More than that, he certainly recognized what Lucian was, too, along with his friends. Should it please him, he could turn every person on this world against them, Last Messiah or not.

But that question seemed to be far from Sharo Khalin's mind. He gave a mysterious smile before turning to the crowds and raising his hands on high. The people roared as one, the sound pummeling Lucian despite the wide-open space. Lucian looked down at the sea of humanity, half-obscured by the dust the parade had kicked up. There had to be *thousands* down there. Perhaps even *tens* of thousands.

"Let us walk away from these masses, brother," Sharo Khalin intoned, as if giving a sermon. "The One knows we have much to discuss."

Lucian saw that he would have to fake things, at least for now. "Nothing would please me more, High Prophet."

The High Prophet inclined his head, leading Lucian toward the doors of the Great Cathedral. A few of the crimson-robed warrior monks fell in behind. Lucian knew he should have felt nervous about following the High Prophet into an unfamiliar place. For all he knew, he was being led into a trap. But for now, however, he needed to learn more.

The coolness of the vast cathedral brought relief from the hot sun, and the dampness of the air reminded him of the caves of Psyche. As the heavy stone doors closed, the din of the crowd was completely shut out.

"Come, let us pray at the altar," the High Prophet said. "The One has been most providential to deliver the Last Messiah at our hour of need."

Lucian had questions, but he decided it was best to play along for now. "Of course. Anything to further the One's Light."

The High Prophet gave a toothless smile. "Your piety is . . . *noted*, Messiah. You are the Light that was promised. The one who opened the Sealed Doors, in accordance with prophecy. The Time of Judgement is at hand."

"Of course," Lucian said, easily. "The One judges all, but those who walk the path of innocence have nothing to fear."

Lucian didn't know why he'd said that, but he also knew it was from the One Book, the scripture on which the entire Oneist religion was based. He'd never read the One Book in his life, and yet he'd recited it as if he knew it front and back. Even the High Prophet blinked in surprise at the quotation.

Lucian realized where the thought had come from. He had unwittingly used the Orb of Psionics to read Sharo Khalin's mind, who had been thinking the same thing. He immediately severed the connection. Hopefully, the High Prophet wouldn't be any the wiser about the slipup.

"Uncanny," Khalin said. "I was thinking the very same thing. For you to know my thoughts as your own is a sign of the One's providence. Verily, you are the one we seek."

By now, they had reached the altar. Lucian knelt, and Sharo Khalin quickly joined him. Lucian didn't bother closing his eyes, opting instead to watch the High Prophet. The holy man's eyes were closed as he prayed intently for fifteen or more minutes. Lucian held his Focus, the closest thing he knew to prayer. He was aware of the Orbs, and how easy it would be to parse the High Prophet's thoughts and get a better sense of things. He could mask what he was doing, be more careful this time.

However, the risk was not necessary, at least for the moment. There would be an opportunity for that later.

At last, the High Prophet stood, and Lucian with him.

"Of course," Khalin said, facing him fully and all but winking, "I know exactly who and what you are, Lucian Abrantes. Just this morning, your face was plastered all over the newsfeeds. Your bomber was last seen crashing on Chiron mere hours ago. And yet, you find yourself here. An impossibility."

"Through the One, all things are possible." Lucian was glad he had thought up that response, but from the High Prophet's unimpressed reaction, it probably sounded more brilliant in his head than in reality.

"Yes. It would seem so." Khalin cleared his throat and spoke gently. "Of course, you must know we Oneists are not against the use of magic, *per se*. Among the Prophets, those you see wearing the white robes, it is called the *One's Gift*. Or more simply, *the Gift*. We are against the use of the Gift by anyone who isn't a prophet. The Gift is the creative force of the universe, and it is the province of the One and his Prophets. When it is not used for the glory of the One, it becomes magic, a heathen perversion. We Prophets lead the Faith, and prophecy has dictated that you, too, are a Prophet, Lucian Abrantes. You have opened the Sealed Doors of the Temple of Light from within, and its glorious light was extinguished this very morning. What's more, is that I have heard whispers from the One himself, that you would come soon. Per his will, the Crusade must begin."

"You said the Prophets can use magic. I mean, the Gift. That means you can, too."

"Ah. But you already knew this, did you not?"

"I did. I was just seeing what you would say."

Sharo Khalin gave a cunning smile. "Yes, Lucian. I am first among the One's prophets. The One's Chosen."

The elder man outstretched his hands, and electricity danced between his fingers.

"So, do you just not use the Gift unless you are around other Prophets? Seems like the secret would leak at some point."

"What secret? We do not practice the Gift openly, but even if we did, those of the One Faith merely see it as the One's providence, a Gift entrusted to his most devout servants. Even the One Book, Lucian, speaks to this. I will admit that our most ignorant followers cannot discern the difference. Magery *is* an abomination, but when used in service to the One, under the precepts of the One Faith, the Gift only enhances the One's glory." He nodded back toward the entrance of the Great Cathedral. "And as for the Holy Warriors, those in the crimson robes, they have taken a vow of silence. They will not speak of it, as they can only talk to their sworn brothers and the Prophets above them."

Lucian looked at the Holy Warriors near the front of the cathedral. Indeed, not one of them had said a word in all the time he had been in here.

"We highly regard our Prophets, Lucian Abrantes, if you will allow me to use your given name. We do not use our Holy Gift unless the occasion calls for it, which is quite rare. All of us are well-trained in its use."

Lucian remembered Fergus's statement about religion and contradictions. "What happens if one of you frays?"

"A corrupted prophet is false, punished by the One for his faithlessness. You need not fear, Lucian. Our Prophets are examined regularly for signs of corruption."

He let the point slide. "Prophets and mages. The Gift and magic. Even you have to admit they are different names for the same thing."

"Never confuse the Prophets with the mages, Lucian. Mages

are of the Shadow. And it is only in recognizing the salvation from the One that a mage might become a prophet, a being of Light."

Lucian tried not to be put off balance by Khalin's use of the words "Shadow and Light." Was it his imagination, or was there a knowing and mischievous glint in the prophet's eyes? But the glimmer was gone as soon as Sharo Khalin looked at the front doors of the cathedral, where Lucian's friends stood surrounded by about twenty Holy Warriors. He realized just how exposed they were, especially his mother, who had no defense besides the sidearm on her belt.

"What about my friends? Would you consider them Prophets or mages?"

"Since they are with you, Lucian, they must certainly be Prophets . . . by default. The One's plans are mysterious, and knowledge of his ways is less important than purity of heart."

Lucian was glad he'd come to that conclusion. It would have been pretty inconvenient otherwise, though something told Lucian that the High Prophet would bend whatever rules necessary to get his way, religion or not. "You mentioned a Crusade. The priest said I was supposed to lead it. I didn't get the memo."

"We can go over the details at a later time. The Crusade will begin soon. Very soon. You have fulfilled the Prophecy of the Last Messiah. That is all that is necessary. As Prophets, our task is to hear the One's footsteps, and to fall in behind as he marches past. So many glorious things have been at work, for decades. The Crusaders have already gathered. The Sealed Doors have opened, the last signal the crusade will begin. We shall return to Earth as saviors, delivering it from the hands of the apostates and unbelievers. Already, your hand smote the wicked Hegemon of the League, sowing chaos. The One has given us these signs, and more, letting us know that *now* is the time for action and brave deeds. The terrible swift sword of the One shall fall upon the Worlds!"

Lucian hoped that wouldn't be happening immediately, because he needed a nap. It was hard to suppress his urge to yawn.

"But you are lacking in food and sleep," Sharo Khalin said. "You have only to lean on me for your every need. As the Voice of God, the One speaks through me. He has yet to tell me what path to lead you on, but he would not lead you here if he did not have a use for you. Until then, you are welcome here. Beyond welcome."

When Lucian heard "the Voice of God," the hairs rose on his arms. He realized, for the first time, that the High Prophet was not speaking figuratively about hearing a voice. That voice could be *anyone*. Perhaps even the Ancient One, the Shadow already taking shape in this reality. The thought was a terrible one, but Vera herself had communed with the Ancient One. If Sharo Khalin were on a similar level, then why couldn't he do the same?

If Sharo Khalin was heeding that voice, he was far more dangerous than Lucian first guessed. All of his exhaustion evaporated as his senses went on high alert.

Lucian cleared his throat, holding his Focus to keep his wits about him. "If you have a ship for me and my friends, that would be ideal. A place for us to rest and recuperate from our long journey."

"We are not ready to attend the fleet in orbit. A splendid sight, Lucian. Its glory will steal your breath! But now is not the time to revel in it. There is a place here in the Great Cathedral where you and your friends can rest. We would be most favored to host you in the undercroft, where the masses won't disturb you. When the time comes for our ascension to the stars, I will summon you."

"When will that be?"

"Quite soon. Once in space, we will take passage together aboard my flagship, *Holy Fire*."

Lucian had to swallow his dislike for this man, at least for now. "I very much look forward to that, Sharo Khalin."

The High Prophet smiled, waving over one of the Prophets, who was younger than the others he'd seen, being middle-aged, with sandy brown hair and a weathered face.

"Brother Nathaniel, take the Messiah to the undercroft and see that he and his companions have rest and nourishment. They are all of the Faith, and to be treated with the same care and attention as you would give me."

The white-robed Prophet folded his hands. "By the One, it shall be done."

"Let your word be good enough, Brother. There is no need to swear, especially by the One."

"Forgive me, High Prophet. I am only exultant over the coming of the Last Messiah."

"As are we all." Sharo Khalin turned to Lucian, clasping his hands piously. "Until we meet again, Lucian Abrantes. It was a pleasure to make your formal acquaintance. It has been most .. . *enlightening.*"

Now, Lucian was completely sure that this was all a show for the High Prophet. There was too much irony in his voice, too much of a tone that said he had the upper hand. The High Prophet didn't buy this codswallop about the Last Messiah, unlike the rest of this planet. If *he* didn't buy it, then what was the point of the charade?

Lucian could only wonder as the High Prophet left by the front doors of the cathedral, his retinue of crimson-robed Holy Warriors trailing behind. Serah, Fergus, and Mira approached Lucian down the center aisle, all of them remaining quiet for now.

"This way, honored Prophets," Prophet Nathaniel said, leading them to an archway behind the altar.

Fergus and Mira arched their eyebrows at this, but Lucian's look told them to play along as they followed Prophet Nathaniel.

3

UNLIKE THE LOFTY CATHEDRAL ABOVE, the undercroft was an almost claustrophobic maze. It was lit by weak sconces and candelabra set into shallow alcoves in the sandstone walls. Brother Nathaniel led them down a confined hallway that seemed to be endless.

"The tunnels extend under most of the City of Zion," he said. "Many apostates and unbelievers can be found not three kilometers down this passage." He looked back and offered a conciliatory smile. "Fear not, brothers and sisters. We are safe here. The Holy Warriors are ever vigilant, and not a drop of unbelieving blood has been spilled within these hallowed halls."

"Hallowed?" Fergus asked curiously.

"Yes. Though the Great Cathedral above us is most impressive, the undercroft is Zion's true beating heart. Indeed, it is the Conclave's meeting place, where the Prophets esteem to rule the Kingdom of the One."

"That's a . . . lofty goal," Serah said. "Almost as lofty as the cathedral above our heads, Sir Prophet."

Lucian opened a link to her. *You're overplaying it. Relax. I've got this.*

As always, Lucian realized he wasn't going to stop Serah from doing what she wanted.

"Indeed, Sister. Long has the High Prophet Sharo Khalin prophesied the coming of the Final Messiah. Though the faith of many was tested at such a bold prediction, the One provides to those who trust in him. That, we must never forget."

Now, more than ever, Lucian was convinced that Sharo Khalin was gifted in Psionics. It was strange, for he had used Dynamism to prove his magical prowess. If he was strong in both, it would speak to his strength as a mage.

"Great works have been accomplished here," Prophet Nathaniel went on, wistfully. "Genius works of writing and theology. Great edicts and proclamations promulgated." They passed a small, humble room on the right, toward which their host nodded. "In that office there, the High Prophet declared the Kingdom of the One not one month ago, formally severing our ties with the League."

"So *that's* why I can't access the GalNet," Serah said.

Prophet Nathaniel frowned. "The *GalNet* is a godless abomination. The High Prophet's Edict of Purity forbade it from our borders long ago, though, of course, filthy pirates have set up black market relays. There are many temptations in the dark recesses of the GalNet, but the One is merciful. When we have sinned, we must turn back to the One. He is always ready to forgive."

"Oh yeah, of course," Serah said. "Forgiveness is next to godliness, or so I've heard."

"I thought that was cleanliness," Mira said.

Lucian had to cut them off. "Anyway, Brother Nathaniel. Where are you taking us now?"

"Your room. I'm afraid the atmosphere here is quite

communal. That means no private rooms. In normal circumstances, women are not allowed here."

"Are we too distracting?" Serah asked.

Brother Nathaniel's cheeks flushed. "Err . . . no, Sister. It is simply the will of the High Prophet. However, we have made an exception in your case, since the Messiah and his companions are above reproach."

"So, we'll all be sharing the same space?" Lucian asked.

Anytime the man talked to Lucian, he was positively gushing. "Of course, Messiah. All shall be to your exact specifications."

"Could you bring us some food, too? Water as well."

"It shall be done. Already, I have instructed our kitchens to prepare a humble feast for your party."

Lucian was wondering how Nathaniel had done that, before remembering that *he* was a Prophet—and therefore, a mage. Lucian, with the Orb of Psionics, reached out to the man's mind, feeling at his Focus. So subtle was his stream that Nathaniel wasn't any the wiser. The man was a Binder, along with being quite capable in Psionics.

"A Binder," Lucian said.

Nathaniel's eyes widened in surprise. "Messiah! Though I am warding myself, you saw through it. The High Prophet was right about you."

"There is no need to ward yourself. I am your friend, as I am to all humanity."

Fergus arched an eyebrow at that, but Lucian figured if he was being called Messiah, he needed to play the part.

The prophet paused for a moment, considering. "Yes, of course. However, I should have you know, Messiah, that we of the Faith don't call ourselves *Binders*. That is a heathen word. We are, instead, Lashers, and Bindings are called Lashings."

"Like you're whipping someone?" Fergus asked.

Nathaniel gave a small, almost sadistic, smile. "Combined with the Gift of Foresight, it makes for quite an effective tool against those who deny the Faith."

Lucian figured Foresight was their equivalent of Psionics. A dualstream of Psionics and Binding could create what most mages referred to as a telekinetic tether, which could be used as a whip, besides grappling objects.

Whatever the case, Lucian found he lost all taste for conversation with the Prophet, as had the others.

They drew up before a humble wooden door.

"These are your accommodations." Prophet Nathaniel gave a humble bow. "I will return with food and drink. I am certain you are exhausted from your long journey."

"Thank you, Brother," Lucian said, smoothly. "May the One guide your footsteps." That was another saying he had gleaned from the Prophet's mind.

The brother bowed even lower, and Lucian was glad he got the hint as he hurried away.

Lucian opened the door, finding a long dormitory filled with eight beds, each containing a small chest of drawers on its side and a footlocker at its end. There was a humble wooden table with two long benches, along with a couple of large clay pots that had to be for what Psion Gaius had once called "evacuation procedures."

"Rotting hell," Serah said, as soon as the door was closed. "These people don't like technology, either! What's with mages and lack of technology? Irion, at least, doesn't seem to think slates are evil."

Fergus chuckled. "I'm surprised you mentioned that instead of the chamber pots."

"For good reason. You're rich if you can afford one of those on Psyche!"

Mira arched an eyebrow. "You're joking."

"Only half. Rot it, why don't they have the *GalNet* here? I'm having some serious withdrawals!"

"Probably because it's a bad influence," Fergus said. "Maybe you should take the opportunity to train your Focus."

"Well, if *you* love Zion so much, maybe you should move here. Seems they like stoic types who are sticklers for rules."

Fergus guffawed. "No, thanks. I'm hardly a stickler, which you should know from my love of gambling."

"And pirates."

"What's *that* supposed to mean?"

"Nothing. Nothing at all."

"Humph. Well, I'll take a nice mansion on Nessus over anything else, with my own dome and parkland. Right next to the Glitz Strip, of course. That way, I can gamble to my heart's content."

Mira chuckled. "You'll be mortgaging that mansion to afford the Glitz. Knew an old captain who blew through his entire pension in less than a month."

"Hopefully, fame and riches lie at the end of this journey, though I'm not holding my breath."

Lucian plopped down on the bed, too tired to take part in the conversation. Such was his exhaustion that he felt himself drifting off almost as soon as he closed his eyes.

———

WHEN LUCIAN AWOKE, there was plenty of food set up on the long table, an assortment of flatbread, hummus, cheese, figs, and olives. It seemed most of the others had eaten. Such was his exhaustion that he'd slept through everything.

While the others chatted, he ate. He knew the food wasn't poisoned because he would have uncovered that intention with his mind-reading. Plus, he was starving. It'd been quite a while since he'd had a proper meal.

All he could think about was what came next. They needed a ship, that much was clear. As things stood, they had no way of getting one. The easiest thing would be to warp back to *Talaria* and then warp the entire ship back here to Zion, but he'd need to find a stretch of land large enough to accommodate it. Not only that, his mother would have to fly into space and hope the Believers wouldn't turn on them. That was a tall order, especially when the entire fleet was orbiting Zion right now. The High Prophet would not allow him to escape so easily.

Despite the new challenges, Lucian was committed to visiting the Mako Academy. The other option—going straight after Xara Mallis without proper training—wouldn't work. He needed to prevent the Joining, and with the Shadow taking shape, the Joining wasn't an idle threat. If the Ancient One merged with him, everything would have been for nothing.

Either he fought Xara Mallis, gained her Orbs, and was powerless to stop the Joining, or he fought her and lost. Neither outcome was what he wanted. He needed training from true masters, and Mako was the only place he could get it. That meant being at the mercy of Sharo Khalin, at least for the moment.

"So, what's the plan?" he asked. "Wait until they take us up to the fleet and pretend I'm a holy Messiah or something?"

"Yep," Serah said. "You're doing a bang-up job so far."

"Thanks. I've just been talking out of my ass, but glad to know it's working."

"If you would allow me to offer a few pointers. When people ask you something, ask a question back. It makes you sound mysterious and wise. Finally, maybe you can use a little Radiant Magic to make yourself glow, just a little. You know, give the people what they want."

"It seemed like Khalin might have been doing that himself," Lucian said. "Remember how he glowed when we were walking up the stairs to the cathedral?"

"Are we sure this place isn't bugged?" Mira asked.

"It isn't," Fergus said. "I already scanned the walls and found nothing."

Lucian had to trust Fergus. If there were any bugs in the room, he would have found them.

"For my part," Fergus continued, "I think Sharo Khalin is being sly. Not all is as it seems, here. There's something else going on. Something that has yet to be revealed."

"That's what I think, too," Lucian said. "He mentioned hearing a voice. He implied it was directing his actions and giving him prophecies."

"You think he's talking to the Ancient One, like Vera?" Serah asked.

"How else could he have known I was coming? The Ancient One knows what I'm doing, and is probably the only one who could have told Khalin I was here."

Their conversation was cut short when there was a knock at the door. Lucian went to answer, revealing Prophet Nathaniel. He inclined his head, clasped his hands, and bowed.

"Messiah," he said. "Are you ready for the ascension?"

Lucian remembered Serah's advice and assumed a pious expression. "Are *you* ready, Prophet Nathaniel?"

Nathaniel's eyes widened, and he seemed to be searching out a deeper meaning in those words. "Yes. I am ready to see the One's plans unfold, and I have prepared my spirit to have a heart of obedience."

Lucian shook his head. Acting mysterious was too much work. "Where are you taking us?"

"You'll be ascending with the High Prophet himself in his transport, along with some of the most esteemed members of the Holy Conclave. A great honor. Is there any last business you need to care of?"

"Is there?" When Nathaniel frowned in confusion, Lucian realized he had taken Serah's idea a bit too far. "Lead the way, Prophet Nathaniel."

"At once, Messiah."

The Prophet led them out of the undercroft, joining a train of holy men, including white-robed Prophets and crimson-robed Holy Warriors. There were also other colors Lucian didn't know the purpose of. Though none of them spoke, many cast him surreptitious glances.

They went up the narrow, circling stairs, emptying into the Great Cathedral above. There, its airy space echoed with the hymns of hundreds singing in celebration. The harmonies reached a crescendo as Lucian entered the vast space, as if they had been waiting for him to belt out the chorus.

When he exited onto the cathedral's broad steps, vast crowds had gathered. They roared when Lucian appeared at the top of the stairs, where the High Prophet himself waited with a knowing smile. Hovering over the city itself were dozens of transports, one of which was lowering onto the porch itself. It roved about twenty meters above their heads, before finding a place to settle in the cathedral's shadow.

"Come," the High Prophet said, stepping up to Lucian and his companions. "It is time."

Though he spoke softly, Lucian could still hear him above the din. They followed him aboard the ship.

They found themselves inside a well-appointed lounge. Sharo Khalin, along with four other white-robed Prophets, all old men with beards, took up their places on lavish couches, while Lucian and his friends sat opposite them. Lucian recognized the Prophet from yesterday who had received him outside the Temple of Light. The two sides watched one another somewhat cautiously. Lucian wasn't sure if these Prophets bought into the racket, or if it was just a means to power. But for the moment, they needed each other. Or so it appeared on the surface.

The ship shifted beneath them, and Lucian watched as the Great Cathedral fell away.

4

SHARO KHALIN CLEARED HIS THROAT. "I think we can all agree that this is . . . unprecedented. Truth be told, I'm not sure what to do. I've spent the night deep in prayer, but the Voice of the One has been strangely silent of late."

"Maybe he's busy," Serah said.

The Prophets on the opposite couch glowered at that. Lucian thought that it probably wasn't far from the truth. Whatever the Ancient One was up to, it wasn't good. Assuming Sharo Khalin was even speaking to him.

"The One's ways are mysterious indeed," Lucian said. "Not even we can guess his intentions."

"Yes, that is so. However, his previous revelations are clear. We must continue the Crusade, despite his recent silence regarding you."

"Of course," Lucian said.

Khalin leaned forward. "You have rested, eaten, and now we can speak. I would like to know more about you, Lucian Abrantes. How did you come to the Temple of Light? In what manner was my prophecy fulfilled?"

"The One has blessed me with a Gift. A Gift no one else has."

Though the expression of the Prophets did not change, Lucian felt their attention sharpen on him.

"And what Gift would that be?" the High Prophet asked, his dark eyes looking almost greedy.

"It is a powerful Gift, but the One has instructed me to not reveal its nature. Our enemies can never learn of my abilities."

"I . . . see. And I assume this Gift would be used to great effect?"

"Verily so," Lucian said. "If the One wills it."

"Lucian Abrantes, there is no need to play coy with us. We are all brothers and sisters of the One here. Whatever revelation the One has given you, we can all receive it."

Lucian hardened his Focus. "And you presume to know the will of the One? You might be the High Prophet, Sharo Khalin, but I am his appointed Messiah."

The Prophets' eyes widened at this, and it was clear they were not used to their master being so challenged. But the High Prophet smiled easily, taking it in good stride.

"As you wish. As you say, I would not presume to know the mind of the One. No man is that great. Not even the Last Messiah."

Lucian remained silent, refusing to be baited. All he wanted was for his followers to doubt the High Prophet, at least a little. That might come in handy soon. He could not undermine the High Prophet's authority in a day.

"I have a reason for asking these questions, Prophet Lucian," Sharo Khalin continued. "The One has revealed some of his will to me, and he has clarified that you have a mighty Gift indeed. He said that a great Miracle would lead the Believers to victory over the infidels. I only wished to find out what that Miracle was so that we might prepare. We will meet soon with the Grand Admiral of the Oneist fleet. He is a brilliant strategist. If he knew the nature of your mighty Gift, the same that allowed you to open the temple doors and fulfill the prophecy, then he might incorporate it into this battle plan."

"Again," Lucian said, "the Miracle cannot be revealed until the proper time. I must insist on this."

The High Prophet did not seem pleased by this. "As you wish."

By now, they were out of the atmosphere, cruising toward a mighty battleship, what had to be *Holy Fire*. Though it was still quite far, Lucian sharpened his vision with the Orb of Radiance. It was at least a full kilometer long, outfitted with dozens of cannons, torpedo tubes, and even the coiled array of a tachyon lance. It shone white by the light of Zion's sun, giving off an almost holy aura.

Within minutes, they were touching down in one of its hangars. The Prophets arose, following Sharo Khalin out, while Lucian and the others followed suit.

They entered the wide hangar, which was busy with activity. The Prophets made their way toward the interior of the ship. Hundreds of gray-uniformed Oneist sailors formed ranks, creating a column through which they passed. Each regiment was led by a crimson-robed Holy Warrior equipped with a shockspear and shield pack. The sight might have impressed Lucian at one point, but he had seen greater things in the Worlds.

"She looks to be of League make," Fergus observed of the ship.

"Yes, Prophet Fergus," the High Prophet said. Though Fergus hadn't once said his name, Sharo Khalin seemed to know it. "The capital ships are out of the League base at Covenant, and that includes *Holy Fire*. What once belonged to our enemies now belongs to the One. Our engineers have retrofitted them for the Crusade. They shall fall like a hammer upon the Solar System."

"I think they have other things on their plate," Serah said. "Like the Swarmers."

"Ah," the High Prophet said, as they passed out of the hangar and into a wide, central corridor. "The Swarmers are the wrath of the One, made manifest. When humanity turns from sin, so will the Swarmers turn from humanity."

"That'll never happen," Mira said.

"No," the High Prophet said, "I suspect not. While the One is merciful, his Final Revelations make clear that the majority of humanity will not be of the Elect. They will feel the One's wrath, even as the One shows mercy to the Elect. In this way, his glory is doubled.

"Yes," Serah said, somewhat ironically. "Death and destruction. Quite glorious!"

Before the High Prophet could respond, Lucian cut in. "Where are you taking us, High Prophet?"

"The bridge. We shall soon be underway. First, the fleet will go at full burn to the Mulciber System, where we will pick up reinforcements. After that, we will continue the rest of the journey to the Solar System."

"How long do you expect that to take?"

The High Prophet gave a furtive smile. "Oh, not long at all. Not with the Messiah on our side."

Lucian kept his face expressionless, but his mind was reeling. The Prophet *couldn't* know about the Orb of Space-Time. If he did, then all his questioning on the shuttle was just for show. The only way he *could* know was if Lucian's suspicions were true: he was talking to the Ancient One.

Lucian couldn't use the Orb to get them *to* Mulciber, since he hadn't been there before. After the fleets linked up, though,

Lucian *would* be capable of creating a portal to the Solar System itself. Through that, the Crusade could easily attack his home planet, catching the League completely by surprise. Would Sharo Khalin ever dare something so bold?

Of course, Lucian had no intention of following through with such a thing. He hoped to be out of here long before that. Surely, the High Prophet knew he wouldn't do that, which made Lucian wonder what his game was. The High Prophet was playing it cool, at least for now, not giving anything away. He seemed utterly confident. If he knew Lucian had access to six Orbs, then confidence was not the right attitude. Sharo Khalin had something up his sleeve for sure, something that said he'd already won.

They entered an elevator, which took them to the command deck located at the top of the ship. When the doors opened, they were greeted by a wide bridge, similar in make to *Volga* in the League First Fleet. There were a couple of dozen officers busy at their stations, with uniforms that were quite similar to the League's. Only the coloration was different; they were orange rather than blue, almost as if no change had been made except for the coloring. Lucian wondered how they could have assembled such a vast armada with such limited resources.

The High Prophet seemed to guess his thoughts. "The Oneists of Zion have not been idle. The Faith has spread far, especially here in the Spinward Worlds. It's sometimes said that if the Trailward Worlds have criminals, the Spinward have saints. The right officers in the right place were all it took to turn these ships over to the One. Hardly a drop of blood was shed. The One will not be denied."

A stalwart, black-bearded man in an orange uniform, decked with many honors, approached the High Prophet, giving a slight bow.

"High Prophet. I would have greeted you personally, but things have been busy here."

"I understand. As the Grand Admiral of the Holy Crusade, you have many tasks appointed to you by the One. You did well to remain here."

The Admiral nodded gratefully. "We will depart soon, High Prophet." The Admiral looked at Lucian, seeming to notice him for the first time. He gave a bow that was almost as deep as the High Prophet's. He had to have carefully calculated that depth.

"Messiah, welcome aboard the *Holy Fire*. Long have we awaited your coming, and we have organized everything for this moment. We will not fail you."

"What is your name, Admiral?" Lucian asked.

"Forgive me. I am Grand Admiral Blackford. Born and raised on Holy Zion, a graduate of the Redemption Aerospace Academy, and veteran of three campaigns, the last of which saw the acquisition of the heathen Evarians into the One's Kingdom."

"The One has blessed us greatly with his leadership," the High Prophet said. "You will not find a better tactician in all the Worlds."

Lucian nodded approvingly. "His dedication is noted."

Grand Admiral Blackford bowed even lower. "You are gracious to say so, Messiah."

"We leave the command of the Crusade in your capable hands, Admiral Blackford," the High Prophet said. "Upon our arrival in Mulciber, the Messiah will play his part, creating the Miracle that will see the One spreading not just among this side of the Worlds, but across the entire galaxy."

"The One will it so," Admiral Blackford intoned, folding his hands in supplication.

Lucian was tired of pretending. "Yes. The Miracle. All in due time."

Blackford smiled graciously. "If you would excuse me, Prophets, I must give the departure orders."

"By all means," the High Prophet said. "Let us not divert you from your duties."

Blackford gave a final bow before returning to the forward view deck.

Lucian watched the bridge officers remain focused on their terminals. His friends and mother stood a short distance behind, along with the members of the Holy Conclave. Lucian could hardly believe he was here, could hardly believe that these people *believed* that this "One" had appointed him to save them.

What was the Ancient One's game? He could still remember that dark shape oscillating in the shadows of the columns not one day ago. All he had to do was close his eyes, and he could see it . . .

"Admiral Blackford?" The High Prophet asked. "Begin when ready."

"At once, High Prophet." He raised his slate to his mouth. "Attention, all who are faithful to the One! The One has gathered us from all the Worlds to enact his glory. From your cradles, you were born to *fight* that darkness. You came from nothing and were born into lives of sin and misery. But the One chose you, saved you, blessed you, and turned you into an instrument of glory. Now, the time has come! Let us drive his terrible, swift sword into the hearts of those who would deny him. Those who had repeatedly closed their ears to his truth. They have turned away from the One; for decades, we have proclaimed his message of salvation and mercy, to deaf ears." Admiral Blackford looked back at Lucian. "But the Time of Mercy has ended. The Last Messiah has come. The Time of Justice has come!"

Blackford's form was practically shaking with zeal. Blackford's deck officers hung on his every word. He was a man worthy of being followed. Lucian would remember that. It might be useful later.

"And now," Blackford went on, "your Holy Messiah, who just yesterday stepped from the Sealed Doors of the Temple of Light."

To Lucian's surprise, Blackford held out his slate for Lucian to give a speech.

Lucian stepped forward and took the slate. He wasn't sure where to begin, but his Focus allowed him to remain completely separated from his emotions.

"Men and women of the fleet," he said. "The end is near. Within months, the fate of humanity will be decided. Whether you're a Believer, or not, that fact is immutable. It's all about to come to a head. I am the Messiah. The Chosen. The High Prophet, for decades, has prepared the way for my coming." He closed his eyes for a moment, then reopened them. Anything could happen after this. "Now, I am here, and I need your help. For without you, this Crusade will fail. I only ask you to be prepared. For anything. This journey will not go the direction you expect, and when plans change, I need to know I have your complete support."

Lucian handed back the slate, not risking anything more. From the Grand Admiral's expression, it didn't seem as if Lucian had said anything improper, but he could feel the High Prophet's icy stare on his back.

But Sharo Khalin said nothing as Grand Admiral Blackford took his slate back. "Ahead full to Mulciber."

Lucian felt the deck shift beneath his feet, a momentary imbalance before the inertial dampening field compensated. *Holy Fire*, along with its surrounding retinue of cruisers and destroyers, advanced out of the orbit of the desert world of Zion, into the black of space.

"Come, Lucian," the High Prophet said, as if nothing untoward had happened earlier. "It would be my pleasure to show you the ship personally." Then, as an afterthought: "Of course, your friends and mother are welcome, too."

Lucian forced a smile. "I would love nothing more."

5

LUCIAN and his companions followed the High Prophet from the Command Deck, along with the members of the Holy Conclave and about a dozen Holy Warriors. Those crimson-robed soldiers remained utterly silent and ready for action at a moment's notice. They were more like droids than men, their stoic expressions almost inhuman.

It seemed strange that the High Prophet was giving them a tour himself, but Lucian wasn't going to stop him. They began near the stern, at the crew quarters that berthed hundreds, where Khalin delighted in showing them the multiple mess halls and recreation rooms. Throughout the ship, advanced weapon systems were never far away, and each station was manned by a dedicated team.

Lucian had only been on League carriers, so this was his first time on a dedicated ship-of-the-line, built for pure fire-power. As such, *Holy Fire* was a sight to behold.

From bow to stern, it took about thirty minutes of dedicated walking down a central corridor that branched into the various systems rooms. Mostly, they passed orange-suited techs, all of whom bowed to their leader as he passed. They also walked by a large number of Oneist marines, who carried particle impactor rifles designed for use in space, which wouldn't endanger the ship with bullets. They also passed more Holy Warriors, who seemed to be watching for signs of general sloth or inattentiveness.

From the Holy Warriors' shockspears and shield packs, it seemed their main function was to fight mages or perhaps even keep the magic-using Prophets themselves in check. It was clear they were personally loyal to the High Prophet himself.

After a couple of hours of the exhaustive tour, the High Prophet took them to a small hangar located amidships, which held a sleek spacecraft that had the same general look as *Ethereal*, with one key difference: toward the stern, it was a fair bit bulkier. That told Lucian, perhaps, the power plant was larger, and therefore *more* powerful than even *Ethereal's*.

Sharo Khalin's face gushed as he gestured toward the shining vessel. "Ah, my pride and joy. This is my vessel, *Fateful Lightning*. It's the fastest ship this side of the Worlds, and may the One witness my words as truth."

A few of the Prophets exchanged glances at that, as if it were unbecoming for Sharo Khalin to swear in such a way. But Khalin was blind to this as he stepped forward, running a wrinkled hand along the glassy, silvery hull.

"It's pretty," Serah said. "I've never seen a coat like that. If *coat* is the proper word."

"It's a refractive hull. Makes it completely undetectable to even the most powerful LADAR systems at distances of over ten thousand kilometers."

"Impossible," Fergus said. "She's far too small to power that, even assuming the larger engine in the stern."

"While it's true smaller vessels don't have the requisite power to deploy a truly refractive hull, *Lightning* is different.

She contains a prototypical engine gained from the skunkworks of Laurentia Base, in the Covenant System. Our scientists are not *sure* how it works. It's impossible to measure exactly what occurs within the power plant, but my scientists surmise the engine is quantum. Perhaps even it splits the individual quantum itself into various sub-particles."

"Impossible," Fergus scoffed, again. "There is no unit smaller than that."

"My scientists suggest it *is* possible, though they are still going through the data secured from Laurentia itself. Whatever the case, the power unleashed by the engine is several orders of magnitude greater than fusion power."

"If that's true," Fergus went on, "then it could change everything!"

"Yes, perhaps so. My scientists have great hopes that they can recreate the technology. Alas, the war makes that difficult, but I am confident this technology will serve the One well."

"How fast does she fly?" Mira asked. "I'm a pilot. That's all I care about."

"Fast," the High Prophet said, with a coy grin. "And not only is she fast, but she can power all requisite systems to support that speed, including inertial dampening to match and artificial gravity, not to mention the aforementioned refractive hull. Either way, its speed is unmatched by all but the most loaded out pinnace. It is practically impossible to track when the transponder is off. As I said before, it will be invisible to most scanners at distances of ten thousand klicks or fewer. What's more, the engine produces little residual heat. It is highly efficient." He shrugged. "Of course, if a ship gets a lock on it in that brief ten thousand kilometer window, it can maintain it. To a point. That's why it comes equipped with *this*."

Sharo Khalin held out his slate and tapped the screen a few times. Lucian almost gasped when the vessel simply . . . *disap-*

peared before him. Instead of the ship, it just looked like an empty hangar. He could only pick out the barest traces of its outline.

Khalin touched his slate again, and the ship shifted back into view.

"What just happened?" Serah asked.

"It's an experimental cloaking screen. The refractive hull can perfectly display the environment the ship finds itself in. Not only will it be *completely* undetectable by LADAR or thermal scans for about thirty seconds. It's enough time to change trajectory and dodge an incoming torpedo salvo." He shrugged. "But even this technology has its limits. Such are the power requirements that the cloaking screen can only be safely engaged for half a minute or so, but then it will need about two minutes to recharge, give or take thirty seconds. It depends on how much the other systems are drawing on the power supply. Of course, in a battle situation, the deflection field will likely be raised, making the cloaking screen of limited use. You might get ten seconds or so of invisibility in that situation."

Fergus whistled. "I've never heard of a deflection shield on a ship this small. I would assume it will deflect energy or kinetic attacks, such as a laser or railgun?"

"That is correct, Fergus. Of course, a railgun will quickly break the shield, but thankfully, they are not very accurate. The shield is highly effective at refracting lasers. Of course, the shield can be bypassed entirely with a torpedo. But an enemy ship will have a difficult time getting a lock inside ten thousand kilometers, even if it does, that's what the cloaking screen is for." He looked at Lucian and gave a wolfish smile. "Of course, since this is *my* vessel, it is verified to my identity. No one else may command it, even if they can somehow bypass the security system. It would be suicide."

Lucian knew that was a not-so-subtle warning to not get

any ideas. But already, he knew that he was going to make this ship theirs. Maybe the High Prophet believed its defenses impregnable, but Lucian already had an idea of how he might get it all the same. During the conversation, Lucian had subtly scanned the man's mind and saw that every detail was the absolute truth.

Lucian stared at the ship and the surrounding hangar, imprinting this exact place firmly in his memory. He left no detail out. He only looked away once he was sure he would remember it well.

"Come," the High Prophet said. "Let me show you to your quarters. There, you will be most comfortable."

They were led toward the stern of the ship, far from the hangar where *Fateful Lightning* was docked. Not that the distance mattered too much, with the Orb of Space-Time.

They were led beyond a heavy blast door and down a short corridor with several such doors lining either side. Lucian didn't want to call it a prison, but it might as well have served the same purpose.

"This special passenger section is for foreign dignitaries and diplomats," the High Prophet explained. "It has access to all the latest entertainment, on a network kept separate from the rest of the ship. We even have simulation pills and a spa."

"A spa?" Mira asked, in disbelief.

Sharo Khalin chuckled. "Needless to say, the crew would commit unspeakable blasphemies to be put up in here."

"Is there GalNet access?" Serah asked.

"Yes, this ship carries a relay, to which guests have access."

"It *does* sound positively sacrilegious," Serah said. "In a good way, I mean."

The High Prophet smiled as if he understood perfectly. "Well, it is not for the Oneists, but rather, our guests who hold to different customs. For now, you are the only ones staying, so feel free to explore the guest wing to your heart's content. You can find the spa and virtual reality equipment just down the hall, not to mention a state-of-the-art gym and pool. And of course, you may call for any food or amenity that is lacking, and it will be provided."

So, they weren't just going to be any prisoners, but *pampered* prisoners.

Sharo Khalin approached the first door on the left, which opened at his approach. As the blast door slid back, it revealed a finely appointed living area that was all but palatial for a military ship. If it weren't for the heavy bolts lining the crevices of the gray, metallic walls, Lucian would have had trouble believing it *was* a ship. There were luxurious couches, in the center of which stood a large holo-table and a built-in kitchen. Several open doors revealed more cabins connected to this main living area.

"I will leave you here," the High Prophet said. "Trust me, you will be perfectly comfortable. The guest wing has everything you could want."

"We *can* leave though, right?" Fergus asked.

"Why would you ever want to? The journey to Mulciber will take no time at all, especially considering the complement of entertainment options. You needn't worry about a thing, at least until we can begin preparations for the Miracle."

"Ah, yes," Lucian said. "The Miracle. To me, this seems more like a prison than a resort."

"I can see how you might think that. But by that definition, wouldn't this entire ship be a prison? None of us can leave it, after all. By giving you this personal space, I'm freeing you from obligations. I want you to focus all your energy on relaxing. A well-earned rest is just what my doctors and psychologists have advised for you."

Lucian had to admit, that *would* be nice in just about any

other circumstance. He had only mentioned it being a prison to see what Sharo Khalin would say. It was beyond obvious that the High Prophet's intentions weren't good, though he seemed to be ignorant of Lucian's abilities. Or at least, *feigning* ignorance. The only way the High Prophet could force him into anything was by threatening the others, so Lucian's main task was to keep alert and make sure no one got separated from him.

"I'll leave you to it," the High Prophet said. "Enjoy your voyage."

6

THE HIGH PROPHET left their rooms, shutting the blast door behind him.

"See ya," Serah said, beaming a fake smile. Once the door finished closing, she added, "don't want to be ya."

"This place is bugged," Fergus said, "though that shouldn't come as any surprise."

"I *still* don't want to be him. Slimier than a rift adder, that one." She cupped her hands and yelled at the walls. "Hey! You suck!"

Lucian waited until Fergus performed a cursory scan of the room. Within minutes, he had located every camera and sound detection device and had fried each one with a basic Dynamistic stream.

"Not even five minutes and you're already trashing the place?" Serah asked.

Fergus nodded, satisfied with his handiwork. "Either they can come to replace them, or admit they were listening."

"All right," Lucian said. "How are we going to get that ship? I felt like the man was teasing us with it."

"That ship is bait," Mira said. "And he intends to catch you red-handed trying to take it. I saw his face when you were talking to the crew. He did *not* like that line about *complete support.*"

"Powerful people dislike having their authority challenged," Fergus said. "Big surprise there."

"Yeah," Serah said. "I thought he might try to fry you with a lightning bolt or something."

"That might not be far from his plans," Mira said. "He just needs a reason. I'd say catching you trying to steal his ship would justify that. He's probably chewing out Admiral Blackford right now for letting you speak to the fleet. That wasn't scripted. The admiral buys into this whole Messiah thing hook, line, and sinker."

"So, the ship is bait, so he can have an excuse to get rid of me?" Lucian asked.

"I think so," Mira said. "You're not who he expected you to be, but he's still playing along like he believes this prophecy."

"I agree," Fergus said. "It's hard to know just how far he believes. He plays his part well."

Lucian nodded. "Like I was talking about back on Zion, I think the Ancient One is influencing him somehow, just as he is influencing Vera. He keeps talking about hearing a voice. We know he is a mage. He showed that at the cathedral. And we know he's hearing a voice that he believes is the One. So, what if the One is the Shadow Lord?"

"Dumb question," Mira said. "But this . . . *Shadow Lord* . . . is the same thing as the Ancient One, right?"

"Well," Serah said, "from what *I* can gather, the Shadow Lord was the fellow who entered the Heart of Creation to take the Orbs, and then he *became* the Ancient One. So now, the Shadow Lord is part of the personality of the Ancient One, so to speak."

Mira still seemed confused. "So, a Shadow Lord is an Ancient One, but an Ancient One is not necessarily a Shadow Lord?"

"Um ... sure?"

"Serah has it right," Lucian said. "I mean, we don't know everything about how it works, but it seems that the Ancient One is sort of an amalgamation of everyone who has once held all the Orbs. That would include the Shadow Lord, and whoever the Second Immortal was. And, by extension, it would include me or Xara, once one of us grabbed all the Orbs. That's what he means by Joining. I would Join with the overall personality. That is, if we don't figure out a way to stop it first." He shrugged. "At least, that's how I figure it. I've been calling him the Shadow Lord because it's close enough to what he is."

"Yes," Serah agreed. "He is *quite* shadowy. Not to mention that *The Shadow Lord* makes him sound appropriately evil, just in case anyone was confused by the fact. It leaves no room for misinterpretation. If I went around and started calling myself *The Shadow Lady*, I'd probably creep out people, even if I'm a nice enough girl."

"You're not taking this seriously enough," Fergus said. "We're talking about an apocalypse on a galactic scale!"

"Well, we have to laugh, even if there's an apocalypse going on. Perhaps it's even the *best* time to laugh."

"You can't stop the apocalypse with laughter."

"Yes," Serah said, sagely. "But one might be able to bear it long enough to figure out *how* to stop it."

"Well," Fergus said, "you may have a point there."

"You should try it, Fergus."

"Try what?"

"Humor. If you make light of something heavy, it becomes much less scary."

"Another one of your proverbs?" Lucian asked.

"Of course!"

Fergus cleared his throat. "Um . . . all right, then. So what are we going to do if the High Blowhard is being possessed by His Lord Shadowiness?"

"That's a good start!" Serah said.

"Well," Lucian said, "if the Shadow Lord is influencing him, I guess that just makes him more difficult to deal with."

"Okay, *supposing* that's true," Fergus said. "What do we do with that information?"

"I'm not sure. I just think it's important to acknowledge the possibility. I don't think there's anything we *can* do. We just have to be careful."

"I just want to know what this *Miracle* is supposed to be," Serah said. "He's mentioned that several times by now."

"That's easy," Lucian said. "Assuming the Shadow Lord theory is true, Khalin knows I can create a portal to Earth. Even if he's *not* being influenced, he knows Yang's fleet traveled from Hephaestus to Chiron instantly, and that *I* might be the reason for that. He wants to join his entire fleet in one spot before I do that. The First League fleet is out of position and will take weeks to get back to defend Earth. During that time, Sharo Khalin can make an incredible amount of demands."

"And how does he intend to make *you* do what he wants?" Fergus asked.

Lucian frowned. "I don't know. He's sure acting like he has an ace up his sleeve, though."

Fergus cleared his throat. "Well, it's easy to see he's acting far too cocky, showing off his ship like that. It's almost as if he believes he can't lose."

"He was telling the truth about that ship," Lucian said. "We just need to beat him at his own game. We have until Mulciber to figure out how to get out of here."

"Why not right now, while they're busy with things?" Serah asked. "It's what they would least expect, right?"

"We need to figure out a way to get that ship unregistered to Sharo," Mira said. "If it's verified to him, there's no way we can control it. No way around that."

"I'm no Radiance hacker," Fergus said. "Emma is, though. Remember what she did with the Orb of Radiance? She not only found the Dark Gate but uploaded its coordinates to *Ethereal's* navigation computer. That required about as much encryption as what we're trying to accomplish."

"Yeah," Lucian said. "But she had the Orb of Radiance."

"Could it work without it, though?" Fergus asked.

"Yes, it might," Lucian had to admit. "If she does have to use it, it wouldn't be for her, you know? The thing is, if I were to warp to *Resplendent* and ask her right now, she wouldn't say *no*. I feel bad about that. Feels like we're just using her when the effects could damage her."

"What if there's no other way?" Serah asked.

"I don't know. Maybe she can try it without the Orb first. We're going to be crunched for time either way. We'd have to defend the ship while she transfers the verification to us."

"And she'd have no hope of transferring it if it's registered on the GalNet," Fergus said.

"Even with the Orb of Radiance?" Serah asked.

Fergus shook his head. "She'd have to rewrite the entire digital history of the ship, across all Worlds. That's impossible. Our only hope is if they registered the ship to a private network. We know the Oneists use a centralized network while detesting the GalNet, which is decentralized. A centralized network is easier to change, but by no means easy."

"Wait," Mira said. "Son, you plan on doing this?"

"Well, nothing is sure yet. In theory, I can create a portal to *Resplendent* and hope she's on board. Borrow her for a few minutes. The Transcends won't be happy about it, but I'm sure Emma would help out if we asked. I wouldn't force her and would let her know the risks. It's not an easy thing to ask."

"I'm also worried about giving her the Orb," Fergus said. "We know how it affected her. If she held it again, even for a minute or two, the effects could be unpredictable ..."

"Yeah," Lucian said. "I know ..."

"Then again," Fergus said, "I'm not sure there's anyone else who is capable of such a stream. Not anyone we can trust, anyway."

"There's another option," Mira said. "Couldn't you just force the High Prophet to sign over the property, with your Psionics Orb or whatever?"

"I could," Lucian admitted. "I'd have to get him alone, and since he's a mage who's likely already on his guard, it would be a fight for sure. I'm not scared to fight him. It's just risky. I might be overwhelmed by sheer numbers."

"Is there ever a time when the High Prophet is alone?" Serah asked. "While he's sleeping, maybe?"

"I wouldn't count on that," Fergus said. "Those Holy Warriors follow him wherever he goes. I know they can't match up to us, but enough of them working together could cause a problem. From their equipment, it seems they are specifically trained to counter mages."

There was another option, too. Assuming they didn't trigger any alarms, Lucian could try to hack the ship himself. He'd never done such a thing before, but sometimes, when he streamed from the Orbs, they provided the knowledge as he needed it. He wasn't sure how it worked, but it had happened more than once. It was almost as if the knowledge came directly to him from the Manifold.

"It's risky," Lucian said, "but I could try to do it myself. I trust Emma more with it, but at least we wouldn't be risking her."

"Are you sure you can do that?" Fergus asked.

"To be honest, no. Getting to the ship itself should be no problem. It's what comes after that worries me. Whatever our plans, something tells me we'd have to improvise at some point."

"They're not going to just let you hack into it without infringement," Fergus said. "That ship is being watched every hour, every minute. We'd have to hold the doors while you figured out the ship."

"What we need is a *distraction*," Serah said. "Only, what could that be? Should we just go for it?"

"No," Lucian said. "We shouldn't rush into anything. We have time, after all. Serah's right. There does need to be some sort of distraction that gives us a chance."

"Like what?" Fergus asked.

"It's a long way to Earth. A lot can happen. We'll be in Mulciber in under two weeks. That's a long time to figure things out."

"We should try to get out sooner," Mira said. "We might not have that long to wait."

Fergus cleared his throat. "If we're headed for Mako, the Mulciber Gate is the shortest journey. Even if *Fateful Lightning* has stealth capabilities, going in the same direction as the fleet is too much of a risk. We can always be detected around Gates, at least for a brief moment, since they only measure a few kilometers across."

Lucian nodded. "That's true."

"We'll have a very narrow window to make the heist work, then," Mira said. "And if things don't work out, we can always get out of here, right?"

"That's true as well," Lucian said. "But if the Manifold

placed the fastest ship this side of the Worlds right in our laps, it must mean us to go after it."

"I agree," Serah said. "But if we snag this one, remember what I said last time. *I* get to name it. We lost the air skiff on Psyche, and we had to give *Ethereal* back, and then we left *Talaria* neglected in the hangar of *Star's Blood*. Let's just try to have a better track record with ships, okay? We have to break the cycle, but as long as we're aware of the cycle, it can be broken."

"Naming it seems a little premature," Fergus said. "We haven't even secured it yet!"

"Dibs," Serah said.

"Sure. Whatever." Fergus looked at Lucian. "Of course, there's the other option. You could just use the Orb of Space-Time to go after Xara directly, right?"

"No, it doesn't work like that. The Orb of Space-Time holds memories of the *locations* where the Orbs were found. It doesn't travel to the Orbs themselves. We still need to figure out where Xara is. But Mako comes first. Otherwise, I'll be powerless to prevent the Joining."

All of them were looking at him strangely. He could tell what they were thinking. Why couldn't he just try as hard as he could to prevent the Joining? Surely, if he resisted with all his power, he could prevent it.

"This isn't just a matter of willpower," Lucian said. "The Shadow Lord is becoming stronger with each Orb I gather. Even now, he could be out there in that corridor, watching and waiting. Wherever I go, he follows. If I were to gather even one more Orb, it might be enough to tip the balance. Hell, even *now* he might make a sudden move, attack my mind while I'm least expecting—"

At that very moment, Lucian gasped as the deck rocked from beneath him.

7

LUCIAN STOOD and went to help his mother. Thankfully, she and everyone else were okay.

Serah frowned. "What in the Worlds is going—"

At that moment, the deck shook again, sending Lucian tumbling to the deck. The ship vibrated for a few moments more before growing steady.

The hiss of air told Lucian that somewhere there had been a hull breach.

"Warning," came an automated male voice from a nearby speaker. "Atmosphere 98%. Blast doors to Delta Quadrant will close in: two minutes, thirty-six seconds. Proceed to Gamma Quadrant immediately."

"It would seem shit has hit the fan," Mira said.

"Let's go," Lucian said.

But when they arrived at the door separating the guest wing from the rest of the ship, it remained firmly shut. When Mira pressed the access panel, it was worse than useless.

"Won't open," she said.

"Atmosphere: 88%. Blast doors to Delta Quadrant will close in two minutes, fifteen seconds . . ."

Lucian raised his hands, and palms facing outward, he reached for the Orb of Thermalism. "Stand clear."

Everyone did so as he unleashed a fiery red stream that instantly caused the hard metal to redden and melt. He also created a shield to keep the heat from escaping. After a few seconds, he'd made enough of an opening, so he reversed the stream. The melted metal door solidified back to its former cool temperature.

"Well, that's one way to go about it," Mira said.

They ran up the central corridor, joining the general retreat from the stern of the ship. As they passed the first intersection, a couple of orange-suited crewmen ran by.

"League heathens," one of them spat. "My buddy over in LADAR said they had a fleet hidden behind Ishamu . . ."

"Impossible," the other said. "How could they be in this system without us knowing?"

His question remained unanswered because, at that moment, another impact heaved the deck from beneath Lucian's feet. This time, though, Serah was ready, streaming an anti-grav aura while they were still in the air, allowing them to fall safely to the deck. With the beating the ship was taking, Lucian was surprised the artificial gravity field had remained intact.

The two crewmen looked at them in shock, all the more so because of the obvious display of magic. But these men were not Lucian's concern. He had his crew to worry about, and the two men ran off ahead of them, anyway.

"It's getting harder to breathe," Mira said, panting for air.

"Warning." The male voice was broken up by the lack of air. "Atmosphere 72%. Blast doors to Delta Quadrant will close in:

One minute, thirty-two seconds. Proceed to Gamma Quadrant immediately."

Lucian stopped in the middle of the corridor. "It's time."

He reached for the Orb of Space-Time. Streaming from every Aspect, he formed an image of the hangar where *Fateful Lightning* was docked. He could only hope that the hangar had remained intact, otherwise, they might be entering a vacuum. A gate opened before him, a sinuous black line rotating counterclockwise to reveal the hangar on the other side, along with the ship in the distance. Air rushed from the opening, blasting Lucian. The pressure on the other side was higher, a sure sign that the hangar was safe.

Lucian held the stream and pushed everyone through. He stepped past the threshold last, then allowed the gate to collapse.

The ship stood before them, ready to be claimed. The only question was, how to claim it?

"Well, well, well," came a voice, from behind them. "Look what we have here. I thought we might have some thieves in our midst."

Lucian turned to find three people: one of the bearded Conclave Prophets who had been on board the transport earlier, Sharo Khalin himself, and a crimson-robed Holy Warrior wielding a shockspear, which immediately became armed with electricity. His shield also powered on, enveloping the warrior in an aura of pure energy.

It was the white-robed prophet who had spoken, judging by the superior smirk on his lips. Sharo Khalin just stared balefully, his expression dark.

"Guess things must be bad for you to abandon your flagship," Lucian said.

"A lucky hit," the High Prophet said, "but not fatal." He

balled his fists, and two twin balls of lightning formed around his hands. "The One has broken his silence. You are a False Messiah, and now, you must pay for your treachery."

Lucian didn't bother responding. He simply shielded Dynamism, while scanning the Focus of the other Prophet. Discovering he was a Thermalist, Lucian shielded that Aspect, making the aura large enough to cover his entire party. Such was the strength of the dual shield that it would have instantly drained his ether without the requisite Orbs.

The crimson-robed Holy Warrior strutted forward, flourishing his shockspear which crackled with electricity. Fergus strode confidently to meet the challenge, even as Lucian extended the range of his shield to envelop Fergus.

The shield instantly nullified the electricity on the warrior's spear. Despite that, he fought Fergus. To Lucian's surprise, the two matched each other strike for strike in a dance of death.

The white-robed Prophet raised his hands, conjuring a column of flame that shot right at Fergus. The Orb of Thermalism barely even registered the impact. The Prophet was a strong Thermalist in his own right; keeping up that column of flame could not have been easy. But he didn't know who he was contending with.

Sharo Khalin simply watched, content to sit back and let his minions do the fighting for him. It was a strange choice, seeing how he was outnumbered, but Lucian didn't question it.

Reaching for Psionics, Lucian pushed the Holy Warrior toward the Prophet just as he released a spout of flame. The Holy Warrior's momentary scream went silent when he was instantly incinerated.

Wide-eyed, the prophet cut off his stream, but the damage had already been done. He opted to create dozens of ice spikes, all floating in the surrounding air, with tethers of Binding

Magic readying to launch them right at Lucian, who he finally recognized to be the greatest threat.

Lucian simply reached for the Orb of Binding and Psionics, all while maintaining both of his shields, and shattered the ice spikes before they could launch. Channeling all his streams into a single point of attack, with Psionics as the ascendant Aspect, he surrounded the white Prophet's Focus, cutting it off from his magic.

Next, he focused on Sharo Khalin, who was still watching without lifting a finger to help his underlings.

"He's too strong!" the defeated Prophet said. "I can't use my Gift, High Prophet!"

Sharo Khalin held up his hand. "How little is your faith, Prophet Galbraith? Watch, and see the glory of the One work through me." The High Prophet turned to regard Lucian. "You will not have my ship, no matter your skill with the Gift. Powerful you may be, but my magic is of a higher sort. Come, let us be reasonable. Even if you were to miraculously win, the ship would not obey you."

"Then we'll do this the hard way," Lucian said. "You're just a pawn of the Shadow Lord."

Sharo Khalin gave a triumphant smile that said he still had the upper hand, despite how things looked. "A vile accusation."

Lucian reached for Psionics. He created a mind control stream, intending to force the High Prophet to give up the ship formally. But Lucian felt unreal resistance, resistance matching the power of his stream aided by the Orb of Psionics. He drew more ether, but it was like trying to knock down a wall with a single pebble.

The High Prophet smiled. "Foolish Being of Shadow! Did you think you could challenge the One? I am a mighty Sorcerer, trained by the Masters of Mako! I learned alongside the likes of

Vera Desai, Xara Mallis, and Ansaldra Dara. Do you think your Shadow Magic can stand up to the One's Light?"

At that moment, Sharo's expression became thunderous. The others gasped from behind him as he transformed before them.

Because now, a shadowy figure was escaping the High Prophet, levitating across the deck in Lucian's direction.

8

LUCIAN CUT off all his streams, opening himself to the Orbs of Radiance and Dynamism. He combined the rush of ether into a single dualstream, which collected in his hands as a gigantic ball of lightning. It shot right into the Shadow.

But the Shadow only absorbed that light, drinking in its power, quivering for a moment as if distributing the energy. Then, it grew darker before floating relentlessly forward.

The High Prophet stood directly behind the Shadow, eyes closed and arms outspread as if he were channeling the abomination. The other Prophet had fled the hangar entirely, deciding to take his chances on the battered battleship.

The deck rocked beneath Lucian, throwing him into the air. He tethered himself downward to keep himself steady. The Shadow was just meters away, and within its oscillating darkness, Lucian could see an orb of light, just like the one he'd thrown at it.

Lucian barely had time to throw up a Dynamistic shield as the ball of lightning slammed into him. He flew backward at incredible speed, only stopping himself with a hasty tether attached to the hangar's ceiling.

The Shadow flew toward him, its dead voice whispering in his mind.

The Joining comes . . .

Lucian pulled himself up to the ceiling, narrowly escaping the Shadow, feeling a trace of coldness where it had almost touched him.

Undeterred, the Shadow floated up after him. Lucian wanted to check on his friends, but such was his focus on the Shadow that he had to trust them to take care of themselves.

I will follow you to the ends of the galaxy. To the ends of time and existence itself! The Joining cannot be undone! It is futile to try.

Lucian had a quick opportunity to glance down at Fergus and Serah, who were trying to take down the High Prophet. An aura of magical energy surrounded him, protecting him from all attacks. He had no idea where his mother was.

Before he could locate her, the Shadow unleashed a dark ball of energy, which Lucian didn't know how to counter. He simply dodged it with another tether, and the dark ball struck the ceiling above, seeming to negate, or perhaps erase, the material it struck from existence. A large section of the ceiling toppled from above, right over where Serah and Fergus were trying to force open Khalin's shield.

"Run!" Lucian called.

Fergus and Serah dove away, just in time for the debris to crash into the deck.

The Shadow gathered another dark orb of magic, shooting it at Lucian once again. He warped out of the way, to the opposite side of the hangar, only for it to blast most of the hangar doors from existence.

Air rushed from the hangar in a whirlwind. Lucian streamed a Binding shield to block the hole before anyone, or anything could go flying out. The pressure drop was incredible, enough for Lucian's ears to ring with pain, and it was much harder to get enough oxygen.

But already, the Shadow was readying another dark orb. Lucian didn't know what would happen if it hit his shield, but odds were, Binding alone couldn't counter it. Rather than edify the shield with every Aspect, he waited.

The Shadow unleashed the third dark orb. As it flew toward Lucian, he created an entry portal directly ahead of him, and an exit portal pointing at the ceiling above Sharo Khalin.

The Shadow screeched its dismay, but it was already too late. When the shadow ball entered the portal, Lucian felt a rush of horrifying coldness. Nightmares and visions filled his mind, challenging his Focus for supremacy.

His portal held. The shadow ball exited the other portal, blasting the ceiling above Khalin.

As it collapsed, the Shadow rushed back to occupy its host. But it couldn't beat the debris falling in slow motion. For a moment, Khalin's shield held, but it buckled under the pressure, burying him.

The Shadow lingered a moment longer before disappearing like a puff of smoke.

A strange quiet fell before the deck rattled again with yet another blast. Lucian could hear the warning klaxons piercing from the decks above, along with the hiss of escaping air. The hangar was freezing, and the pressure continued to drop. They didn't have long to make it to safety.

Panting, Lucian pulled himself toward Fergus and Serah with another tether. "Everyone okay? Where's my mom?"

"Over here!"

Mira was standing in the doorway of *Fateful Lightning*, which had somehow opened during the fight.

Lucian didn't have time to question how it happened. "Let's get out of here."

They ran into the ship, gaining access to a long central corridor. Mira ran toward the bridge. Lucian noted tighter quarters than what he was used to. This was the smallest ship he'd been on, probably meant to crew ten or fewer, and yet everything was sleek and modern, which made sense if it was indeed a prototype of a new League design.

Mira took up the pilot's seat while everyone piled in behind her.

"Well," she said, "let's see if this Sharo fellow was blowing smoke out of his ass."

She hit the power toggle, and to Lucian's surprise, the dash lit up and the engine immediately thrummed. There was no warm-up period, as would be the case with a typical fusion engine. It seemed ready to fly right off the bat.

Mira nodded approvingly. "Ship is locked, loaded, and ready to blast."

"Let's get off this ship, and do it fast!" Serah added.

Mira peered through the front viewport. "And the Shadow Dude was kind enough to create an opening for us."

"I'm just wondering how you got the ship open in the first place," Lucian said.

"I don't know," Mira said. "I just kept trying the access panel, and eventually, it accessed. Let's just hope the ship works the same way. The Prophet talked up a big game that we wouldn't get it working."

"I just hope he's dead," Fergus said.

"Almost *anyone* would be dead after getting buried like that," Lucian said.

"It certainly seemed to stop Mr. Shadow Man," Serah said.

The entire ship rocked as another attack pummeled *Holy Fire.*

"Why aren't we moving?" Fergus asked.

"I don't know," Mira said. "Controls are unresponsive . . ."

At that very moment, something seemed to click because the ship lifted off. *Fateful Lightning* floated toward the opening in the hangar doors, as light and graceful as a feather.

"All right, we're rolling!"

As soon as the ship left the hangar, Mira tilted it downward, revealing a scene of battle. The source of the exterior explosions soon became obvious. The Believers' fleet was engaging a small, but dangerous, force of League ripsaw fighters. Several larger capital ships, also of League make, floated a short distance away near an icy moon, what Lucian assumed to be Ishamu. Looming behind that moon was a ringed gas giant with a green, poisonous hue.

"All right, strap in," Mira said, cracking a smile. She was in her element. "Let's see what *Lightning* is capable of."

Like a bird of prey, *Fateful Lightning* fell upon a squadron of ripsaws from behind, that had the orange coloring of Believing vessels. Mira opened the cannons and blasted them with railgun fire. Two ships went up in spouts of flame that quickly dissipated in the vacuum of space. Mira jerked *Lightning* away, pressing another button on the control stick.

"Hope this works," she said.

To Lucian's surprise, the Believing ripsaws weren't giving chase. It took him a moment to realize why: the cloaking screen was engaged. A status bar indicated they had about twenty seconds of invisibility left.

Mira took the opportunity to shoot off a couple of torpedoes from *Lightning's* tubes, which lit into a heavy destroyer that was wreaking havoc on a League cruiser. The destroyer immediately broke apart. *Lightning* flipped dizzyingly, heading in the opposite direction.

The cloaking display powered off as Mira weaved around a

squadron of League heavy bombers. Almost immediately, *Fateful Lightning* became the target of at least twenty torpedoes, the soonest of which would impact in mere seconds.

"They don't know we're on their side," Mira said. "Shit, shit, shit!"

"Mom, don't worry. Those won't be your last words."

Lucian streamed from the Orb of Space-Time. He focused on the moon in the distance. Milliseconds before impact, the scene suddenly shifted . . .

. . . and the icy surface of Ishamu loomed before them, toward which *Fateful Lightning* was shooting at nearly full blast.

Mira angled the ship away from the surface, the G-forces becoming unreal for a moment. Lucian created a reverse Gravitonic aura to take the edge off. Within seconds, they were facing the green gas giant in the distance.

"All right, we're alive," Mira said. "But we're still too close to the battle. We need somewhere to hide out. Wait for this to blow over."

Lucian felt a moment of vertigo, both from the dizzying battle and warping the ship even a short distance. He'd barely had time to gather his ether, and yet, the action had been completed in seconds. The Orb of Space-Time had become incredibly powerful with all but two of the original Orbs.

Mira guided *Fateful Lightning* down to the surface, engaging the cloaking screen once again, now that the system had repowered itself. It was enough cover to settle the ship on a stretch of icy flats riddled with cracks.

"You sure know your way around this ship," Fergus observed.

Mira leaned back in her seat. "Thankfully, the navigation menus are basic League software common to all ships. It's a bit different, but not by much."

In the distance, a geyser was issuing a stream of liquid water that immediately crystallized into ice. Above them, there was no sign of the battle.

"How long should we stick around?" Lucian asked.

"Long enough for them to forget about us," Mira said. "After that, I can fly us to wherever we need to go. Fuel reserves look good. That should get us pretty far."

"Well, if the engine is quantum-based, what fuels it?" Fergus asked.

"Seems it takes helium-3, just like any other ship," Mira said, exploring the ship's database. "How it uses that fuel, I can't say. Maybe there is some sort of fusion going on, along with something else that amps up the power levels. Whatever the case, I can get this ship to Mako, no problem. We might need to refuel one time, but it's doable."

As soon as she finished saying that, the entire ship went dark. There was ominous silence for a moment, followed by the hiss of air rushing off the bridge.

"It's venting us!" Mira cried.

Lucian immediately threw up a Binding shield to cover the doorway to the bridge, preventing any more air from escaping. The display flashed on while an emergency siren blared. The display gave a top-down view of the ship. Every compartment but the bridge flashed red, showing a complete vacuum.

Fergus cleared his throat nervously. "I . . . have a theory."

"Well, care to explain?" Serah asked.

"The High Prophet was telling the truth. Maybe we *can* fly the ship, but the ship was letting us do that because it was in immediate danger. Now that it's safe, it's trying to kill us."

"Kill us?" Serah asked. "We're on a bloodthirsty, murderous ship?"

"Well, it's probably programmed to kill anyone who isn't the High Prophet, or anyone he doesn't permit to fly it."

"That theory makes sense," Mira said. "Ships are only operable if the owner is on board, or at least licensing it. It might have let me pilot it to get it out of danger because it would be programmed to save itself."

"So, how do we fix it?" Serah asked. "We're going to run out of air in here, eventually."

"We can always transmute more with Atomicism," Fergus said. "But eventually, we would be forced to warp ourselves out."

Lucian wasn't going to give up that easily. "If we can get this ship working for us, that would be ideal. We aren't going to get any closer to Mako than this, and we won't find a faster ship." He looked at the others. "I'm going to have to get Emma."

"What about your shield, though?" Serah asked. "It's going to disappear if you leave!"

"Fergus, can you hold on long enough? Maybe Serah can work in confluence with you. I just need an hour or two."

"I see no other way," Fergus said. "Just make it fast, all right?"

"Yeah, I know." He looked at all of them. "So, I know it's a bit cramped in here, but don't stand where I am right now *at all*. I'm not sure what would happen if I opened a portal right on top of someone when I come back."

"Yeah," Serah said. "Not a pleasant thought."

With that out of the way, he nodded. "Well, here goes nothing."

He imagined the bridge of *Resplendent*. It occurred to him that the mages might not even *be* there anymore, or worse, that the ship might have even been destroyed in the battle with the Golden Pirates.

But Lucian had nothing else to go on. If he wanted *Fateful Lightning* to be *their* ship, he needed Emma.

The image of *Resplendent's* bridge grew larger in his mind. With a stream of magic, he left *Lightning* behind.

9

THE BRIDGE of *Resplendent* was cold, dark, and abandoned, but otherwise intact. Outside the viewport was a planet, along with other ships of the Consolidated League First Fleet, sharing the same orbit on low power. The boundless blue ocean made Lucian think it was Volsung, at least at first. Only, the coloring was off. Volsung's waters would have been a brighter blue, while the water here was dark, almost violet in hue. Only a few, scattered gray islands dotted its surface.

The only other planet it could be was Oceanus, a first world in the Sirius System. It was a single Gate jump from Alpha Centauri, so it was conceivable that the Fleet could have been moved there for some reason, or at least, a portion of it.

If that was Oceanus, then he had just learned something new about the Orb of Space-Time. Though he had formed his memory of *Resplendent's* bridge while it was in Chiron's orbit, it didn't seem to matter that the ship was now in Oceanus's orbit. What mattered was the memory of the place itself, no matter the new location the place found itself in.

He supposed he should have figured that out by now

because technically, *everything* was in motion relative to each other. That was just the nature of the cosmos.

The only sound was the rattle of the life support vents. He reached for the Ether, discovering that there were no mages nearby.

Lucian reached out with the Orb of Psionics, seeking Emma. To his relief, he found a connection within seconds.

Emma? Are you on Oceanus right now?

Lucian! Yes, where are you?

On Resplendent. *I just warped myself here. We need your help with something.*

Help with what? The Volsung Mages are on Admiralty Base right now. It's on the surface. We're doing joint training with the League Planetary Forces. Seems they expect a ground campaign at some point. Never mind that, though. If they find out you're up there, you could be in serious trouble!

They won't catch me, Emma. Listen, is Transcend White down there? I need to speak with her. I want to clear some things up, but I don't have much time.

Yes. All of us are.

Well, how can I get down there? Can she send up a ship or something?

I'm not sure. Listen, though. You're kind of . . . wanted, for killing the Hegemon. What makes you think she'll agree to a meeting?

About the Hegemon, I might be partially responsible for that, but it's more complicated than it seems. Transcend White knows what was going on with him.

What was going on, then?

Vera was possessing him somehow, even though he's not a mage. Transcend White and I found this out after we talked for the last time.

Are you serious?

I was just trying to get Vera out of his head, but somehow, she took control of him and even transferred her magic to him. It ended up being a fight. It's hard to say who ended it. Every pirate on that bridge was gunning him down.

That's insane. Why would she sacrifice the Hegemon like that?

She was done using him. If I'm to blame for his death, it will drive a rift between me and the League forever. It just makes it that much more likely for Xara to finish her plans.

Sorry for doubting you. It's just everything is falling apart now, and everyone is blaming you for it. I'm just annoyed because I've been having to defend you without a shred of evidence to back me up.

I'm sorry. It's just impossible to get everything right.

Believe me, I understand. Look. I can talk to her about you. And you said you needed my help, too?

That's right. Do you think you can hack over the ownership token for a ship using Radiance?

That's impossible.

What if it's on a private network? No GalNet.

What person would be stupid enough to register their ship to a private network?

The High Prophet Sharo Khalin. The GalNet is outlawed within the Believers' borders.

Did you steal the High Prophet's ship?

Yeah, it's a nice ship, except it might be trying to murder us. The security system just vented every compartment, and Serah and Fergus are holding it with a Binding shield.

And you're just now mentioning this?

So, think you can do it?

He could all but hear her sigh. *Fine. But no promises.*

―――――

WITHIN THE HOUR, a small shuttle had docked in *Resplendent's* hangar. When the door opened, it revealed a familiar face.

"Khairu! You're a sight for sore eyes."

She gave a terse nod. "Talent Lucian. I wish I could say the same."

Lucian strapped in. "If I explained the situation, I'm sure you'd forgive me."

She didn't ask for elaboration as she backed the ship out of the hangar. Only once she had the course plotted for Admiralty Base, which seemed to be a platform floating on the ocean, did she respond. "It's hard to believe the damage you've done in such a short time."

"If I'm a wanted man, then how is Transcend White going to speak to me?"

"In secret. You must hide your face with your hood and stream a concealment ward."

Nothing more was said after that. The transport flew toward the planet, lurching through layers of turbulent gray clouds laced with lightning. When they broke through, a torrential downpour pounded against the ship. It was only when they were a few hundred meters from the surface that Lucian could make out artificial lights, on what appeared to be a large structure rising above the turbulent waves on high struts.

Khairu landed on a concrete landing strip, which was being whipped with sheets of rain. Lucian could feel the surface heaving beneath them.

They exited into the rain, and by the time they entered the structure, Lucian was soaked to the bone. Standing there, ready to receive him, was Transcend White, her dark eyes thunderous with barely repressed anger. Lucian supposed she had a lot of reasons to be mad at him.

Khairu bowed her way out, leaving the two of them alone. Transcend White only watched him, waiting for him to break the silence.

"I'm sorry for how things happened," he said. "It got out of my control."

It sounded lame, but there was nothing more he could say. When she finally spoke, her voice was icy.

"I told you the Hegemon was beyond you."

Lucian met her gaze. "I was just doing what I thought was best. Mistakes happen."

"Mistakes *happen*?" she said, her voice going colder. "The League teeters on the brink of destruction. I don't know what you were trying to accomplish here, but now, we can't even *meet* openly. To mention nothing of Psion Gaius . . ."

"I regret his death, Transcend White. But it was a risk for you to send him."

"How did it happen?"

Lucian thought back to the fight with the basilisk in the volcano and didn't know what to tell her. If he told her that the fear of battle broke him, would it ruin her memory of him?

"He fought bravely."

Something in Transcend White's eyes seemed to know he was lying. "Gaius was never a fighter. Brilliant in his own way. But perhaps it was a mistake to send him."

"It's hard to say. He pulled his weight. I was coming around to him at the end."

"A pity. And the others?"

"All alive."

"Is there a reason you've come alone, Lucian?"

Lucian shrugged. "It's easier. I need Emma."

"She's told me already, along with everything else you said."

"So, you understand our situation. Even now, Serah and Fergus are fighting to stay alive. My mom is mixed in it, too."

"There are certain things we must discuss first. Your friends can wait an hour more."

That was easy for her to say. But if it was the price of getting Emma's help, he would wait.

Her face grew suddenly somber. "My sister is dead."

Lucian felt an intense shock. Had it been from the wound he'd inflicted, or perhaps when he'd expelled her Focus from the Hegemon?

"I see your reaction," Transcend White said, "and no, you are not responsible for it. I don't know how she met her end, but I am sure of it all the same."

"How do you know?"

"The brand she placed on you has changed its signature," she said. "It's passed on to a new owner."

"A new owner?" He wanted to ask "who," but he already knew the answer. The answer was obvious. "Xara?"

Transcend White nodded gravely. "Perhaps Vera was weakened by her outright possession of the Hegemon. Perhaps Xara saw an opportunity of some sort. We just don't know. It goes to show that when we act rashly, terrible consequences can occur."

"I *had* to act rashly. The stakes—"

"—You know *nothing* of the stakes. We barely survived the destruction above Chiron! You brought a pirate fleet into the First Worlds! *Whatever* were you thinking, Lucian?"

"Did the Pirates win?"

Transcend White shook her head. "We barely secured a truce, about an hour after the blood of thousands was shed. The new Hegemon, Kirsten Madi, is on her way to Chiron right now."

"I hope she's better than Palmer."

"She is . . . effective. But probably not effective enough."

"And Admiral Yang?"

"As part of the truce, she's been given stewardship of the

Hephaestus System. It's . . . simpler that way. For the moment, she's committed her forces to defend the League. We will see."

"Isn't that a good thing?"

From her silence, it seemed Transcend White was far more cynical than him. And perhaps she was right to be.

"So, Vera's brand never went away," Lucian said. "It passed on to Xara. When I saw you on Volsung, you said Vera's death would dissolve the brand."

"I don't know everything, Lucian. But I can make a guess. If Vera can transfer her Focus across light-years to a non-mage, using a brand that she's set up, then her abilities far surpass anything I could have imagined. She is getting assistance from the Ancient One."

"There's a lot I need to tell you about that. I've . . . got the Orb of Dynamism now."

Transcend White's betrayal of surprise was only a slight widening of her eyes. "That was where you went, then?"

Lucian nodded. "The Orb of Space-Time seems to hold the same memories I had on Psyche. Only these are clear enough to be like my own memories. I was able to use that to travel directly to it."

"Remarkable," Transcend White said. "And presumably, you can do so again to claim the final two Orbs?"

"No. They only go to where the Orbs were originally located, not to the Orbs themselves. At least, that's how I *think* it works. But even if I could jump straight to Xara, I wouldn't do it."

"And why not?"

Lucian quickly took the time to explain to her about the Shadow that was following him. Now that he had six Orbs, it had become more than the voice haunting him, but an actual presence he couldn't get rid of. He finished by updating her on their current situation, being somewhat hostage to an advanced spaceship that was trying to kill them. Assuming it was fixed, it could get them to Mako in record time. There, he hoped to receive training that would prevent the Joining.

Once he was done, Transcend White frowned in thought. "You're right to go to Mako. Get there, no matter the cost."

"That was the plan. I figured they might know something about how to stop this Joining."

"Perhaps. But just as important is removing Vera's brand. The Sorcerer-Ascendant of High Cloud Temple is perhaps the most powerful sorcerer in the Worlds, rivaling even Xara and Vera. If there is anyone who can remove your brand, it's him and the Council of Elders. I'm afraid that if your brand isn't removed, defeating Xara Mallis will prove impossible. Even if you have more Orbs than her, she'll be able to read your every action before you execute it. She, too, has trained under the Masters of Mako. You will need their training if you are to survive. Theirs is a magic that the Volsung Academy dares not to teach. A higher kind of magic, you might say."

"You mentioned that removing the brand could kill me."

Transcend White nodded gravely. "It may. But if you don't remove it, you will certainly die, anyway. You must go to Mako. Find Lakhmu. He is the Sorcerer-Ascendant there."

"Lakhmu. I'll remember that. Except we're stuck because we're at the mercy of Sharo Khalin's spaceship. I need Emma to transfer its ownership token to us."

"Emma . . . is a promising Radiant, and has shown a talent for hacking various information systems of high complexity. Perhaps she can get *Fateful Lightning* to work for you."

"That's what I was thinking. But only if she wants to. If she doesn't want to do it, then I'll have to try myself."

"That would be dangerous." Transcend White pondered it for a moment. "I'll see if she wants to help."

"I appreciate that. And . . . . I'm sorry about Gaius. I really am."

"I need a new Psion," Transcend White said. "As strange as it might sound, I would have chosen you, if not for the strange situation we find ourselves in."

Lucian couldn't help but widen his eyes. "*Me*?"

"For practical reasons. There is the obvious question of overall strength. You are the strongest mage in the Worlds, bar none. And having that rank will give us more options. As Psion White, only the Transcends would outrank you."

"Some might say I allowed Gaius to die to take his position."

"Maybe so. But you're the most powerful Psionic on the Academy's rolls. To not ask you would seem a slight."

Lucian supposed that was true. "So, *are* you asking me?"

She gave a strange smile. "It requires an oath of loyalty, seven-sealed before the Spectrum of Transcends."

"All right, then. Absolutely not."

"I thought as much. But having the position of Psion White would put you in a position to ascend to Transcend. Perhaps even as high as Transcend White. Gaius was going to be my successor upon my eventual death. And perhaps my death will not be so eventual. I am quite old, one of the few mages left who remembers the dark days of the Mage War, and even before. None of the Transcends are strong enough to be White, aside from Transcend Red, but she hasn't the proper temperament for leadership."

"I understand your point, but I would never allow myself to swear that oath."

"As you wish. I will leave you here since we don't have anything more to discuss. I will speak to Talent Emma and give her the option to rejoin you. For that matter, I'll put the matter to Psion Khairu as well."

"I would welcome both."

Transcend White nodded. "Get to Mako in one piece. I'll tell Sorcerer-Ascendant Lakhmu to expect your arrival. Good luck, Lucian. And a word of advice . . . don't come back. I've already risked too much by speaking to you."

"I understand, Transcend White. Good luck to you, too."

10

TEN MINUTES LATER, Transcend White was gone and both Emma and Khairu joined Lucian in the atrium, Emma in her Talent robes with a green sash and Khairu in her resplendent yellow Psion robes. Lucian couldn't help but notice Emma's drawn face, as if she'd been through many trials since their last parting. Lucian felt a stab of guilt at that. But he supposed he carried his own lines now. Khairu's face, too, seemed older and wiser, and steelier than ever.

"Transcend White told us the basics," the Yellow Psion began, "but it's up to you to explain the rest."

So, Lucian caught them up on everything. Lucian concluded with their situation on *Fateful Lightning*. By this point, two hours had passed since he'd warped from there.

"So, it's up to you guys," he finished. "It would be great to have you both back, but I'm leaving it for you to decide."

"I'll help," Emma said. "Such as I can."

Lucian felt instant relief. "That's great." He turned to Khairu. "What about you, Psion Yellow?"

Khairu seemed to consider for a long moment. "I'm sorry. I can be of more use here."

Lucian wasn't surprised. He would have welcomed her help, but Emma was more important. "That's fair. How are Linus and Plato doing?"

"Still training," Khairu said. "It'll be a while before they're ready for action again."

It was hard for Lucian to imagine *either* of them subjecting themselves to the Academy's rigor, but it was either that or going back to the Isle of Madness. Maybe they would have preferred that option, but it was too late to go back.

"I should go," Khairu said. She faced Emma. "Good luck, Talent Emma."

Proper as ever, she gave a nod to Lucian before leaving the two of them alone.

"We better hurry," Emma said. "Your friends are likely wondering where you are."

Lucian couldn't argue with that. Everyone was probably wondering if something had gone wrong. "Ready?"

"Ready as ever."

Lucian reached for the Orb of Space-Time. Recalling an image of the bridge, the exact spot he'd left behind, he opened the portal. From their position, they could see into the bridge itself, along with Serah and Fergus's surprised faces.

Emma's eyes widened at the sight. "You figured out a new way of warping."

"Hey!" Serah said. "Get over here! We're at our wit's end."

Lucian took one step through, right onto the bridge. Emma followed shortly after.

As soon as Lucian allowed the portal to wink out, the sound of the storm on Oceanus died away, replaced by the icy silence of the moon. The air on the bridge was stale. They probably didn't have much oxygen left.

"I need access to the terminal," she said. She just noticed Mira. "You must be Mrs. Abrantes?"

Mira smiled. "Just Mira, hon. We're glad you're here."

"Of course."

Mira allowed Emma to access the controls. When the terminal wouldn't turn on, Emma mouthed a curse and gave it a jolt of electricity. The screen flashed on, and within seconds, there were numbers and letters on her screen, none of which made sense to Lucian.

With a start, Lucian realized she was already streaming. Green magic surrounded her hands, with both of them placed on the computer screen and accessing the information network within. Her eyes were closed, her face a mask of intense concentration.

While she worked, Lucian took over the Binding shield, changing it to a brand so that he wouldn't have to maintain an active stream.

Within half a minute, the lights were back on, and the life support system hummed smoothly. Another minute later, Emma had the door system back online. She shut every door on the ship, the compartments pressurizing with alarming speed.

"Damn, she's good," Serah said. "Way to go, Emma!"

"Don't break her concentration," Fergus said.

Indeed, it seemed as if everything was already working. But Emma concentrated on some final bit for the longest time. Her entire body shook as her arms quivered on the monitor, and she was clearly in the middle of some epic struggle. The lines of numbers and letters sped into a blur.

At last, the engine powered on fully. She opened her eyes and let out a breath. The terminal showed the default touch-screen menu.

"Done," she said. "It was . . . difficult. But thankfully, it *was* verified on a private server. Luckily, the League never registered it at all. I erased all transponder data and obliterated the ownership token from existence. I also removed all access codes to the Believing network. Under no circumstances will it reconnect to that, but that shouldn't be an issue unless someone were to make it remember the codes. The danger should be completely gone once one of us registers it."

"Excellent!" Fergus said. "She'll fly, then?"

"She'll fly."

"Emma, you're amazing," Lucian said.

She looked around. "What kind of ship is this, anyway? It's like nothing I've hacked before. League software is mostly the same, but it was tampered with by the Believers. Rather crudely, I might add. The energy coming from the engine is unreal."

"It's a new League prototype," Fergus said. "At least, according to what the High Prophet told us. It'll get us to Mako faster than anything else, which is why we went through the trouble."

"I can assure you, that's true," Emma said. "I was able to use some of that engine power to brute force the verification. Anyway, we're going to need a new name for the ship to register the ownership token to someone's profile."

"Register it to Lucian's," Fergus said. "If he dies, we have bigger problems."

"Thanks," Lucian said. "I've always wanted to own a starship. *Really* own one."

It was the culmination of a lifelong dream. Even if that dream was useless growing up in the slums of Old Little Havana, it was coming to pass. Or so it seemed. Despite everything, the very idea of it was exciting.

"The look of power on your face is almost terrifying, Lucian," Serah said.

"That's Captain Abrantes to you."

"Does this mean I don't get to name it?" Serah looked at Emma. "I mean, if anyone deserves the honor, it's probably Emma . . ."

"I'd probably name it something boring, like *Aurora*. That's the planet I most identify with. Or maybe *Sani*, in honor of my birth world."

"Well, I can't compete with that," Serah said.

"No, by all means. You can name it."

"Really? Great! Because I have an awesome name." She looked around, all but rubbing her hands together. "How's *Blood Wyvern*? The wyvern is the fiercest predator on Psyche, but the *blood wyvern* you'll only find in the Riftlands." She looked at Lucian. "Those are the ones you killed there, on the day we met."

"They were tough customers," Lucian said. "Without the Orb of Binding, I'd have been toast."

"Tough, fast, *and* majestic," Serah said. "That's what this ship is. *Blood Wyvern* it shall be!"

"All right," Emma said, with a laugh. "We can key it into the transponder right now. As soon as we're in GalNet range, it'll automatically verify."

She went ahead and typed the name in.

"Wait," Serah said, walking up. Making sure the name was to her specifications, she nodded and tapped the verify button.

"How's it feel?" Lucian asked.

"Feels rotting good. I finally got what I wanted! Now, let's not lose this one, okay?"

He couldn't imagine how they could, given the ship's capabilities and his own. And they hadn't really "lost" any of the other ships. *Ethereal* was safe in *Resplendent's* hangar, while *Talaria* was safe in *Stars' Blood*. At least, as far as Lucian knew.

"Well, maybe we should break here," Fergus said. "Have a

crew meal or something while we wait for the battle overhead to blow over."

Lucian had almost forgotten about that. "Any updates there?"

"Well," Fergus said, "I can set a receiving ward, but I didn't want to do so while holding the Binding barrier. I still need some time to recover from that."

"This engine barely lets out any heat," Mira said. "As long as we stay quiet, no one will find us. Of that, I assure you." She stood. "Think I'm heading to the galley to get some food prepped. Welcome aboard, Emma. You made quite an entrance."

"Thanks," she said, her cheeks reddening a bit.

Within the next thirty minutes, they were sitting at the table and eating. It almost felt like old times as everyone filled Emma in on the details Lucian didn't have time to explain earlier.

On Emma's end, they learned the First Fleet was still in orbit around Alpha Centauri, but the mages of both Volsung and Irion had retreated to Oceanus for training, along with the League Planetary Forces. They were simulating the defense of a space-to-sea orbital invasion. There were reports of Swarmer vessels descending on Malon's oceans and floating, being used as mobile bases from which to strike the planet's coastal cities. The planet was almost sure to fall in a matter of weeks, meaning Astravan was the next target.

Beyond Astravan was Alpha Centauri, perhaps three to six months away from being attacked.

The discussion of the war put a damper on their conversation, but there was no way to avoid the subject. At some point, though, everyone decided it was time for bed.

When they woke up, they could take stock of the battle and decide on the best course of action.

11

LUCIAN AND SERAH were shocked from sleep by the shriek of the ship's klaxons.

"What's going on?" Serah asked sleepily.

"I don't know. Hopefully nothing crazy."

Lucian threw on his boots and walked to the bridge. Fergus and his mother were already there. All of them stared out the forward viewports, which were caked with a layer of ice several centimeters thick.

"All right, what's happened?" Lucian asked.

"My guess is the moon is passing through the rings of the gas giant," Mira said.

"Hold on a sec," Lucian said. "I'll get the suit on."

Lucian stepped off the bridge and within minutes, he was suited up and entering the airlock. When he pressed the exit button, the door wouldn't even budge. It was probably locked up by the ice.

He reached for the Orb of Thermalism and streamed onto the door itself, getting it just hot enough for the ice to melt on the opposite side.

Finally, the door opened, revealing ice as far as the eye could see. A fine, blue haze covered the sky, through which he could see the green gas giant.

Lucian started down the ramp, almost slipping. He turned to see the ship encased in what amounted to an ice tomb.

Reaching for the Orb of Thermalism, he surrounded himself with a heat aura that encompassed the entire ship. Through the reddish haze, the ice melted fast, most of it sublimating instantly. Within seconds, the ship was free of its coffin.

"Good work," his mother said, in his earpiece. "Get back on board. We need to talk about what comes next."

Once back on the bridge, Lucian saw that the dash was lit and the engine was thrumming with life. Emma was awake, too, drinking a thermos of coffee, along with Serah, who was still rubbing the sleep from her eyes.

"Perfect timing," Lucian said. "We need to talk about our next steps."

"I thought the plan was Mako," Emma said.

"It is. We just can't leave until the battle has cleared up. I assume since things were quiet during the sleep cycle, we're good on that front."

"You're right," Mira said. "Mostly quiet, but that could be because we're on the opposite side of Sanctity now."

"Sanctity? That the name of the gas giant?"

She nodded. "We're more than two hundred thousand kilometers from where the battle took place. Unless there's a ship within ten thousand kilometers, we're practically invisible. And we always have the cloaking screen."

"Who won the battle, then?" Serah asked.

"That remains to be seen," Mira said. "Wide-band newsfeeds say the Believers won. Seems like the League was just a small strike force. All that could just be propaganda."

"So, what do you think?" Lucian asked.

"I say let's get off this snowball."

Lucian nodded. "All right. Burn full for the Mulciber Gate."

Not a moment later, *Blood Wyvern* was lifting off the icy surface of Ishamu.

———

WITHIN MINUTES, they were on a trajectory to the Gate. All was quiet on the ship's scopes. Nothing lurked out in the darkness of space, and *Blood Wyvern* was speeding up at a startling rate.

It would only take seven days to exit the Zion System for Mulciber, and a further five days would see them into the Covenant System. The star systems were not on the small side, either, both comparable to the Solar System. *Blood Wyvern* was just that fast.

As they traveled, they got more details about the battle. According to news reports, the Believers had easily destroyed the League flotilla. The League had intended it as a sneak attack on Zion. Either way, the League fleet had gone up in dust, and the Crusade was still on a trajectory to the Mulciber System. By this point in the acceleration curve, *Blood Wyvern* was comfortably ahead of the Believers' fleet.

As far as the High Prophet Sharo Khalin, he was injured but recovering quickly, praise be to the One. The Messiah turned out to be false and was to be hunted without mercy.

"We *saw* that rubble bury him," Lucian said. "How could he *possibly* be alive?"

"Knocked unconscious?" Serah asked.

"No way to know for sure," Fergus said. "Looks like all we can do is settle in for another long journey."

Serah sighed. "All right. Trying not to let that sentence make me barf, but I'll deal with it."

"For my part," Fergus said, "it's *exactly* what I want."

"Same," Emma said. "Boring is good."

"I have to agree with that," Mira said. "It means we get to live another day."

"Welp," Serah said. "I'm going to see if I can continue my character. I had some skill points to distribute."

"I hope you remembered to save that data to your slate," Fergus said.

"Duh," she said, holding it up. "I have *several* backups." Her eyes suddenly widened as she reached into her robe pocket. "Oh no. Oh *no, no, no . . .*"

"What?" Lucian asked.

"My sim pills. They're in the cabin on *Talaria!*"

"Well," Fergus said, with a chuckle, "maybe you can look at it as an opportunity to join the rest of us in reality."

"But I don't want that!" She turned to Emma desperately. "Emma, do you have any spares?"

"Sorry. I had to ditch mine before rejoining the mages."

"No . . . this can't be happening . . ."

"It'll be all right," Lucian said. "I'll get you some pills at the next stop."

"At the Mako Academy? You've got to be kidding me. If it's anything like Volsung, they probably live like they're in the Stone Age."

"You can play games with me," Mira said. "Do you like trivia?"

"*No*, I don't like trivia!"

"I don't see what the problem is," Fergus said.

"I'm sure we still have plenty to do. I noticed the wardroom table converts into a holo projector. Movies are more my speed, anyway."

"I guess," Serah said. "Maybe I'm overreacting just a bit . . ."

"Maybe," Lucian said.

Serah eyed him critically. "Or maybe I'm not."

"You're right. You're not."

"As long as we're not dying, that's a plus for me," Mira said.

"Well, maybe you guys are right," Serah said. "I should look on the bright side. It's almost like old times again, except better. Traipsing across the galaxy, killing bad guys, partying in dance clubs, finding shiny treasures . . . this list goes on and on!"

Lucian laughed. "Maybe the real treasure is the friends we made along the way."

Emma shook her head. "When did *you* get so corny?"

"It's true, though," Serah said. "For everything bad that's happened, there's been a lot of good, too. Emma's back, for one. And Lucian's mom is alive! We just need Linus and Plato."

"Yes, they lighten the mood a bit," Fergus said. "Although the ship's food stocks would not survive Plato too long."

"Who *cares* about that?" Serah asked. "Lucian can just get us anything we want with that Orb of his. We can eat like royalty every night!"

"I won't risk using the Orb unless I have to," Lucian said. "It could have unintended effects."

"You kids are silly," Mira said. "I think what's important is that we're all alive, and will be for the foreseeable future. Let's just focus on getting to Mako in one piece."

"Well said," Fergus said. "Though I'd hardly say I'm a kid. I'm about six months away from my fortieth."

"Well, you look young for almost forty, if you don't mind me saying," Mira said. "At least you're not on the wrong side of it like me."

"Doesn't look so wrong to me," Fergus said.

His mother smiled, and all Lucian felt was horror. "Are you *kidding* me? I'm right here."

"Well," his mother said, "we have to listen to you and Serah's cringey remarks. Take it as a lesson, son."

"And I have to listen to *all* of it," Emma said. "I'd rather we just focused on the mission. Whatever everyone wants to do on their own time is none of my business."

"Interesting," Serah said. "Very interesting. Fergus, if I might be so bold. It seems my previous theory is holding water. More than water."

"What theory?"

"You have a thing for pirate ladies."

Lucian held up his hands. "All right, that's enough. New subject, and that's an order from your captain."

"Who made *you* captain?" Serah asked teasingly.

"Me. *I'm* the rightful owner of this ship."

"Technically, the ownership hasn't been verified on the GalNet yet," Emma said. "But I'm willing to stand behind that point. For the sake of crew morale."

"You kids are dramatic," Mira said. "I think Emma has a point, though. I still don't know what's happened since we jumped out of AC, so I'd like to ask her some questions."

"Sure," Emma said. "What do you want to know?"

"For one, what are the Swarmers up to now?"

She hesitated a moment before answering. "It's . . . not looking good on that front. While the Swarmer fleet in Hephaestus was completely obliterated, the main bulk of the Fringeward Swarmer fleet is besieging Malon. They're expected to have full control of the system within weeks, if not days. The Coreward Swarmer Fleet has taken over Beal and is on its way toward Pontus."

"Pontus," Fergus said. "Just one Gate from Psyche itself."

Emma nodded. "That fleet could be in Psyche within a month or two. Depends on what they do, and how fast they go. It's worse than that. There are reports of attacks in the outlying Border Systems. Of course, it's hard to separate rumor from fact. It's impossible to verify facts. Of course, at the Border

Gates, there are no defenses to speak of. As many as a dozen or more outlying colonies may have fallen by now."

"A dozen?" Mira asked, in shock.

Emma nodded. "The Fringeward Fleet has slowed its advance, which is why the League is redeploying to Archea. That's where Hegemon Madi hopes to hold the line, shoring up League defenses at Archea, Alpha Centauri, and Arion."

"While leaving the rest to burn," Fergus said.

"The situation is dire. There isn't enough defensive infrastructure in the outer systems for the League to use. And they can't get there in time, anyway. Even if they tried, it would leave other, more populated worlds open to attack. There's no option but to fall back and try to hold the line."

"Even that may prove pointless," Mira said, despondently. "Chiron is the only world with a comprehensive orbital defense network. There used to be talks of building defensive platforms in Archea, Volsung, and Arion. But of course, it was just all talk and no action. That's the League Assembly for you."

"Any estimates on how long it'll take for the Swarmers to get to the First Worlds?" Lucian asked.

Emma shrugged. "Some say as little as two months, in the case of the Fringeward Fleet. After all, a section of the Fringeward Fleet broke off to go after Hephaestus, so it's clear they recognize that world's strategic importance. Without you, Lucian, it's doubtful even Admiral Yang can hold it. And with the collapse of Carthago Corporation, Hephaestus has become a mostly useless asset."

"They must be rioting by now on Hephaestus Station," Fergus said.

"The situation is bad," Emma said. "There are riots everywhere, not just Hephaestus. Especially in the Mid-Worlds and Border Worlds. Not even martial law is enough. It's not just Zion that's broken off from the League. Other worlds have gone their own way after empty League promises to defend them. Everyone recognizes the Hegemon has no clothes."

"In other words," Mira said, "shit has thoroughly hit the fan."

Emma nodded. "That's an apt way to put it. Whatever law and order there was even a month ago has completely evaporated. The best thing would be to go straight to the Mako System."

"That'll be impossible with our fuel levels," Mira said. "This prototype engine is like a black hole. According to my most recent calcs, we can make it as far as Covenant to refuel. That's a Believer world. Assuming we can top off there, getting the rest of the way to Mako should be smooth sailing."

"It takes normal helium-3, right?" Lucian asked.

"Yep, one hundred and twenty standard fuel units. A large tank for a ship this size, but not large enough. It'll cost a pretty credit to fill up, especially in times like these."

Fergus shook his head. "We still have access to our old account. Still a little shy of five hundred credits in there."

"That should cover it," Mira said. "One would hope, anyway."

12

FOR THE NEXT FIVE DAYS, things were quiet. But the second they passed through the Mulciber Gate, the ship's dash chimed with a hail request.

"Must've locked onto us in just the nick of time," Mira said.

Lucian felt his skin go cold. Anytime they'd gotten a hail request in deep space, it was always bad news.

Everyone was on the bridge within a minute. Gaining distance didn't seem to make the request go away, so it was likely the ship had gotten a scanner lock right on the ship. It must have happened as they'd passed through the Gate during the narrow window it would have been possible.

"Why is it not giving the ship name and specs?" Lucian asked.

"No transponder," Mira answered.

"Wonderful. Accept it."

It took a few seconds before a slick male voice spilled out of the speaker.

"Greetings, and thank you for using our Gate! For a small fee, we'll let you continue on your way."

"Who is this?"

"This is the Mulciber Transit Authority. Unfortunately, I must insist on the gate tax. Recent regulations were put out by the Prince himself."

Mira muted the mic. "Bullshit. Mulciber is Believing space, and if anyone had a tax, it would be them."

"So, it's a pirate," Lucian said. "Anything on our scanners?

"No," Mira said. "They must have been sitting cold for a long time. Waiting for a sucker to pop out and run along their trajectory . . ."

"Don't take *too* long to decide," the pirate said, amiably. "You're going quite fast, I must admit, but nothing can outrun a torpedo."

Lucian unmuted the mic. "I agree. Better hope *you're* fast."

There was silence for a moment. The pirate hadn't expected that.

"Please sync six hundred and twenty-five credits to the address I'm sending on short-band. As soon as the funds clear, we'll be happy to let you go."

Lucian unmuted the mic. "Six twenty-*five*? You've got to be kidding. No one has that kind of money."

"Someone with a nice ship like that does. Someone who's gone dark so as not to be found by certain authorities. So, what'll it be?"

"I'll give you one hundred. Final offer."

The pirate laughed. "I'm afraid my rate is non-negotiable."

"Come on, man. I don't want to waste my torpedoes on you."

"I am confident in my ship's point defense cannons. And your own ship is too small to have point defenses."

"You're wrong about that," Lucian said.

"We do have point defense *and* torpedoes," Serah insisted. "The best in all the Worlds."

The pirate guffawed. "So, shall I take this as a refusal?"

"I got an idea. Instead of shooting a torpedo, how about you shove it up your ass?"

"I see. You will regret those words."

Instantly, the dash lit up with two incoming torpedoes as communication was cut off.

"Looks like he means business," Serah said.

"Two torpedoes," Mira said. "On a 20g acceleration curve. God, we're dead. One minute, thirty-seven seconds to impact."

The pirate sent out another hail request. Mira pounded the accept button.

"Lucky for you, I can power off the torpedoes," the pirate said. "However, that will cost you a thousand credits."

"Get bent," Lucian said. "We have a lock on your ship, and you're about to lose your precious torpedoes, anyway."

"A bluff. You have less than a minute to decide, Captain. This has been a most unfortunate exchange, but I'm prepared to see it through to the end."

"Turn off that blowhard," Lucian said.

Mira cut off communication. "Cloaking screen is ready. Enough of a charge to give us thirty seconds of invisibility."

"Turn it on fifteen seconds to impact, then change trajectory."

"Aye-aye. Thirty seconds to impact as of now."

"What if this cloaking thing doesn't work?" Serah asked.

But Lucian was already gathering his ether. They would have backtracked if that was the case. There was no way around that. But hopefully, it wouldn't come to that.

"All right," Mira said. "Here goes nothing."

Mira engaged the cloaking screen and tilted the ship slowly upward.

Out the forward viewscreen, Lucian could see two lights

fast approaching. Within seconds, both were lost to view. The blip only lasted a microsecond.

The cloaking screen unpowered, and everyone watched the screen to see if the torpedoes would turn back.

"They've lost signal," Mira said, letting out a breath.

"How close are we to their ship?"

"Coming in hot," Mira said. "We'll be on top of them in five minutes. Going far too fast to get an accurate shot with rail-guns, though. Torpedoes will be required."

"We could just leave them there and go on our merry way," Fergus said.

Lucian knew that would be the most prudent course. And yet, a large part of him wanted to turn the tables. Perhaps it was a need for revenge. Simply, he was tired of being jerked around by pirates.

"Send out a hail request," he said. "See if we can shake them down for something."

Within moments, he answered the request.

The pirate's voice was angry. "How did those torpedoes miss? What did you do?"

"Here's your situation," Lucian said. "In less than two minutes, your ship will be dust. Maybe you have PDCs, but we have enough torpedoes to brute force our way through them."

"I see. And what do you want, Captain? I'm sure we can work something out."

Lucian was about to tell him to give everything they had when the scanner registered two more torpedoes shot their way.

"It was foolish to broadcast to us, Captain," the pirate said, smugly. "This time, you will not escape so easily."

"So much for working something out," Fergus said.

Mira cut off communications. "Never trust a pirate."

Lucian was not concerned in the least. The cloaking had recharged and was ready to be used.

"Ten seconds to impact," Mira said.

Mira flipped on the cloaking screen once again and changed the trajectory. The torpedoes shot off into space, completely missing.

"Okay, *now* they're dying," Lucian said. "Fire everything."

Mira promptly obeyed. Within seconds, four lights shot from *Blood Wyvern's* tubes.

This action caused a frenzied hail request to come in, which Mira answered. "Yeah, who's this?"

The pirate's voice was practically a wail. "Oh, Great Captain! Spare our miserable lives. We'll give you everything we have. Over one thousand credits!"

"For our trouble?" Lucian asked. "Make it five thousand."

"Captain, I assure you . . ."

"The torpedoes will reach you in about a minute. Don't take too long." He nodded to his mother. "Send them the wallet link and cut off communication."

Mira did so, and Lucian opened his slate wallet. Much to his surprise, the balance changed almost immediately. They were five thousand credits richer.

"Damn," he said. "Should've asked for more."

"We're not going to let them live, are we?" Mira asked.

Lucian considered a moment. If he left these brigands alive, they would only terrorize whoever else passed through. From the way they'd fired four torpedoes like it was nothing, business must have been pretty good.

"One minute left to impact," Mira said. "Window closing soon."

"I say let them die," Serah said. "I'm tired of these filthy pirates."

Lucian agreed. It didn't feel bad to double-cross double-crossers, especially when it had been their lives at stake. They all watched on the LADAR screen as the torpedoes hit their target. From the way all four detonated, it seemed the pirate captain was also lying about his vaunted point defenses.

"Well," Mira said. "This has been quite the profitable venture."

Lucian blinked, hardly believing that such a precarious situation had turned into such luck. This ship was the real deal and had dodged incoming torpedoes not once, but twice. Maybe it was luck, but Lucian didn't think so.

Lucian's slate pinged. When he opened it, he found that the transaction had been reversed.

"Slimy little bugger."

"What?" Serah asked, looking over his shoulder.

"He set the transaction to reverse once we cleared his ship."

"Wait," Serah said. "It's bouncing back!"

Indeed, the money *was* back in Lucian's account. He didn't know *what* was going on, but he felt the need to secure the funds, and quickly before it was routed out again.

"Send it to my wallet," Fergus said.

Lucian did so immediately. To his relief, it cleared and veri-fied within seconds.

"What just happened?" Serah asked. "Why did it do that?"

Emma cleared her throat. "My guess is it *can't* reverse back. He's no longer alive and whatever network he was using got shot. Since the funds have nowhere else to go, they defaulted to the last known wallet. Which was Lucian's."

"So it would have been fine," Lucian said.

"Most likely, yes," Emma said.

"Wait," Serah said. "Does this mean we're five thousand credits richer?"

"Seems so," Fergus said. "That will more than cover fuel or

anything else we might need. Add that to Gaius's money and we can live comfortably indeed. For many years."

"That would be great news if the entire galaxy weren't going to rot," Serah said.

"Yes," Fergus said. "There is that. Still, it's better to be optimistic. That money will be useful, no doubt of that. Operating a starship gets expensive. Especially prototypical ones."

"The money isn't spendable until it's confirmed on the GalNet, anyway," Lucian said. "The Mulciber System is under Believing control, so it might be a while before we reach League Space again."

"I'm sure the credit network is still running on whatever net the Oneists have in place," Fergus said. "It's the only currency accepted universally, from Terminus to Sulisto."

Lucian knew he had a point. "Here's to getting through the Mulciber System with no more drama."

13

LITTLE HAPPENED over the next five days as they passed through the Mulciber System and into Covenant.

"Fuel is low," Mira began, "and the only major orbital in the system is Port Grace, above Covenant itself. If we dock there, our ship will almost certainly be recognized, even with the new transponder we're running."

"Any options?" Lucian asked.

"Well, I've been looking farther out. Five days away, there is a fuel platform in the orbit of Amol Dasi, a gas giant quite distant from the central sun. But it's the closest to the Sibir Gate, which we need to pass through to get to Mako."

"Refueling so far from civilization is risky," Fergus said.

Fergus had a point. Being in the outer Mid-Worlds was bad enough, but typically, the outer planets of a Mid-World system like Covenant were a haven for piracy. Not always; gas giants often had fuel platforms to service gas mining operations, but it was always a risk to consider.

Normally, Lucian would have chosen a station far closer to a major population center like Covenant, a world home to some fifty million people. However, docking at a Believing stronghold was certainly a risk, and probably the greater one.

"It's risky," Lucian agreed, "but docking at Port Grace would be even riskier. There's no question we need to refuel to capacity to make it the rest of the way."

Lucian wished he knew how to fabricate star fuel, as many Atomicists did. Perhaps if he had the Orb of Atomicism, he could figure out a way to do it.

Much to Lucian's relief, the vast sum of money had been fully verified in their account, along with the ship ownership. *Blood Wyvern* could be considered fully his, and neither the League nor the Oneists could do anything about it. Money was also a problem of the past, at least for now.

The bad news was, with the reports hitting their newsfeed every single day, Lucian wasn't sure how much security credits could bring.

Over the next few days, they began the process of slowing down, and by the fifth day, Amol Dasi was dominating the forward viewscreen. It looked like a pearl floating in the black, not unlike Cupid in the Psyche System, minus its baleful red eye.

"Where is this station, anyway?" Mira asked. "It would be just our luck if it wasn't there anymore."

The thought hadn't occurred to Lucian. This *was* a rather remote system, so information wasn't always reliable. The Covenant System was almost distant enough to be considered a Border World, and within living memory, it *had* been a Border World. There was little infrastructure outside of Covenant itself and the few small habitats orbiting it.

"There it is," Mira said, taking manual control of the ship.

The platform was tiny against the backdrop of the massive planet. And shabby. It barely looked like it could hold itself together, and was probably built when the system was first colonized decades ago.

"That thing's from before the Mage War," Fergus said.

"We need fuel," Lucian said. "And they have it."

Serah whistled. "You *sure* about that, Cap?"

"We have no choice," Emma said. "What's the worst that can happen?"

"Well, I can think of several things . . ." Serah began.

"They just sent us a docking code," Mira said. Her eyebrows arched. "Prices look . . . surprisingly reasonable. Just under a cred per unit."

"In *these* times?" Fergus guffawed. "That's too good to be true. Out this far, it should be twice that!"

"Maybe they're close to a refinery," Emma said. "I did some research on this system. High concentration of Helium-3 in this planet's atmosphere. The best in the Spinward Worlds. It's not *too* unbelievable."

"Humph," Fergus said, skeptically. "We'll see."

"Hailing their code." She clicked the confirm button on the display screen. "Amol Dasi Fuel Station, this is *Blood Wyvern*. Requesting permission to dock and refuel."

The reply only took a moment, which Lucian thought was a good sign.

"*Blood Wyvern*," came a friendly, female voice. "Welcome, and permission granted. Please dock at platform two. Uploading docking codes to your link."

"Thank you," Mira said. "We'll see you soon."

"Long way from home, eh?"

"You might say that."

"We'll get you topped off, no worries. We mostly get miners out this way. More He-3 in Amol Dasi's atmosphere than anywhere in the League, and that's the truth."

Mira shut off the mic. "Chatty, isn't she?"

"Probably aren't many people out this way," Emma observed.

Even if nothing seemed amiss, Lucian knew not to take anything for granted. Not after *their* luck.

"One little thing," the platform operator said. "With the troubles and all, the price going out on wide-band is a little out of date. It'll be a cred and two hundred per unit. I'm afraid there's no room for negotiation."

Lucian wanted to argue his point, not for the sake of saving a few sub-creds, but to maintain the illusion that they were not a rich target, despite the obvious luxury of their ship. A rich man wouldn't quibble over that, at least to Lucian's mind. Someone with money troubles would.

"That's what you advertised," Lucian said, doing his best to sound irate. "You can't just make a promise and pull the rug out from under people. That's not how you do business."

"It is out this way," the operator said, easily. "I'm sorry, but them's the breaks."

He huffed. "Fine."

"Glad you see things our way. See you soon."

The communication cut off as *Blood Wyvern* wrapped around, entering a narrow hangar and settling down. Lucian noticed that there was a set of hangar doors ahead of them as well as behind, probably to allow ease of access. As soon as the hangar was shut off to the vacuum of space, it began pressurizing. After a minute, the air vents stopped pumping, and a team of four grubby men in blue jumpsuits entered the hangar.

"Better go out and meet them," Lucian said. "I'll call the bridge if we need anything."

"I'll come, too," Fergus said.

Lucian was grateful for the backup.

They exited and Lucian noted three men holding the long

fuel line, while the lead man, who had an oily face and a slimy smile, approached.

"You with the League, friends?"

Lucian shook his head, not seeing the point in lying. Besides, being with the League out here was more likely to be a liability.

"Huh. Don't recognize your ship model, but seems to be in the League swoop class."

Lucian wanted to tell him it wasn't his business, but he didn't want any drama. "Just fill it to capacity, please."

The man nodded, seeming to catch his drift. "All right. No worries there, boss. We'll have her topped off before you know it." He nodded back toward the bridge. "You can wait in there if you like. This might take a few hours."

"A few hours?" Fergus asked. "You guys don't seem that busy."

"This pump's old," the man said, with a shrug that said it couldn't be helped. "Between you and me, our boss is a cheap bastard, and we don't get enough business out here to upgrade. With the war and all, it's hard to get the parts."

"I think we'll just wait out here, thanks," Lucian said.

The man smirked. "Suit yourselves. Open her up, and we'll fill her up."

Lucian called the ship's bridge. "Pop the fuel cap."

A moment later, a panel slid from the underside of the ship, and men moved in tandem to refuel. Within the minute, the old pump built into the wall was rattling.

Once all was secured, the men stepped away for a smoke break, talking in low voices. Nothing seemed amiss. Lucian thought *maybe* he was being paranoid, but he had good reason to. Every time he ended up in one of these places, everyone tried to fleece him for all he was worth, or worse.

Lucian was relaxing a bit when there was a disturbing pop coming from inside the ship.

Lucian rounded on the men. "What the hell was that?"

The men immediately ran to the pump, cutting it off. Lucian drew himself up, hoping the anger on his face would be enough to get them to stop screwing him around.

The lead man stepped up, his face embarrassed. "Err . . . what kind of engine did you say you have?"

"Does it even matter? It runs on he-3, just like every other rotting starship in the Worlds!"

The man nodded knowingly. "Ah, but this is one of them *newer* ships. We're putting in the wrong type of fuel, I'll warrant."

The blast door slid open, revealing Serah. "Hey! They blew a hole in the containment sphere!"

"What?" Lucian asked, now *seriously* pissed off.

The lead man held up his hands, as if in affront, then looked at Lucian. "Sir, your uploaded engine specs say you required *standard* star fuel. If you had just told us of your particular engine situation, this could have been avoided."

Lucian had had enough. He reached for the Orb of Psionics and Binding, and lashed out at the man's mind, making no pretense of hiding his abilities. He needed to find out what was happening, and *fast*. A stream of violet magic left Lucian's fingers and surrounded the man's brain. The man went catatonic as Lucian searched his thoughts.

The other men cried out in shock, but Lucian worked fast. He gleaned everything he needed to know in about three seconds.

They had unleashed tiny nano-bombs in the star fuel. They hadn't intended on destroying the containment sphere, but merely to gum up the works, to force them to use a "mechanical team" to fix it. Once the team was on board, they planned a takeover of the ship, killing anyone on board. They had already done this to a dozen other vessels and had made quite the profit in selling them on the black market in the Sibir System.

By the time Lucian had learned this, the ruffians were reacting, reaching for impact handguns hidden in their jumpsuits. The door leading into the rest of the station also opened, revealing more toughs bearing impact rifles.

Lucian sighed. "Here we go again."

14

LUCIAN SENT a kinetic wave hurtling toward the four toughs directly ahead. In the space station's low gravity, they went flying toward the far wall. Still holding the Orb of Psionics, Lucian raised a shield, deflecting the impactor impulses that shot from within the station itself.

The pirates inside decided to cut their losses, shutting the blast door into the station.

Lucian knew what came next, but even so, he wasn't prepared for the sudden opening of the hangar doors. Together with Fergus, not to mention the four pirates he had blasted with the kinetic wave, he flew toward the opening.

He redirected his Binding shield to tether himself toward Fergus, and then surrounded them in a Binding aura, along with some of the station's air. Lucian panted, not sure of how much air he'd managed to grab. Not enough, apparently. The four unlucky pirates hurtled into space.

But now, Lucian and Fergus were well outside of the hangar, the doors of which were closing. They were crafty bastards, Lucian had to give them that.

He streamed Binding Magic, tethering them toward the deck of the hangar right next to the ship. They shot forward, and as they passed through the closing doors, it pincered the Binding aura. Lucian added additional strength to the tether, pulling them the rest of the way to the deck.

The air was freezing within the bubble. Lucian reached for Thermalism, adding its power to the aura.

Now, they just needed air. Lucian was already feeling faint.

Thankfully, the blast door to the ship opened, giving them access to the airlock. They walked on and the door slammed shut behind them.

Air blasted in the chamber, and Lucian allowed the dual-streamed Thermal-Binding aura to fall. Both he and Fergus sucked in air greedily.

The door ahead opened, admitting them to the ship. Lucian heard Serah shouting a curse sternward, so he went in that direction. In the engine room, Serah, Emma, and his mother were surveying the damage. There was a hole about half a meter wide, right where the fuel line connected with the containment sphere. The black, spherical engine within was completely visible.

"Radiation risk?" Fergus asked.

Mira shook her head. "The ship shut down as soon as we started fueling. The fuel tank is still intact, surprisingly, and we're at ten percent capacity. Probably enough to squeak out a journey to Covenant, if it weren't for this gigantic hole."

"How are we supposed to get a whole new *containment sphere*?" Serah asked.

Lucian surveyed the situation. "We've got bigger problems. We're stuck in a vacuum, and there are about half a dozen guys in there thinking about the most efficient way to kill us."

"What even *happened*?" Serah asked.

"I read one of their minds. They had some nano-bombs in

the fuel line. They planned to clog the engine, giving them an excuse to come on board and take over the ship. I'm guessing something about our engine didn't play nice with it. They were just as confused as us. They wanted to kill us and take the ship intact, not incur a costly repair."

"And you figured that out just by shooting some magic at them?" Mira asked.

"More or less. They probably thought I was trying to kill them right there and then, which is why they started to fight back."

"What now, then?" Emma asked. "Abandon ship?"

That would certainly be the safest option. Within seconds, Lucian could open a portal to anywhere in the Worlds he had been before. But that would mean admitting defeat, and they would have wasted this time traveling for nothing.

Lucian couldn't accept that. "This is an actual fuel platform, with actual fuel. We just need to take over the station and get it for ourselves. I know from my psychic stream that there are six pirates left, including the lady who talked to us."

"Maybe we should reach out again," Serah said. "Come up with some kind of deal?"

Mira sighed. "The fact that they're not hailing us means they've probably given up on diplomacy."

The alarm klaxons suddenly blared. Lucian ran to the front of the ship and looked out the forward viewports toward the interior station doors. They had cracked open a bit, and a couple of men in EVA suits were setting up a massive railgun battery aimed directly at the ship.

"So much for diplomacy," he said.

There was no time to get into his suit, so he ran to the airlock, surrounding himself in a Binding aura to keep his supply of air contained. He opened the door and stepped into the station, reaching for the Orb of Dynamism and combining it with his Binding aura, even as the men continued setting up their railgun emplacement.

The magic collected before him in a massive ball of electricity. The men scattered and ran, leaving the railgun. Lucian unleashed the stream of chain lightning, completely frying the gun. Letting go of Dynamism, he kept Binding open, creating a reverse tether that would keep the doors from closing. As soon as he passed through the crack, he released the tether, allowing the doors to shut behind him. He combined Psionics with his Binding shield, to counter the impactor pulses they would surely use against him.

He had time to register two separate, shabby corridors before something blasted him in the side. His aura cracked under the force, and he went flying. He used a tether to right himself, but still ended up slamming against the bulwark.

He hastily strengthened his shield, just in time to eat another blast. This time, the shield held.

He looked down the corridor to see the same two men as before, each holding heavy impactor rifles. Lucian reached for Dynamism, setting his anchor point directly between the two of them. Lightning leaped from his fingers, covering both men from head to toe in electricity. They screamed inside their helmets as they went down, writhing on the deck. Had it been a normal Dynamistic stream, it would have petered out by now, but combined with Binding Magic, the lightning swirled around them like a storm. By the time the lightning vortex ended, the men were long dead.

Lucian heard clomping on the deck from behind him. He whirled to see a large, bearded man with a long, metallic shock baton just a few meters away. Lucian streamed reversed Dynamism, forcing the baton to clang to the metallic deck. Weaponless, the man turned tail and ran, but not before Lucian tethered his legs together.

The man writhed on the deck, unable to escape. Lucian walked forward calmly, holding his Focus to divorce his mind from the act of killing. With a thought, he extended his shockspear and made quick work of it. Letting him live was too much of a risk, especially knowing there were three pirates left.

Lucian felt Serah trying to reach out with a Psionic link. *What's up?*

What's up? You go in there, guns blazing, and that's all you can manage to say?

What else am I supposed to say?

I don't know. Telling us what the hell is going on will be a start! Can you open the doors for us? The hangar is repressurized now.

Lucian made his way back to the entrance, pressing the entrance button. They slid open, revealing Fergus, Serah, Emma, and his mother, all in EVA suits, the mages bearing shockspears while his mother held her own impactor rifle. The sight of that shocked him a bit, but from the way she held it, it seemed she knew how to use it.

"Where are the bastards?" she asked, her voice projecting from outside her helmet.

"Three down, three to go. I'm not sure where they are. Not yet, anyway."

Fergus's eyes shone with green Radiance. "I can answer that." He pointed to the right. "They are just down that corridor, beyond that door. I believe they've barricaded themselves in some sort of control room."

"Let's move, then," Lucian said.

The voice of the woman who had hailed them spilled out of an intercom system. "Please, there's no need for violence. Have a full tank. On us."

Lucian ignored the plea and continued toward the door.

"Five hundred credits, too," she added. "Uplink your wallet code and it'll be done. We don't want no trouble."

Lucian was just a few paces away from the doors.

"Damn it, you think it's easy to be a pirate? Don't make us kill you!"

Lucian raised his hand toward the door, which glowed with molten red light. Screams and shouts emanated from beyond. A few impactor pulses warbled the metal.

Lucian increased the power of the stream until rivulets of molten metal flowed along the deck. By now, the upper half of the door was gone, revealing a small command center. A few pulses blasted off Lucian's shield, which he expanded to include everyone around him.

Power. So much power. His heart sang with it. The desire to draw even more was almost irresistible.

So he did. He reversed the Thermal stream, cooling the molten metal almost instantly. He walked forward, adding the power of the Orb of Dynamism to his shield. Even as he ate shot after shot of the pirates' rifles, their eyes going wider and wider, he collected that energy in his shield, streaming it toward his hands. He held it there for a moment, allowing it to collect, before releasing it as a single white laser. He swept the command center from side to side, and such was the energy unleashed that it instantly obliterated the three pirates.

It also obliterated the wall beyond them, which opened the small compartment to the vacuum of space.

Before anyone could go flying off, Lucian let go of his extraneous streams, blocking the doorway with a Binding shield. He turned the shield into a brand by wrapping it with Psionic Magic. Only then did he let go of all of his streams.

His mother watched him wide-eyed as he walked deeper into the station.

"Where do you think you're going?"

He turned back around. His Focus still pulsated within his

mind, absorbing his emotions. It was hard to feel anything but the tasks that needed to be done. "We need to finish filling up."

"What's the point?" Mira asked. "You saw the containment sphere. It's completely shot!"

"We'll find a way. We *have* to find a way."

"You think there are any more bombs in the fuel?" Fergus asked.

"That was a one-time thing," Lucian said. "The rest of their fuel reserves should be clean."

"Mira is right," Emma said. "We need to replace that sphere, but it's not just something you can find. It has to be made to the right specifications . . ."

"Lucian could use a binding shield on it," Serah said doubtfully.

"Do we want to do that for the rest of the journey?" Fergus asked in disbelief. "That engine puts out *a lot* of power. It would take more than Binding to keep it sealed. The stream would almost certainly need to be active to be of adequate strength. Even Lucian has to sleep."

Even if Lucian *could* do it, if such a shield weakened for even an instant, it would cause the reactor to overload, leading to a near-instant death. That was what happened when containment shells broke in fusion engines, anyway. If this quantum engine was even *more* powerful, it stood to reason that they would be obliterated even *more* instantly.

Despite Lucian's power with the Orbs, he didn't want to test his Binding against that.

Instead, he had another idea. A strange idea that he wasn't sure would work.

"What?" Emma asked. "You've thought of something."

"Yes. But first, I need to perform a little experiment."

15

LUCIAN and the others explored the station. With all the vermin exterminated, there wasn't much to find. A few cabins, all accessible from a central, spinning ring, and three other fuel platforms besides the one they were using. They found a small transport, a dated hunk of junk which Mira estimated would take a month to get to Covenant, and thrice as long to reach Mako.

The crew settled into the break room. Inside was a coffeepot, with an old brew that was acrid from sitting on the burner for so long.

It was time to see if his idea would work.

Lucian took the coffeepot, dumped its contents in the corner, then slammed it onto a nearby table, just hard enough to crack the glass.

"What are you doing?" Fergus asked.

"Stand back a bit," he said. "I'm not sure, yet."

Before anyone could ask anything more, Lucian reached for the Orb of Space-Time. But rather than use the usual forward stream, a stream that would fold space and create a portal, he created a *reverse* stream, as he had during his battle with Xara on Nai Elyn. He surrounded the coffeepot with a dark aura.

Nothing happened. But Lucian felt the potential. He knew intrinsically that everything within that aura could be treated as time-malleable. It simply required another Aspect to provide direction. Lucian thought back to his battle with Xara Mallis, how he had reversed her fusion reaction by sending it back in time, but he couldn't remember the Aspect he'd combined with Space-Time to do that.

And then, it came to him. He combined the reverse Space-Time stream with a reverse Binding stream.

At last, the cracked coffeepot became surrounded with black, sinuous lines, creating an opaque shell. Everyone watched in amazement as that shell floated across the room, retracing its journey from the coffeemaker. It was as if Lucian were pressing the rewind button, but only for the coffeepot and everything in it, while everything else stayed the same.

When the pot settled in its previous place, Lucian let go of the stream. The black shell dissipated to reveal the coffeepot, unbroken. The only difference was that there was no coffee inside it.

"How did you do that?" Emma asked in amazement.

"A reverse Space-Time stream combined with reverse Binding," Lucian said. "Space-Time Magic made it time-malleable, while reversed Binding pulled it backward."

"You . . . turned it into a tesseract," Fergus said.

"A what now?" Serah asked.

"A fourth-dimensional object," he said. "At least temporarily."

"What the hell does *that* mean?"

"Even I'm not sure entirely what happened," Lucian said. "I just know it works. If it works on a coffeepot, it'll work on a ship."

"Wait," Mira said. "You're going to send the *containment sphere* back in time?"

"That was the idea. Just an hour or so back, to where it wasn't broken."

"I see your point," Fergus said, "but that might be dangerous."

"How so?"

"Remember the coffeepot? It went back not only in terms of time but *space*."

"Meaning?" Serah asked, her brow scrunching.

"The containment sphere would not only go backward in time. The containment sphere, along with the engine, would appear in the space that *corresponds* with that time. If you catch my meaning."

"So, what does *that* mean?" Emma asked.

"It means that while the containment sphere might return to its previous, unbroken state, it would also do so in a different location. Much like that coffeepot. So all we'd do is transport the containment sphere, and the engine it holds, outside our ship."

"Yeah, that sounds bad," Serah said.

"Remember, all things are in motion," Fergus continued. "For example, this station is orbiting Amol Dasi, right? And Amol Dasi in turn is orbiting its parent star. And that parent star is orbiting the center of the galaxy. And our galaxy is moving outward—"

"—Okay, I see your point," Mira said. "So, can't we just wait on the ship, and wherever the ship goes, we go, too?"

"Yes," Fergus said. "However, unless Lucian can create an exception for us with the Orb of Space-Time—a *time shield*—if you would, we would *also* get sent back in time and space. So we'd go back to our former selves, and likely, lose all our memories up to the present point. While time around us will have moved normally, we would still be stuck in the past, with none of our memories beyond the point Lucian streamed us back to."

"Are you rotting *kidding* me?" Serah asked.

"So, what would happen, theoretically?" Lucian asked. "If I could create a time-shield, that would require an additional aura surrounding everyone while they are on the ship. That's a lot of magic, even for me. That coffeepot didn't require too much, but we're talking about an entire starship, going further into the past than I sent the coffeepot."

"First, no one is asking a very basic question," Emma said. "Is there another way to do this without playing with time travel? Doing it on a coffeepot is one thing, but we're talking about doing it to *ourselves*?"

"This is all theoretical," Fergus said. "It's fun to talk about, but I wouldn't advise it in reality."

"Well," Mira said. "We're not repairing this ship, and there's likely no one who can besides the ones who built it. They're either dead or working for the Believers now. It's either this or that hunk of junk we found on platform four."

"So, you're *for* this?" Emma asked.

"Not all of us have to go back on the ship," Lucian said. "Maybe just me. The rest of you can stay on the station and be immune from this theoretical memory loss. Then you could just explain what happened to me."

"You'll need a pilot," his mother said. "I'm willing to try, so just me and Lucian will go. As soon as the time travel is done, you can link to our ship transponder. Naturally, we'll answer it."

The others looked at each other, unsure.

"There's Atomicism," Emma said, doubtfully. "I'm sure a good Atomicist could duplicate the material of the containment sphere and plug the hole."

"That would take a lot of magic," Fergus said. "And isn't a

simple thing. None of us are even Atomicists, and it would require Lucian creating a portal to find one."

"I doubt Transcend Orange would want to help us," Lucian said. "And the only other Atomicist I know is probably being mind-controlled by Queen Ansaldra right now."

"We just went through a lot," Emma said. "Let's not rush into anything. Maybe we should rest up a bit. Let ourselves recover."

"That's the best idea I've heard yet," Fergus said.

Lucian realized something that no one else seemed to be considering. "Maybe we *shouldn't* wait. After all, the longer we wait, the further back in time I will have to send the ship. And the more unpredictable things become."

"What do you mean?" Mira asked.

"Well, if we rested four hours or so, for example, then the original point I'd have to send the ship back to would be further in both time and space. For all I know, that amount of magic could be impossible to stream. We won't know until we try."

"Are you good for it?" Emma asked, worriedly.

Lucian nodded. "I still feel strong. The Orb of Space-Time is being powered by five other Orbs now. It is capable of a lot more."

"So, Mira and Lucian are going back," Fergus said. "Which means Emma, Serah, and I will stay on the station."

"I want to go back, too," Serah said.

"No," Lucian said. "I won't risk anyone unless I have to."

"Rot that. If something happens, you might need my help."

Lucian knew there was no convincing her otherwise. "All right. Serah, too."

"And what do *we* do?" Emma asked. "I mean if it doesn't work?"

Fergus's face became solemn. "Well, I suppose we'll have to

take that transport and locate Lucian's Orbs somewhere in space. Then one of us will have to finish the job."

"Let's not think about that," Serah said. "It'll work. You'll see!"

Fergus sighed. "As much as I hate the idea of time travel, I don't see any other way. We know it works. At least, with coffeepots."

Everyone just looked at each other, as if to ask if this was really happening.

Lucian broke the silence. "What other choices do we have? We've already established that a Binding shield on the sphere would be too dangerous, and probably pointless, if any actual damage to the engine occurred."

"Lucian is right," Emma said. "If we're going to do it, we'd better do it soon. The longer we wait, the harder it'll be."

Despite all the terrible things that *could* happen, perhaps the risk was worth it. Not only would it solve the problem of the shot engine, but it was a tool they could use in the future, should the occasion call for it. Who knew? Maybe they'd get to keep all their memories after all, and even if they didn't, they'd accounted for that.

The fact was, they still needed this ship. The only other option was the shabby transport they had found that wouldn't get them to Mako in time.

"Let's go," Lucian said. "It'll be done before we know it."

16

AS THEY STOOD before the ship, Lucian tried not to think of the things that might backfire. All the same, they were stuck here unless they had a functioning ship. The only other option was using a portal to go to Transcend White and beg for a ship. But she had told him not to come back, and Lucian would die before subjecting himself to that embarrassment.

Five Orbs backed up the Orb of Space-Time now. He had to trust it was strong enough to do whatever he intended. This was, perhaps, his greatest test yet.

He entered the ship with his mother and Serah. They went to the bridge, though Lucian supposed it didn't matter *where* they stood, as long as they were on the ship.

"Well," Serah said. "If something goes wrong, I just wanted to tell you guys something."

"It won't go wrong," Lucian said.

"Let me say it, anyway. If we end up getting sent back a year or two, it was nice knowing you."

"I won't send us back that far." Despite his words, Lucian

felt doubt pulsating within him. He drew a deep breath. "Everyone ready?"

"Let's get this over with," his mother said.

Before he could talk himself out of it, he reached for the Orb of Space-Time, feeding it magic from all five of his Orbs.

Technically, he only needed Binding and Space-Time to complete the time reversal, but streaming from all five of his other Orbs would make the process go faster. He just had to make sure he pulled with the Orb of Binding and Orb of Space-Time while setting the aura large enough to cover the entire vessel. Difficult, but he was confident he could accomplish that much.

He maintained complete Focus, holding the streams steady and allowing the magic to fill the Orb of Space-Time. The aura was the correct size, just large enough to surround the entire ship. He realized there would be a fundamental difference between this stream and what he'd done with the coffeepot. With the coffee, he'd been standing outside the area of effect, but this time, he'd be standing *within* it.

What happened if he lost his memory while going back in time? What if he no longer remembered the reason he was doing it?

That meant he had to prepare everything in advance. He'd have to trust the Orbs to impart the knowledge on how to complete the stream.

He worked by instinct, delving into the Manifold itself. He streamed a torrent of magic, not allowing the stream to activate until it had the requisite amount. The stream had to complete itself, even without him to mind it. Lucian had never tried such a thing, but it was necessary.

When he judged it finished, he released the stream. And chaos ensued.

There was no proper word to describe what happened next,

or perhaps, *before*. It was a constant sense of bewilderment as memory after memory slipped away. The human brain had evolved for eons to make sense of its world by creating stories drawn from images, filling in the gaps as needed with fabrications of its devising.

In short, his brain had no way of processing or comprehending what it was like to travel through the fourth dimension, in a direction that should have been impossible.

Everything he saw was completely forgotten by the time he reached the preceding one. He saw himself walking on the ship. He was in the space station break room with Serah, Fergus, his mother, and Emma. There was a coffeepot. A stream of magic. A broken coffeepot. Him spilling the coffee. Grabbing the coffeepot. Walking into the room.

He kept getting yanked backward, shocked into compliance, only to forget why he had been shocked in the first place. There was always another image, another goal, another objective, completely forgotten in the next instant as he went irrevocably backward.

Pieces of the space station reassembled themselves. Bodies reintegrated before him, a white laser entered his hands, and impactor pulses bled back into guns. He was running backward, but still, the time stream worked, pushing him further and further back at an advancing rate.

He was out in space now, surrounded by an aura of Binding Magic. He was shooting back toward the station. Some men were firing at him. He was on the ship again . . .

On and on it went, a kaleidoscope of madness. Lucian wanted to scream, but he was watching himself from the outside.

In the end, though, it *did* end, and the blur of images was completely forgotten.

LUCIAN STOOD with Serah and his mother on the bridge of *Blood Wyvern*. There was a moment of blankness, an intense sense of déjà vu such as he had never known. He hadn't had such a feeling in years. It reminded him of the fraught days before he had fully emerged as a mage.

"You okay?" his mother asked him.

Lucian shook his head. "Yeah, sorry. I just . . . have this weird feeling. It's gone now."

Serah stood beside him, looking similarly dazed. "Yeah. Me, too."

"You were saying something?" Lucian asked his mother.

"Yeah. About the station. They just sent us a docking code." Her eyebrows arched. "Prices look . . . surprisingly reasonable. Just under a cred per . . ." She frowned. "Huh."

"What?" Serah asked, looking at the readout.

"The time window just changed. Said we'd be arriving at the station in four minutes. Now it's two hours and fifty-nine minutes!" She looked out the viewport. "And I could swear, the planet itself is a bit farther away, too."

Lucian looked up and was shocked to see that she was right. "That's impossible. Maybe it's a glitch?"

"Where are Fergus and Emma?" Serah asked, looking around the bridge. "Were they *not* just standing here a second ago?"

"That's *really* cheap star fuel," Mira said. "A little suspicious, if you ask me. Let me call the station back." Mira sent a hail request.

"Forget that," Lucian said. "What's up with the time? Even my slate is saying we're two hours ahead of where we should be!"

Serah reached for the intercom. "Fergus? Emma? Get in here."

At that moment, the station answered Mira's call.

"About time," Mira said.

"Don't be shocked," came Fergus's voice from the speaker.

Lucian couldn't feel *anything* but shocked. "Fergus? Are you playing with the intercom?"

"No," he said, sounding delighted. "Holy rotting hell, it worked!"

"*What* worked? What are you talking about? Is that coming from the station?"

"It's the station all right," Mira said, her face as white as a sheet. "How the...?"

"Lucian, Serah, Mira," came Emma's voice, "I'm here, too. You're going to have to listen closely. None of this will make sense, but it's all going to be explained in a second. You just went back in time approximately three hours."

Lucian's jaw dropped. "Uh...what?"

"I guess you don't remember anything which we thought might happen," Emma went on. "Anyway, you need to take this on faith. Fergus and I are already on the station. It turned out to be a trap, and there were six pirates on board. They destroyed the engine and containment sphere with a nano-bomb in the fuel line."

"She's telling the truth," Fergus said. "Lucian ended up clearing out the station. Long story short, there's no other ship on board. No useable ship, anyway. So, we decided it was best to send Lucian back in time with the ship, along with Mira and Serah, so that the engine would repair itself."

Lucian did a double-take. "Damn." He turned to Serah. "Hear that? I cleared out the station all by myself."

"Sounds like it was future Lucian, not you."

"Whatever."

"Emma and I remained behind to explain the situation," Fergus went on. "So, all that's left is to dock and fill her up." He paused. "Can you confirm the engine is intact?"

Lucian, in a daze, walked sternward. Within the minute, he had confirmed that the engine and containment sphere was completely intact and functional.

"It's fine," he said, once he'd come back.

"Good," Fergus said. "I'm sending you the docking code for platform three. We landed at two last time, and it's pretty shot to hell. If you need to confirm the facts, you'll see the station itself."

"We just time traveled . . ." Mira said.

Some of the bewilderment was going away on Lucian's part, but he still felt a thrill of exhilaration. Before, with Xara Mallis, he had reversed time around a fusion stream she'd attempted. But now, he had discovered it could work on people.

He was still a bit confused about how things had happened, but he supposed the others would explain when they got there.

Mira pulled the ship into the dilapidated station. Within minutes, they had docked and pressurized in a small hangar. Emma and Fergus came out of the station to greet them.

"So, how was it?" Emma asked.

"How was what?" Lucian asked.

"Time travel."

"I don't remember anything. I remember getting this weird sense of déjà vu about fifteen minutes ago, and then suddenly, things didn't make sense anymore. The time was off, and the planet was in a slightly different position."

"Want my review?" Serah asked. "I do *not* recommend time travel. Not at all."

"I guess you didn't go *back* in time, technically speaking," Fergus said. "Just your ship and everything *on* the ship went back, while the outside world remained the same. Just like with the coffeepot."

"The coffeepot?" Lucian asked.

"All in due time, my friend," Fergus said. "Come on. There's a breakroom inside. We'll explain everything you missed."

So, they told them everything. Once all was explained, Lucian had trouble believing it had happened. The experience was truly bizarre.

After thinking for a long moment, he broke the silence. "There *has* to be a better way to go about it in the future. A way to preserve memories. We might need to do it again. It's too useful."

"Is that even possible?" Emma asked.

"I have no idea."

"We got the fuel line ready," Fergus said. "We'll be topped off in about an hour."

They filled up the ship, and this time, there were no bombs in the fuel line, which in Lucian's mind, was always a plus.

Soon, they were on board again, having taken the liberty to restock their ship with the fuel platform's supplies. They had a full store of water and food, more than enough to see them to Mako and beyond.

"All right," Mira said. "We've got enough in the tank to get us to Mako."

"Let's get out of here," Emma said.

Within the minute, they were off again, wrapping around Amol Dasi in the direction of the Sibir Gate.

Due to a fortuitous aligning of the Gates, the rest of the journey would only take fifteen days.

17

A FEW DAYS LATER, they cleared the Gate into the Sibir System. Almost as soon as they were in Sibir, the dash lit with an incoming wide-band message. But rather than the usual white blinking button, it was red.

"Distress beacon," Fergus said. "In a system like this, I wouldn't touch that with a ten-light-year pole."

"Why not?" Emma asked. "A true distress beacon is hard to fabricate. It has to come from a verified code."

"Well, you're right about that. We already know how far we can trust the natives. We've gotten up to speed, and slowing down again would add days to our journey."

"It's League law that the nearest vessel has to stop and help a ship with a beacon," Mira said. "They aren't thrown on casually. As Emma said, the codes are unique, coming directly from a transponder logged with the League Transit Authority. Pirates are not likely to have one unless they salvaged one from another ship that hasn't been verified as offline. That switch can only be thrown once."

"Meaning?" Serah asked.

"The odds of it being genuine are reasonably high."

"Scanners in that direction?" Lucian asked.

"We've already locked on. Ten million klicks away. Fifteen minutes at our current velocity." She focused on the readout. "Looks like a basic civilian transport, by the name of *Strobi*."

"Like a liner?" Fergus asked.

"Something like that. Answering will allow the vessel to pick up our transponder code and ship specs. If we want to stay off LADAR, we should keep moving."

"Answer it," Lucian said, unable to help his curiosity. If they wanted to go invisible again, they could cut off communications and use the cloaking screen.

A male voice spilled out of the speaker, somewhat emotionally. "*Blood Wyvern*. Thanks for picking up. We're in dire straits, here. I'm Captain Jovanovski, of the *Strobi*. We're a refugee vessel out of Pallas. We ran out of fuel days ago. I burned us into a stationary orbit around this system's primary with the last of our fuel reserves, but we have nothing left."

Lucian frowned. If this guy was lying, he was doing a good job of it. "How many refugees?"

"I've got over a hundred souls on board. Women and children, mostly. Barely escaped the slaughter in the Pallas System. But there's no fuel to be had. We already had to fight off one vulture. Pirates boarded us and we lost most of our men during the defense. I know I'm taking a tremendous risk here, leaving the beacon on, but we have no other hope. Hell, you might be pirates, too, for all I know. Your ship name doesn't inspire much confidence, but the specs seem like they might be League-make. We're out of options now. Our rations are running low. We'll be completely out in seven days . . ."

The man trailed off, seemingly at a loss for how to continue.

Mira muted the mic. "We're coming in too fast, especially if they're in a stationary orbit. Slowing down and getting back up to speed will make us lose both time *and* fuel. I don't think it's doable."

"Is there anything we *can* do?" Serah asked. "If so, I say let's do it!"

"How much fuel would we burn?" Lucian asked. "How long would it take? Run the numbers."

"Okay. Navi-computer should come up with a solution soon." She input the command, and within seconds, a course had been plotted.

"If we were to start right now, we'd be there in about ten hours. Would require a lot of circling and burning full to max inertial dampening capacity. That, plus getting back up to speed, would deplete half of our fuel."

"Wow," Lucian said.

"That's the fastest we could do it. If we slowed the rate of deceleration, it wouldn't use as much fuel."

"How about a one-day deceleration?"

She ran the numbers again. "About an eighth of our tank. Of course, getting back up to speed would take about as much."

"Enough left to make it to Mako?"

"If you pick Option B, yeah. No problem. Depends on how much fuel that liner wants. They're heavy ships. Tanks in the thousands of fuel units, usually."

Lucian nodded, then unmuted the intercom. "Captain Jovanovski, we need more information. How much fuel do you require?"

"Enough to get us someplace safe. Covenant is where we're bound. We'll need about forty units of fuel to make it to safety."

Mira muted the mic again. "Our tank holds one hundred and twenty units, and we're still almost at capacity."

"Does the math work out?" Lucian asked.

"Math is sketchy. Showing we'll have enough to get to Mako

by a razor-thin margin. And that's assuming no further slow-downs or detours."

Lucian ground his teeth. Over a hundred lives in his hands, and yet if he stopped to help them, hundreds of *millions* could die to the Swarmers. The answer was obvious. They should keep moving.

And yet he couldn't bring himself to abandon them if there was a chance it was real.

"Please," the captain begged. "We'll give you everything we have."

"*Strobi*," Lucian said, after unmuting the mic, "we barely have enough to make it to our destination. And in these times, there's always the chance that this is a trap."

"I'm aware of that," he said, his voice growing increasingly desperate. "I will transmit time-stamped images. Videos. Whatever proof you require. Just name your price."

Already, the ship's network was registering incoming pings. Lucian didn't bother looking. They *could* have fabricated the evidence, but it would have taken a great deal of effort. Judging by their encounter on the fuel platform, Lucian couldn't discount the possibility.

He muted the mic again. "Thoughts?"

"Well," Mira said, "five minutes have passed since we registered them. The arrival window is shrinking."

"We're not just going to leave them to die, are we?" Serah asked.

The others were silent. Fergus was looking out the viewports with a blank expression, while Emma seemed troubled.

"*Seriously*?" Serah asked. "These people need our help. So, we should help them!"

"It's a huge risk," Emma said. "Space . . . is a cold place. To survive it, you must be even colder."

"I'm with Emma on this one," Fergus said. "I won't sleep

well for the next few nights. But our mission is greater. Being stationary next to another ship creates risks. They may attempt to sabotage us, just like the fuel platform. Or another pirate could swoop in before we have time to react."

Mira nodded, apparently making her opinion known.

Serah watched Lucian with wide blue eyes, afraid he would agree with the rest. He knew to leave them to their fate would make her lose respect for him. He would no longer be the man she thought he was. Even given the risks.

But she had nothing to fear. Lucian wasn't going to leave those people behind for a second.

"We're stopping. Yes, I'm tired of being stabbed in the back. And maybe that is what will happen again. Space is cold. You're right, Emma. At the risk of stretching the metaphor too far, or being cheesy, there are stars in space, too. We need them for light and warmth, and without stars, life wouldn't be possible. Human empathy must be guarded, precisely *because* space is cold. If there's a chance we can save those people, that's what we need to do."

Serah smiled, and even Emma was nodding. "I respect that decision."

Fergus shook his head. "I think you're making a huge mistake, but I understand your reasons. I've got your back, whatever the case."

Lucian nodded. He felt at peace with the decision. It didn't matter what anyone else thought.

He unmuted the speaker. "*Strobi*, we'll discuss payment when we get there. See you soon."

Before Jovanovski could respond, Lucian broke the connection.

"Engage the new trajectory?" Mira asked.

Lucian nodded. "Do it."

"Twenty-six hours now," she said. "They won't see us coming until we're almost on top of them."

"That's as it should be," Fergus said. "If their intentions are bad, we don't want them to know the hour of our arrival."

"Are we going to make them pay?" Serah asked.

"We don't need the money, so no," Lucian said. "Information, maybe, if they have it. We can't let them think we'll help them for free."

"Smart," Mira said.

"Whatever the case, you're doing the right thing," Serah said.

Strangely, it didn't *feel* like the right thing. He could very well be risking his friends' lives or even his own.

Emma was already looking at the images and videos the captain of *Strobi* had uploaded.

"Is it bad?" Lucian asked.

She nodded. "Looks legitimate. The ship's loaded beyond capacity. Unreal squalor. It's no wonder they ran out of fuel . . ." She shut off the stream of images and videos.

"I'll take your word for it." Lucian had to keep his state as emotionless as possible. "Either way, we should get rested up. An hour out, we should get in our EVA suits just in case. Arm yourselves with weapons you're comfortable using."

18

THEY ALL STOOD on the bridge of *Blood Wyvern* as they approached *Strobi*, a boxy civilian transport that had seen better days. It looked as if it could comfortably hold thirty or forty souls. If they had crammed well over a hundred, the ship's systems would be at their breaking point. The times were truly desperate in the Border Worlds.

As good as Jovanovski's word, it was in stationary orbit, completely at the mercy of any vessel going by. Lucian was relieved to find the vessel alone. The distress beacon would attract the wrong ships like sharks to blood.

The dash lit with an incoming hail, which Lucian answered.

"Thank God you're here, *Blood Wyvern*. After you cut off, I wasn't sure you'd come."

"*Strobi*, for our security, we need you to set your ship into low-power mode before we complete the docking maneuver. Life support and interior lights only."

Lucian waited for a response, which took longer than he would have liked. Mira pulled the ship alongside the *Strobi* but didn't move to join airlocks.

At last, the captain responded. "*Blood Wyvern*, I understand your sentiment. But we have many women and children on board, not to mention heavy articles and baggage. I'm afraid powering off completely would cause a panic that could lead to mutiny."

"I must insist. Tell your people that if they want to be saved, you must comply."

"Captain, morale has never been lower. We can refuel the ship while running, and I have my safety to think about. The people will simply not stand for it."

Lucian was becoming less impressed by the moment. "Captain Jovanovski, I've spent a great deal of fuel to slow down and assist. I don't like wasting my time. If you refuse to comply, then I will have no choice but to leave you to your fate."

Jovanovski's response was instant. "Please, *Blood Wyvern*, have mercy! I will do exactly as you specify."

Mira muted the mic. "Gee, that wasn't hard."

Lucian shook his head. Of course, he knew he should just leave right now, but there was something else about the situation that seemed off. Those pictures and videos had been genuine enough, at least by Lucian's estimation. He found it unbelievable that, with their lives at stake, they wouldn't want to power down the ship temporarily.

Jovanovski's words weren't adding up. And Lucian intended to get to the bottom of it.

"Captain Jovanovski, follow my exact directions. If you fail to comply, you'll have more than a mutiny to worry about."

There was a long pause, and then a sigh. "Very well, Captain. How do you want to go about this?"

"First, I understand that these are troubled times. I'm willing to give you twenty fuel units for information."

"Captain, we need forty."

"Twenty. It will see you to the Covenant System. We ran the

numbers for your ship specs. Even accounting for your passengers, twenty units are enough to get you to Covenant."

"Of course, we are willing to take whatever you can offer. But if you are willing to supply us with the full forty, I have certain things I can offer to sweeten the deal."

"Like what?"

"To be blunt, Captain, we are carrying far too many aboard. If you're bound for Sibir, perhaps you might be interested in a few refugees? We have some promising individuals on board, and the Slavers of Sibir are always looking for fresh meat."

Lucian could hardly believe what he had just heard. "Are they, now?"

"I would not speak so candidly, captain, if the situation were not dire. With less on board, we would stand to go farther and not starve on the voyage. Furthermore, it's the best situation for all. Any refugees you receive would be better . . . *cared* for, under another master you found in port, rather than me. If you would excuse the crudeness of my speech."

"That's a hell of a way to put it," Mira grumbled.

It didn't take much thinking to figure out just what he was dealing with, here. These were no refugees. They were slavers, taking advantage of the chaos in the outer systems to try and make easy credits. These bastards had been so greedy that they stuffed their ship with far too many people, causing them to run out of fuel.

"Not interested," Lucian said.

"I see you are a noble man, Captain. But we have no credits to spare, and human lives are the only things we have to barter with. I would normally not do so, but my back is against the wall."

Mira muted the mic and looked at Lucian. "This man is a slaver, son."

Lucian nodded. "I figured that out, but I still need to play along. There might be a chance to save those people." Lucian unmuted the mic. "I understand perfectly, Jovanovski. I'm sure we can agree. You said you had how many on board?"

"One hundred-and-two refugees, women and children all. As I said before, most of the men perished in a boarding operation we suffered three days ago."

"Convenient," Emma said, quietly enough not to be heard.

Lucian could already piece together the real story. Likely, Pallas was under threat from the Swarmers, and these slavers had posed as a means to escape. Desperate people gave them their money, only to enter a life of slavery. The men had either been killed or hadn't been accepted as slaves to begin with. It filled him with a fury such as he'd never known. Playing it cool was only possible by taking firm hold of his Focus.

Jovanovski cleared his throat. "I would be willing to part with ten refugees of my choosing. Don't worry, all are young and would fetch a good price in any market." Lucian could feel the man's slimy smile through the speaker. "Or, keep one or two for yourself, if you like. I'd offer you more, but your ship is quite small, and I doubt you could fit them without jeopardizing your fuel reserves."

"I want twenty," Lucian said, feeling sick that he had to feign negotiations over something so horrid. "And *I* get to pick."

The captain of the *Strobi* went silent for a moment. "You've put me in a difficult position, Captain. I cannot risk letting any other soul on this vessel, in case your intentions are ill. I'm afraid you'll have to be content with whoever I send to your ship."

"As you've so eloquently put it, your back is against the wall. If you want the full forty units, that's what you have to agree to. And I want to see these refugees in person to make sure I'm getting a good deal."

Lucian heard other men's voices, apparently arguing with the captain.

After a moment, the captain came back. "*Blood Wyvern*, you've got yourself a deal. Just open up your fuel cap, and we'll take care of the rest."

"First, we need to link up. I'd like a tour of your vessel. To make sure everything you've said is true."

"Of course, of course. That can be arranged. I'll allow you to complete the docking maneuver. We will speak in person soon."

Mira mimed barfing as she closed down the channel.

Fergus grunted. "He bought it hook, line, and sinker."

"I want you ready to disengage at a moment's notice," Lucian said to his mother. "If I'm on board *Strobi*, I can always get back on my own."

"You're not going in there by yourself," Serah said. "They're going to double-cross you."

"I don't doubt it. I'll take Fergus. This guy seems like a huge creep, and that's putting it lightly. He won't be as suspicious if it's just men."

"It would feel good to put him in his place," Serah said.

"In time," Lucian said. "We need to size them up first. We're already here, so let's be heroes."

Fergus's eyes shone green with Radiance. "Plenty of thermal signatures on board that ship. He's probably not lying about the number of people."

If that was true, then the situation was truly despicable.

Over the next minute, *Blood Wyvern* and *Strobi* linked their airlocks. Lucian looked at his mother.

"If you need to break the connection, do so. *Serah* can let me know what's going on with a Psionic link. As soon as you get the signal, don't hesitate. Fergus and I can handle ourselves."

She nodded. "Got it. Good luck, son."

They walked to a small operations chamber next to the airlock. Fergus grabbed an impactor rifle. They were practically the only gun option that was "safe" to use on board spaceships. Lucian just kept his shockspear handy, but well-hidden in his pocket. A shockspear without a built-in battery pack would give away the fact that he was a mage, and that was a card he wanted to hold close.

Lucian nodded, touching the shockspear haft hidden in his jumpsuit pocket. "Ready to roll?"

"As ready as I'll ever be. What's the plan, then?"

"Just follow my lead."

"Translation: you have no idea."

"Here's the plan. Feel them out, and when we get the opportunity, kick some ass and save some lives. How's that sound?"

"I . . . almost feel sorry for them."

"That's one of us."

The airlock clicked, a sign that the slavers were waiting in their airlock on the opposite side. Lucian pressed the access button, and the doors slid open.

Three gruff-looking men with hollow expressions waited on the other side of the airlock. Lucian could almost smell their stench before he saw them. Like Lucian and Fergus, they were fully suited.

The center man was larger than life, at least two meters tall with a wide build to boot. He held a heavy particle impactor, pointed down at the deck for now, that from the looks of it could obliterate Lucian and Fergus instantly. But Lucian was confident he could raise a Psionic shield in time to neutralize the threat.

The one on the right was tall and rail-thin, with a long face and long, greasy hair. The final slaver had jet-black hair and a cadaverous complexion. Both wore shock batons on their belts, with hands not far from their weapons.

The big guy, who Lucian assumed to be Jovanovski, nodded toward his weapon almost apologetically. "Forgive me, Captain. In times like these, we must be so careful. I feel a little better that you had the same idea." He smiled apologetically, though Lucian didn't doubt that if Fergus had been stupid enough to not bring weapons, these men would have tried to walk all over them. "I'm Captain Jovanovski."

"Captain Abrantes," Lucian said, not bothering to lie.

The man frowned for a moment as if that name tickled at his memory. But he smiled easily. "Captain Abrantes, I'm confident we can work out our issues. I have two other men back there, suited up as well. They will complete the fuel transfer. Do you have any other crew on board?"

"Three," Lucian said. "They will remain behind to monitor the transfer."

"Very good. I'm pleased that you've told the truth because we already knew there were at least three others on board. I feel more comfortable moving forward with this transaction, knowing your honesty."

Lucian frowned at the way he was framing that as if they were parties on an equal footing. Captain Jovanovski was completely confident that Lucian wanted those captives as much as he wanted the fuel.

"I trust that you are ready to see the captives?" Jovanovski pressed. "I think we both know what we're dealing with here, so perhaps it's best we drop the whole refugee business."

"Of course," Lucian said easily, even as his gut churned a bit at the idea.

Jovanovski didn't seem to catch onto Lucian's true feelings from his pleased smile. "I think you'll be most satisfied with what you find. True, they are in a rough state, but the quality will be unsurpassed. Especially since I've agreed to give you the right to choose."

Lucian maintained control of his composure. The captain was testing him to see how he would react. There was no longer any pretense. Lucian was here, his ship locked in, and now Jovanovski wanted to see if Lucian would take the deal. If Lucian betrayed any sign of disgust, he would tip his hand.

Lucian held his Focus, both to have easy access to his magic, and to keep his expression emotionless.

"We're ready to have a look. Twenty captives. No less."

The man frowned a bit at first but completely erased it with a smile. "Of course. I could give the first five now, and the rest after the fueling is complete."

"Unacceptable," Lucian said, firmly. "Ten of my choice now and the rest after."

The man's face tensed for a moment before becoming completely smooth. Lucian had the feeling that in any other circumstance, the fighting would have long broken out. However, Jovanovski needed fuel, and if he planned to betray Lucian later, that would have to wait.

"Very well." He barked an order at his two lackeys. "Imeri. Dauti. Show the captain and his associate to the cargo hold."

Normally, such a move would be suicidal. Cargo holds tended to be separate from the rest of a vessel, usually below the main deck on transports like this. They could be locked in and extorted.

Though Lucian knew such a situation wouldn't be any danger to him or Fergus, he had to pretend as if it were. The captain was testing him.

"Bring the captives to the main deck, please. One by one."

"You are a hard man to please, Captain Abrantes."

Lucian picked up his slate, making a show of calling the bridge. "Ready the ship to disengage." He was about to turn when Captain Jovanovski held up his hands placatingly.

"Good captain! Forgive me. We'll do as you ask. We can only do five at a time, for security reasons."

"Where are your two other crew?"

"In the cargo hold. They are readying things for your viewing."

"Captain Jovanovski, I have an alternate idea. As a show of good faith, I would ask you to board our ship and leave your weapon here. Fergus here will accompany you to our wardroom, where you'll be treated most comfortably. This is the only way I'll feel comfortable going into the cargo hold on my own. That is only fair, considering your crew is armed with shock batons, and I have nothing."

From the captain's expression, it was clear he didn't like this idea. But at Lucian's hard glare, there was no other way forward.

"Very well. Forty units of fuel, for twenty captives of your choosing. A captain for a captain. How can I argue with that?"

Lucian nodded. Slowly, the pirate captain dropped his weapon, well out of reach of his two crewmen. Fergus stepped out of the way and nodded toward the open airlock of *Blood Wyvern*. When the captain was aboard, Lucian opened a connection to Serah.

Fergus is coming back with the captain. Under no circumstances let him leave the ship. Don't do anything yet or reveal yourselves. Not until I signal it.

Her response was immediate. *Got it.*

The doors of both ships shut, leaving Lucian alone on board *Strobi* with the two crewmen.

"All right, then," the lean, mean-looking one said with a menacing air. "Follow us to the hold."

Lucian did so, steeling himself for what he knew must lay head.

The interior of the ship was dingy, dilapidated, and ill-lit. A sour smell clung to the air, a stench the cold temperature didn't do much to soften. Layers of filth had accumulated in the corners, and the life support vents rattled as if the system were on its last legs.

Lucian felt none too easy as he was led down the claustrophobic central corridor. He couldn't imagine how terrified the captives below must be. The corridor made a sudden turn, where there was a heavy blast door. The lanky man placed his hand on the palm reader and the door slid open.

The stench of unwashed bodies and human waste was practically unbearable. He could hear the sounds of whimpering. Lucian's stomach turned, but he had to go on. He had to see this through.

The two slavers watched him for a reaction, and clearly, some of his dismay was evident on his face. They had the gall to *smirk*. They nodded toward the opening as if challenging Lucian to go first.

He couldn't wait until they were both dead.

"After you," Lucian said, neutrally.

"As you wish." The two men headed down the narrow stairs, and Lucian followed.

Nothing could have prepared Lucian for what he saw. He had never seen such abject misery, such horror. Three rows of captives were chained to the deck on their backs, in almost complete darkness, presided over by two slavers with shock batons. One of the crew threw on the lights, and the people groaned at the sudden shock of brightness. Captain Jovanovski had been as good as his word. All were women and children, looking at him with a strange mixture of horror and hope. Some just looked listless, as if they had given up living long ago.

Lucian clung to his Focus more closely, not allowing himself to feel. He *couldn't* feel. This was but a small taste of the evil that lurked in the Worlds. How many vessels just like this were crossing space right now, unknown and unheard because of the recent chaos?

Already, some of them were piecing together what was happening and were begging for him to choose them.

He simply couldn't stand it anymore. There seemed little point in keeping up the charade.

"What'll it be?" the lean one asked. "We don't have all day."

"Enough, Imeri," said the one with dark hair and emotionless eyes. Dauti, if Lucian remembered right. "The useless captain is as good as dead. It's time we took things into our *own* hands. Just like we talked about."

At that moment, Lucian noticed that all four men were looking at him dangerously, with hands on their shock batons. That was all that stood between him and liberating these people. Four men and a weapon that was all but useless against him.

It was going to be a beat down.

"Tell me," Lucian said. "How would you like to die?"

The men looked at each other, for a moment unsure, before they laughed.

"*You* will be the one dying, fool!" Dauti crowed.

"There's fire, of course. Freezing. Lack of air. Of course, I could force you to kill each other. That might be interesting. Or I could compress you until you implode, but that's rather messy."

"You talk too much."

They circled toward him. Lucian backed toward the stairwell, not for his safety, but to get them as far away from the captives as possible. He didn't want them getting hurt.

He opened a Psionic link to Serah. *Disengage the ship.*

It didn't take long for the order to be followed. Lucian felt the deck shift beneath him.

Dauti gave a cruel smile. "They are abandoning you, Captain."

"And you don't have any fuel."

The man paused, the fact seeming to register for the first time. The guy certainly was stupid.

"Clearly, you jumped the gun and didn't think this through," Lucian said. "Then again, you're the ones who were bright enough to load a ship beyond capacity and run out of fuel."

The man snarled. "What do *you* know? I'm sure your crew will be willing to make a deal."

Lucian was getting tired of this. "No, because they understand the value of loyalty. So, who wants to die first?"

The two men who were still nameless seemed to be the first takers. The larger of the two charged Lucian, his shock baton sending out a tendril of electricity. Lucian raised a Dynamistic shield just in time, and the man's weapon overloaded and sent him convulsing and screaming on the deck.

"Energy shield!" Imeri said.

They didn't even know the half. The downed man recovered, but now he was backing away toward the others.

"I don't see no shield pack," another said.

The chained captives were all watching him, some even trying to break their shackles to get at their oppressors. Lucian would have freed them with his magic if he'd only known how. However, it would be easier, and safer, to focus on the slavers first.

"Ready to renegotiate?" Lucian asked.

"It's just a shield, you fools," Dauti said. "Just get past it and attack!"

"You first," Imeri spat.

Lucian shook his head. "You guys are talking as if you have a chance."

"Wait him out," Dauti said. "A battery that small can't last long."

"I can wait here all day."

"He's toying with us," said the one who had taken a shock, his eyes wide and fearful. "He's going to kill us all!"

"I'm going to kill you first if you don't shut your trap," Dauti said. "Just wait, all patient-like."

That was when Lucian extended his shockspear with a metallic whir. From the collective widening of their eyes, they finally figured out the truth.

"Psycho," Imeri said, his face going pale as a ghost.

Lucian stepped to the side, nodding toward the stairwell. "Up the stairs. Come on. Chop, chop."

At first, they didn't obey him. So, all Lucian had to do was approach them from the side, taking care that his Dynamistic shield didn't touch any of the captives. He left space for the pirates to escape, even jabbing his spear a few times to get them moving.

The pirates scuttled up the stairs like rats fleeing a sinking ship. The last one tripped over his own feet, his faithful companions shutting the door above. He banged on that door, howling. He looked over his shoulder, his eyes wide with terror.

"Not to worry," Lucian said. "I'll get that."

The man cowered in the corner as Lucian pushed against the door with a reverse tether, increasing the force until it bent. At last, after a few seconds, the door exploded outward. The man scampered away, whimpering.

Lucian reached the top of the stairs and turned down the central corridor. Another blast door barred the pirate's progress, and he beat against it futilely. At Lucian's approach, he was sobbing. He turned and got down on his knees.

"Please," he said. "I beg you . . . I've had a hard life. I had no choice but to do this. Please . . ."

Lucian opened a connection to Serah. *How's the captain?*

We have him in the airlock. Beating against the door like crazy. I'm afraid he might make a dent in it.

Take out the trash. I'll be back soon.

Will do.

Confident that the matter was taken care of, Lucian regarded the man for a moment. Then, he streamed Binding at the door, blasting it open to find the other three pirates waiting for him beyond. Dauti was holding Captain Jovanovski's massive impactor rifle. He bore a wicked smile.

"Boom."

Lucian raised his Psionic shield just in time to eat the blast, but unfortunately for the hapless slaver in between them, the impactor pulse didn't care about his life circumstances. Lucian's shield, thankfully, spared him from being soiled by the explosion of body parts, organs, and blood.

Now was the time to stop pulling punches. He threw his spear, tethering it to Dauti's chest. It buried itself deep, causing the man to drop the gun and go down. Lucian tethered the spear back.

The two remaining slavers fled toward the bridge. Lucian tethered their feet together, making them spill to the deck. He held the stream, even as they fought each other in their pointless bid to escape.

Lucian stood to the side and raised his hands, aiming for the airlock.

"Your carriage awaits."

They wailed as he gave them a strong kinetic push, slamming against the airlock's outer door. Lucian walked to the control panel and closed the inner door.

He watched them through the window for a few seconds, so that they would have a moment to experience a fraction of the terror they'd inflicted on their victims. Both were begging him for mercy, but through the thick door, their pleas went unheard. It took a few seconds of punching the terminal screen for Lucian to find the command to open the outer door.

With one last look in the airlock, he pressed the button, and they were out and away, on a journey to join their good friend Jovanovski.

Lucian streamed electricity along his spear, cleaning it of accumulated blood and gunk. Once done, he reopened his link to Serah.

All clear. Link up the ships.

19

WITHIN A FEW HOURS, the captives were unchained and tearfully thanking Lucian for saving them, once reality had sunk in. Many refused to believe they were free, distrusting Lucian almost as much as the slavers. Lucian didn't blame them, but they seemed more willing to trust his mother, so he let her take over.

None of them could pilot, so Mira programmed a simple course that would put them in orbit above Covenant, where hopefully they could find further assistance. They transferred the forty units of fuel that would see them there safely.

They were that much poorer in fuel, and it was time they would never get back, but at least a hundred and two lives had been saved from lives of slavery. Lucian would never find out their fates. It was up to the stars.

After it was all over, they gathered on the bridge to see the vessel depart, its large thrusters burning on a path for the Covenant Gate.

"Hope they make it," Emma said.

"Me, too," Mira said. She turned back to the pilot's terminal.

"New course plotted for Mako. Seventeen days, most of that time getting back up to speed. We'll have ten units of fuel by the end of it."

"No more detours, then," Fergus said.

"Hey, we did a good deed," Serah said. "We should be patting ourselves on the back."

"That whole situation was beyond horrible," Mira said. "In all my years in the Fleet, I've never seen something like that."

"Welcome to the Spinward Mid-Worlds," Fergus said.

"I don't expect I'll ever come here voluntarily again," she said.

From everything they had been through, it certainly seemed a rougher part of space than the Trailward Mid-Worlds, but it could also be a sign of the times.

"Whatever the case, Fergus is right," Lucian said. "There will be no more stopping, no matter what. Let's just hope those folks make it somewhere safe and sound."

The rest of the journey through the Sibir System proceeded without incident. Though their passage was peaceful, the news beaming from the greater galaxy was not. From the newsfeeds, smaller Swarmer fleets had infiltrated nearly every Border System. Nothing more than a few raiding vessels, aiming at whatever ships they could find, though the news was reporting a new, major incursion at the Eroth System, toward galactic north.

That was too far away to worry about, though. After traveling a few days longer, they learned that distress beacons were par for the course, at least in this system. In the ten days through Sibir, their ship logged no less than seven of them. Even if *Blood Wyvern* had the requisite fuel, Lucian knew stopping was useless. Even Serah admitted as much. There was too much pain and suffering in the galaxy to try and stop it all.

Most, if not all, of those distress beacons were surely pirates lying in wait for an easy mark.

It was a relief to pass out of such a pirate-infested system and into Mako, where things were much quieter. Almost eerily quiet. The planet had no habitation outside of its main world, without even the most basic of orbital platforms.

It took seven days to decelerate into orbit around the planet, a heavily clouded, tropical world that was mostly unfit for human habitation. However, the higher elevations were famous for their cloud forests and were the only place cool enough for small settlements to have established themselves. The planet's only inhabitants had come to Mako to disconnect. Besides the odd exile or hermit, there were sizeable communes of nova-naturalists, who advocated for a complete return to a preagricultural existence. On Mako, at least, there was enough food variety to make such a transition possible, and the planet's biochemistry was kind to Earth plants, at least at higher latitudes.

For the most part, however, the planet was a vast, unexplored wilderness, with a population of no more than twenty thousand across the entire surface. They at least had the coordinates for the Mako Academy.

"Prepare for atmospheric entry," Mira said.

They broke through thick cloud layers that never seemed to end. After falling for quite a while, the ship slowed, with no sign of the surface below.

Then, out of nowhere, treetops appeared in the forward viewport, only a couple of hundred meters below them. Jagged hills and cliffs stretched in every direction, all covered thickly with high trees that were remarkably Terran in appearance. Between two of those hills, Lucian spied what appeared to be a deep lake.

After one last hill, there was a small landing strip at the

base of the next rise. *Blood Wyvern* lowered smoothly down, alighting on the surface.

"So, I never asked," Serah said. "Is the atmosphere breathable, at least?"

"Completely," Emma said. "However, it might be warm and humid. We should avoid the lowlands. They regularly have wet-bulb temperatures exceeding thirty-five Celsius during the day."

"What's that mean?" Serah asked.

"You'll cook alive, slowly and painfully," Fergus said. "Your body can no longer naturally cool itself in those conditions, no matter how much water you drink."

"How hot *is* it out there?"

Emma checked the data readout on her slate. "A cool twenty-eight Celsius."

"It's not even sunny, though!"

"Perhaps it will cool off when we go higher," Emma said. "The academy is at the highest point of the mountain ahead of us."

Serah sighed. "All right. At least the gravity isn't too bad. I can manage."

"We should head up," Emma said. "The climb is steep, and nightfall is four hours away."

From Lucian's research, the day and night cycle here was faster than Earth's, at about sixteen hours. The inhabitants compensated by going through a complete day and night cycle before going to sleep, only to experience the inverse arrangement upon waking up.

They exited the ship, all wearing Talent's robes except for Mira. The warm and humid atmosphere, tinged with the spicy scent of alien vegetation and damp earth, almost made Lucian feel as if he was drowning. It would certainly take some getting used to.

"Holy hell, it's hot," Serah said.

"It's the humidity," Fergus said. "It'll get better once we're higher."

They found a narrow mountain trail weaving through the trees. Every surface shone with dew, and water constantly dripped from the thick canopy above. There was no wind, which only added to the stifling atmosphere. It didn't take long for Lucian's entire body to be coated with sweat.

It was already getting cooler, though. Ten minutes later, they were halfway up the mountain's north face, and a slight wind made it chilly. In every direction, Lucian saw green hills, foreboding clouds, and the odd call of an unknown creature.

"This world's quiet," Fergus said. "Serene. I can see why they built their academy here."

"Volsung was quiet, too," Emma said. "But there was always the surf on the cliffs. I can still hear it in my dreams. But here, there's a stillness. Maybe it's the clouds and the trees, or the lack of wind. This is a place where thoughts are the loudest things."

Lucian thought the description apt. The silence was so pronounced that it seemed no one wanted to disturb it as they continued the climb.

It took a couple of hours to reach the top. The trees came to a sudden end, allowing Lucian to spy a series of thickly sloped pagoda roofs. When the path leveled, they stood before a great temple, assembled from the local trees. It was built upon a thick wooden platform, onto which steps ascended. Statues of strange creatures and hooded men were carved into the thick, supporting pillars with amazing detail. The roofs and awnings, all at different levels, were too numerous to count, while long, narrow windows looked upon the forest from above. Smoke rose from various points, though there were no people to speak of, at least standing out here.

All of them paused for a moment to admire its surreal beauty, such a stark contrast from the forlorn Volsung Academy and the corporate feel of the Irion Mages' Tower.

They approached the main set of steps, which curved into the yawning entrance. They passed into a labyrinth of wooden hallways beset with carved figures, pillars, and reliefs. There were depictions of mages at meditation, strange beasts and plants Lucian had never seen, budding flowers, rivers, and trees. A haze of incense filled the air, but there was no sound, nor any sign of a person.

"What now?" Mira asked.

"There's someone here," Fergus said. "Somewhere."

At that very moment, a man in brown robes appeared before them. He didn't enter the hallway through a door, or drop from the ceiling. He simply *appeared*. And so did six others, three to his left, and three to his right. All wore those same brown robes.

"Err . . . hi," Lucian said, awkwardly. "Is one of you Sorcerer-Ascendant Lakhmu?"

The short, bald, and wizened man standing at the forefront shifted on his feet. He had a mischievous gleam in his brown eyes. He carried a short, gnarled stick to aid his walking. That was why Lucian was surprised when, as quick as lightning, the elderly man raised a withered hand and pulled Lucian forward with a tether.

Lucian immediately countered the tether, sending the man flying back. But as this was happening, the sorcerer to the man's right was streaming an anti-gravity aura around Lucian, lifting him ten meters off the ground. But before he could protect himself against *that*, another sorcerer shot a fireball at him, which he barely deflected by raising his hand.

The other three mages were fighting Fergus, Serah, and Emma, and handling them easily. And by now, the original mage, the old man, had recovered and was surrounding Lucian with a Binding shield. Even with the Orb of Binding, Lucian had trouble reversing the old man's stream.

The other mages added their strength to that stream, making it even harder for Lucian to break out. Other Aspects only lent to its strength.

The old man watched Lucian through the sheer surface as if trying to figure him out.

"Let me out of here!" Lucian said. "Don't make me level this place to the ground!"

The old man just chuckled. Angry, Lucian reached for his Focus, but to his shock, they had completely cut his connection. In the heat and chaos of battle, he'd allowed his Focus, the most vital aspect of himself, to become vulnerable.

As soon as he recognized this error, the shell dissipated, and all the sorcerers stepped back to observe him. He had access to his magic once again, but since he was no longer being attacked, he didn't stream.

"What was *that* about?" Lucian asked.

"What do you *think* it was about?" the old man asked, with a gap-toothed smile that almost bordered on asinine.

"You don't want us in here? Fine. We can go." Lucian turned around and walked back to the others. "Come on. Let's get out of here."

His mother looked at him incredulously. "We came all this way, and we're turning back *now*? With what fuel?"

Lucian realized she had something of a point. He hadn't meant to leave. Not really. When he turned back around, the seven sorcerers were simply watching him, watching for him to say something. They had called his bluff. It was hard not to feel like an utter fool.

"What do you want with me?" Lucian asked.

The old man chuckled, clasping two hands on his belly. "What do *you* want?"

"What is this, some sort of test? I don't have time for that. The Worlds are going to hell right now, in case you haven't noticed. Why can't you just greet me like a normal person? Why humiliate me?"

"Is *that* what happened, Chosen?"

Chosen. So, they were at least acknowledging what he was. "I don't know. Maybe a little."

The elderly man grunted as the other sorcerers just watched him quietly.

"This *is* the Mako Academy, right?" Lucian asked.

The man gave a serene, knowing nod. He chuckled again, though Lucian didn't see what was so funny. It was as if he didn't know, or care, that humanity was on the brink of destruction.

"I'm sorry if I did something wrong," Lucian said. "Something to have offended you. But I have nowhere else to turn. I've been told that the Sorcerers of the Mako Academy are the most powerful mages in the galaxy." His cheeks burned for a moment. "If you handled me that easily, then even I have to admit that much."

"Even *you*?" the man asked, amused.

Lucian ignored his question. He realized the man had done nothing *but* ask questions ever since he'd arrived. He looked back at the others, who seemed to be just as confused. Serah, however, was smiling, as if she found the old fellow funny.

"You there," the old sorcerer said, pointing his walking stick at Serah. "Come here."

Serah approached, not seeming to have any fear, considering the level of power the Mako sorcerers had displayed.

He looked at her from head to toe, and it seemed under his

scrutiny, Serah showed her first sign of embarrassment. "I know. It's bad."

The man arched a white, bushy eyebrow, but said nothing more. "Not hopeless. Fear not. You've come to the right place." The old man waved the others over. "Come, come. Don't be shy, now."

Once all had gathered around, the old man surveyed his audience, and drew up importantly, almost as if he were addressing a lecture hall filled with three hundred people.

"I will explain things clearly to you. I've been waiting for many months for your arrival. Yes, long before even *you* knew you were coming. I am powerful in Psionic prophecy." He gave a high, tittering laugh. "What you experienced *was* a test, a quick way for me to measure your abilities. We have a long road ahead of us indeed. Yes, a long, long road. Pray that we run quick!"

"How long?" Serah asked.

"That remains to be seen. The first lesson of a sorcerer is to guard your mind, always. There is nothing more precious in all of creation than your mind and the realities your mind can manifest."

After he said this, he gave a sidelong look at Lucian, as if to remind him he should be doing so right now. Lucian supposed the time for humility was about to begin. He streamed a Psionic ward. The old man nodded, satisfied.

Fergus shifted his feet. "I suppose you must be the Sorcerer-Ascendant, Lakhmu?"

"You suppose correctly, Fergus."

"And the others?" Mira asked.

"What others?"

Lucian frowned. "Those six other sorcerers standing around you. They are all looking at you right now."

"Are they?"

Lucian looked at them to be sure. They most certainly were. He didn't understand why Lakhmu was playing coy.

"Take another look, Chosen. Look closely. Tell me what you see."

Lucian did, examining each sorcerer. He approached the closest one, a middle-aged man with distinguished, handsome features and slate-gray eyes. The man watched him sternly, not shifting his feet. Lucian reached out for the man's Focus, only to find that there *was* none. A non-mage? But he had *seen* him stream. Had Lakhmu, like Vera, switched his Focus to another man, a non-mage?

The mystery was solved when Lakhmu closed his eyes, and a shimmering Psionic ward dissolved from all around them. Lucian let out a gasp as the scene shifted. He was still in the temple, but it was worn, weathered, and ill-lit, with vines and creepers choking its interior surfaces. The statues and monsters looked sinister in the shadows, and the only light came from shallow recesses filled with flickering flames. Outside the windows, rain slashed against the jungle, and the forest swayed and groaned as if in duress.

And the other sorcerers had vanished entirely, leaving Lakhmu alone. This time, he was no longer smiling, but quite somber. The others looked around, shocked at the sudden change.

Lucian looked around, bewildered. "What did you just do? I thought this was an Academy, but now, it looks like ruins. What happened to the others?"

Lakhmu shrugged. "I can tell you that. But first, you must answer me. Do you submit yourself to my training or not? Do you wish to challenge the Psion of Darkness, or to go your own way?"

Lucian frowned. Certainly, this environment was less impressive than what he had seen at first. Was Lakhmu living here alone? And yet, he had conjured an entire scene, even an entire *battle*, making Lucian and his companions believe it was the truth.

"I'll be trained," Lucian said. "But I will submit to no one."

Lakhmu's pudgy face grew stern. "You must yield to gain, young mage. And many times, accepting a low place puts you in a position to gain." He tittered. "Something to think about."

Lucian sighed. Had he come all this way just to become Lakhmu's errand boy?

"I want to learn magic, Sorcerer-Lakhmu. *Powerful* magic. And I need to learn it fast to defeat Xara Mallis, to gather the Orbs and return them to the Heart of Creation. If you can't help me with that—"

"—I can," Lakhmu said. "But only if you will help yourself."

"Can you remove the brand Vera Desai placed on me?"

The man regarded him critically. "I . . . can do that. But you must be trainable. You are a mage now, Lucian. But should you submit to me, I'll induct you into the higher mysteries of magic. A mage cannot defeat Xara Mallis. Only a sorcerer can. A *powerful* sorcerer."

"What's the difference?"

The old man smiled. "Everything. The road will not be easy, but you can become powerful. You must leave your conceptions of magery behind and stop playing with shadows. You must see the world as it is. More importantly, you must see yourself as *you* truly are."

"How long will that take?"

"It's not a question of time. It's a question of conquering yourself."

The others watched him, seeming to await his decision. As did Lakhmu. Lucian's heart was racing at the idea of entrusting his life to this man, who was apparently to become his mentor if he wanted to learn more.

Despite his misgivings, he had come all this way. He needed answers.

"Okay," Lucian said. "I will . . . submit myself to your training. I want to defeat Xara Mallis. I . . . want to conquer myself."

"Good. Then we begin."

20

IT WAS as if he were a Novice all over again, only ten times worse.

Lucian would spend the days mostly without magic, repairing the fallen Cloud Forest Temple. He did the work without complaining, with a humbler heart than he'd had only a few short days ago.

For some strange reason, though, it was easy to be at peace here. This world was quiet. There was no GalNet access, no light pollution, and no extraneous noise. The only sounds were of nature: the swaying of trees, the chirping of birds and strange creatures from the forest, and the gentle rainfall. The rain came in the evening, usually, and mostly, it fell gracefully in the seventy percent Earth gravity. It was hard to believe that just beyond this alien sky, the Worlds were falling apart.

Despite the dilapidated state of the temple, there were chambers beneath the main surface that were dry and warm enough. And it was here that Lucian and the others would ask Lakhmu questions. And the old sorcerer would tell them stories, often to the sound of the night rain falling softly above them, or if it was during the day, the sounds of life emanating from the surrounding forest.

"So, what happened here?" Lucian asked. "Why are you the only one left? Why is the temple in disrepair?"

Sorcerer Lakhmu sighed heavily and seemed to collect his thoughts for a moment. "It . . . was a slow decline. The start of it was the Mage War, of course, but the rot started happening before."

"There was fighting here?"

"No, Lucian. It was not with tachyon lances, or fire, that our temple fell. It was our training."

"Your training?" Serah asked.

Lakhmu nodded sagely. "We trained Vera Desai and Xara Mallis when the Volsung Academy would not. We trained Ansaldra Dara, among others, who rose to the Council of the Wise of the Starsea Mages. They took our greatest lessons and mysteries and used them for power, rather than to achieve the highest good."

"And what is the highest good?" Lucian asked.

The man gave a knowing smile. "To be one's true self. All else stems from that."

"Why did you train them to begin with?"

"I saw the kernel of potential within and wished to cultivate it. That is what I've done with all my students. But perhaps it was hubris that I took them in. The Transcends of Volsung had exiled them, and perhaps I should have been more cautious." He shrugged his bony shoulders. "But the instruction of magic was at a crossroads. My training is of the Old Way, which is far more powerful than the New Way, which other places call the Path of Balance. Before the war, we trained many students. But when the war was over, the League forced us to stop our training."

"But you're still here," Lucian said. "You mean to tell me

you've been in this temple by yourself for fifty-plus years? And everyone still seems to think you're open for business."

"It shows you how easily people are deceived, even those who think themselves clever. People see what they want to see, Lucian. You should remember that."

Lucian was just confused. "But . . . why? What's the point?"

"We are not there yet, young mage."

"Those other sorcerers you conjured, though," Lucian said. "Who were *they*?"

"They were past sorcerers who graced our halls. All are dead, either by war or by the fraying."

"But you've survived, despite training in the Old Way," Emma said.

"Yes. Again, our training was misguided. It led to great power, but that power was not tempered with truth or goodness. It was misguided intellectualism, without an object. Knowledge for the sake of knowledge can lead to some evil places."

Fergus cleared his throat. "Knowledge is good though, isn't it, Sorcerer Lakhmu? With knowledge, we can do many things. Some would argue that knowledge, comprehension of reality as it is, is the highest good."

Lakhmu shook his head with a smile. "The highest good is not comprehending it, Fergus. It's doing it."

"Doing *good* is the highest good?" Lucian asked. "Sounds overly simplistic."

Lakhmu chuckled. "Yes. It is simple. But it's also complicated."

"I don't know about all that philosophy stuff," Serah said. "But from what I can tell, Master Lakhmu, you seem happy in a way that most mages are not. Maybe there's a reason for that."

"I have accepted myself as I am, Serah, and it took a war and the death of all my friends to realize that. I was trying to unlock the secrets of creation, thinking that the ends justified the means. I deemed that the knowledge unlocked would save so many more than were destroyed in the path to gain it. But I was denying myself and my truth, and that was the path to despair. The most common form of despair is not being who you truly are."

That made Lucian himself wonder: who was *he*? Was he in danger of sacrificing himself, who he was, to achieve something supposedly higher? That was what Vera, Xara, and even Ansaldra had done. All had been students of this man. What had caused them to go wrong? Was it his teaching, or something else?

"How can you accept yourself, then?" Serah asked. "I know who I want to be, but I can never. . . *be* that person, if you know what I mean. I'm . . . too far gone, you might say."

Lakhmu looked her fully in the face. "Be who and what you are, Serah. There is nothing else. Live your life. Learn, love, eat, drink, spend time with friends."

"But the galaxy is going to hell," Lucian protested. "How can we just relax if we don't rise to stop it? Should I just give up everything and retire? That sounds nice, but I'm the only one who can stop the Swarmers."

Lakhmu chuckled. Lucian felt annoyed. It hardly seemed something to laugh about.

"What's so funny?"

"Forgive me," Lakhmu said. "When I was your age, I would have never said these things. But after the Mage War, after its destruction, in the pits of despair, I looked up, opened my eyes, and saw reality as it was. And you know what I did?"

"What?" Mira asked.

He chuckled. "I *laughed*. And I haven't stopped laughing since."

Lucian was incredulous. "So, we save the Worlds with *laughter*?"

"You are up against a great evil, Chosen. That is why I am here. To teach you to fight it. To teach you to find your truth. You do not fight evil with evil, but with goodness and truth."

"How do I do that?"

"You are already on the right path. You have come here and have humbled yourself. I have seen into your heart, and your intentions are pure. But you also face great darkness, a Shadow that marks your every step."

"How do you know about that?"

Lakhmu laughed. "You seem surprised? If you haven't learned that I am a great sorcerer, a man who understands life's hidden forces, then you haven't been paying much attention."

"Why do you use that word to describe yourself? You say *sorcerer* instead of *mage*. You still haven't fully explained that."

"Words are not arbitrary things, Lucian. A mage uses magic according to a set of rules. A sorcerer conjures realities from the Manifold and becomes the master of reality. Rules do not confine the sorcerer as they do the mage."

Fergus frowned. "But magic *has* rules. Radiance is my primary. That makes me a Radiant. If I dualstream it with Binding, the stream will require four times as much ether, and combining it again with Dynamism, for example, would require nine times as much. Forward and reverse streams combine in different ways, and produce different effects. It is the mage's part to study such phenomenon, to interpret them, and to do so safely that limits the effects of the fraying."

Lakhmu laughed. It seemed it was his default response. "You're right, Fergus. It *is* a mage's lot to do that. But it is only one way of interpreting magical reality among many. That school of thought has overtaken the masters of Irion and

Volsung. Some believe in sorcery, but precious few can practice its realities."

"What do you mean?" Lucian asked.

"Take Sorceress Ansaldra, for example. Does she limit herself to mere magery? She works great evil on the distant world of Psyche, maintaining countless brands that never seem to dissipate. More than that, she can transfer her Focus and live as another person. How can she do that if she is following the rules of magic, as understood by the wise masters of Volsung and Irion?"

"Okay," Lucian said. "Then how does she do it?"

"Imagination is the beginning of creation. Will what you imagine. Imagine what you desire. And at last, create what you will."

"I don't understand. The magic of rules, what I learned at Volsung and other places, makes sense to me. But you're saying that I can create my *own* rules?"

"You become what you understand," Lakhmu said. "Understand this, and you understand everything."

"I *don't* understand, though. How can I be made to understand?"

"Life has hidden forces you can only discover by living."

"Living? Am I not doing that right now?"

Lakhmu's face sobered. "No, Lucian. You are *dying*."

That had not been the answer he expected. "What do you mean? I can't get the fraying anymore. That's not what you mean, is it?"

Lakhmu shook his head. "You are not dying physically. You are being driven toward a goal, a despair, that is not of your devising. You will not discover that until it is too late."

"You're acting as if it has already happened."

Lakhmu's eyes became sorrowful. "There are many mysteries, many magics, of which I know little. But as I look into your eyes now, that is what I see. Despair."

Well, so what? Of course, Lucian couldn't be happy if he was supposed to be the rotting hero of the entire galaxy. If Serah was doomed to die from an incurable disease, if everyone around this fire would die if he failed in his mission, if all of *humanity* would die, how could he *not* despair? It was all on his shoulders.

And this man's solution was just to laugh it all off?

He had to force himself to be patient. To understand. "Tell me. What must I do?"

"Life can only be understood by experiencing it. It must be lived forwards, but understood backwards."

"How does that help me if I can't figure things out until I'm older?"

Serah put a hand on his arm, perhaps sensing his mounting frustration.

"You've only just arrived," Lakhmu said, at last. "But I will leave you with this before we sleep. Face who you are, the bare facts of your existence, and the truth of that will change who you are."

It sounded like something Vera might have said to him, once upon a time. Had she gained some of her philosophy from this old sorcerer? But Lakhmu, to Lucian, seemed to understand more than Vera. To have a different way of viewing things. His goals and motivations were certainly different, and perhaps that amounted to everything.

"Good night," Lakhmu said. He rolled over, turning his back to the fire.

The rest of them followed suit.

21

THROUGH THE NIGHT, Lucian's dreams were troubled. The Shadow was there, chasing him through the rifts of Psyche, the glaciers of Halia, the scarred wastelands of Hephaestus. It seemed he could get no reprieve.

And yet he knew the Shadow was a part of him. And he could never run away from himself.

He awoke, not feeling rested in the least. Lakhmu was cooking a pot of stew over a low flame, along with a kettle of hot water. The air was damp and cool, and the green forest was silent and still. All was gray from the thick layer of clouds that never seemed to dissipate.

"Sleep well?" Lakhmu asked.

Lucian shook his head. "Nightmares."

"Hmm. Well, try some of this tea. It may help."

Lucian drank the green tea. It was bitter, though sweetened by the sprigs of some local plant.

"What do you eat here, anyway?" Lucian asked.

Lakhmu chuckled. "Oh, a little of this, a little of that."

The others were just now rousing at the sound of their conversation.

Lucian watched the stew, what seemed to be a mixture of Terran crops and local herbs. He looked at Lakhmu, who was now whistling, and wondered how he could be so happy living here all by himself.

"What are we going to do today? I thought I might sweep out the entry hall."

Lakhmu chuckled. "Your fervor for chores is commendable. However, I know that's not what you truly want to do."

"Well, that's all I've done so far, so I figured—"

"—It's time for your training to begin, Lucian Abrantes. There is no time to waste."

Lucian felt hope upon hearing this. Finally, it seemed Lakhmu acknowledged the Worlds were falling apart. Indeed, they might not even have enough time to train before the Swarmers fell upon this very star system.

The others stayed behind while Lakhmu led Lucian out of the dilapidated temple and toward the trees.

"So," Lucian said. "What do you do for fun?"

Lakhmu laughed, as if delighted by that question. "Well, I have many hobbies. I love to cook, to go for long walks. And of course, to visit my friends in the lower villages." He shrugged. "I don't spend much time here at this temple. But it seemed the proper place to begin your training. So, I went to meet you here."

"There are villages?"

"A few. Most of them are in the cloud forest at lower elevations. Warmer than here, but quite bearable. They have a simple way of living. Their lives are harder than most in the Worlds, but their spirits rest easier."

Lucian wondered whether Lakhmu had gotten some of his

space hippie inclinations from the nova-naturalists. "Where are we going, then?"

He shrugged. "I don't know. Just seeing where life leads us. That's what life is about, isn't it?"

Lucian hoped it led to him becoming a better mage. Or better yet, a sorcerer. "You said Vera, Xara, and Ansaldra all trained here before the Mage War."

"That's right."

"And you were here."

He chuckled. "That's also right."

"If you don't mind me saying, you've been around the Worlds for a while, but I'm having trouble keeping up with you."

Indeed, Lakhmu set a fast pace through the undergrowth, weaving down the green mountainside. "People underestimate what fresh air, regular exercise, and good food can do for you. That is magic no pill can capture."

"I guess. Well, what I meant is, you must have been young when Xara and Vera came here."

"Oh-ho, I certainly was. I was in my thirties when Vera and Xara came for training. We sorcerers made a practice of delving the Manifold to unlock its secrets, even after the practice was forbidden elsewhere. If new knowledge was to be gained, it had to be gained here. In that way, we attracted the greatest and most ambitious minds."

"Did Arian come here?"

"Oh, yes. I was truly young then, but already inducted into training under Sorcerer Ishtar. A powerful sorcerer, he was. *Very* old school. Arian, however, didn't train with us specifically." Lakhmu looked at him curiously. "Though it was a long time ago, I still remember him as if it were yesterday. Those memories are reawakening even now, perhaps because I sense something of him in you."

Lucian felt goosebumps at that. He knew why Lakhmu would feel such a thing. Lucian had yet to share his story with him. Mostly, because Lakhmu seemed to think it was immaterial, at least for the time being. But it was clear that Lakhmu sensed something about the Orb of Space-Time.

Lucian thought now was as good a time as ever to lay the whole thing out. And for the first time, Lakhmu seemed ready to listen.

For hours, Lucian talked as they followed the trail into the lower valleys, the forest becoming more wild and untamed. Though Lucian could hear wild creatures in the woods around them, nothing larger than an insect made itself known.

The ending of Lucian's story timed itself with reaching the bottom of the mountain, where a stream ran in a rocky clearing. Two other trails branched off, and the remains of a fire were evident.

"This is a meeting spot between various naturalist tribes," Lakhmu said, seeming to not want to comment on Lucian's story for now. "It's as good a place to stop as any."

Lakhmu set to work setting up camp, getting a fire going, and weaving a bed of thatched leaves near it. A quick traipse in the woods revealed a bounty of herbs and edible plants, which the old sorcerer added to his cookpot, along with some cuts of meat he'd packed in with them.

As they waited for the pot to boil, Lucian looked at Lakhmu, whose eyes were hooded with thought. He got the feeling he was digesting Lucian's story, figuring out what to do with it.

It was only after they had eaten, and night had fallen over the narrow valley, that Lakhmu said anything.

"That's quite the tale, and I've heard many in my long years. That you are still here, optimistic for a brighter future . . . it greatly speaks to your character, young man."

"What do you make of it all? Why is this Shadow following

me? Who is the Ancient One, anyway, and how is he able to talk to me?"

"Vera would know that more than me, but she is no longer alive to tell us. And I fear it was Xara who murdered her."

"How would you know that?"

"Because I know Xara's nature. Yes, she idolized Vera, and in so doing, became an even more extreme version of her. Vera would kill to serve her idea of the ultimate good. Xara would do ten times that, though she would never admit it to herself."

"What would Xara have to gain by killing Vera?"

"That, I can't say. It's only an emanation of the Manifold."

"What do you know about the *Alkasen*? It seems that my goals and theirs align, but still, they're killing humanity. It seems like they should be throwing everything they have at Xara Mallis."

"And where *is* Xara Mallis? Do they know?" Lakhmu chuckled. "The *Alkasen* are powerful, and their Emissaries can use magic, as you have seen before. But they are not *all-powerful*. They cannot locate a single sorceress, especially if that sorceress is trying to keep herself hidden. They attack humanity for one simple reason. You and Xara, on the deepest level, want the same thing for humanity: salvation. The only thing that differs is how you mean to achieve that."

"I don't understand. Shouldn't they be *helping* me?"

"If both of you want to save humanity, the easiest way to move things forward, from the *Alkasen's* perspective, is to *attack* humanity. This will inspire both you and Xara to fight for the Orbs. And if that fight somehow alerts them to your presence, all the better."

Lucian supposed that made sense, and it was not something he had ever thought of before. It explained why the Emissary, Silumko, hadn't killed him. Because not all the Orbs had been gathered yet, it was better to release Lucian, that he or Xara might find them all. If ever the two of them got close together again, it might attract the *Alkasen* to attack, as it had in the Nai Shairen System.

Lucian frowned. "That's why they followed us through the Dark Gate. The Orbs attracted them to us." Lucian's eyes widened in realization. "They might even be attracted to me *now*. Just before we came down on Mako, we got all these reports of Swarmers attacking the Spinward Border Systems. Is it because *I'm* here?"

"Maybe so. Your very presence causes a powerful reverberation in the Manifold, like ripples going outward on an otherwise still lake. Not even a Radiant ward can completely conceal your whereabouts, especially with the number of Orbs you now possess. But if you and Xara were to come close, they would home in on you like a beacon."

"Of course they would." Lucian sighed. "I have to kill Xara, take her Orbs, and get rid of them as fast as possible. Find the Heart of Creation. The thing is, I'm not sure that's the right move anymore. I mean, it will end magic forever. And if magic ended forever, the Gates would stop working, right? That would be the end of humanity as we know it."

"Better the end of humanity as we know it than the end of humanity."

"But Xara has her own point. She wants to fight the *Alkasen* to the bitter end, even if it means merging with the Ancient One."

"She wants to rage against the dying of the light." Lakhmu chuckled. "That's Xara, all right. But in the end, a war with the Ascendant Beings would fail. They are of the Light Realm, and we are of the Shadow. Not even the Orbs can change that. The Ancient One attempted to become an Ascendant Being, but he needs Xara—*and* the Orbs—to complete the transition."

"Or *me*."

"Yes. Or you."

"I just don't know what to do. I'm lost. It's hard to have faith that answers are just going to drop from the sky. It seems we've gotten no new information in a long time. Nothing that changes the equation, anyway. Either I go to the Heart of Creation with the Orbs, or I take Xara's path."

"Perhaps more answers will come," Lakhmu said. "There is more to discover, after all. You are still in the middle of your story, and you can only discover the rest by continuing your journey. I'm afraid I can't help you any more than that."

Lucian hung his head. "I was afraid you'd say something like that."

Lakhmu yawned. "That's enough talking for tonight. Tomorrow, we will continue our training. Your true test has yet to come."

With that foreboding sentence, Lakhmu turned and fell asleep. Uneasily, Lucian did likewise.

22

WHEN THEY AWOKE, it was evening. They had talked through the previous night and had slept through the morning. Lucian could never get used to the day and night cycles here. It was like Volsung, only in reverse.

After they'd finished eating and packing up, Lucian faced Sorcerer Lakhmu.

"So, when do I learn to stream?"

He chuckled. "Tell me. We talked about a great many things last night. I want you to answer an important question for me. Even with everything going wrong, do you still have hope for the future?"

Lucian wasn't sure how to answer. "I do. It's hard, though."

"Having hope is paramount. Working toward a better future, even if you can't see it yet. There is no truth more universal."

"So I have to believe in hope or something?"

"No, not believing. *Doing.*"

"I feel like I'm *doing* already."

"You are on the right path," Lakhmu conceded. "But no one knows a man's end until he reaches it."

"What's *that* supposed to mean?"

"Despite everything you've done, Lucian, you are still only potential. Just as Vera, Xara, and Ansaldra were only potential when they came to be trained here. And yes, even Sharo Khalin."

"Sharo Khalin trained under you?"

"Yes. He was . . . an interesting case. Powerful." It seemed Lakhmu didn't want to say anything more on the subject. "In the end, all of them failed the Test."

"The Test?"

"That comes later."

"Okay. Well, you haven't told me how to stop the Shadow, and you haven't told me anything about how to prevent this Joining. If I find all the Orbs, he says it's inevitable. Is that true, or is he just lying?"

"If you are not ready, Lucian, then yes. The Joining will be your fate. Long ago—ten million years ago—the Forerunners completed the First Gate, opening the way to the Heart of Creation. The Shadow Lord, who already dominated the Forerunners, wanted to use the Manifold to cement his power. He entered, finding the Orbs gathered in the Septagon, and claimed them for himself in the Ethereal Crown."

"The Ethereal Crown?"

"It is the natural state of the Orbs. When gathered in one's Focus, they manifest as a crown, a crown that follows the Chosen like an aura. It is unbreakable, except by one method: the death of the one wearing it."

"That's what happened to the Shadow Lord. The Alkasen defeated him. His crown was broken." Lucian frowned. "Wait. How do you know all this stuff, anyway?"

He gave a mysterious chuckle. "I delved for these truths. I will show you how."

Lucian shook his head fiercely. "Delving is dangerous. I know from experience."

"Yes. There are . . . dark forces in the Ether. The Manifold holds the Focuses of all mages, dead and alive, evil and good. In the Ether, dreams become reality. But so do nightmares."

"The Shadow Lord is in the Ether."

"Yes. And he is in the Shadow Realm, too, as you well know. In the end, it won't matter. Light or Shadow, he can follow you anywhere."

"How do I defeat him?"

"You must pass the Test. You can only defeat darkness with light and truth. If you pass the Test, you will have both."

"What Test is that?"

"I will show you when you are ready. Delving is an effective tool, and it is the heart of being a sorcerer. You should not fear it. As long as your heart remains true to yourself, no evil there can touch you. Otherwise, you will be forever bound by the rules of the Shadow Realm."

"What do you mean? I have so much to learn, Lakhmu. I know almost nothing of Dynamism, for example, and yet with the Orbs, it's like I intrinsically know what to do. Why is that?"

"And what do you think you're doing when you use the Orbs?" Lakhmu asked, all but winking. "You are *delving*, Lucian. The Orbs are not the power in themselves. They are merely the keys, keys that grant access to the Manifold, as if you were truly there and could stream unabated, along with power incorruptible."

"I see. And you know all this from delving, too?"

Lakhmu nodded. "Yes. But as my long life winds down, I've found I wasted a lot of it searching for knowledge when I could have simply been enjoying myself. Perhaps, in a way, this compulsion carried over in my teachings to my pupils. Perhaps it's what set them down the path that led to the Mage War."

"Knowledge is good, though. It's what we do with it that matters."

"Maybe so." Lakhmu grew even more serious. "Are you ready to continue your training, Lucian?"

Lucian nodded. "Yes."

"Then follow me. Our lesson continues in the Ether."

"The Ether?"

"Assume your Focus. Reverse stream Psionics, until the Shadow Realm falls away."

Lucian did so, and within moments, the world was replaced with the Ether. Multicolored lines swirled around objects, and everything shone brightly as the sun. Despite that brightness, Lucian had no problem looking at it.

Lakhmu stood before him, a resplendent, angelic being. He was no longer an old man, but the perfect image of glory, godlike. Lucian knew this to be his true form, the form that cast the shadow in the reality below.

We are in the Ether, Lakhmu said, his voice entering his mind. *The Light Realm. You have assumed control of your being of Light. This is what you do when you delve. Whatever you do here will also happen in the Shadow Realm below us.*

Lucian realized Lakhmu didn't mean the Shadow Realm was *literally* below them. He meant it was on a lower plane of existence. The Ether looked just like the real world, only brighter, and he could see the swirling ether that was invisible from the lower reality. That ether eddied, seeming to be attracted to the two of them standing there.

Using the Ether like this is the chief difference between a mage and a sorcerer. A mage is common. They are confined to the Shadow Realm, and their Focuses are the only thing that may coexist in both

Light and Shadow. However, they cannot experience what we are experiencing now. To do so would lead to their instant deaths.

Why am I just learning this difference between mage and sorcerer? How come no one told me this before?

The masters of the Mako Academy—of which I am the last one left—are the only ones in the galaxy who note the difference, along with those they trained, of which only a few still exist. Vera knew it, as does Xara, but both would keep such knowledge to themselves. Ansaldra Dara acknowledges it, as she bears the title Sorceress-Queen rather than Mage-Queen for good reason. Indeed, the Ancients noted this difference as well.

I see. Lucian realized that as far back as meeting Vera for the first time, she had emphasized a difference between Shadow and Light, and even then, had possibly been preparing him for this knowledge before the Transcends of the Volsung Academy could get a hand on him.

That said, Lakhmu went on, *not even a sorcerer can stand this place forever. It's a place where ultimate conviction and hope are paramount. Without either, your Light form will be overwhelmed, maddened by dark forces beyond conception. That leads to the fraying.*

Then what is the point of being here? If magic can be streamed from the Shadow Realm, why use the Ether at all?

There is true power here, despite its danger. Indeed, before the time of the Mage War, even before the time the fraying was known, the Ether was the higher calling. A calling few were capable of. This led to many deaths. In fact, the Transcends originally took their names for their ability to access this realm as we are now. They transcended the lower reality to stream from this one. In the Shadow Realm, a mage is bound by rules. In the Light Realm, rules are bound to the sorcerer. Whatever changes here, changes in the Shadow Realm below us. Imagination itself allows the sorcerer to circumvent the rules that bind mages.

That's how Ansaldra can control so many with her streams, Lucian said. *She created them from here.*

Precisely. And there are things you can do here that would otherwise be impossible.

Like what?

That is for you to discover. Imagine it, and the Manifold itself will teach you. Just as your Orbs can teach you in the lower realm. That learning is but a shadow of what they are truly capable of.

Lucian remembered what Lakhmu had said earlier. *Imagination is the beginning of creation.*

Lucian allowed his imagination to run free. He imagined a floating fireball, and instantly, it appeared before him. He didn't stream Thermalism and Gravitonics in the proper configuration to make it work. It simply *worked.* He felt both streams flowing through him, though that of Thermalism was endless, while Gravitonics would eventually peter out. He also felt the Orb of Space-Time working, filtering the impurities that would have otherwise come from Gravitonics, to create a pure stream.

This is amazing, Lucian said.

Amazing. And dangerous. You must control your thoughts and emotions here. They attract attention.

Lakhmu saying that only made Lucian think of the Shadow Lord. And, of course, thinking of the Shadow Lord made him coalesce like a gathering storm cloud just behind Lakhmu.

We leave, the old master said.

Lucian let go of his Psionic stream, and once again, the Shadow Realm returned. It was fully night, now, and looking at the place the Shadow Lord had been gathering just before in the Light Realm, there was nothing.

Lakhmu watched Lucian closely. "You have seen what is possible. In the Shadow Realm, the rules of magic are the most important thing, working almost like a science. However, in the Light Realm, there are no rules, only potential and the overall strength and belief of the sorcerer. Faith becomes more important than skill and even knowledge. But for it to work, you need an unassailable foundation that cannot be shaken."

"Xara Mallis is a sorceress, then? Then how was I able to defeat her on Nai Elyn? Not to mention Vera."

"In truth, Lucian, that has more to do with fortune than anything else. You gained the Orb of Space-Time, and you had some help from your friends, who are powerful mages in their own right. Emma having the Orb of Radiance was not something they counted on, either. It was enough of a surprise for you to get access to that Orb, something they could have never planned against, or even suspected. It was enough, at least, for them to cut their losses to fight another day. Had you not found that Orb, Lucian, you would have been soundly defeated."

It was enough to give Lucian a chill. "They have access to something I was barely even aware of."

"You've delved the Ether before," Lakhmu said. "When there were times of desperation, you entered the Ether to stream magic that would have been impossible otherwise. The Orbs sensed your need and elevated you to the Ether, if only temporarily. But the action was uncontrolled, and the more uncontrolled it became, the greater the danger. For when you are in the Ether and not defending yourself, you become an easy target. And with your discovery of the Orb of Space-Time, I imagine the Shadow Lord has become even more desperate. He desires nothing else than to wear the Ethereal Crown again, to rule over all existence, for all time."

"I have to stop him," Lucian said. "I need to become a sorcerer."

"That is why I'm here. You are to be my last student. If you are not the Chosen of the Manifold, then there is nothing left to fight for."

"How am I supposed to defeat Xara, then? I know I have

more Orbs than her, but she has more knowledge. More experience. She could probably still beat me."

"The ability to secure ourselves against defeat lies in our own hands. But the opportunity to defeat the enemy will be provided by the enemy herself."

Lucian could only wonder what that opportunity might be. "That tells me nothing."

"It is a battle of minds as much as magic, Lucian. What shall win, your ideas, or hers? Whose truth is stronger, more righteous, better? Which champion will the Manifold reward more? For we are not the source of magic. The Manifold is."

"The Chosen of the Manifold," he mused. "Has the Manifold truly chosen yet?"

"I wonder that myself."

"I feel like we're just puppets dancing on the gods' strings. The Ascendant Beings being those gods. What if all this is just . . . *entertainment* for them?"

"Yes, it very well could be. But if they consider the Orbs to be of the Light Realm, our suffering might simply be their punishment."

"If that's true, then they're not the good guys, either."

"Dangerous words. Dangerous ideas."

"Well, what do you think?"

"I think," Lakhmu said, "that it is time we continued our training."

23

UNDER THE TUTELAGE of Sorcerer Lakhmu, Lucian experienced reality such as he had never known it.

Psionics was not the only way to occupy the Ether. Any Aspect would do, and the direction of the stream didn't matter. All that mattered was the intent of the stream and the belief that it would happen.

After his first time occupying the Ether, Lucian could never hold himself there for long. Of course, the Orbs made accessing the Ether easy, but remaining there long enough to influence things was the hard part.

In the past, he avoided delving out of fear of the Shadow Lord. There was a sense he didn't belong here, an internal angst that told him he needed to escape. That anxiety would grow and manifest the darkness of the Ancient One.

But despite his repeated failures, Lucian would try again and again. Lakhmu trained him to control his emotions and expectations, to let hope and imagination be his guide rather than fear and despair.

After dozens of failed attempts, Lucian sighed and sat down

on a rock. "I need more knowledge, Lakhmu. I need to know how to stay in the Ether."

Lakhmu laughed. "No. You need *less* knowledge."

"Less?"

It reminded him of something Vera had told him long ago. That if he ever went to the Volsung Academy, their way of doing things would make him forget everything she had taught him. Perhaps his way of understanding magic, even his way of understanding reality itself, was standing in the way.

"Yes, Lucian. You must orient yourself with what you must do, not with what you must know."

"Think less, do more?"

"Yes."

"Okay. But I can't ignore the dread I feel when I'm in the Ether. I'm a being of Shadow, and the Ether is for beings of Light. It's a place for the dead, for those who are gods. Every moment I'm there, there's this . . . anxiety, I guess. It's obvious I don't belong there."

"That is the key. To live with anxiety, you must have *passion*. A goal toward which you're working, something more powerful than any anxiety. That goal is your truth. It's not necessarily a logical or final answer. But it must be true to you."

"My truth. What could that be?"

Lakhmu chuckled. "Don't try too hard to think about it. You don't choose your purpose. Your purpose chooses you."

"My purpose." He shook his head in frustration. "My purpose is to gather the Orbs and bring them to the Heart of Creation."

"You sound bitter about that."

Lucian wanted to throw up his hands in frustration. "Well, it's not what I would've chosen for myself. It means I'm going to die, probably. But I *have* to do it because no one else can."

"If it's not something you truly want, then the Ether senses that."

"What can I do, then? I know I shouldn't trust anything Vera said, and yet she said the key was to accept my reality, whatever it was. To learn to be happy with it." He frowned. "Yet I'm struggling with my reality. My reality isn't something I want to live with. And Serah will die if I fail . . ."

"If you could live any life, what life would that be?"

"I would end all this. I would stop the fraying. I would make the Swarmers go away. I would bring peace to the Worlds. But not for its own sake."

"For whose, then?"

"For Serah. For my mother, Fergus, Emma, and everyone else. And . . . I don't want magic to end. That would kill billions potentially. I don't want what Xara Mallis wants, either. But I *also* don't want what the *Alkasen* and the Ascended Beings want, either." Lucian looked at Lakhmu hopelessly. "That's my truth, as near as I can figure it."

Lakhmu nodded sagely. "You are a guardian. A protector. And yes . . . a hero, though you don't see it. All you must do is embrace the truth of who you are to your core. If you run from that truth, if you allow yourself to be subjected to another's truth, that is the path of darkness and eternal despair. The stakes are more than just humanity. It is your very happiness, Lucian. Your very soul. Embrace your truth, and then the rest of your path will be set before you. Nothing will stop you. You are the Chosen of the Manifold, Lucian. But you must also choose yourself. And when you choose yourself, you will know the way."

"The Chosen will know the way." Lucian frowned. "And what if the Ascended Beings don't want my truth to become reality?"

"The Ascended Beings don't control the Manifold. They

were birthed from it, just as you are, though they occupy the Light Realm and you the Shadow. The Manifold responds to truth, whatever form that truth takes. When there are multiple truths, the strongest truth wins. It is the nature of reality. And the strongest truth is the one we choose."

Lucian stood and nodded. "The strongest truth. My truth is, I want it all. I want to save Serah. I want there to be peace. I want the *Alkasen* to leave humanity alone. I want magic to remain, or at the very least, for the Gates to still work." He paused. "I want everything, and nothing less."

"I hear the strength of your words. They are the words of a sorcerer. Uncompromising. Remember, the crucial thing is to find a truth that is true *for you*. An idea for which you will live and die. You must throw the full weight of your being in its direction, committing to it fully, regardless of reason or intellectual certainty. You must do something for the sake of itself. To take a leap of faith. That is the soul of magic. True magic is not bound by rules or laws. Faith is the soul of a sorcerer."

Lucian nodded. "Xara has her truth. Ansaldra does, too. I don't agree with either of them. But now, I have mine. Such as I've figured it, anyway."

"Do you feel at peace, recognizing it?"

Much to Lucian's surprise, he did. He had always been afraid to want everything, figuring he'd have to sacrifice someone or something for the greater good. Perhaps even sacrifice *himself*. But he had to think higher. To fight for the most hopeful outcome.

Maybe it wasn't achievable, but he had to try all the same.

"Yes," Lakhmu said, with a smile. "You begin to understand. Let us continue training."

———

IN THE FOLLOWING DAYS, Lucian began having fun with magic, perhaps for the first time in his life. But it was by no means easy to change the way he had been doing things for the past few years.

"You must believe you *belong* in the Ether," Lakhmu said. "You and the Ether are one. You must let your truth shield you from its darker influences."

"How can I make it more natural?"

"You're trying too hard. Don't try. Don't work. Your truth is inside you, waiting to be released."

Counterintuitively, these words made Lucian want to try even harder. To force his truth to the forefront. He wanted to intellectually understand it, at least until he remembered Lakhmu's teachings.

You must get yourself oriented with what you must do, not what you must know.

You don't choose your purpose. Your purpose chooses you.

The highest good isn't comprehending it. It's doing it.

"Do you *want* it, Lucian? Do you truly want it? You're trying to try, and trying to try is the same as not caring."

"I want it. I want to save Serah. I want to stop the *Alkasen*." He paused, and almost shuddered at the words that came next. "I'll stop the Ascended Beings themselves if they get in my way!"

The world before him fell away, replaced with the multicolored, dreamlike reality of the Ether. But he no longer felt disoriented here.

He felt as if *he* were its master. *He* was an Ascended Being, at least at this moment.

Lakhmu's light appeared beside him, a spark compared to Lucian's radiance. The Ether swirled around Lucian, drawn into him as if he were a black hole absorbing light.

The Chosen rises to the mantle! Lakhmu said.

Lucian felt as if he could bend the Worlds to his will. For the first time, it felt like he got it. *This* was what streaming was supposed to be like.

He was the Chosen of the Manifold. *He* knew the way. Even if he lacked two Orbs, it wasn't about the Orbs. It was his belief. His truth.

Never forget who you are, Lucian. Never forget this moment. Do you know the way, Chosen?

Lucian was heady with realization. For the first time, everything was clear. He had the power, but he'd *always* had it. The forces against him had always seemed too great to challenge, something he could barely fight off.

Now that he'd realized the truth, he had to do something with it.

He reached through the Ether, toward the Orbs of Atomicism and Gravitonics. They were on . . . *Psyche*? They formed in a flash in his mind. There was no room for doubt.

That was when Lucian felt a force push against him. He realized what that force was.

Xara Mallis.

It isn't time to face her, Lakhmu said. *You must first pass the Test.*

She was much too far for Lucian to fight from here. She was defending herself from his influence, and he from hers. That he had found her at all only showed that even she couldn't defend herself at all times.

But now she had seen him. She also knew what he was capable of. She would know what to expect going forward. Just as he had sensed her Orbs and location, she had sensed his.

He retreated from the Ether and returned to the campground they had been using for the past two weeks. Both he and Lakhmu stood in silence.

The old master looked at Lucian somberly, and Lucian

thought he would scold him for doing something so dangerous. But he said something else.

"The time has come, Lucian. You are ready for your last trial. The Test will cement your truth in your heart so that you'll never forget it. Upon its completion, you will no longer be a mage. You will be a sorcerer." He looked to the sky, as if seeing something there that Lucian couldn't. "But there is little time."

"What is this Test?"

"There are places in the Shadow Realm where the Ether is stronger. Trained as you are, you will be able to find it. But you must go alone, and face it alone. It will be dangerous."

"Could it kill me?"

Lakhmu nodded gravely. "Yes. It has killed before, in the past. Not just in body, but in the soul. I can say no more of it because the trial differs depending on who undergoes it."

Lucian nodded. "I see. Then that's what I'll do."

"This is who you were born to be, Lucian. Remember everything I've taught you, and until you return, I shall be silent."

"Thank you, Lakhmu. For everything."

But as good as his word, Lakhmu didn't respond. He seemed strangely solemn, as if he recognized the danger Lucian would soon face.

Lucian turned from him. He ascended into the Ether, reaching out to feel for the source of power Lakhmu had mentioned. To his surprise, he felt it pulsating in the distance far beyond the trees ahead, beckoning like a beacon.

Lucian left the campsite behind, walking east down a narrow trail into the forest.

24

AS THE DAY faded into night, Lucian streamed from Radiance to better see. The forest was a rich tapestry of life, an ecosystem as complicated as the rainforests of Old Earth before the great mass extinctions of the 21st century. He passed stands of Terran fruit trees intermixed with native plants, but it seemed as if the plants were working in harmony with one another rather than competing.

He followed a fast-moving stream running down a narrow rivulet, a conduit through the lush greenery. He pulled himself along with tethers, weaving his way down the stream into the lower lands. The air grew heavier, hotter, and more humid. It was almost like breathing in a sauna. He remembered Emma's warning of wet-bulb temperatures that were intolerable to humans during the day, but that wouldn't be a threat until sunrise, which was a few hours away. But the lower he went, the hotter it got. Eventually, he created a reverse Thermal ward to help keep cool.

He reached a point where he had to diverge from the simple path. He tethered himself above the rivulet, which had by now grown into a fast-moving river, bushwhacking directly through the trees with his thermal-branded shockspear.

After a few minutes of this, the ground suddenly gave out from under him.

Before he could even react, he was on his back in some sort of pit, surrounded by trees that were leaning over him. The ground beneath him was shifting, funneling him further down from the surface. Something wet, slimy, and acidic coated his arms, burning fiercely.

He warped himself out of the trap, returning to the precipice above, over which he had stepped just seconds earlier. Several dozen trees were writhing like tentacles, reaching out to grasp him.

Lucian raised his arms, and the organism was immediately consumed in flames. A great screech resounded, echoing throughout the forest, but Lucian only dialed up the intensity of the fire, using Gravitonics to create a whirlwind. A bubble of reverse Thermalism surrounded him, keeping him cool even as the inferno raged.

After a few seconds, there was nothing left but a charred crater and ash borne by the wind. When Lucian returned to the Shadow Realm, smoke poured from the depression the organism had once occupied.

The pain in his right arm finally registered, where the saliva of this plant-like organism had seared him. The damage wasn't as bad as he thought. Painful, but it would heal, given time.

He reached out again, using Dynamism to draw water from the moisture-rich atmosphere, washing off the acid as best he could. He dried it with some large leaves hanging from above.

The threat neutralized, he tethered himself across the charred depression and continued on his way.

EVEN WITH THE reverse Thermal ward, it was sweltering by the time the sun rose, burning hot from above. At some point, he reached the bottom, finding himself standing above a still lake. He touched the surface, and much like the surrounding air, it was hot to the touch. But this lake was near where he needed to go.

He followed the shoreline until he reached a small inlet with cliffs rising high on either side. Using Gravitonics, he streamed a series of discs across the surface of the water, and soon found himself before a deep, dark cave.

Despite the heat of the surrounding air, he felt a chill upon seeing that. The trial of becoming a sorcerer was before him. Vera had stood here before, as had Xara and Ansaldra, among others who bore the title of sorcerer. They had all faced some sort of Test and had gone down a different path than the one Lakhmu would have hoped for.

Now, it was *his* turn to prove himself, to remain true to this purpose.

When he entered the cave, it was like entering the yawning mouth of a primordial beast. Every breeze made the hot, humid air feel like an exhalation, and the fetid stench of rotting vegetation within made Lucian's stomach turn. Still walking on the surface of the steaming water, Lucian lit a light sphere, dialing up the brightness to high intensity. Strange insects, long and skeletal, shied away from the light, scuttling across the ceilings and walls toward dozens of porous openings.

Lucian allowed himself to be led by the pulling sensation, which felt very similar to the pull of an Orb. If another Orb popped up after all this time, it would not have surprised him in the least.

The water ended, and Lucian stepped out onto a dark shoreline. He entered the Ether, sensing he was close to the source. Immediately, ether streams swirled along the walls of the cave, racing around him. All the lines were coming from the tunnel ahead, a river of ether.

The ether eddied toward him, attracted by his power. Ahead in the dark tunnel, he saw two large, lizard-like creatures guarding the passage, both still as statues.

Lucian sensed their ill intent before they even attacked him. Atomicism and Dynamism combined in his fingers, and twin forks of orange lightning shot from his fingertips, instantly vaporizing both creatures.

Lucian continued forward, coming to a massive pit from which the streams of ether flowed. Lucian stepped over the edge, levitating down with an anti-gravity disc. He stepped lightly on the ground and continued walking, where the ether was even thicker.

Despite the power pulsating within him, he sensed a dark presence ahead. What he knew was to be his Test. He firmed his resolve, and with utter calm, stepped into a new chamber.

A bright light shone in the center of this chamber—and before that light stood a shadow, the shape vaguely familiar. The shadow oscillated, forming the image of an old woman wearing a cloak, with completely white eyes and a superior smirk.

Ah, Vera said, her voice entering his mind. *I was wondering when you'd arrive.*

Despite holding his Focus, Lucian couldn't help but be unsettled by her presence. It was almost enough to send him reeling out of the Ether entirely.

I thought you were dead, Lucian said.

I am not. I've never been more alive.

How are you here? This is impossible.

Nothing is impossible when the Manifold wills it. Her smile evaporated. *I am not here in the Shadow Realm. Step out of the Light Realm, Lucian, and you would perceive me only as a shadow.*

The same Shadow that has been chasing you since the Temple of Light on Zion.

Lucian readied himself to attack, but he still needed to learn more.

That was you?

Me. And . . . others. The Ancient One is a powerful being. We are many, and our power is great.

What are you talking about?

Even in death, I have achieved power unimaginable. When Xara slew me, she took the short end of the stick. But soon—very soon— she will join us. As will you.

I will never join you.

It is inevitable, Lucian.

Is this the Test? Resisting your call to power? That's hardly a test.

Vera was silent. *There is much you don't understand, Lucian. Much that can't be revealed, for you have to complete your path. You think you're near the end of your journey. You think you will destroy Xara, that you will save yourself with your new sorcerer's tricks.* She all but cackled. *How wrong you are! How little you know!*

Tell me what you know, then. Don't keep me in suspense.

I have gained great knowledge. I understand all! All those who have joined with me and the Ancient One are now as powerful as an Ascended Being. How foolish I was before, and how blind. But now, there is nothing that can stop me! I know good from evil, for I have tasted the fruit of the garden.

The highest good isn't knowing. It's doing.

That fool Lakhmu has gotten to your head. He's a crazy, deranged old man, far past his glory days. Before, I was an old woman grasping at straws. And now, I see the grand plan, what has been set in place since the dawn of creation. There is no escaping that plan. You are but a pawn, ignorant. A two-dimensional creature who cannot conceive of depth, destined to ping and pong off two lines forever. That is . . . until the Joining. I will lift you from your constraints. And like me, you will see and know all.

I will never believe a word you say.

That, too, is according to plan. If you truly wish to go off script, then say in your heart that you wish to complete the Joining now. She laughed. *You will not, Lucian. You are an ignorant Being of Shadow who thinks he can stream the power of gods!*

You're off your rotting rocker. You got yourself killed, and now you're trying to gloat? A gloating ghost. That is your legacy, Vera. You wasted your life on a false idea, and you died for it. I've never seen anyone cope as hard as you. It's sad.

Cope? There is only fate. There is only the Manifold. Regret, yearning, and wishing for a different outcome, even pining for our subjective truths, as that jester Lakhmu would peddle, are all the height of folly. What is beautiful, what is loved, and what is necessary, is only achievable by accepting and loving one's fate, not pining for false idealism. For the first time in my life, I have fulfilled my destiny.

You're a ghost lady, sent back to haunt me. Great. What kind of destiny is that? If I were you, I'd be livid I got such a raw deal.

You understand nothing, Being of Shadow! I see it so clearly now. It was darkness in my old life, but now, I understand fully. I regret nothing because everything happened for a reason. And yes, I love what has happened. I would have done no differently, not if I had the choice to relive my life repeatedly for all eternity. I would endure every hardship, every sorrow, and subject myself to every pain to achieve what was necessary. This is the only true path to happiness, to love. All idealism is false in the face of necessity. And the Ancient One is a necessity. None can stop him! Even the Ascended Beings quail at the coming storm. The Joining comes! It is your fate, Lucian, as it was mine. It is the fate of all magekind! You must love your fate, Lucian, or necessity will force you to love it in the end.

Lucian just watched, wondering just how long she would go

on. It seemed Ghost Vera loved the sound of her voice even more than Real Vera. *Is that all you have to say?*

I'm quite done. How can I expect you to understand? I thought I would tell you if only because one day, you will realize I'm right.

Ah, now it makes sense. You just want to say I told you so. Very noble. I thought being a ghost would make you rise above your baser instincts. Apparently not.

Fool. Glory to the Ancient One. Glory to the Shadow Lord!

Before Lucian had the chance to tell her how very evil that sounded, her Shadow shifted and dissipated. He expected that to be that. However, the Shadow coalesced again, creating a most disquieting shape. Lucian stared for a long time, but there was no denying it.

It was *himself* he was seeing. A shadow version of himself.

25

UNLIKE VERA, his Shadow was not long-winded, and in fact, was utterly and chillingly silent.

Lucian extended his shockspear, surrounding it with Radiance. At the same instant, his Shadow self extended its shockspear, an ethereal one that was darker than midnight, seeming to drink in the light of the surrounding chamber.

Lucian stabbed his spear, and his Shadow countered with its own. As soon as the two weapons met, Lucian's was atomized from existence.

The shockwave sent him hurtling back. Such was the force that Lucian had no time to resort to his usual method of securing himself with a tether. His body became ethereal, sailing through the wall of rock behind him. He slowed himself with a tether connected to the floor of the chamber ahead. He rocketed forward, landing there and snapping back.

The Ether had allowed him to dodge death, but now, he no longer had his shockspear.

The Shadow twirled its spear of darkness, rushing to meet

Lucian. Streams of ether pulsated from the source, entering the Shadow and seeming to give it power.

Lucian had to take the fight outside this chamber. Though Lucian did not have the Orb of Gravitonics, the source of power in this chamber seemed to function like an Orb, giving him access to a massive amount of ether.

He streamed Gravitonic Magic at the ceiling, reversing the flow of gravity. Immediately, both Lucian and the Shadow fell upward. Before they could land, Lucian shifted the flow of gravity *sideways* toward the entrance tunnel. Both he and the Shadow fell in that direction into the chamber of water near the entrance of the cavern.

Farther from the source of power, gravity reverted to its normal direction. He and the Shadow fell toward the water, the Shadow entering it first.

Lucian reached for the surface and instantly turned it into a solid surface of ice. He could see the Shadow lurking beneath that ice, completely frozen within. Lucian paced the ice, wondering what to do next.

A second later, the Shadow shattered the ice and surged toward him, forcing Lucian to tether himself to the ceiling. The Shadow floated, extending its shockspear of darkness toward Lucian. At its tip, a spout of liquid fire shot out.

Lucian raised his hands, catching the fire and absorbing its power. He then shot it back.

The Shadow dispersed for a moment, dodging the blast and reappearing just a few meters to the left. Magic coalesced at the tip of its spear again, a combination of Atomicism and Dynamism. Lucian shielded the death lightning that forked its way across the chamber.

The Shadow gave up the attack and shot forward at lightning speed, extending its shadowy spear. Lucian opened a portal, connecting it to somewhere above the orbit of Volsung.

But before the Shadow slipped through, an aura of black magic surrounded it, which made it go *backward*.

Lucian realized it was going back in time, though for him, time seemed to proceed normally. He didn't have time to be shocked that the Shadow *also* had access to Space-Time Magic. He shifted the portal forward, knowing the Shadow would not remember to dodge.

At last, the Shadow proceeded forward again, except this time, it entered right into the portal. Lucian closed it from behind.

The cavern was left in silence. Lucian allowed himself to float to the ice surface below him, which was already glittering from meltwater. He was just about to allow himself to slip out of the Ether when a portal appeared directly ahead of him.

The Shadow surged forward, its long spear impaling Lucian in the stomach.

A wave of shocking coldness overwhelmed him. Not pain. Just coldness. He felt the Shadow shifting within.

The Joining comes!

Lucian raged against it. He needed to get this Shadow out of him. But already, it was writhing inside him like a snake.

You cannot resist. We are inevitable.

Lucian reached for every Aspect, feeling defiance such as he had ever known. He became ethereal, streaming with everything he had. He would *die* before he allowed this thing to control him.

He radiated light, that light spreading and piercing even the surrounding stone of the cavern. Nothing could withstand it, and had he been physically present in the Shadow Realm, that light would have obliterated him from existence.

The Shadow clung on within him, stubbornly refusing to let go.

The greater the Light, it taunted, *the greater the Shadow cast.*

Lucian refused to listen. Evil could not overcome the resisting soul.

He drew even more ether, more power. The source obeyed, streaming all its ether through the Orb of Radiance. The Orb itself was a blinding light, a supernova exploding. Lucian clung to the spear, but so far, it was still stuck in place.

At last, there was nowhere else to hide. The light overwhelmed the Shadow, splitting it with beams of light. Lucian reached for one of those beams, recognizing it to be the spear of shadow. Only it was no longer an instrument of darkness, but a weapon of light. Lucian grabbed it, gripping it in his right hand.

He drove the spear into his Shadow. It emitted a piercing scream. With that action, the source of power closed off, and the Shadow disappeared.

Lucian was thrown from the Ether. When he opened his eyes, he was standing on top of a heap of ruins, and the air was choked with dust.

But piercing the haze was a glorious light that he still held in his right hand.

Lucian reentered the Ether and floated upward to escape the surrounding dust. In the Ether, nothing remained to haunt him. The Shadow had vanished with the closing of the source of power. He was sure the Shadow still existed, but it had failed in Joining him. But it would try again someday. While he had defeated his Shadow, the same was not true for the other sorcerers who had visited this cave.

Lucian floated high above the desolation he'd created. The cave was simply . . . *gone*, along with the lake. It was as if a meteor had impacted the landscape below him. Never in Lucian's life had he streamed such power.

And for the first time, he noted what he held in his hand. A spear. Not just any spear, though, but the same spear the

Shadow had carried with it from the source of power. Only instead of being a weapon of shadow, it shone white with an almost holy aura. Lucian realized it was like an Orb, an object that existed in both Light and Shadow, a spear of ether itself. He held it now, knowing that if he wasn't who he was, it would have destroyed him at its touch.

And he knew that with this weapon, he could destroy the Shadow that haunted him.

Lightspear. A voice seemed to enter his mind from the Ether beyond.

He didn't know who the voice was at first, but the memory returned to him. *Rhana?*

Take it and drive it into the Hearts of Shadow.

Hearts of Shadow. Could that be what he'd just fought, and were there more than one? He had so many questions. Where had the spear come from? How was he even speaking to her right now? Whatever the case, the spear seemed to be his now. He was the Chosen of the Manifold, and because of that, this spear had chosen him. With it, he could destroy these Shadows, if ever they tried to Join him again.

For now, he was content to hold it as the wind swept around him. For the first time, he realized he was floating. He wasn't using a tether, but simply manipulating gravity itself within the Ether. If he so chose, he could fly.

He turned, facing the high, green mountain from which he had come. From its peak, smoke poured upward into the sky. He recognized a weak pull at his mind, a pull he'd been oblivious to during the battle.

Serah?

Lucian! The Swarmers are here! Where are you?

I'm coming. Hold on.

Lucian shot across the sky toward the site of Cloud Forest Temple, Lightspear in his hand.

26

LUCIAN SHOT DOWN from the sky like a meteor, landing in front of the burning temple with a thunderous boom. The *Alkasen* surrounded the complex, along with some of their smaller, angular vessels. Like the Emissary, they had dark blue, lizard-like skin, tall forms, and clasped shockspears in their reptilian hands.

As one, each of them turned to face him. Dozens upon dozens of them.

His heart thundered in his chest, not for his own sake, but for that of his friends and Lakhmu. For now, there was no sign of them.

The *Alkasen* converged on his position with lances of lightning, fireballs, ice spikes, kinetic waves, and other magical attacks.

Still in the Ether, he approached, shielding every attack with barely a thought.

The three closest *Alkasen* dove for him, their speed aided by tethers, and their weight amplified with Gravitonics. Lucian held out Lightspear, lacing them with death lightning that obliterated them in midair.

Other *Alkasen*, as if of one mind, charged him. Lucian created a sphere infused with Binding, Gravitonics, and Space-Time Magic. The beings flipped feet first into the air, right into that spinning sphere that pulsated with potential. Lucian reversed the streams, shooting the *Alkasen* off at unreal velocity. Some flew toward the flames of the temple, others over the trees into the far distance.

By now, only a few of the beings were standing their ground, while the rest were fleeing onto their ships. Some of those vessels were already retreating into the sky.

Lucian reached out for the closest one, lacing it with Binding and Psionic Magic. It shattered in midair, followed shortly by an explosion that gave off a blast of unreal heat.

That left only two who fought as bravely as they did pointlessly. Lucian untangled their magical defenses and shattered both with Lightspear.

Every threat extinguished, Lucian stepped out of the Ether. Lightspear dissipated from his hand as the fires of the temple burned bright, and the acrid smoke from its burning timbers made him want to choke. He reached out, trying to locate his friends.

He ran toward the tree line and came upon Fergus, Emma, and his mother, all leaning over Serah's fallen form.

"No!"

When they parted for him, he found Serah lying on her back, blood pouring from a wound in her abdomen. It must have happened just before his arrival. She wouldn't last, not without an advanced med-pod and medicines.

"What do we do?" Fergus asked, his voice just barely holding back panic. "Rotting hell, they came down so fast! There was this light in the distance, and then *they* were here."

"Stand back," he said. He touched Serah's face, and her blue eyes opened and found his.

"Took you long enough," she barely managed.

She coughed, and blood sputtered from her mouth. She had minutes left, if not seconds. There was no time to waste.

Lucian knew exactly what he needed to do. Even if his Focus was about to collapse from what he'd done over the past few hours, he had to push himself even harder. He focused on only one goal: saving Serah.

Magic from every Aspect responded to his need. Every Orb fired on. An aura surrounded Serah's form, cocooning her body and making it impossible to see her.

But he could feel her pain. He soon realized that she had lied to him about the fraying. It didn't just hurt sometimes. It hurt *all* the time. She had only spared him the truth to keep from breaking down and losing hope.

It was not just her skin. It was in her organs and even her bones. Even without the stab wound, she'd only have weeks before the rot reached her brain.

He knew there was no way to cure her. But he had the power to do something else.

Now that he was a sorcerer, now that he held Six Orbs, he was sure he could do it. He could bring her back to her old body and *also* save her memories.

I am the Chosen of the Manifold. Without Serah, I refuse to go a step farther.

But it still required Serah's approval. Already, she was unconscious, but Psionically linked with him.

Serah . . . I have to do this. Do you trust me?

Can you do it?

Yes. You are everything to me. Without you . . . I'm nothing.

He could see her smiling in his mind's eye. *Do it, then.*

With that, the stream began. He saw the world through her

eyes, and her memories joined his own, at least for the time being. He would give them back as soon as the ravages of time reversed themselves.

As he streamed, he knew her such as he'd known no one before. He understood everything that had been lost in translation. She was his love, just as he was hers. And love would prevail. It would save her because his love for her was his truth.

Serah was nothing but a cocoon of blinding light. In the Shadow Realm, that light would be too blinding to look at, but in the Ether, Lucian could see Serah transforming before him. The fraying wounds crawled down her neck, revealing healthy skin. It retreated up her arms, down her shoulders, off her chest and legs and back. It retreated until it was only a slight wound on her arm, as big as the day he'd met her. Getting rid of that wound was the hardest part because he had no memory of her before.

But he insisted it happen. And stubbornly, it *refused*.

I won't stop until I've finished. Even if I die.

The Manifold knew it to be true. A cataclysm of magic worked through him, all converging on that wound until it was the size of a kernel. Then a grain of sand. And finally, it was microscopic.

But even microscopic was too large. It would only grow again. It had to *all* be gone.

With a last burst of magic, Lucian cried out, and the brightness subsided.

Serah stood before him, healthy and new. Completely healed. Two years of ravaging, all gone.

But her mind was still empty. She was nothing but a shell. Until he returned her memories, she was no one.

Lucian infused them back into her mind. When he returned the final one, he let go of the stream.

The magic complete, he was hurtled from the Ether and

into the Shadow Realm. He fell to his knees almost blacking out.

But he forced himself to remain conscious. He had to see if it worked.

She was still lying on her back, and the others crowded around her, looking at her in wonderment. Lucian stumbled forward, and when he looked down at her, he couldn't help but gasp.

She was healed. Her pain was gone, her skin flawless. She was younger than the Serah he had met in the Riftlands, at the beginning when the fraying had begun to set in. And she would have all her old memories.

But only if she woke up.

He kneeled and clasped her hand with both of his own. "Serah? Please..."

Her eyes remained closed.

He linked with her mind and could feel activity there, but no conscious thought. Had something gone wrong?

But it was at that moment that she coughed, and her eyes blinked open and found his. She frowned in confusion.

"Am... am I dead?"

Lucian laughed. "Far from it." He gathered her in his arms, and he felt tears come to his eyes.

"I feel . . . different." She looked at him for an explanation. "Where am I? What is this place?"

"We're on Mako. Do you remember what happened?"

He helped her stand since she seemed to have trouble supporting herself. If he had taken her body back in time, of course, she would not be used to heavier gravities, having only lived on Psyche. Her face was the same, minus a few lines and smaller scars. She had been older than him before, but now they were probably close to the same age, at least physically.

"I . . . don't know. I remember being . . ." She struggled to remember. "I remember Halia, Volsung, Archea Station, Isis . . ." She frowned. "After that, it's a blur. I remember a tower . . ."

"Irion," Lucian said.

"Yes. Irion. I just remembered. And Aurora . . ." Her blue eyes became bewildered. "Memories are flooding back all at once."

"Amazing," Fergus said.

She looked at him in surprise, seeming to notice him, and the others, for the first time. "I'm so confused right now. How did we find ourselves here?"

Lucian smiled. "At this rate, you'll remember everything in a few minutes. Just hang on."

"Lucian, what *happened* to me? For the first time in forever, I feel . . ." She struggled for the word. "Good. *Alive*. And my skin isn't on fire." She shook her head. "I don't know. It's all so confusing."

"It'll all make sense, I promise. Have you looked at yourself yet?"

"What do you mean?"

He reached for the sleeve of her Talent's robe, and drew it back a bit, revealing her unmarred skin. She just stared, unbelieving.

"Is this a dream?"

"No. It's real."

"I had these aches in my knees, and they're completely gone, too."

"With Lakhmu's training, your fraying is gone."

She looked at him blankly. "Lakhmu? Who's that?"

"You'll find out soon," Lucian said. "I underwent training with him, and now . . . I'm a sorcerer."

"A sorcerer?"

"Some mages can stream from the Ether directly. The rules

are different there. You might even say there *are* no rules if you're strong enough."

"And *you* are?"

Lucian nodded. "Yeah. No doubt about that. That's how I healed you."

Her eyes remained wide. That fact seemed to just be registering. "You *healed* me?"

He touched her face. "It's true, Serah. You're safe now."

"I . . . don't know what to think. You didn't just heal me. You took away other things, too. I had this crick in my knees. I guess from all the jumping around I've been doing. It's gone. How did you manage it?"

"Remember the coffeepot yet?"

She frowned. "The coffeepot? What would that have to do with anything?" She paused. "Well, I'm remembering more now. The basilisk! Rotting hell, that tore me up."

"Maybe we can talk about it later. We need to find Lakhmu."

"Lakhmu. Your teacher, right?"

"Yes. I have to make sure he's okay. We were just attacked by the *Alkasen*."

"Rotting hell!"

"They're gone now. Don't worry."

Lucian reached out for Lakhmu and was happy to discover he wasn't too far away.

He looked at the others. "Serah and I will be back."

"Be careful," Mira said.

"We'll be here," Emma said.

Lucian and Serah skirted around the side of the temple to find Lakhmu standing at the edge of a cliff, his robes swaying in the breeze. He wasn't looking toward the temple, but the setting sun in the west.

Lucian ran toward him. "Lakhmu. I'm glad you're all right."

Lakhmu turned to him and Serah, giving a somber smile.

"I passed the trial. The Shadow attacked me, and—"

"—You need not elaborate. Long ago, I had a prophecy. That the true Chosen of the Manifold would bear a spear of light, forged from the Ether itself. Not one of my pupils has returned from the Test with this token."

Lucian reached out his hand, and with a mere thought, Lightspear solidified in his hand, shining like starlight. Serah's eyes went wide at the sight. Even Lakhmu's eyes grew wide, and then strangely sad.

"You have passed the Test. Well done . . . Sorcerer-Ascendant."

Lucian frowned. "Sorcerer-Ascendant? Isn't that you?"

Lakhmu ignored his question, at least for now. "Not for much longer, Lucian. There is still the matter of the brand Vera placed on you. I must erase it for good. You cannot face Xara Mallis with it active."

"Is it possible to remove it?"

"Yes. However, you cannot remove it from yourself. It requires another. And it requires sorcerous magic rather than rule-bound magery."

Lucian nodded. "All right, then. I'm ready when you are, Lakhmu."

"Then enter the Ether with me." He looked at Serah. "Perhaps it's best for you to step back, Serah. I'm . . . glad that you are well. Though Lucian is strong in magic, he still needs you. More than you will ever know. Take care of him."

She nodded. "I will."

After Serah had stepped back, Lucian and Lakhmu delved into the Ether.

27

THIS TIME IN THE ETHER, it seemed different.

Lucian didn't feel its power. There was only a sadness he couldn't explain. The source seemed to be Lakhmu himself, though he didn't understand why.

There is something I must tell you, Lucian.

What's that?

You have fulfilled my prophecy and have become more powerful than even you dreamed. But despite your power, you must remain humble. Give a person power, and you will see who that person is. Who will you turn out to be? I have hope, Lucian. But that is all I can have. Soon, you will go. Your training is complete. Lakhmu watched him for a moment. *Are you ready?*

Lucian nodded. *I think so.*

One more thing. Though we've only known each other for several weeks, I'm proud of how far you've come. Long have I doubted my prophecy, that I would train the Chosen himself. And it is good to feel hope again, so close to the end.

What do you mean by the end?

I once believed my role in the Worlds would be greater. In the

Mage War, I led armies, commanded fleets, and was considered among the wise. I was not wise, though. Despite my foolishness, despite my students turning to evil, I was still well-esteemed, and many believed I might rise to be Hegemon. A Sorcerer-Hegemon. But, after seeing billions die, worlds destroyed, and after seeing the Tragedy of Isis . . . I withdrew. I realized so much that was wrong in the Worlds was because of me.

Lakhmu, they made those choices, not you.

Yes. They stopped listening to their truths, and instead, subjected themselves to another's. That darkness lives in us all. I don't know anything, Lucian, even now in my old age. I lost Vera, Xara, Ansaldra, and even Sharo. At one time, I wondered whether all four might be the Chosen. I had nearly given up hope. Until you came. The point is, I have many regrets. But as you hinted, perhaps it couldn't have happened any other way. You might not be standing here today otherwise. It is not my part to right the wrongs of the past committed by myself and others. The Manifold has chosen you for this task. You passed the trial. You hold Lightspear. And now, for my last act, I will dissolve the brand Vera placed on you, so that you can face Xara without fear of her undermining you.

His last act? He couldn't mean . . .

But already, the old sorcerer was streaming, and there was nothing Lucian could do to stop it.

Seven Aspects—red, orange, yellow, green, blue, violet, and silver—swirled around Lakhmu. They all combined into one, multicolored stream, leaving Lakhmu's form and attacking a shadow within Lucian's Focus.

And he realized, for the first time, that this was how the Shadow had found him. Since Vera was a part of the Shadow, it could mark his every move. It happened as early as his time on board *Ethereal* in the Nai Shairen star system, but as he gathered more Orbs, the Shadow became more fully formed.

Perhaps the Shadow hadn't been ultimately defeated, but

after this, it could no longer follow him.

All became white as the colors obliterated Lucian. He felt himself floating in an endless sea, and after a long time, he returned to the Shadow Realm, his reality.

Lakhmu stood before him on wobbly knees, collapsed to the ground, and rolled on his back. His eyes were closed.

"Lakhmu!" Lucian kneeled at his master's side. The old man's eyes fluttered open, though the cause of his injury was not readily clear. But Lucian knew whatever he had done had given him a grievous injury.

"Lucian," he rasped. "Or shall I say . . . *Sorcerer* Lucian?"

"Wait," Lucian said, remembering the Orb of Space-Time. "I can save you . . ."

Lakhmu held up a deferring hand. "I have . . . served my purpose. And even if I wished to live . . . such powerful magic takes its toll. Perhaps you love me, as a student loves a teacher, but that love isn't as strong as your love for her. For that reason, the magic would fail. Love is the bridge between imagination and reality. Everything is nothing without love. Besides, for what reason would I go on? I am ready to depart from this world. I was merely . . . hanging on a few moments longer, hoping to speak with you one last time."

"Why not continue living? You could help us, Lakhmu."

He shook his head, a sad smile stretching across his wrinkled face. "Eternity calls for me, Lucian. And soon, I will answer. My life, for all its trials and mistakes, will not end in despair, but in hope. Of all my apprentices, you passed the Test. You battled the darkness and won. You have surpassed Ansaldra and Sharo. You have surpassed Vera and even Xara Mallis. Without embracing your truth, you wouldn't have been able to best the Shadow. And now, you must take that truth and leave this world. Never forget it, Sorcerer. Your truth will give you strength to stand against all darkness."

"I won't forget it, Lakhmu."

The sorcerer's eyes became filled with tears as his body convulsed. But despite that great pain, he made himself continue. "Be the hope for the Worlds, Lucian. That is your purpose. To fight for life. To fight for humanity. To fight for *her*. You have seen it now?"

"Yes. But . . . I haven't finished my training. Yes, I passed the Test, but there is so much left to learn. So much for you to teach me."

"Remember. The highest good is not knowing, but doing. You must now *do*, Lucian. That is all there is to it. I . . . can teach you no more. You must follow your truth, trust it to the very end." Lakhmu looked at him closely. "When I breathe my last, you will be the Sorcerer-Ascendant. You will be the last of the Mako Sorcerers."

"Lakhmu . . ."

"The hourglass has run out for me. The last grains are floating down. All the things in life that were loud, all the things that seemed so important and inviolable . . . they are coming to an end. The world and its realities grow still, as eternity is still." He coughed, and blood dribbled down his chin. But he resolutely struggled to continue. "There is only one thing that matters, in the end."

"What is that?"

"Whether or not we have lived our purpose." He reached out a gnarled hand. "Be happy, Lucian. Trust yourself. Have faith in goodness, and goodness will manifest. That is the Sorcerer's Way. Happiness is all I wish for you. And happiness is all you must wish for yourself."

With that, Lakhmu gave a small, peaceful smile, then drew his last breath.

Serah watched him, too, tears in her eyes. Lucian felt himself break down right there. Lakhmu had passed on, returning to eternity and the Manifold. All that was left was his organic body. Just a mass that once held Lakhmu, but no longer was him.

"I . . . remember everything now," Serah said. "If anyone's lived a purposeful life, it's him. There is nothing to mourn on his part. Just ours."

Lucian nodded. "What should we do with him?"

"On Psyche, we simply bury our dead."

Lucian nodded. "We'll do that, then."

They returned to the campsite and hastily dug a grave, marking it with a stone. With Lightspear, Lucian etched the following words:

HERE LIES LAKHMU,
    Sorcerer, Teacher, Friend.
    He died with hope,
    His purpose fulfilled,
    His truth realized.

LUCIAN HAD LEARNED everything he needed to know to face Xara Mallis. The prospect filled him with fear. He knew Xara would be more powerful and prepared than she had been on Nai Elyn. And she knew he was coming.

But as Lakhmu had said, he had to trust himself. He had to remember his love for Serah, his love for his mother, and his love for his friends. Love was the bridge between imagination and reality. The Sorcerer's Way.

They lifted off the planet, leaving the ruins of Cloud Forest Temple behind. As Lucian watched the last of the trees recede into the heavy clouds, he knew he would never be the same.

28

"INCOMING SWARMER FIGHTERS," Mira said, as soon as they locked into orbit.

"Swarmer fighters" was an understatement. There was an entire carrier, with the same rock-like exterior as the ones around Hephaestus. Ship after ship escaped the cracks riddling its surface, all shooting green lasers in *Blood Wyvern's* direction.

Mira dodged the first couple of shots while the deflector shield ate a couple more. Delving the Ether, Lucian manifested a Radiant shield that enveloped the ship. From the Ether, he no longer had to see where the shield was going, because he could see through the walls of the ship itself. Despite dozens of lasers pelting Lucian's shield, it was in no danger of collapsing.

"Orders?" Mira asked, anxiously.

"Get ready to jump."

Reaching for Space-Time, Lucian opened a portal directly in front of the ship, where a violet-tinged world could be seen floating against the backdrop of a large, white gas giant with a single red eye.

"Oh, no," Fergus said. "Here again?"

But they were already through, and the portal closed behind. Things were utterly quiet as they coasted toward the Mad Moon.

"Xara is here," Lucian said. "I'm not sure where exactly. But it probably won't be too hard to find her."

"What is she doing here?" Mira asked.

Lucian knew the answer, though he hadn't thought about it until now. "She needs an army."

"An army?" Mira asked. "To fight the League?"

"Eventually, yes. She has to start somewhere. Where else to get mages but a mage prison planet, especially if you offer them a way out?"

"I don't see *any* way out," Emma said. "Unless she somehow intends to take control of the Wardens. Is such a thing possible?"

"More than possible. It's her plan."

"And what about Ansaldra?" Fergus asked.

"She's either Xara's ally or an obstacle. We'll only know when we get down there."

"I'm surprised the Wardens haven't hailed us yet," Mira said.

"I'm shielding the ship. They won't see us, even if they're within sensor range."

"I'll take your word for it. Where are we headed?"

Lucian looked at Serah, who was watching the violet-shrouded surface below. A few pointed peaks were visible above the clouds. They were over the moon's far side. Below them would be the Riftlands.

"We need a place to settle down, to assess," Serah said. "Maybe we can head to Kiro Village. It's a safe place, and they might know more."

Lucian nodded. The village had exiled her for her condition, but now she was no longer fraying. Even they couldn't deny her. According to the laws of the Deeprift, she could return, but it couldn't be an easy thing for her.

"How do you feel about that?" he asked.

"I'm . . . not too thrilled, to be honest. The last time I saw my old man . . ." She shook her head. "It wasn't a pleasant conversation, but I can't think of a better idea."

"Maybe this is a chance for reconciliation," Emma said.

Serah remained silent at this prospect.

"It would be good to return to Kiro," Fergus said, at last. "I've grown beyond it. But to visit with the Elders, to tell them what our little quest for the Orb of Psionics turned into . . ." He chuckled. "It would be something."

"Serah is right that it may be a safe place to learn about Xara," Emma said. She looked out at Psyche as if in disbelief. "I can't believe we're *here*. I get to see this place with my own eyes. I've had more than a few nightmares about it."

"The dangers are overstated," Lucian said. "Well, maybe not, but we should be safe enough."

At least, until they had to deal with Xara Mallis.

"Can she detect us?" Emma asked, apparently thinking the same thing.

Lucian shook his head. "She will as soon as I lower my concealment ward. Something I don't plan on doing the whole time we're here." He turned to look at everyone. "I . . . just want everyone to be prepared. When we left Kiro, Ansaldra's men were just days away from attacking."

"Maybe we can help them," Emma said.

"This would have been about a year ago," Lucian said. "Who knows what we'll find?"

"All right," Mira said. "Just let me know where to put the ship down."

Even Lucian was unsure of that. "Did the scanners log the surface's topography?"

"Difficult with the clouds. But I'm detecting a deep canyon, as well as some other minor ones. Everything else is hazy."

"Go to the deep canyon."

It had to be the Deeprift. The Deeprift extended for hundreds of kilometers, so it would be impossible to know just where Kiro was in all that. He'd have to rely on Serah to find the way.

"Detecting a station in orbit below us," Mira said. "Engaging cloaking screen."

As they flew toward the atmosphere, Lucian spied a space station circling beneath them, along with several docked ships. They were completely oblivious to their passing, all the more so as Lucian masked even their thermal signatures.

By the time the cloaking screen powered off, they had broken through the clouds. They were descending toward a violet sea, and in the distance rose towering white cliffs stretching from north to south as far as the eye could see. The waves pummeling the cliffs were *massive*, an effect of the low gravity and Cupid's influence on the other side of the moon. The constant crash of the surface created a mist that seemed to hang eternally over the surface of the water.

He remembered Serah and Fergus telling him travel by sea was impossible on Psyche. After seeing this with his own eyes, he fully understood why.

They drew level with the canyon, passing over the cliffs, from which an enormous waterfall tumbled into the tumultuous ocean below. It was the beginning of the Riftlands.

Mira flew into the opening. *Blood Wyvern's* shadow fell onto a fertile river valley filled with farms and villages. To his surprise, there were people down there. They fled at the sight of the ship passing above them.

"I know exactly where we are now," Serah said. "This is

Mistfall, the eastern border of the Riftlands. From here, it's probably another fifty kilometers to Kiro."

"Tight quarters," Mira said. "All right, I'm going to lift out of here so we have more room to maneuver. Following the rift."

Lucian watched as she weaved between sharp mountains obscured by clouds. Off to the right, he spied a flight of wyverns, about a dozen circling a pointed peak. Mira had no choice but to keep the ship within the rift—if she went any higher, it would become impossible to tell where they were.

Serah watched out the forward viewscreen intently. "It's almost unrecognizable from above. Kiro lies halfway up the Deeprift, in the middle of the Great Ascent."

"What's the Great Ascent?" Lucian asked.

"Well, from the sea, the Deeprift is wide and more or less even. The Great Ascent is where it slopes upward. It's the roughest part of the rift."

"I see. So keep looking out for the area where the rift gets shallower?"

"That's the idea."

Within ten minutes, the canyon walls had become narrower, so that there was hardly room for the ship to maneuver. And below them, Lucian could see cultivated terraces with few places flat enough to land. Far below was a rushing river, the stream that had carved this rift over tens of millions of years.

"Set down here," Serah said. "Wherever it is, it's probably a day's walk from Kiro, if not less."

"Will do," Mira said.

When they lowered to the ground, *Blood Wyvern* powered off, just short of a cliff that overlooked the canyon below.

"Any idea where we are?" Lucian asked.

"We'd have to walk around a bit," Serah said. "But from the

landscape, we're pretty high up. Wyvern country. There won't be many people around."

"I can open a portal to Kiro. We can just leave the ship here."

He led them outside. The rocky, foggy terrain reminded him of his first night on Psyche. The night he had met Serah.

She seemed to be of a similar mind as she breathed the air in deeply. "Brings back memories. The gravity feels right here. Familiar. No smell of wyvern dung either, so that's a plus." She looked at Lucian and nodded. "All right. I'm as ready as I'll ever be."

With a mere thought, he opened the portal, locking onto a memory of just outside Kiro Village. Serah was the first one through, followed by the rest.

Once Lucian allowed the portal to close behind him, he saw that the palisade in front of the gate had been expanded, with new towers and even a shallow ditch in front of it. For all that, though, there were no guards in those towers. He got a sinking feeling as they approached, with Serah far ahead of the rest of them.

"Hello?" she called. "Anyone home?"

There was no response. Nor was there the smell of fire coming from within the cave itself, something Lucian had noticed last time he was here.

Serah got a running start before leaping the palisade with a gravity-assisted jump. Lucian did the same, clearing the wall in one smooth movement. Once on the other side, it was as he had suspected. There was no sign of life, and the cave was dark and quiet.

"Doesn't look good," Serah said.

Lucian infused the entire cave with light. It looked much the same as before, its buildings still intact. They were empty.

"Abandoned," he said.

"But why?"

Lucian shrugged. "Beats me. It has to be related to Xara."

"It's hard to imagine Xara coming here. It's the middle of nowhere, in Psyche terms."

"Well, we left the palace in ruins," Lucian said. "But maybe we could learn something if we head to Dara."

"Let's get out of here, first."

They hopped over the wall again, landing neatly by the others. From the widening of Mira's eyes, it seemed she could never get used to magic being used right in front of her.

"Abandoned," Serah said. "We need to go to the Golden Vale. See what's going on. If Xara is anywhere, it's there."

Mira pointed up the trail. "Hey, someone's coming."

Lucian looked, and sure enough, an elderly man with a walking stick was arriving out of the fog. He seemed to bypass Kiro entirely, set on some other destination. He looked their way curiously for a moment before continuing on his journey.

"Hey, wait up!" Lucian called.

The man stopped and waited for them to approach.

"How do ye do?" he said.

"Where is everyone?" Lucian asked. "Is Kiro gone?"

The man frowned, curious. "You new here?"

"I guess you could say that," Lucian said, not wanting to go into details.

"Well, I don't know how *that* could be, seeing how they've stopped all the prison barges. You're in the wrong place at the wrong time."

"Why's that?" Serah asked.

The man looked at her with interest. "That's a Rifter accent if I've ever heard it. Where are you from, girl?"

"Here. I've been away a long time, I guess you could say."

"Hmm. Well, it's about time for lunch, if you guys care to

listen. Give me news, such as you have, and I'll give you mine. My name's Isaavi."

"That sounds like a fair trade, Isaavi," Fergus said.

So, they sat right there, sharing some of the food they had packed, and the old man shared his. They learned things had changed mightily in the Riftlands, in the last few weeks especially. The Chosen of the Manifold had come, he said, and she was ruling from Dara in the Golden Vale. She had come from the stars in thunder and glory, fulfilling Ansaldra's prophecies.

Except now, Ansaldra was on the run, holed up in the south. Things had turned quickly against her, as disgruntled nobles and people hailed Xara as a liberator.

"But Queen Ansaldra ain't having none of it, no sir," the man went on, taking a huge bite of Lucian's instameal, something that approximated poutine, complete with gravy and curds. He smacked his lips. "My, where'd you get vittles like this?"

"Err . . . never mind that. Anything else?"

"Well, there's war in the Golden Vale. All of Psyche at war! And the Chosen is winning. Xara Mallis has come back from the dead! She's calling her new country Starsea. Queen Ansaldra does *not* like that. Well, methinks Ansaldra doesn't like the idea of *not* being in charge, if you catch my meaning. Well, it's hard to know exactly what's going on. I'm much too old for the recruiters to care about me. But most of the villagers have up and left. All of Kiro went with them, and the old ones went to Mistwatch by the Sea. Some of the old ones, though— the mages—joined Xara."

"That would be my dad," Serah said.

Isaavi's eyes widened at that. "Your father is Elder Ytrib?"

Serah nodded. "That's right. And the last place he needs to be is a battleground."

"Well, most of the Rifters got sent by airship several weeks back. Those who were deemed unfit to serve were sent down-rift." He nodded toward the empty village. "The Starsea Mages want every mage fighting for the Chosen. Needless to say, things ain't going too well for Ansaldra. Word is, she's holed up in her Summer Palace on the Sea of Eros, down in Malia. She still has control of things in the southern half of the Vale but is losing ground fast. Most folks are more than happy to take up arms against her."

"I bet," Serah said. "But Xara isn't a good choice, either."

"Well, I see your point, but good luck convincing people of that. They say she's the Savior of the Stars. Even most of Ansaldra's nobles went over to Xara when they saw her powers. The ones who weren't completely mind-controlled by Ansaldra, anyway." He cleared his throat. "Anyway, that's all I know, either way. What news do you have for me? I can tell you are starfarers, too. That food didn't come from anywhere on this moon."

Lucian gave him a fifteen-minute spiel of what was going on outside the Mad Moon, and the old man listened, fascinated. He figured he owed it to him, anyhow.

Once finished, Lucian had one more question to ask. "So, where might we find the Kiro villagers?"

"Well, Starsea took control of the airships, you see. I'd look in the Golden Vale, at the battlefront."

"The front?" Serah asked, her voice rising. "My dad's almost in his seventies!"

"Well, I don't know you can get there fast enough."

By Lucian's reckoning, it was time for them to get going. "Thanks for the information, Isaavi."

"The Golden Vale is far, young man. Have a care, for things aren't the same on the Mad Moon anymore." He cackled. "One might say it's gone even madder."

"We'll keep that in mind."

They waited for the old traveler to pack up and lose himself in the fog before they even thought about what to do next.

"What now?" Mira asked.

"We can't go to the front lines," Fergus said. "Even with a concealment ward, it's too much of a risk."

Lucian had to agree with him there. "Nowhere on Psyche is safe. But the safest place would probably be behind enemy lines. Knowing Ansaldra and Xara are fighting each other is good information. It gives us a potential ally."

"*Ally*?" Serah asked. "She'll try to kill you the minute she lays eyes on you!"

"I should have said *temporary ally*. And honestly, I don't think she'll kill us. She needs our help, and maybe we could use hers, too."

"Seriously?" Serah asked. "She and Xara deserve each other. Good riddance to both!"

"Except it's a battle Ansaldra will lose," Fergus said. "As soon as she falls, nothing stands in Xara's way of uniting all of Psyche. And with the mages *and* the Warden fleet above, they will cause some real damage. We have to stop Xara before she takes out Ansaldra."

"Yeah, but when will that happen?" Mira asked. "That man's information is probably out of date. Xara might have won the war already!"

"Well, I know someone who *could* help," Lucian said. "If he's alive . . ."

"Jagar?" Serah asked. "Lucian, I'm hopeful too, but we have to be realistic."

"Well, we know Ansaldra is alive, so *she* survived the palace's collapse. If that's true, it's possible Jagar survived. We should leave no stone unturned."

"I couldn't have put it better myself," Fergus said. "Jagar would be a good source of information, assuming he's alive. As far as Ansaldra, she's certainly the lesser of two evils. She can help us against Xara. If it were just Xara by herself, that would be one thing. We could just go straight after her. But she has an army of thousands at her back, and what's more, it seems she's reformed the Starsea Mages. Who knows how many of *them* are fighting for her?"

"Airships, too," Emma said.

"I suppose you have a point," Serah said, grudgingly. "But *helping* her? Maybe we need to go the assassin route. Find out where Xara is, and then, *bam*! Even *she* needs to sleep, right?"

"Risky," Fergus said. "One shot, and then the jig is up."

Mira cleared her throat. "I don't know much about this besides what you told me. Having more information would be useful. Do we know where this Malia place is, anyway? And what about this Jagar? How do we go about finding him?"

"Malia is in the southern part of the Golden Vale, on the Sea of Eros," Fergus said. "The second-largest city on Psyche. It shouldn't be difficult to find by air."

"As far as Jagar, I can reach out for him," Lucian said. "If he's alive, I can sense him."

"Without Xara sensing *you*?" Fergus asked. "That would take a lot of magic."

"It would, but I don't think we have a choice. He's the only source we can trust. If I reach out for him and find nothing, we can always go straight to Ansaldra as a backup."

"And Selene?" Serah asked.

"Well," Lucian said, "if things are the same as when we left, then she is still being possessed by Ansaldra. Not much we can do about that if we need Ansaldra's help . . ."

"Keeping the spaceship hidden will be the hard part," Mira said. "We have the cloaking screen, but its uses are limited. It won't stop the engine noise."

"Maybe there's a place we could hide it that's not too far

from Malia," Lucian said. "Maybe an isolated mountain or something. Is there anything like that down there, Serah?"

"The land's mostly flat in the south. A lot of forests and swamps, though. And you have to be careful of the forest dragons, of course."

"Forest dragons?" Mira asked.

"Yes," Serah said. "They're endemic. Highly poisonous, too. I'd much rather face a couple of wyverns than a single one of those things."

"Are there people in this forest, anyone who could report our ship?" Lucian asked.

"Not in the deeper parts. If we come down at night, it's probably doable. Then again, isn't all this pointless if Xara already knows we're here? What if she's detected our ship already?"

Lucian had to admit it was a possibility. Going into the forest would be a needless risk in that case.

"We won't try to hide," he decided. "She'll find out I'm here, anyway, if she hasn't already."

"Okay," Mira said. "What's the plan?"

"Jagar is a long shot, but we should at least try that first. If we don't hear from him, then we talk to Ansaldra."

Lucian knew things were about to come to a head. But he had to remember Lakhmu's teachings. He had to trust himself.

Recalling the image of the terrain just outside the ship, Lucian opened a portal back. Once through, they entered *Blood Wyvern* to plot their next moves.

29

MIRA PILOTED them above the southern half of the moon, which was mostly open water. It would be unlikely for Xara's airships to range so far. From the wardroom, Lucian delved the Ether.

He recalled Jagar's image and sought a connection. It had been about a year since they'd seen each other, though it seemed much longer. It was hard for Lucian to recall his grizzled face, gray beard, and hooded eyes.

There was no connection. He was about to give up when he received a vision. Jagar was riding on top of a wyvern, a determined expression on his weathered face. It wasn't just any wyvern, though. It was the same creature they'd found by his cabin on the Sandsea.

Akhekh. This vision wasn't a fluke. Jagar was alive and well.

Jagar? It's Lucian. Can you hear me?

Lucian felt hesitation on Jagar's part, followed by a feeling of disbelief. *Lucian? Boy, is that you?*

Yeah, it's me. I'm back. I was hoping you'd be alive.

Rotting hell, lad! Listen, you've come back at the wrong time.

There was a pause. *Wait. Don't tell me the League caught you. How could you let them do that?*

Jagar, you know me better than that. I'm here to stop Xara Mallis. Maybe Ansaldra, too.

There was a long silence. Lucian thought he'd lost him.

Finally, Jagar responded. *Listen. I can't talk like this. This link is too risky. I know you're masking it, but Xara is wily. Meet me at the Valley of the Faithful. It's in the Mountains of Madness. It's a place where neither Ansaldra nor Xara can find us.*

Where is it?

It's hard to say exactly, but it's about five hundred kilometers south of Dara and the Pass of Madness, in a long green valley on the eastern side of the mountains. As you get closer, you'll know.

Lucian wasn't sure how that would be possible, but he supposed he could figure it out when they got closer.

I assume you have a ship? I saw you blasting off on one while I was making my escape.

Yes, but it's a different ship now.

You can explain it when you get here, boy. Just don't be surprised when you land.

Lucian didn't have the chance to ask what he meant. The connection fizzled out.

He ran to the bridge, and his mother looked at him questioningly. He picked up the intercom.

"Everyone, to the bridge. Jagar's alive, and we're going to meet him."

———

THE RISING sun cast the towering Mountains of Madness in gold. *Blood Wyvern* idled above a deep, green valley in between the eastern and western ranges. There were only a few large valleys in the Mountains of Madness, but this was the largest one they'd seen. It had to be the place Jagar meant.

Of course, it was impossible to tell if it *truly* was, but things became clearer when Mira pointed out the forward viewscreen.

"Something's moving down there."

Lucian looked at a sharp mountain top cloaked in cloud. Indeed, the cloud seemed to move. Reaching for Radiance, he focused his vision until he could make out the finer details.

"Wyverns," he said. "Hundreds of them."

And they were all coming their way.

"What could they be doing?" Fergus asked.

But Lucian's eyes picked out what none of them could see. One of those wyverns was carrying a person.

"It's Jagar," he said.

At the realization, Lucian realized Jagar was trying to open a Psionic link.

Lucian? Follow us to the valley.

As one, the cloud of wyverns turned back toward the mountain.

"They want us to follow them," Lucian said.

They followed the wyverns into the long, green valley. Its walls were sheer, with waterfalls cascading down from melting glaciers. It was indescribably beautiful, a truly wild place that was impossible to access on foot.

Within fifteen minutes, *Blood Wyvern* settled on a rocky plateau. They exited to find thirty of the frightening beasts facing them not twenty meters away.

And in the middle of them rose Akhekh, the largest wyvern by far, who carried Jagar.

Jagar slid off the side of the wyvern in one smooth motion that belied his age, landing lightly on his sandaled feet.

Serah ran toward him. "Jagar!"

The two hugged, and Jagar chuckled. "Serah Ocano. I'm glad you're okay, kid."

She pulled back. "How did you get out? We thought you were dead!"

By now, everyone else had caught up. Fergus clasped Jagar's arms, while Lucian watched from behind them with a smile. Jagar had guided them across the western sands of Psyche. Without him, they would most likely be dead.

"I'm sure we all have stories to share," Jagar said, "but if you haven't figured it out by now, things have gone to rot here. As if they weren't before."

Serah watched the wyverns curiously. "Um, how haven't they killed you, yet? If you don't mind me asking."

"We're allies. We both want the same thing."

Lucian knew the answer to that. "The death of Ansaldra?"

Upon speaking the Sorceress-Queen's name, Akhekh and several of the closer wyverns glared at Lucian dangerously.

"That's right," Jagar said. "And believe it or not, the wyverns are at war with each other, too."

"Really?"

"We should head up to the caverns. Talk it over. Though your ship is quiet as far as spaceships go, it won't fit up there."

"What do you suggest?" Lucian asked.

"Pick a wyvern. Normally, they wouldn't consent to it, but I've assured them you can be trusted. You want the same thing as they do."

Lucian remained silent at that. He didn't like Ansaldra, but he might still need her. If the wyverns and Jagar wanted to give her justice after he'd dealt with Xara, then so be it.

"So, they'll let us ride them?" Serah asked. "Voluntarily?"

"Some won't, no matter what. But any of these around Akhekh are amenable. It's dangerous to be out in the open like this. I'd tell you to move your ship, but there's no other place to land it here."

"I . . . might just stay with the ship," Mira said. "No way I'm flying one of those things."

"Come on," Fergus said. "You can fly with me. I won't let you fall."

"I don't know . . ."

"Don't worry. That big one there with the black wings looks like it can carry us both."

"It's not far, anyway," Jagar said. "I don't believe we've been acquainted."

"Mira Abrantes," she said, holding out a hand. "Lucian's mother."

Jagar's bushy eyebrows rose appraisingly at that. He took her hand, lifting it and giving a slight bow. "Well, any family of Lucian's is welcome here in the Valley. But now I'm most curious about the developments outside this world."

Jagar's eyes went to Emma next.

"This is Emma Almaty," Lucian said. "She's a good friend and a talented Radiant. I've known her since my Volsung days."

"How do you do?" Emma asked properly.

"Miss Almaty, good to have you here. With you guys here, we can finally make some progress!"

Serah was already walking up to the small wyvern to the right of Akhekh, as bold as could be. She climbed up and sat between the sharp spikes on its back. "Well, let's get this show on the road."

Lucian took the wyvern to Akhekh's right, a large, dark beast who didn't seem thrilled to bear him. Then again, Lucian didn't know what the creature was thinking.

By the time Fergus and his mother settled on the wyvern next to Lucian's, Jagar took up his spot on Akhekh, towering over them all. As soon as he was situated, the wyvern gave a running start and took to the air. The others ran after it from behind.

For the second time, Lucian got to experience the wonder of flying high on the wind, with the cool breeze rushing around him. The green valley and its river ran beneath.

They headed for the western wall of the valley, a near-vertical mountain face riddled with cliffs and caves. Soon, they were landing on one of these cliffs which held the wide entrance of a cave, the interior of which became lost to darkness. Even *more* wyverns were at rest, all looking at the newcomers with either interest or animosity.

As soon as they were off their wyverns, they flew into the air above the valley or retreated into the darkness of the caves. Lucian couldn't help but notice a fetid stench emanating from within. Maybe Jagar was friends with them, but that didn't stop them from being the apex predator of the Mad Moon.

Thankfully, Jagar didn't seem to have a mind to go deeper into the cave. There was a small fire, down to coals now, which he fed with fresh logs and a burst of Thermal Magic.

"Tea, coffee, *kra*? I have all three."

"Coffee," Mira said. "Make it strong."

"Coffee it is."

Over the next few hours, Lucian told him what happened after Psyche. He'd told the story so many times that he had it down to an art by this point. He condensed the information and expected Jagar's questions, all while adding newer points.

A few hours later, Jagar knew as much as any of them and began telling his tale.

"Ansaldra had me on the ropes. Honestly, I think she was toying with me more than anything. Trying to get me to come back to her side." He shook his head. "When she finally realized I wouldn't do that, she truly meant to kill me once and for all." He paused, taking a deep drink of his coffee. "That was when the very foundations of the palace shook. The ceiling collapsed, rubble piling between us. I ran like the wind. I saw some light and went toward it. That's it. I got out. By and by, I found myself above the ruins of the palace. Looking at the devastation, I knew finding her would be impossible. And the guards were already circling the ruins like sand shrikes. If she was alive, I would have to come back and fight another day."

"She survived, too," Fergus said. "That man we met in the Riftlands said as much."

"I know that much. Her body didn't survive, but her mind did. They say she's taken the guise of a beautiful young woman."

That confirmed Lucian's suspicions. "Selene. We need to make that right."

"That's what I figured, too. Things are faring poorly for Ansaldra. But I know Xara Mallis. She will be just as bad for Psyche, if not worse. You wouldn't believe the tales about her, Lucian. They say she has dark magic that has made her more powerful than ever."

"Dark magic?"

"I'm only repeating what I've heard others say. I've scouted out Dara and asked around. If the stories are to be believed, if any mage stands against her, she just . . . *absorbs* their power."

Lucian frowned. "Absorbs?"

"Yeah. Absorbs. This dark aura surrounds her, and a stream leaves the other mage. It goes inside Xara, and . . ." He shook his head. "The mage just falls dead. And Xara gets stronger."

The mere idea of it was nothing short of terrifying. How many mages had already died? Had that been Vera's fate? If Vera's powers had been combined with Xara's, she was much stronger than Lucian imagined.

"No wonder Ansaldra fled," Emma said. "She doesn't stand

a chance."

Lucian cleared his throat. "So, how does this *absorption* work? Does she get all the mage's power? Just some of it?"

Jagar shook his head. "You're acting as if I know. I'm only repeating what I heard. If true, though, we have our work cut out for us."

That was a vast understatement. "She knows I have six Orbs, and she only has two. She also knows I'm coming for her. She'll want to reach Ansaldra, defeat her, and absorb her powers. Ansaldra is the most powerful mage on this world, and if she gains access to her abilities, even the Orbs might not be enough to stop Xara."

"Maybe so," Jagar admitted. "To make matters worse, most of the wyverns have joined Xara after she promised them the entire Riftlands. That's part of the reason you found it abandoned. Xara moved its population to the Golden Vale. Most Rifters are eager to see Ansaldra deposed, no matter the price."

"My father and the Elders of Kiro are with them," Serah said. "Do they know they're going to lose their homes to the wyverns after the war?"

"It's hard to know which side Xara is playing," Jagar said. "It just shows she can't be trusted. The only thing she cares about is reforming the Starsea Mages, and she intends to start on Psyche. The Wardens are completely useless in stopping her. Of course, they probably don't know she's here, and think there's some internal mage war going on."

"You said most of the wyverns are helping Xara," Lucian said. "Do you mean they're *fighting* for her?"

Jagar nodded. "They are allies. At least for now. Those wyverns respect her strength. The only ones who are *not* fighting for her are in this valley right now."

"So, what side are *they* on?" Serah asked. "Surely not Ansaldra's."

"They are non-aligned. They don't like Ansaldra, but neither do they trust Xara, after what I've told them. And yet we can't fight them both."

"You plan to let them kill each other?" Fergus asked.

"Well, that *was* the plan. But Xara is dominating the fight. The only way we can keep them fighting is by lending Ansaldra a helping hand." He laughed bitterly at the prospect. "Good luck convincing the wyverns of that."

"That would be difficult for you, too," Lucian said.

"Aye. That it would. There's no good answer here, Lucian. But maybe with you here, we'll have more options."

"From what I gathered, time is running out," Lucian said. "How long until Xara gets to Malia?"

"Even now, she's conquered everything of note. All except Malia in the south. She's still consolidating her armies, airships, and wyverns. All to make one final push that will fall like a hammer. It could be days away. No more than two weeks, but my guess is, it'll take on the order of a week or so."

Jagar looked at Lucian soberly. "Of course, if Xara knows you're here, she will move faster."

"We need to get moving as soon as possible. Do you think the wyverns will work with me?"

"You've told me your plans for Ansaldra. You hope to use her against Xara. They will just want to know what happens after the battle, assuming Xara is defeated."

"I'll leave that to you and the wyverns," Lucian said.

"She will want guarantees if she is to work with you."

"She has no choice *but* to work with me."

"That may be so, but as long as she has something you want, she can always hold it over you."

Lucian saw that much was true. "I don't know what's best, Jagar. I just want to stop Xara. You need to convince the wyverns she's the bigger threat."

He stared into the flames, brooding.

"How many wyverns are here?" Serah asked.

"About three hundred in this valley alone," Jagar said. "It's hard to say, but Xara has four or five times the number. And Ansaldra none, aside from the few her Psionic Mage-Knights have wrangled."

Lucian stared into the flames and thought for a moment. "Jagar, I don't know the right choice. So far, we've talked about just going straight for Xara and trying to knock her out. But surrounded by wyverns, mages, and soldiers, it would be too risky. I need to isolate her somehow."

"That's not too likely," Jagar said.

"What do we do, then?"

"Well, I might convince the wyverns of the Valley to follow you. Maybe. But I doubt they'll be keen on killing themselves in a suicide attack. They're smart enough to know when they're being used as cannon fodder."

"Well," Mira said, "if we had any torpedoes left, we might launch a couple at her army. It would be brutal, but it might get the job done."

"My dad and every villager of Kiro are in that army," Serah said. "Not to mention tons of other people who are caught up in it."

And Lucian had the thought that even *that* wouldn't be enough to stop Xara, outside of a direct hit she never saw coming. Even if she couldn't protect her army, she could save herself. She had saved herself during the Siege of Isis, after all.

There didn't seem to be *any* good answers.

"I don't know how you feel about this, Jagar," Lucian said. "I certainly wouldn't ask it of the wyverns. Even if she's on the ropes, Ansaldra has resources. Maybe the best way of getting to Xara is by strengthening Ansaldra's position. At least temporarily."

Jagar gritted his teeth. "Well . . . perhaps it *could* be done."

"Seriously?" Serah asked.

He gave a slow nod. "Akhekh would follow me anywhere. And I might convince some other wyverns to bring you as far as the Shadowed Forest. But they dare not fly any farther than that."

"Couldn't we use the ship?" Lucian asked.

"Not without being seen, no. Xara's airships are everywhere, and if she finds yours, she will know it's you. If you landed close to Malia, someone would see it." He nodded. "Aye, wyverns are best, under the cover of night. As the wyvern flies, the Shadowed Forest is a two-day journey from here, and the land in between is little-populated and untouched by the war. And wyverns are not as strange a sight as a spaceship."

"What about people *riding* wyverns?" Lucian asked.

"The wyverns won't let an airship close enough to see them," Jagar said. "You have nothing to fear. But a wyvern offers nothing for free." Jagar stood, and everyone else with him. "It would be best for only Lucian to come. To be frank, your presence is only being tolerated for my sake. I have told them already that you are the true Chosen of the Manifold, not Xara. They wish to test that claim."

30

JAGAR LED Lucian deeper into the caverns. They passed pods of wyverns along with the picked-over remains of past meals. The wyverns gave Lucian eerie stares. Their eyes were either all-black or all-white, the latter seeming to glow in the darkness.

Though the creatures couldn't speak, Lucian knew he wasn't welcome here. The feeling of despondence only grew the deeper they went.

At last, the cavern opened up, revealing an underground stream. That stream ran around a small island, on which Akhekh sat. He stood tall on his strong two legs, with his vast wings outspread for balance.

Lucian approached the island, stopping just short of the stream. More wyverns filed in from behind, forming a ring from which it would be impossible to escape.

Lucian remembered what Jagar had told him. The wyverns only respected strength, so he had to show he was strong. Not just in magic, but in spirit.

"Reach out to him," Jagar said. "He can't open the connection to you, but you can with him."

Lucian nodded. He formed a Psionic link and found the connection instantly.

Akhekh, Lucian said. *I need your help.*

The wyvern snarled. What came into Lucian's mind was not exactly *words*, but images and ideas conveyed instantly, with nothing lost in translation.

Why should we help you, human?

The way "human" was expressed let Lucian know exactly what Akhekh thought of the word. To the wyverns, humanity was comparable to excrement. And that excrement had come to Psyche and had spread across its surface, an unabated wave of filth driving the wyverns from the fertile valleys rife with game, to the cold highlands of the rifts and the high mountains.

The message was clear. Whatever Lucian offered for the wyverns' help had to make up for at least a part of that. There was only one thing that would be acceptable. One person who was viler than the rest.

Ansaldra had to be brought to justice.

I'm strong enough to defeat her, Akhekh. But I can't do it alone.

Ansaldra is powerful.

I'm stronger. Much stronger. But we must defeat Xara Mallis, too. If Ansaldra is bad, then Mallis is worse.

Akhekh's all-white eyes consumed him for a long moment. *Xara Mallis is strong. Strong enough for most of the wyverns to throw in their lot with her. She promised the Riftlands to us.*

If you believe in Xara so much, then why aren't you helping her?

Akhekh hissed. *We do not offer ourselves for empty promises. You must prove yourself.*

How?

Prove your strength. Show us you can destroy Ansaldra.

You're missing the bigger picture. What do you think Xara will do if she wins and you're the only wyverns who didn't help?

A long silence stretched between Akhekh and Lucian. He was thinking things were hopeless when the wyvern resumed the conversation.

Jagar's faith in you counts for much, human. Though it is against tradition, we will grant you one boon, hoping you will fulfill your end of the bargain.

What's that?

We will take you to the heart of the Shadowed Forest. Let that be your test of strength. Southeast lies Ansaldra's city of Malia. If you can emerge from the forest alive, then you are strong enough for us to follow into battle.

I will not fail.

Your metal wyvern can remain here. We'll take you there. But . . . we will require one hostage.

Hostage?

They will be treated well. As well as we treat Jagar. They can remain on the metal wyvern if they so choose.

Lucian was about to protest until he realized this might not be a bad thing. His mother would be safe, and she had no business being in a dangerous forest filled with poisonous dragons.

I agree.

Then your word is sealed.

The wyvern seemed to want nothing more from him, turning and heading deeper into the cave. Jagar approached him from the side.

"So?"

"They'll take us to the Shadowed Forest, but they want one hostage to remain behind. To ensure good behavior, I guess. They say if I can escape, then that'll be proof enough of my strength."

"Well, that's better than I'd hoped. Who will stay behind?"

"My mom. She'll put up a fight, but she'll be safe here. And maybe once I prove myself, the wyverns will let her come with the ship."

"Very good. Should we deliver the news?"

Lucian nodded. Together, they headed back to the front of the cave.

———

MIRA WAS ALREADY CROSSING her arms. "No way. *Uh-uh.* I'm not staying behind, and that's that."

"Well," Lucian began, awkwardly, "*someone* has to."

"And what? I'm the most useless, right?"

"You're hardly useless. You're our pilot, and we can't lose you. Besides, I just don't think it's a good idea for you to be in a dark forest known for its poisonous dragons."

She gestured to the cave behind them. "What do you think *this* is?"

Lucian wasn't sure how to respond to that.

"I'm roped into this now, and you're not getting rid of me that easily."

She was being stubborn, as usual.

"Mira," Fergus said, "it's a two-day flight on the back of a wyvern."

"I can handle it," she snapped. She nodded to Jagar. "*He* can stay behind."

"I don't count as a hostage," Jagar said. "Besides, the wyverns want me to go."

"Oh, to make sure we stay on the straight and narrow, huh?" Mira asked. "Well, that's smart of them, I guess."

"You don't have to stay in the cave," Lucian said. "You can stay on the ship."

"As if that helps. I'm just supposed to sit by myself, doing *nothing*, while all of you are risking your lives? I can't even go anywhere because the Wardens will detect me."

"I don't know what else to say. Look, I don't like it either, but it's going to be dangerous, Mom."

"I know that. It's just . . . hard to stomach, I guess. You being out there, while I'm stuck here . . ."

"I'm sorry. I know it's hard, but you won't be stuck here forever. You can join the fight when the time comes. When the wyverns fly out, maybe you can, too. But I absolutely *cannot* allow you to come with us. If something were to happen to you, it would be my fault. I couldn't forgive myself for it."

She let out a heavy sigh, but after a time, she gave an accepting nod. "Fine. Well, logically, it's what should happen. I know that. I just don't like the idea of it. How will I know to help you when it's time?"

"I can always come back and let you know. Just keep the engine room clear. That's going to be our warp-in point if we ever need to come back. It'll be fine, Mom."

"You're fighting Xara Mallis, Lucian. This might be the last time I see you."

Lucian shook his head. "Don't talk like that."

There was a long silence, and finally, she seemed to relent. "All right. I'll stay."

She sunk into a sullen silence. Lucian didn't blame her.

"Well, we should probably rest for the rest of the day," Jagar said. "We can get started at night under the cover of darkness. I can get the wyverns to fly us back down to the ship if it's more comfortable sleeping there."

"No need." Lucian was already opening a portal back. Jagar's brown eyes went wide at the sight, and even the wyverns seemed perturbed.

"Rotting hell, boy. What is that?"

"A portal. Don't you remember me talking about it?"

"I do. Still. Doesn't look natural." He frowned in thought. "Why can't we just use *that* to go straight to where we want?"

"I can only go places I have a memory of."

"Oh, yeah. Well, you can't expect me to remember every rotting thing you told me. I still think I'll fly down on my own. How do I know the Jagar that pops out the other side is the same fellow as me?"

It wasn't a thought that had ever occurred to Lucian. If that was the case, then it was too late. "Suit yourself. We've been using them, and we're still here. Just know that you might have to use it someday to get out of a tight spot."

"Well, I think I'll pass the time up here for now, if you don't mind. Never been one for spaceships, and being on one is just going to give me bad sleep. I'll see you down there this evening."

Everyone else went through the portal and back to the ship.

"Good to see he's alive and well," Serah said.

"His story is remarkable," Emma said. "A reformed Starsea Mage, *and* a member of the Council of the Wise?"

"Who also wants to take revenge on his wife," Fergus added.

"*Ex*-wife," Serah said. "Either way, he won't rest until he's had his vengeance. It's almost romantic."

"I think that's the complete opposite of romance," Emma said.

"I suppose our sensibilities are different on the Mad Moon."

"I have to say, this place isn't what I expected," Emma said. "It's quite beautiful."

"Hey, I'm glad you agree," Serah said. She smiled as if she'd gotten an idea. "Emma, maybe when all this is over, we can start a tourism company or something. Or better yet, a theme park!"

Emma laughed. "Lucian, maybe you can put that pirate money to good use."

"I'll consider it," he said. "A lot of liability issues, with the wyverns and all."

"Come on," Serah said. "We can make people sign something. And hey, it seems like the wyverns might be the good guys. People would pay a bundle to ride on one!"

Lucian couldn't help but laugh at that. "You have an imagination. I have to give you that."

"I think I'm going to get some sleep," Fergus said, stifling a yawn. "After dinner, of course."

"Same here," Mira said.

No one stayed up too long after that, choosing to get some rest.

31

THE NEXT EVENING, Jagar was waiting for them, along with four wyverns, of which Akhekh was the largest.

Mira stood on the boarding ramp to see them off. It was hard for Lucian to meet her eyes as he climbed atop his wyvern, who seemed to tolerate more than welcome him. His mother couldn't hold back her tears, as if he were going off to die.

For all he knew, he was.

"I'll be fine, Mom. Don't worry about me."

She shook her head. "You don't have a kid, so how could you understand?"

Lucian didn't have anything to say to that.

"Just don't do anything stupid," Mira said. "I love you."

"I won't. And—*whoa!*"

Before Lucian could say anything more, the wyvern took off at a run. It wanted this humiliating errand over with. It was all Lucian could do to hold on. Akhekh was to blame. The great wyvern had already launched itself off the edge of the plateau, causing the other wyverns to follow suit.

Within seconds, all were airborne, flying side by side toward a pass between two high mountains.

By the time Lucian turned around, his mother had become small with distance. She held up a single hand in farewell, which he returned.

"I love you, too."

He knew she couldn't hear the words, but he wanted to say them all the same.

They flew toward the dark eastern sky. It was cold in the heights, made even colder by the gusting wind. Those gusts came from the mountains behind, filling the wyverns' wide, leathern wings and providing additional speed.

It was an hour before they were past the mountains entirely. Far below them spread a jagged landscape of hills and canyons, cloaked in darkness.

With Radiance, Lucian could make out forests as far as the eye could see, along with a few winding streams snaking their way away from the mountains. The horizon seemed too near, a fact he had forgotten about being away from this world for so long.

The night passed uneventfully. They flew high enough that their passage could not be seen from below. There wasn't much chance of that, since this was a wild area of Psyche. He wasn't exactly sure where they were, but it was probably southwest of the Golden Vale since the landscape was rough and uncultivated.

When daylight broke in the east, they found a resting spot in the hollow of two large hills, whose sides were sheer enough to be an unlikely camping spot for people.

They set up camp while the wyverns went hunting. Little was said as they made a small fire and ate their dinner, a vegetable stew with caro pepper and some fish Lucian had tethered from a nearby stream.

Sleep came quickly and easily. When evening came around again, they set off southeast toward the Shadowed Forest.

The clouds were thicker on the second night, and the temperature far warmer than the foothills of the Mountains of Madness. Hills gave way to flat boglands, filled with soggy ground, still ponds, and wide, overhanging trees. Lucian hoped this place wasn't their destination.

The boglands were soon replaced with forest, with twisted, swamp-like trees, though at least the land seemed less sodden. The canopy extended as far as the eye could see in all directions, and there were various streams, all making their way east.

Just as the gray lit the eastern horizon, the wyverns glided toward a low hill rising above the thick forest. Their journey by air had ended. The trees were far too thick to see any potential threats, much more a forest dragon.

Almost as soon as they were off, the wyverns took off for the west. The only exception was Akhekh, who watched Jagar a moment before following the rest. Some communication had passed between them, but it was not for Lucian to ask.

They stood on that hill, surveying the Shadowed Forest to the horizon. This was the only hill, sheltered above the eaves of the forest.

Jagar grunted. "It'll be bad. Without Lucian, I wouldn't expect to survive this journey. Give me the Westlands and Fire Rifts above this rot any day."

Of course, Lucian could enter the Ether and brute force their way through this forest, or even tether everyone across the treetops. That would require separating people. Even for a minute or two, that could prove fatal. It would also be difficult to mask such a large discharge of magic from Xara. Though Lucian had his concealment ward up, after a certain point, it became impossible to hide magic if the streams grew large enough.

"How far are we away from Malia, Jagar?"

He shrugged. "It's been decades since I've been on this part of Psyche. The Shadowed Forest stretches a thousand kilometers east to west. It ends at the Golden River. I'd wager they dropped us a couple of hundred kilometers from the city. That's a guess, though."

It certainly didn't sound promising, and Lucian saw he would have no choice but to use magic if they wanted to get to Malia anytime soon.

"Are there any roads?" Emma asked. "That would make things go faster."

"Not this far out," Jagar said. "When people travel the forest, they use the rivers. But coming this deep is suicide. No one goes beyond the Webwood, and that's fifty kilometers from the river."

"Maybe that's what we should do," Lucian said. "Use a river. There's one over there, off to the south. Looks wide enough to navigate." He looked at the others. "Does anyone know how to make a boat?"

"Aye, I can," Jagar said. "All you need is a log and a lot of time."

"Well, maybe Thermalism can help," Emma said. "I read about it one time. Old Earth cultures would use fire to carve out a tree trunk. A dugout canoe. It's primitive, but if it worked for them, it could work for us. No way we can push through this forest. Lucian could even tether the boat downstream. That could make it go even *faster*."

"It's not a bad idea," Jagar said. "It would avoid the forest itself. But the waterways are dangerous, too. You never want to fall in, especially on the slower parts. Lots of nasty monsters lurking underneath."

"Monsters on land, monsters in the river," Fergus said. "Which poison do we pick?"

"The one that's faster," Lucian said. "I say let's try this dugout canoe idea first."

"All right," Jagar said. "If we angle southeast, we should hit that river after a klick or two."

The river was within sight of the hill. It would be simple to stream everyone down one at a time. But Lucian was not merely a mage. He was the Sorcerer-Ascendant, trained by Lakhmu himself.

He could warp everyone, and he was strong enough to conceal the action.

"Everyone, stand around me," he said.

"What are you doing?" Jagar asked. "Our own two feet will serve just as well."

"That forest will take hours to cut through," Lucian said. "If we warp down there, it saves everyone from being separated."

"I don't *want* to get warped."

"Just close your eyes," Lucian said. "We don't have time, Jagar. Even now, Xara could be sieging the city. If she's allowed to break into the city and absorb Ansaldra's power, it will make her too powerful to stop."

Jagar's face darkened at that prospect. "I . . . know you're right, boy. If it's what's needed, then I'll let you do it."

Lucian nodded gratefully. "Nothing bad will happen. I promise."

With Jagar appeased, Lucian focused on the riverbed in the distance, using Radiance to give him a view that was clear enough to connect the two points.

Then, using the Orb of Space-Time, he surrounded himself and his companions with a veneer of black magic.

In the next instant, they stood by the fast-moving river, the rushing water nearly at his feet. Tall trees overhung each side of the river, while the undergrowth was impassable. It was immediately clear that bushwhacking their way here would have been impossible without Thermal Magic.

Jagar blinked, dazed, then shook his head. "That was something."

Emma was already getting started on the canoe. "Here's a nice tree." She gave it a light kick.

"Looks like it has potential," Fergus agreed.

"How are we going to get it down?" Serah asked.

Emma cleared her throat and cracked her knuckles. "I've got it."

After everyone was out of the way, she raised both of her hands, from which a thin green laser sliced the trunk clean through. She angled it so that it fell on the shoreline with a thunderous crash.

"Nice work!" Serah said. "Now what?"

"Just do what I say," Jagar said. "We'll have a canoe before we know it."

Over the next few hours, they fashioned the vessel. They cut it the right length with a laser, even carving a curved bow and stern to help with water resistance. Lucian used Thermalism to burn the inside and Psionics to remove the ash. He increased the intensity as far as he dared, and smoke billowed into the air.

Once finished, he cooled the interior rapidly.

The vessel was complete and didn't look half bad, at least by Lucian's estimation. While he'd been working, the others had crafted some crude paddles. While Lucian intended to use tethers to guide the vessel downriver, having the paddles would help. There was even room to stow their gear.

"I'm impressed," Serah said, wiping her brow. "Good job, team."

"Now, for the moment of truth," Fergus said. Before anyone

could say anything, he pushed the vessel into the rushing water and hopped in.

"Hey!" Serah said. "Where do you think you're going?"

Taking his paddle, he turned the thing around, but now it was facing sideways while still going downriver.

Lucian pulled the vessel back with a tether until it was back on the shoreline. "Now, we need to *all* sit in it. I hope it doesn't sit too low."

"It shouldn't," Jagar said. "In Psyche's gravity, it should be perfectly balanced."

Soon, all five of them were sitting in the vessel, along with their gear. Lucian and Fergus pushed it off the shoreline and sat in the back of the canoe.

It floated perfectly downriver.

"Huzzah!" Serah exclaimed. "Malia, here we come!"

They rounded a bend, and Lucian saw a distant tree trunk. He created a tether from the bow of the canoe to the base of the trunk.

Instantly, the canoe sped up, the bow even lifting a bit as it skirted downstream.

"Whoa!" Emma said. "Careful with that!"

Lucian let go once they got to another bend. The team paddled madly to turn in time before crashing into a rock, but Lucian saved the canoe with another tether, aimed at a tree on the left. Once things were steady, Fergus nodded approvingly.

"Not bad. This might not take too long. And the river will only get wider and more navigable as we go downstream.

"Let's hope so, Fergus," Jagar said. "Just go easy on the magic, Lucian. If we go too fast, we'll lose control and be tossed into the river. We're safe as long as we are above water. Mostly."

The next few hours passed without incident. The sun fell behind them, and the river was gentle. Lucian's tethers had them going at the speed of a motorized boat, and he'd only slow them down during bends or narrow stretches. Schools of fish teemed in the shallows, chased by larger fish that had long, spear-like noses, like swordfish. Groups of flat, plastic-like creatures floated on the river's surface, similar to jellyfish. Sometimes the groups would be quite plentiful, up to a hundred, but thankfully, they could divert course away from them.

The river soon became a maze, a web of waterways eddying around various islands. The water was shallow, with sandbars that slowed them down. If it weren't for Lucian's tethers, they would have had to get out of the boat itself.

When the sun went down, the sounds of the river grew louder, and high-pitched shrieks emanated from the trees on both sides of the river.

"What the hell is that?" Fergus asked.

Jagar shrugged. "Just keep paddling."

Emma was out of breath. "So . . . tired . . ."

"Same," Serah said. "When are we going to take a break? We've been at it all day."

"Not outside the boat," Jagar said. "Somewhere in the middle of the water, where at least we might have a fighting chance of escaping."

"We can't go on like this forever, can we?" Serah asked. "What if we have to keep it up for a week or more? Rotting hell, that's a horrible thought!"

"We've made good progress," Jagar said. "And I have some idea of where we might be."

"Where's that?"

"This appears to be the start of the Webwood, and if so, that means we're getting close. The hard part is finding our way through. They say people enter this place, never to return."

"That's comforting," Emma said.

"We'll be fine," Lucian said. He was happy that they were

getting close. "So we just need to get past this Webwood, and then we're home free?"

"Well, it's not that simple. The Shadowed Forest is dangerous, however you slice it."

"I say let's push through, then. I don't want to stop here at night."

They wove around various islands. There was nothing but this swamp in all directions. It would have been easy to lose all sense of direction, but Jagar had a good sense of the stars above. When the tree cover was too thick to see the sky, Lucian combined Radiance and Dynamism to get a sense of the moon's magnetic field, using that as a guide. Psyche's magnetic field was weak compared to most other worlds, being dominated by Cupid's magnetosphere mostly, but Lucian was sensitive enough to discern the difference.

As the sun rose above the eastern trees directly in their faces, three streams combined into one. Somehow, they had found their way through the Webwood.

Lucian was about to tether them downstream when, at the junction of the waterways, a great ripple fanned across the surface of the water. That ripple turned into a wave, and then a fountain. The canoe would have keeled over if not for a tether Lucian placed on a nearby tree.

But the wave was the least of it. From the source of the disturbance, a massive, angular reptilian head rose from the muddy water, along with a long snout lined with razor-sharp teeth. A long, snakelike neck extended from the surface. The beast grew larger and larger as more of it was revealed, with the displacement of water pushing the canoe onto a nearby shoreline.

They escaped the canoe and stood to face the massive monster, who rose on four thick legs supporting its massive body, lined with green scales from head to tail. That tail was swishing now, with a long spike protruding from its end.

The poison dragon of the Shadowed Forest opened its cavernous maw, unleashing an unholy bellow that shook Lucian to his bones.

32

LUCIAN ENTERED THE ETHER, knowing that its use might tip off his location. He had bigger concerns at the moment. Like the massive green dragon staring him down, and now shooting slimy green poison in his direction.

He warped everyone onto the opposite side of the river, the spout of green liquid landing where they had been standing not two seconds before. The canoe was soaked from bow to stern, rendering the vessel completely useless.

Lucian reached for Gravitonics, instantly floating high into the air. He had to distract the dragon from the others. He reached out his hand, summoning Lightspear. The ethereal weapon manifested itself, shining resplendently. He shot himself at the dragon's head at lightning speed, spear extended.

The dragon dodged, opening its mouth to catch Lucian as he passed. But Lucian surrounded himself in an aura of fire. The dragon's head snapped back as it let out a high shriek.

Lucian flipped in midair, flying in for another attack. He collected a ball of lightning on the tip of Lightspear, unleashing it at the dragon. It let out a roar of pain as electricity sizzled down its body. It threw back its massive wings, beating at the air. The gust of wind it created was surprisingly strong, pushing Lucian back.

The dragon began lowering itself into the river, apparently no longer liking its chances.

But Lucian didn't plan on killing it. He created a link to the creature's mind. There was resistance—*great* resistance—but its strength was no match for Lucian's sorcery, especially after he had weakened it.

The mind control secured, he levitated toward the dragon and landed on its back. He secured the ward with three other Aspects, ensuring it wouldn't fall for a very long time.

He stood on the dragon's back, catching his breath. It remained still and docile, waiting for Lucian's command.

Lucian looked at the shoreline, where the others were watching in awe.

"Hitched us a new ride."

He made the dragon turn toward them, and water sloshed in their direction, soaking them from head-to-toe.

"Seriously?" Serah asked, who was now soaked to the bone.

"Sorry about that. Who wants to come up first?"

"Are you sure it's safe?" Emma asked.

"Of course. I'm not breaking a sweat."

Lucian pulled Serah up. The creature below them was so big that it could fit everyone without issue. It took some balance, but there was no danger of falling off. The dragon wouldn't move unless Lucian allowed it.

He pulled the others up. Once everyone was secured, he instructed the dragon to start downriver. Obediently, it went, using its massive tail to propel itself downstream.

"Your powers are incredible, boy," Jagar said. "They are not to be believed. When you controlled those fire wyverns, I didn't think that could be topped. The green dragons of the Shadowed Forest are the proudest creatures on Psyche. Wyverns are hard enough to control, but no one has *ever* done what you're doing now."

"Lakhmu taught me well."

"Not even Lakhmu could have done this. Perhaps Ansaldra could if she had a mind to, but even that, I doubt." He eyed the wide river ahead of them, lined on both sides with jungle. They were almost high enough to see above the trees. "It won't be long now."

"Let's hope we don't run into anyone," Fergus said. "This tale would spread for miles around."

"No one would stick around long enough to see us," Jagar said. "It's strange for this dragon to be close to the end of the forest. It might've been hunting. Perhaps that junction of waters would be the perfect place to catch prey."

"Well, it certainly worked out for us," Serah said, patting the dragon's back. "What should we name him? Stampy?"

"It could be a *her*," Emma pointed out.

"Good point," Serah said.

"This dragon is our ride, and little else," Fergus said. "We'll be parting ways soon, so don't get attached."

Serah sighed. "You are *such* a buzzkill."

Lucian had to say, riding on the back of a dragon above the still surface of the river was the best way to travel on Psyche. Kilometers flew by at a rapid pace, and the dragon never seemed to tire. Lucian had no difficulty holding the mind control ward, and it could last for weeks if he wanted it to. All the other creatures of the forest fled at their approach.

By mid-afternoon, the forest had become less wild, and the river gentler. Smoke rose in the distance. They were getting close to human settlements. Lucian spied a small village on top of a hill and committed it to memory.

"It's time to get off," he said.

Lucian tethered everyone to the shoreline, then sent the beast back upriver. Despite the distance, he had no trouble holding the ward. Normally, holding wards became exponentially more difficult with distance, but any ward created with sorcery rather than magery behaved differently.

Lucian dissolved it when the dragon was a fair distance away, leaving them alone on the shoreline with nowhere to go.

Lucian already had a plan. He recalled the image of the village and opened a portal to it. By now, it was dark, and hopefully, that darkness would cover them when they came out the other side.

They passed through, finding themselves at the top of the hill. The land was brighter up here, though the sun had already set over the eastern hills. No one was around, thankfully.

But the mere act of coming here was all Lucian had wanted. He now had a memory of this town, something strong enough to travel to with a portal.

He was utterly exhausted, and he knew he wasn't the only one. Serah was practically nodding off standing up.

"Anyone up for sleeping in a real bed tonight?"

"A bed?" Fergus asked. "What are you talking about?"

In answer, Lucian opened a portal to the plateau outside *Blood Wyvern*. "Back on the ship. I have a memory of this place now, so I can get us back here once we've had a good night's rest."

"Brilliant!" Serah said.

Jagar grunted. "This Space-Time Magic creates some strange possibilities . . . but I can't argue with it. It would be safer to pass the night in the Valley."

"Let's move," Fergus said. "Before someone sees."

———

WHEN THEY APPEARED on the plateau, the ship wasn't there. Lucian looked around, but there was no sign of it. A tendril of fear snaked in his stomach.

"Are we in the right spot?" Emma asked.

Jagar looked around. "Yes, this is the right place. If she's gone, that means the wyverns are, too."

Fergus looked into the star-filled sky, his expression worried. The plateau was utterly silent.

"She *wouldn't* have left unless something was wrong," Lucian said.

Several high screeches sounded in the air. Lucian looked up to see shadowed forms circling above by the dozen. More shrieks pierced the night as the wyverns descended toward them.

"They attacked the Valley," Jagar said, drawing his shockspear. "There's no other explanation."

There was no point in fighting them. Lucian *could* do it, but killing these wyverns would require a huge discharge of ether.

So, he surrounded everyone in a Space-Time aura, forming an image of the first place that popped into his head. He didn't know what made him recall the Spire in the Burning Sands, but there was no time to think of anything else. A portal would have used less ether, but the warp was faster.

As soon as he had a connection, Lucian completed the warp. And not too soon, as a pair of wyverns were seconds away from tearing into them.

Sand blasted him, as did the heat. He created a Binding and Thermal shield against both, covering everyone around him. Though it was daytime on this side of Psyche, the sand was so thick that it was impossible to see. With Radiance, Lucian pierced through the storm, spying the shelter of the Spire itself.

He pushed his way forward. As soon as they passed the threshold, they found themselves inside the vast Spire. Lucian took in the sight, and could hardly believe they were here. It would serve as a temporary shelter, far removed from where anyone could find them.

"Never thought I'd see this place again," Fergus said, looking around. "Brings back memories."

"Good ones, I hope," Emma said, looking around.

"Not so much."

"I have whiplash," Jagar said, blinking drearily. "This kind of magic doesn't agree with old bones."

"Let's get some food in you," Serah said. "You'll feel better."

Jagar gave a doubtful grunt.

As she set up a fire, Emma looked around. "This is where you found the Orb of Psionics?"

"Yeah. About a year and a half since we first set out across the sands to get back to civilization. Seems like a lifetime ago . . ."

Surveying the tower's interior, it was quite similar to the tower on Nai Elyn. The sand was scattered across the floor, far more than the last time he was here. Without the Orb to protect it, the tower was just another ruin. The ethereal glow that had once protected its surfaces from the ravages of time was completely gone.

Despite the situation, he couldn't help but think about his journey up to this point. Over three years had passed since that fateful day he'd discovered he was a mage. He'd begun at twenty, not wanting to embrace who and what he was. Now he was twenty-three, though, but with everything he'd been through, he felt decades older. It certainly showed in the lines of his face, which belonged to a man he no longer recognized.

"What made you choose to come here?" Fergus asked.

Lucian shrugged. "First place that popped into my head." He faced the others. "I'm going to leave you guys here for now. I didn't want to warp everyone onto the ship, since the space is limited. I have to make sure my mom's okay."

"Don't let us keep you," Emma said. "Be careful."

"Be back soon."

He opened a portal to the engine room of *Blood Wyvern*.

As soon as the portal closed, the deck heaved below him. He planted himself with a Binding disc, designed to do nothing more than keep him from falling.

There was too much commotion for his mother to hear him, so he waited for the ship to steady before letting go of the disc. He forced his way to the bridge. When he was close enough, he hollered.

"Mom?"

"Lucian?"

He made it, finding his mother flying the ship as if her life depended on it.

He strapped in beside her. "What's going on?"

"League Wardens, that's what! These wyverns came out of nowhere and started attacking the Valley. I had no choice but to pick up and leave. Of course, the Wardens caught my engine signature. No helping that. Lost most of them in the mountains, but there's still four left, and I've run out of mountains."

"Well, we can fix that."

Lucian imagined the airspace directly above the desert Spire, allowing his magic to feed into the Orb of Space-Time. He entered the Ether, surrounding the ship in enough Space-Time Magic to complete the warp. Lucian couldn't be bothered about being detected by Xara. Saving his mother was more important.

The next moment, *Blood Wyvern* was getting buffeted by the sandstorm. Mira deployed the deflector shield while Lucian warded the ship across all spectrums, rendering it invisible to radar, LADAR, and thermal scans.

"God, that was a trip," Mira said. "You came along just in the nick of time."

"Call it instinct."

She frowned at the display. "Scanners are showing this building in the distance."

"Yeah, that's where we are," Lucian said. "You can put the ship down in front."

"What are you doing out here? This is still Psyche, right?"

"Yeah, just the opposite side of the moon. It's safer. We were just going to spend the night here before warping back."

"I can never get used to jumping around like this. You could make the perfect conman, you know? Or a burglar or thief."

Lucian laughed. "Would you be proud of me if I did that?"

She shrugged. "Well, you could do anything and I'd still be proud of you. I'm your mom."

"I'll keep that in mind. Are you all right after that chase? Did the ship take any damage?"

She laughed. "Nah. Not with me at the controls. And I'm fine. I've been through worse, trust me. The worst part was thinking I'd have to keep it up forever."

Within minutes, they had settled down and Mira powered off the ship. Without the deflector shield, sand once again blasted the hull, but *Blood Wyvern* was more than capable of taking it.

"We're camping out in the tower for now," Lucian said.

"Why don't you guys come on the ship? It'll be a lot more comfortable."

Lucian couldn't argue with that. He went to the blast door, but as soon as it slid open, the others were already waiting outside. They must have heard them landing.

"What happened?" Serah asked.

"The Wardens found the ship. Luckily, my mom saved it

with some plucky maneuvering. And of course, I warped it here."

"What about the wyverns?" Fergus asked.

"I don't know. Hopefully, they got somewhere safe."

Jagar was quiet, his face despondent. Even he didn't know.

"Hey, we'll figure things out tomorrow," Lucian said. "We just need some food and sleep, right?"

Fergus prepared some food for the crew. They ate, no one talking much, and went straight to bed. Such was Lucian's exhaustion that he was asleep almost immediately.

LUCIAN AWOKE to find Serah was gone, though the sheets were still warm on her side. He rolled over, but when she didn't come back after a few minutes, he got up. He sensed that she'd gone toward the tower.

By now, the storm had died, revealing the unearthly beauty of Psyche's Planetside sky. Above them, Cupid loomed, its watchful red eye baleful. It was almost as if he had stepped back in time. As turbulent as those days had been, they were strangely nostalgic. He and Serah had only just met, and he couldn't help but think of their journey together, a journey that had taken them across entire worlds.

He found her standing to the side of the Spire's entrance, and he knew why she was awake. Though the desert sands had risen high above it, it was the approximate location of Cleon's grave.

She looked up as he walked toward her. He wrapped his arms around her.

"You think your magic can bring *him* back?" she asked.

It was a strange thought, and one Lucian would have never considered. "I think even magic has its limits."

She looked at the sands for a moment. "Well, his Focus has passed on by now. I think . . . he's at peace. Maybe we shouldn't mess with that." She gave a light laugh. "He was so *annoying* sometimes, complaining every step of the way. And yet, in the end, he became a hero."

Lucian nodded. "He accepted himself before I did."

"Maybe he knew he was going to die. When you accept your death, all the rot falls away. Only truth remains."

"Maybe so."

"What if you *could* bring him back, though? Assuming he'd be the same old Cleon as before. Would you do it?"

"I don't know. It's . . . a strange thought."

"You saved me when I should've died."

"Well, that feels different," he said. "I would've done anything to keep you from dying."

"What if you could make a portal, not to go to a different place, but a different time? What if you could go back and *stop* him from dying? Would you?"

"Where is all this coming from, Serah?"

"It's just hypothetical. I probably would."

"I don't even know if that's possible . . ."

But as Lucian thought about it, he grew more disturbed. Who was to say it *wasn't* possible? He was a sorcerer now, and if he could imagine it, he could make it so. He already knew how to move particular objects back using a reverse time aura. Could he do the same forwards? Could he just straight-up *time travel*?

"I'm surprised I've never thought of that," he said. "But then you have things like the butterfly effect."

"What's that?"

"It means over a long enough time, even small things can

produce crazy effects. They say that even the flutter of a butterfly's wings, over a long period, can change the weather on the opposite side of the world in ten thousand years, or something like that. Chaos theory."

"So if you were to go back and save Cleon and bring him here, it would change the present?"

"Possibly. Our reality might shift in fundamental ways. If I saved Cleon, it might give Ansaldra the extra seconds she needed to stop us. I'd be her puppet. Fergus might even be dead. Or both of us."

"But how do we know the reality you'd travel back to is *our* reality? Maybe saving Cleon in the past would just create a new reality in that timeline, while ours would remain unaffected. Maybe, as far as our reality is concerned, the past doesn't change. So, any change made to the past creates an alternate reality that has nothing to do with us."

Lucian couldn't help but chuckle. "Maybe so. But how could we possibly know? We'd have to try."

"Is there some flaw I'm not seeing? If I had your power, Lucian, I would go crazy with it. You're more of a thinker, but I would just do things as I see fit."

"That can be dangerous."

"I know," she said, somewhat glumly. "I have whims. If it were me, I'd just be curious and want to see if I could time travel. I would go into the past and find everyone I've ever lost. I'd explain the situation, and tell them to come with me if they wanted to live."

"That sounds like the premise of a holo-film," Lucian said.

"I'm serious, though. You think I'm joking, but I'd probably be creating these butterfly effects all over the place. Probably ruining reality. Eventually, the universe would just stop existing. It would give up trying to keep everything straight. Then,

I'd have to create a portal to a whole *new* reality, one where I hadn't messed anything up."

Lucian laughed. "Or I could just send Xara to another reality. Make her someone else's problem."

"Seriously, though. You probably have that kind of power if you wanted to use it. That's the power *every* mage would have if Space-Time Magic ever got out of your hands. I'm just one person, Lucian. What happens if thousands of different mages have access to this magic? Didn't Arian say that would happen if you gathered all the Orbs?"

It was an uncomfortable thought. "Maybe they wouldn't have the power to do it. Space-Time Magic is ether intensive and requires a lot of it to function. Even moving a couple of seconds into the past would probably be enough to exhaust most mages completely."

"Maybe," Serah said. "We won't know until you've got all the Orbs, right?"

Assuming that even happened. What Jagar had told him about Xara was terrifying. If she could absorb the power of other mages, along with Vera's powers, he might not have a chance. If she got to Ansaldra first, it might be game over.

They both stood there for a while, lost in thought. Originally, Lucian's goal had been to return the Orbs to the Heart of creation. To end magic once and for all.

But that was before he'd learned that the Gates would stop working. The Ancient One had told him that, and even if he wasn't to be trusted, that information needed to be verified.

Keeping the Orbs was just as bad. It meant war with the *Alkasen*, and not only them but the ones who had sent them. And it also meant holding off the Ancient One, preventing the Joining. He had a tool for that now: Lightspear. But Lucian had the feeling that driving that ethereal weapon into the heart of the Shadow was easier said than done.

Lucian remembered his resolution on Mako, the truth he'd arrived at. The idea of fighting for everything had given him power such as he had never known. He couldn't allow humanity to be destroyed, just as he couldn't allow it to be ruled over by the Ancient One, who was hell-bent on using Xara Mallis to absorb the power of any mage he came across.

If there wasn't an obvious solution, then he had to force one.

"Let's get back to the ship," he said. "As far as Cleon . . . let's let him rest."

"Okay," she said. "Sounds good."

They headed back to *Blood Wyvern*.

———

ANOTHER FEW HOURS LATER, with the crew rested and dawn just minutes away, everyone gathered at the pillars outside the Spire. Mira stood at the top of the boarding ramp.

"So, am I just supposed to wait here? There were already several quakes last night. Will it get any worse?"

"Hard to say," Jagar said. "It might. The Wardens might detect you if you power on the ship."

"They already know we're here," Lucian said. "They probably won't look for you here, but I wouldn't take the chance."

"No guarantees, then," Mira said. "Well, I can handle myself regardless. Don't worry about me." She looked them all over. "Well, what are you waiting for? Don't you have a universe to save or something?"

"We'll be back before you know it," Lucian said.

"Yeah, I'm sure. Go kick ass." Though she was putting on a brave face, Lucian could see the fear behind her eyes. It was easier to pretend he wasn't about to get *his* ass handed to him.

He tried not to focus on that as he imagined the jungle

village they'd left behind, creating a portal there. Through the vertical plane, he could tell it was nighttime. He stepped through, feeling the arid heat of the desert replaced by the sweltering humidity of the jungle.

Once everyone had passed, he allowed the portal to close behind him, shutting out the bright desert.

Lucian led the way out of the village, where a road led the way east. He had no problem seeing at night, and there was no one on the road, so he took turns tethering everyone one at a time down the trail. It was easy to fall into the rhythm of it. He could have tethered multiple people at once, but he was already holding a concealment ward and didn't want to stream too much. They were getting close to Malia now, and by extension, to Xara.

They passed several other villages on the riverbank. The river was wider, stretching hundreds of meters across. It was empty of craft, and smoke hung in the air. The acrid smell only grew more powerful as they walked.

After several hours, they entered the remains of abandoned towns, some already sacked by Xara's troops. Shells of buildings remained, and some ruins were even smoking. From the lack of bodies, Lucian guessed the citizens had abandoned this area days, if not weeks, ago.

They saw similar devastation in the countryside. Broken carts, abandoned goods, and finally, bodies left to rot. Judging from their sickly stench, they had been there for a few days at least.

Jagar watched the scene grimly. There was nothing to say. There was only the horrible realization of war and all its evil. It was but a fraction of the pain unleashed by Xara Mallis, and it was too much at that. No end justified such butchery. And yet, Lucian knew billions had died because of Xara's leadership not only now, but during the Mage War.

Lucian felt anger such as he had never known, especially when passing the bodies of children, dead next to their mothers and fathers. There were dozens of them. All massacred.

This senseless violence demanded justice. Xara hadn't likely done it herself, but her actions had caused it.

Lucian no longer cared if he was seen or heard. All that mattered was reaching Malia as quickly as possible. For all the evils Ansaldra had exacted on Psyche, she was not as bad as this.

He could not allow Xara to leave this world alive.

34

AS THE SUN rose above the surrounding forest, they found themselves before the white gates of Malia. The terror of the countryside seemed far away from this place. Its white stone walls and circular towers were sturdy, suggesting purity and resplendence that belied the truth of how it was likely created, with the labor of the Daran Empire's slaves.

Marring the pristine white walls were hundreds upon hundreds of tents and shanties assembled outside, refugees fleeing the crisis. As they wove through the squalor, it was impossible not to notice the people's thin and haggard forms. Their hollow, expressionless eyes followed Lucian and the others.

"Why can't they go inside the city?" Emma asked.

"They are likely keeping the people out to better withstand the siege," Jagar said, bleakly. "That way there are only so many mouths to feed."

Emma's face went ashen. "What happens when Xara's army comes?"

Jagar gave a bitter laugh. "You think Ansaldra cares about that?"

They arrived at the gates, made from solid steel and at least ten meters tall. They remained resolutely closed. Two of the Queen's Mage-Knights stood before the mighty doors, both wearing conical bronze helmets and colored robes. The left-hand one had a red cape and the other a yellow. A Thermalist and a Dynamist, then. Behind them stood a squadron of Hoplites, all armed with bronze armor and spears, about a dozen in all.

The Thermalist, who had a gruff, unwashed exterior and stubbled face, approached Lucian. "Sorry. Gate's closed. You'll have to continue on your way."

"Continue on our way to where?" Jagar asked. "There's nothing but the sea beyond Malia."

"Not my problem," the Thermalist said. "You can set up in the camps if ye please."

These two would prove no obstacle to Lucian, but he gave them a chance, anyway. "We need to speak with Queen Ansaldra. We are allies, and we've traveled a long way to be here. Ansaldra will deal harshly with you if you don't give us a hero's welcome."

The two men looked at each other and broke into laughter.

"You ain't seeing her Majesty, kid," the Thermalist said. "I'd sooner face Xara and her flying demons! Come on, enough with the jokes. We have duties to attend to."

Lucian sighed. "I must insist. I don't want to force the issue, but I will not hesitate to do so. If you can't take me to Ansaldra directly, then surely, I can speak to your Mage-Lord?"

"Piss off," the Thermalist said. He nodded toward his Hoplites, as if permitting them to deal with Lucian as they saw fit.

Lucian sighed. "I *tried* to be polite."

The hoplites stalked forward, brandishing their spears.

"Plan?" Emma asked, backing away a few steps.

"I'll handle it," Lucian said. "Just stall them a bit."

He delved into the Ether. Immediately, he became surrounded by an aura of Gravitonic Magic. He leaped high into the air, flying over the wall. He glimpsed passing guards and Mage-Knights, who were too shocked to do anything but watch with slackened jaws.

Below him spread a city of small and medium-sized white stucco buildings with red-tiled roofs. Cobblestone streets curved around hills, and the city spread on both sides of the wide river, which emptied into a vast sea filled with tumultuous waves. A stately fortress rose above the rest of the town, where the sea met the river on the western bank. That had to be Ansaldra's Summer Palace.

Lucian adjusted his flight path to fall on an isolated roof of the palace. He landed lightly and opened a portal to the front gate, revealing the sight of Jagar arguing with the Mage-Knights. Lucian was glad it hadn't come to blows.

Both of the knights stared at him in shock, along with the Hoplites.

He whistled at his friends. "Gate's open, come on in."

The others poured through, Fergus even giving a mocking salute to the guards as he did so. The soldiers just stared in disbelief.

With everyone on the roof, Lucian realized that this news would not take long to reach Ansaldra's ears. That was why Lucian intended to reach her first. He turned toward the central tower, seeking her out with his Focus. Her presence emanated from within the high central tower.

Jagar was already trying an exterior door, but it was locked. Lucian simply pushed on it with a reverse tether, blowing it off its hinges.

As they passed into the palace, Ansaldra's presence filled Lucian's mind.

You know, Lucian, you could have reached out to me earlier instead of going through all this trouble.

Well, I tried to tell the guards at the gate that I needed to speak to you, but they wouldn't let me in.

They wouldn't? Well, perhaps I will have their heads for that. This is a grave insult to the true Chosen of the Manifold, after all.

That's unnecessary. Where are you, anyway?

Why? So you can kill me?

No. I'm here to help.

There was a long silence as Ansaldra seemed to consider this. *You came all the way here to help me, Lucian? I'm truly flattered. You must feel something for me after all.*

This isn't about you, Ansaldra. It's about stopping Xara.

I see. Well, you may find me in my tower. I will call off my guards. For now.

"She's upstairs," Lucian said.

Lucian led everyone down a stone hallway, which accessed a wide set of spiraling stairs that circled up the central tower. Footsteps signaled the approach of a couple of Mage-Lords, with violet plumes and capes. Leading them both was Jarvis Tian, castellan of the Golden Palace, though now, Lucian supposed, he had gotten this job. A troop of Hoplites was also there for backup.

Jarvis seemed to be the one in charge, approaching with an air of confidence, his mustache drooping and his nose upturned in the air. In the last two years, the man had put on weight, and his face bore new lines.

"Queen Ansaldra has summoned you to her solar." When he noticed Jagar, he recoiled as if he were a poisonous viper. "What is *he* doing here? Guards! Arrest him."

The Hoplites moved, while Jagar reached for his spear.

Lucian surrounded his party with a Binding shield. The Hoplites frowned, not wanting to push into Lucian's shield.

"He's a friend," Lucian said. "He stays."

"He's not a friend of her Majesty!"

"He stays."

Jarvis heaved a heavy sigh, as if he had the most demanding job in the Worlds. Lucian thought that probably wasn't too far off the mark. The castellan turned to the Mage-Lords. "No need to escort him out, gentlemen. It would probably prove ineffectual. However, keep a close eye on his companions. Only by Ansaldra's order are they all allowed to be near her."

Lucian turned to the others. "You guys will be okay for a moment, right?"

"Of course," Serah said. "More than okay."

Lucian nodded at Jarvis. "Lead the way."

"Please. Follow me."

Lucian followed Jarvis, turning off the main staircase for another one, this one taking them to the side of the tower. At last, the stairs ended at a door that Jarvis unlocked.

When the door swung open, Lucian found himself in a spacious chamber of white stucco surfaces decorated with serene paintings, colorful rugs, and plush furniture. Reclining on a low couch, next to an open window that admitted the cool breeze from the Sea of Eros, was Queen Ansaldra, in possession of Selene's person.

She looked no different from what Lucian remembered, but there was something in her beautiful expression that told him he was dealing with Ansaldra rather than Selene. Perhaps it was the slight, superior smirk on her lips, or the way her emerald eyes gazed at him far too hypnotically.

"My dear Lucian," she said, rising languidly. "You moved the Worlds to return to me in my hour of need."

"I'm not here for you, Ansaldra. I'm here for answers."

"Well, for you, I can supply them."

Lucian ignored the obvious flirtation. "Xara Mallis must die."

She smiled. "Oh my. Tell me more."

"I need guarantees."

"Lucian, slow down. You're too eager. It's a bit . . . off-putting. Flattering. But still . . . *off-putting*."

Lucian was fast losing patience. "Ansaldra, I just passed dozens of dead bodies in some town to the north of here. If we don't move and move now, thousands more will die. Now is not the time to lie down on a couch!"

Ansaldra chuckled. "Noble. You remind me of Jagar when he was a young man. Of course, I corrupted him in time."

This was worse than useless. Lucian had expected Ansaldra to be a little more accommodating, a little more reasonable. A little more desperate.

"You thought I would be desperate," she went on, all but winking. Had she read his mind, although he had guarded his thoughts? "But you forgot one important thing. I am the Sorceress-Queen of Psyche. The rightful ruler of this world is *me*. I would *die* before giving up my place. I don't care how desperate the situation is. This is *my* queendom."

"Xara doesn't care about that. You *will* die, and that will be the end of that. But if we work together, at least you have a chance."

"Why work with me at all, Lucian?" She sounded almost bored. "What do you have to gain? You've already taken my home. Even my old body died during the collapse of the Golden Palace." She chuckled at that last one. "Although *that* wasn't much of a loss. Over the past two years, this form fits me like a glove. I feel like myself again."

Lucian wasn't sure what to say to that. One condition of his help was that she'd have to give up possessing Selene. But she had no other body to return to.

"Here's the situation," Ansaldra said, growing serious. "My advisors and I expect Xara's army to be here as soon as tonight. You must have come out of the Shadowed Forest because there's no way you would have gotten by the front lines. We've given up everything up to the city walls. They have yet to close the noose, but any day now, they'll show up. Most of my cities are flocking to her banner. Even the rotting *wyverns* fly for her. They outnumber us ten to one, if not more. There is no hope of victory, Lucian. None."

"Then why don't you surrender? Or is there some sort of plan?"

"*Plan?*" Ansaldra gave a bitter laugh. "There's *no* plan. I planned to wait for the city to be surrounded, and then challenge Xara directly, as impossible as that seems. Sorceress against Sorceress, for the fate of Psyche! It's almost poetic. But that would be a losing battle. Even if Xara consented, she would leave nothing to chance. They not only have the wyverns but nearly every airship in the empire, not to mention tens of thousands of soldiers. They even gathered those brutes from the Riftlands, not to mention the Western wastes. We only have a few airships that are low on ammunition for the cannons. We only have four thousand soldiers manning the city, and only a hundred Mage-Knights and ten lords and ladies who have remained loyal."

"I thought you had a lot of them branded. They're turning on you?"

"It's worse than that, Lucian." For the first time, her nonchalant façade dropped, and Lucian saw fear in her green eyes. It was subtle, but it was there all the same. "There are . . . reports. Reports of Xara having a new kind of magic. A magic that can directly attack a mage with no counter. It instantly kills them, but not before drawing every bit of ether they possess."

"I . . . heard the same thing. From Jagar."

"It's impossible to say exactly what is happening. But Xara is far more powerful than she was during the Mage War, and that should terrify us all. It's not just the Orbs, Lucian. It's not just her sorcery. It's something else entirely. A darker kind of magic, perhaps something outside the Aspects themselves, or perhaps composed of all of them. I faced her once in battle, in Tolivo up the river. What I saw defies words."

"Explain it as best as you can."

"There was great rending in the Ethereal Background. If ever she faced a mage, the fool was sure to lose. She would absorb their very power. The Focus itself. It all became hers."

"How many has she absorbed?"

"That's hard to say. Any who refuses to follow her gets their powers absorbed. Even Vera must have fallen in that way, for there is no sign of her on this moon. That's the best I can figure it. No one can replicate that stream. It's a sorcery given by a darker power."

"The Ancient One."

From the darkening of Ansaldra's expression, it seemed she had some notion of him already. "If Xara has Vera's powers, along with my mages, I fear we have already lost. The force that's possessing her . . . the Ancient One, as you've called him . . . you cannot resist him. Not even by sorcery. A higher magic is required. Not even your Orbs will be enough, Lucian, for his very Focus is bound to them. Indeed, even if you gather them, this will cause his Focus to overwhelm your own."

"It's not over yet. I just came from Mako, where I received training from Sorcerer Lakhmu himself."

"Lakhmu." Ansaldra's face became strangely nostalgic. "I didn't know he still lived. How is he?"

"He's . . . dead. Vera had placed a brand on me. He removed

it, and the action took his life. By the time I realized what was happening, it was too late."

"I see. Well, even if you've had Lakhmu's training, it isn't enough. Even I can boast the same, and yet I cannot withstand her power."

"I passed the Test, Ansaldra."

Her eyes widened at that before her brow furrowed in thought. "The Test." She watched him curiously for a moment. "Xara claimed she passed the Test, and in that way, won Vera and me to her side. Though Lakhmu insisted she hadn't, we saw her unreal power and witnessed her revelation."

"What revelation?"

"That she would find the Orb of Atomicism on Isis."

So, *that* was what had started it all.

Ansaldra continued. "All these decades later, a puzzle piece falls into place . . ." She looked up at Lucian. "Her power was such that we believed Lakhmu was mistaken. But it all becomes clear. The power she inherited in the cave was not *her* passing the Test. She took on the Ancient One, along with Vera."

"And you?"

She shook her head. "I . . . did not follow through on the Test. I got there, already severely weakened from the journey. And I just couldn't finish it. So, I lied to Lakhmu." She laughed. "I was just a young girl, then."

"What did Lakhmu say?"

"He knew the truth, of course. So when I learned Xara had passed the Test and had proof to boot—at least, proof that satisfied my naïve understanding—I gave up everything to follow her."

So that let Ansaldra conveniently off the hook. If she was telling the truth—something Lucian doubted—then only Vera, Xara, and Sharo Khalin had been marked by the Ancient One in that cave. He drove each student to separate purposes, to fulfill his own ends.

And all but Lucian had failed in their trial against their Shadows.

"What *is* that cave, anyway?" Lucian asked. "Why is the Ancient One's presence just waiting there to possess anyone who comes by?"

"Not just anyone. *Mages.* And not just those who use magic, but those who have ascended to use sorcery. The source of power is what might be called a Joining."

Lucian felt a chill at that word. "That was how it was supposed to happen. I was supposed to lose."

"Indeed. I already expect your next question. Why would Lakhmu send his most promising pupils there? After all, he never went himself." She smiled. "What, that surprises you? It was all for his prophecy that the one who passed the Test would be the Chosen. But unwittingly, sending his students there only gave birth to death and destruction. Without sorcerer vessels, the Ancient One could have never touched the galaxy. The *Alkasen* would have returned, of course, but the Mage War was not likely to have happened. Starsea is the Ancient One's dream, not any dream of Xara's, though the two of them are likely so knit together by now that she doesn't know where she ends and he begins."

That line gave him a chill. He remembered the columns within the Temple of Light, where the Shadow had said something very similar: *Where you end, Chosen, I begin.*

"Yes. The Ancient One tried to possess you, and it seems you have resisted. For now. If you deal with Xara Mallis, you are dealing with him."

"But doesn't the Ancient One know about Lakhmu's prophecy?" Lucian asked. "It seems he already knows I'm the

Chosen. If he didn't believe so before, he certainly does now. So why use Xara?"

Ansaldra was looking at him as if he were stupid. "Because, Lucian, she is useful. She is a means to get to *you*. But tell me. What exactly happened during this Test? What proof do you have that you passed it? How do I know you are not being influenced by your Shadow, trying to trick me?"

She seemed utterly calm for someone who thought she might be facing this possibility. Lucian saw she would need to see the evidence.

So, he held out his hand. A line of light materialized there, blinding to behold. Ansaldra raised her hand, streaming a Radiant shield to block that light. But from the way she was squinting, it did little good.

By the time he fully summoned it, its radiance subsided, allowing Ansaldra to look at him, this time with awe.

"This is Lightspear," Lucian said. "I fought the Shadow, the same one possessing Xara. The source of power spawned it in that cave by the lake. He attacked me with this spear, only it was dark then. We had a battle of wills, I guess you would call it. In the end, I made the spear mine, and it turned into this. I heard a voice speaking to me from the Manifold. It told me to drive this spear into the heart of darkness. And I drove it into my Shadow and vanquished it."

Lucian allowed the spear to dissipate. The bright sunshine pouring in from the window seemed dim in comparison. For once, Ansaldra didn't seem to have anything to say.

"I hold six Orbs now. Xara only has two. I also hold Lightspear, a weapon made from ether itself. It has already proven that it can destroy the Ancient One's Shadows." He watched her intently. "All I have to do is drive it into Xara's heart."

"Six Orbs . . ." Ansaldra said. "Remarkable. But Xara herself has two. I know, for she has displayed unreal power with Gravitonics, not just with Atomicism."

"I not only have the Orbs of Binding, Psionics, Radiance, Thermalism, and Dynamism. I also have the Orb of Space-Time. The Lost Aspect."

Her eyes widened at that. She stood and watched him intently. "Lucian, listen closely. I prophesied long ago that the Chosen would come to this world, that we would join forces. It would seem that prophecy is being fulfilled, though not in the way I imagined."

"We don't need to defeat her army, Ansaldra. We just need to defeat her. She doesn't know I'm here yet. She doesn't know I have Lightspear. She doesn't know that Lakhmu named me Sorcerer-Ascendant. All she knows is that she can no longer use Vera's brand to sense me. I passed his Test, and have proven his prophecy true." He made a fist. "I can defeat Xara. I *will* defeat Xara."

"Sorcerer-Ascendant." She gave a small smile. "That title among the Mako Masters doesn't simply go to the ones they wish."

"What do you mean?"

"If he passed that title to you, then it's because he judged *you* more powerful than Xara herself. Lakhmu could sense his pupils, even when they've gone off. I daresay the three of us women—Vera, Xara, and myself, sorely disappointed him, not to mention Sharo, who never joined the Starsea Mages, but forged his own path. Jagar was the weakest of us all. He desired to be the Sorcerer-Heir and would train day and night. Lakhmu's refusal to let him undergo the Test drove him to the Starsea Mages. One might say it drove him into my very arms."

"Seriously?"

Ansaldra nodded. "All that is the distant past. Jagar, too, is a sorcerer, but not on the same level as us. He never found his core truth." Her eyes became somewhat sad. "Well, that's a lie. What's the harm in telling you the truth? His core was me, always. When I became someone he no longer recognized, well, he lost that core. He hasn't been the same since. I broke him, and only now, when everything is lost, do I realize that."

"You act like you're proud of that or something."

She gave a devious smile. "Well, you must admit it *is* flattering. I don't think there's love anymore. How could there be? But he's lost his sense of self. Why else would he go hide in the wastelands, intent to mope until the end of his days? Now, his only friends are wyverns."

"And me. What's the point of talking about this? We need to talk about Xara."

"*You* will face Xara, Chosen, not me. Frankly, none of us have the aptitude. You have convinced me somewhat, though I remain skeptical." She nodded regally. "I will help you, such as I can. As you said, you don't need to defeat her entire army. I'm sure if you make your presence known, she will make hers known as well."

There was a knock at the door.

"Enter," Ansaldra said.

Jarvis opened the door. "Your Majesty. The rebel army is just hours from the city. We have sighted wyverns and airships in the southern skies."

"So soon?" she asked, drolly. She turned to look at Lucian. "They were going at a slow and steady pace for weeks, Sorcerer-Ascendant. But now, they are flying like the wind. Are you *sure* they don't know you're here?"

"I suppose it's possible."

"Well," she said, "let's make it a battle for the ages, then."

35

WITHIN HALF AN HOUR, the din of cannons from Xara's airships pounded against the alabaster walls of Malia. Wyverns screamed in the sky, smoke rose from the landscape beyond the city, and Ansaldra's brave soldiers and Mage-Knights hurled bolts and fireballs into the skies from the ramparts.

Lucian watched from the highest tower in Malia outside of the Summer Palace. For now, it was only an aerial assault meant to weaken Malia's defenses. A great mass of men and siege engines appeared on the distant horizon, tromping over charred farmland. Already, the tents outside the city were ablaze, and the fate of its unfortunate residents was unknown.

Lucian felt a moment of vertigo, a sense of unbalance from within. He reached for Psionics to block the attack, and despite his power, it required far more magic than he expected.

"You okay?" Serah asked from next to him.

"She knows I'm here."

Fergus stared into the distance. "Do we have any way of figuring out where *she* is?"

A thunderous boom sounded from well beyond the walls. A

shockwave emanated from somewhere in the forest, barreling outward at the speed of sound, flattening trees for fifty meters in all directions.

"I think we have our answer," Emma said.

The fallen trees were now floating in the air, supported by the magic of the Orb of Gravitonics. There were dozens of them, all massive and likely centuries old. They just kept floating higher and higher.

"Brace yourselves," Lucian said.

The trees stopped ascending into the sky. Lucian knew, without having to read the stream, that those trees would fall hard and fast on the outer walls.

He sprang into action, flying at incredible speed. He summoned Lightspear in his right hand just as Xara hurled the missiles against the outer walls. They all converged on a single spot next to the gatehouse.

Delving the Ether, Lucian pulled up on a nearby rooftop. He opened a portal right where the trees were going to fall, opening an exit portal above the forest from where Xara had launched the trees. He made the entry portal as wide as he could, ether roaring through him to accomplish his bidding.

There was a series of resounding cracks as multiple trees slammed into the wall, moving so fast that they broke the sound barrier, even igniting into flame because of the friction caused by air resistance. Men screamed and died as the wall crumbled before the onslaught. Despite this, perhaps half of the trees passed through the portal, crashing into the land from which they had originated.

Dust billowed out from where the wall once stood, making it difficult to see. However, Lucian's Radiance-enhanced vision could discern that the wall had been completely obliterated, leaving Malia open to attack by Xara's ground troops. Swarms of wyverns were descending on hapless defenders, while Xara's airships inched forward, maneuvering into position. The forerunners were already turning broadside to unleash their thunderous destruction.

There were hundreds of wyverns, dozens of airships, and tens of thousands of men and mages, all marching toward the gap in the wall.

Lucian reached out for Xara, and to his surprise, found a connection.

Fight me, Xara!

Aren't you the hero? Why cower behind those walls? Come meet me on the field of battle! I can tell my men not to interfere.

She was baiting him into a trap. And yet, what *else* could he do? Every second he hesitated, more people died. The wyverns were already rampaging in the skies above the city. Two circled down toward him.

With a frustrated growl, he latched on to both, shattering them both in tandem. Blood and viscera rained from above, which he avoided with a side-stepping warp.

Lucian was just seconds from being devoured by another wyvern. He created a portal in front of it, and a portal directly behind him so that when it entered, it skipped him entirely. As soon as the wyvern was safely past, he latched on to its mind, using a Psionic brand to bend it to his will. He commanded the wyvern to wheel back and land on the rooftop next to him. The wyvern promptly did so, its eyes violet-shrouded.

He jumped on with a gravity-assisted jump, and the wyvern flew north against the tide of invaders.

A few more wyverns diverged from their attack paths and focused on Lucian. He dropped one of them to the ground with a tether amplified with Gravitonics, while he threw Lightspear at the other. It pierced the wyvern's chest, flying straight through without pause. The wyvern screeched as it spiraled to the ground. Lucian willed Lightspear to return to his hand. Soon, the wyverns learned to stay far away from him.

On his left, an airship was turning to face him, its cannons ready to unload. He raised Lightspear on high, gathering Thermal and Dynamistic Magic at its tip. Using a tether, he connected the magic with the hull of the ship.

Instantly, flames covered the entire vessel. It tipped forward, even as men jumped overboard, preferring to die from falling than burning.

Ships and wyverns cleared the space surrounding him. He wondered what was going on, until he saw *her* hovering right in front of him, her dark cloak billowing behind, and her shockspear infused with lightning. It was hard to tell from the distance, but she seemed to be smiling.

He hardly had time to react as she flew at him with unreal speed, but that attack was a feint. A Gravitonic aura pushed down with unbelievable force.

Rather than contest the stream, Lucian tethered Xara, and she fell after him. He felt her trying to dislodge the tether, but he only increased its power, drawing her closer and closer to him, even as he fell. There was a moment of panic on her face. If Lucian was going down, she was going, too.

At the last moment, she released him, and Lucian was floating once again. But the tether was still active, and Xara couldn't break free.

With a grimace, her left hand became wrapped by orange Atomic Magic, with her right surrounded by yellow Dynamistic Magic. Lucian already knew what was coming. If the death lightning struck him, he would be obliterated.

Lucian surrounded himself with a Dynamistic and Atomic shield, which deflected Xara's attack. Lucian pulled her ever closer with the tether. She was just meters away.

She drew back her shockspear, its tip enshrouded with

magic designed to pierce Lucian's shield. Lucian released the tether, gaining some space. But rather than face him, she shot off, right over the fortifications of Malia as her troops breached the walls.

Rather than give chase, Lucian warped back to his friends. Only when he arrived, they were no longer there. He could immediately see why. The airspace above the city teemed with wyverns and airships. Fire rained from the sky, winged beasts dove into the streets, attacking fleeing civilians, while the airships' cannons blasted the towers and outer walls of the Summer Palace.

But of Xara, there was no longer any sign.

Serah? Where are you guys?

Inside the Palace. The throne room. Where the rotting hell are you? This place is getting blasted to smithereens!

Headed that way. Along with Xara Mallis.

Rotting hell!

Don't worry. I'll be there soon.

Lucian warped to the stairway just outside Ansaldra's solar. He got there just in time for a squadron of Hoplites, led by a pair of Mage-Knights, to run past him. Their eyes went wide at his sudden appearance. Lucian wondered what would have happened if he warped just a couple of seconds later, right as they were over his current position. He got the impression the results wouldn't be pleasant.

"Where's the throne room?" he asked.

"This way, sire," the lead Mage-Knight said.

"Go," Lucian said.

The soldiers led the way down the stairs, which opened into a hallway that was both long and wide, decorated richly with a red carpet, elegant paintings, and stained glass. They were only running a few seconds when one of those windows shattered, and in came four blue-robed mages on tethers.

The next moment was chaos, with the Mage-Knight who had spoken to him immediately dying when a reverse tether threw him against the wall. The Hoplites formed a shield wall, spears out, while Xara's mages focused on the final Mage-Knight.

Lucian floated above the Hoplites and blasted the blue mages with a kinetic wave. Once the hoplites recovered from their shock of seeing him levitate, they fell upon their foes and brought things to a bloody conclusion.

Lucian didn't have time to hang about, instead choosing to run down the rest of the hallway. Thunder and explosions sounded from outside, while screams emanated from the court-yard below. The city was falling far faster than he would have ever guessed.

Serah's voice entered his head. *Lucian! Where are you?*

Almost there.

He tethered himself to the far wall, where two of Xara's Mage-Knights appeared from around a corner, each wearing the yellow robes of a Dynamist. Even as Lucian flew, they raised their hands and sent lightning in his direction. He raised a Dynamistic shield, adding Radiance to reflect the attack. They screamed as lightning ran through them.

Lucian ran past them and through a wide archway into the domed throne room. There he found dozens of Mage-Knights, all gathered around Ansaldra, who stood in the middle of them all. There were also about eight Mage-Lords and Ladies, all wearing battle robes. Fergus, Serah, Emma, and Jagar waited with her, none of them seeming happy about it.

Every head turned in his direction as Lucian approached the center of the room, the Mage-Knights parting to make way.

"Good, you're here," Ansaldra said.

"Now, tell us your plan," Fergus said to Ansaldra.

"I will." Her green eyes took in her audience. "We can only

match Xara if we *stand together*. Not even Lucian alone can hope to face her. She's too powerful."

"I just did," Lucian said. "She just avoided me and flew into the city."

"She can *fly*?" one of the Mage-Lords asked, an older man with a trim goatee, who wore bronze armor over his robes, along with a green cape and plume.

"That, and other things that are far more terrifying," Ansaldra said. "She has the Orbs of Gravitonics and Atomicism. She can do much worse than fly, of that I assure you!"

"What's your plan?" Lucian asked. "We don't have much time."

"Yes. I've gathered my most accomplished mages. Along with your friends, of course. Xara has the power of who knows how many mages, along with her Orbs. If we hope to contest that, we must join streams, and lend the power of our Focuses to one individual only. A champion who can face her on equal terms."

"My life for yours, Ansaldra," a nearby Mage-Lady said. "Our Sorceress-Queen must stand against the invaders."

Ansaldra smiled graciously. "I appreciate the vote of confidence, Mage-Lady Laurelyn, but I shall not be the Focus of the confluence. That would be Lucian Abrantes. Lucian, the Chosen of the Manifold! He shall lead our collective stream."

The Mage-Lady gave Lucian a look of disdain. "My word! This young brute, this *barbarian*, is to lead our defense? My Queen, I have followed you to the ends of Psyche, but this I simply cannot condone! Ever since the first settlers of Psyche, my family has pledged allegiance to your name. If I might be so bold . . ."

Ansaldra raised her hand, and with a Psionic-Binding dual-stream, twisted the noble lady's neck, snapping it thoroughly.

The nobles let out a collective gasp. Even Lucian couldn't hide his shock.

"Does anyone else have something to say?" Ansaldra asked.

No one did.

It was at that moment that a great crash resounded from the ceiling above. Stone and masonry rained down. Lucian reached out his hands and pushed the falling debris back, saving the ones below from harm. But the walls simply kept falling, and there was no way Lucian could levitate it all.

"Help him, you fools!" Ansaldra screeched.

Lucian felt a sudden influx of power. At first, a few streams joined him, and then many. He delved into the Ether, having no problem getting that massive amount of power to do his will. He reversed the gravity streams bringing down the palace, launching the masonry high into the air, and pushing it Psionically so that it wouldn't fall on top of them. Then, he launched himself upward, Lightspear extended, using Radiance to pierce the cloud of dust.

Xara floated before him, a shining, resplendent figure. Wyverns and airships swarmed around them, but they did not approach. It seemed they intrinsically knew anyone who got in the way was liable to be killed.

Lucian was close enough to shout and make his voice heard. "You can't hide, Xara!"

Xara simply smiled. "Oh, is that what this looks like to you? I'm shining like the sun, while *you* were cowering behind those useless walls. Why don't you just give up? It would make this far simpler."

"After how far I've come? Keep dreaming."

"About what I expected. Do you know how powerful I've become, Lucian? I have something greater than even the Orbs. Not even you can stand up to it!"

"Is that supposed to scare me or something?"

Instantly, Lucian felt himself become heavier, but he warped aside to throw off the Gravitonic stream. He tethered Lightspear right at Xara's heart, but she dislodged it with a Binding shield of incredible power.

Lucian willed the spear back as Xara held out her hands, creating a sphere of orange and gray magic. Lucian reached out, reversing time around the dualstream. It petered into nothing.

"You did that easier this time," Xara admitted. "I can see that fool Lakhmu's touch."

Xara shot a column of fire from her spear, which swirled into a fiery tornado. Lucian absorbed the impact easily with the Orb of Thermalism.

"Is that all you've got?" he asked.

But while she had distracted Lucian with the fiery vortex, Xara was tethering someone toward her. It was Emma. She floated next to Xara, locked in a Gravitonic aura, her body seeming to be in some sort of stasis from aiding Lucian's Focus.

Lucian roared, but he couldn't undo the stream.

"She's helpless," Xara crowed. "Imagine how much harder this fight will be when her magic is no longer yours to command, but mine?"

Xara's body became wrapped with darkness, almost as if a Shadow were being cast over her. Lucian flew forward with reckless abandon, extending Lightspear. The Shadow retreated at its light, and Xara cast Emma toward the ground.

Lucian slowed Emma's descent, levitating her back to the throne room. Meanwhile, Xara was already pulling other mages toward her, two of the nobles from the throne room below. Within seconds, the Shadow extended from her body, absorbing the ethereal light from both of their floating forms. Once done, she cast their bodies aside against the ruined palace.

Emma had just been seconds away from sharing their fate. With her safe, at least for now, Lucian faced Xara again. A stronger version of Xara than before, who had the power of two more mages under her control.

"Now," Xara said, her face exultant, "let's see how powerful you are, False Chosen."

36

THEY BATTLED high over the devastation of the Summer Palace of Malia, trading shots with neither gaining an advantage, even as they laid waste to the city beneath them. Within hours, Malia had transformed from a beautiful city of pristine white towers to a smoking heap of ruins.

But as the battle raged on, Lucian discovered he had a key weakness: his friends. Any time Xara targeted them, it forced him to retreat to protect them.

Xara attacked him with every Aspect, and only with sorcery could Lucian counteract her. He no longer thought of *how* to counter her attacks. If he thought about it, he would die. He simply *did*, his sheer determination enough to mount a stunning defense.

At last, they were both floating above the palace again, all but leveled except for the throne room, where Lucian had created a sort of stasis shield, a self-sufficient brand bound by every Aspect. It was a significant drain on him, even with the magic of the mages at his disposal. But there was no other way to keep everyone safe.

Such were the extremes of their battle that it was more a fight for access to ether, which could only resupply itself so much in their general area. It wasn't as much a question of skill, but will.

And Xara's will was strong. She was a shining light, a continual fountain of ether. As was Lucian.

Xara levitated for a moment, seeming to consider her next move. Lucian floated before the highest tower of the Summer Palace, now broken at the top.

Xara had mostly kept herself detached, fearing Lightspear and shooting streams from a distance. That was why Lucian was surprised when she flew straight at him, spear extended. He used the Orb of Psionics to push her back. But as he did so, a Psionic shield surrounded her, a shield of surprising strength. She was throwing everything into that shield in some desperate gamble.

Lucian changed tactics, surrounding himself with an aura of fire. She neutralized that fire with a Thermal shield. They circled in the air, stabbing and swinging their spears at each other, each adroitly dodging.

Xara blasted him with a kinetic wave, one strong enough to eat through his shield. It knocked him a great distance back, which gave Xara enough of a reprieve to fly toward the barrier protecting his friends. She stood on top of it, raising her hands high and streaming an orange and gray orb with all her might, infusing it in the tip of her spear. If allowed to ignite, the fusion reaction would be strong enough to shatter the barrier for good.

Lucian shot forward, Lightspear extended, while reaching for the Orb of Space-Time. He could see Serah through the barrier, her eyes closed and kneeling as if in prayer. An ethereal glow surrounded her, a line of pure ether extending from her and permeating the barrier to enter Lucian. She looked at peace.

He only had one option left. It would mean giving up all the extra power of the mages inside the barrier, but he no longer had any choice.

Just as the bomb was about to go off, Lucian shot toward Xara, readying his magic. Just before he made contact, he imagined the scarred surface of Isis, the plain before the mountains that contained the Starsea Sanctum.

Within the instant, they were no longer on Psyche, but hundreds of light-years away. Lucian drew a fresh infusion of ether from this new landscape before Xara could do the same. She was just moments away from unleashing her fusion bomb; not even she could stop that reaction now.

He had to get away, but he couldn't gather enough ether in time to jump back to Psyche. He instead imagined the interior of the Starsea Sanctum and was there in an instant. It was silent, his rapid breathing the only sound in the darkness.

And then, there was a great rumbling that only grew louder with the passing of seconds. Lucian surrounded himself with a seven-sealed stasis, the only thing he judged strong enough to protect him from the incoming shockwave.

Within seconds, it was upon him. A wall of rock, fire, and pure energy blasted into his shield. Despite the shield's incredible strength, it shook like a leaf in a hurricane. Lucian flew up and away, along with all the debris of the mountain and Starsea Sanctum. Lucian was sure that there had never been a manmade explosion as large and deadly as this.

He kept flying up and up, and it was impossible to see through the debris surrounding him. He was shocked when he was *still* flying, even a few minutes later. The stasis held. The force of the explosion had been enough for him to achieve escape velocity, to be in *outer space.*

Up here, the debris cleared enough for Lucian to see the surface below him. He released all but the Binding and Atomic Aspects of his stasis ward, freeing up ether to warp him back down to the surface.

What he found was a massive crater, along with a pall of thick, radiation-infused dust. He shielded the residual heat and radiation of the blast, and with Radiance, began his search for Xara.

He found her resting a few kilometers away, behind a ridge that offered some protection from the dust. Almost as if she *hadn't* put everything into that attack just a few minutes before, she rejoined the melee, though with less vigor.

He pushed Xara with a kinetic wave, as far as he could to create some distance. She didn't seem to have the magic to block the attack and flew backward at incredible speed. She quickly gained control and landed on her feet. She raised her hand and sent a lance of fire and lightning in Lucian's direction. He shielded Thermalism and Dynamism, eating the impact. He added Radiance to the shield, causing the magic to be reflected at Xara. She did the same thing, which caused the stream to remain suspended in the air between them.

Xara cut off the stream, probably having depleted her ether reserves. While she was infusing herself with more, the lines of light entering her from all around, Lucian knew this was the time to strike.

He tethered himself to the ground right in front of her, extending Lightspear. She dodged adroitly, flashing her spear to drive into his back as he passed. But Lucian was ready, warping himself back a few paces to dodge the blow. He came at her again while she was still in motion.

A kinetic push sent him hurtling back. He softened his landing with a tether, but Xara pushed him into the ground crushingly. He warped away before any damage could be done, right next to Xara. Before she could react, he imagined an environment that even *she* couldn't escape.

He streamed the ether to complete the connection. His truth had to be more powerful than hers. That was all there was to it. If it was, he would win.

Within the next moment, they were floating within the cone of the great volcano of Hephaestus. Taking a page out of Xara's playbook, Lucian streamed a gravity aura around her, sending her crashing down. That was worse than useless. She countered it without breaking a sweat and instead sent *him* hurtling down into the magma.

Lucian surrounded himself with the strongest Thermal and Binding shield imaginable right before he entered the bubbling surface. He felt the intense heat and pressure, but both Orbs kept him safe. Still delving, he waited, using Atomicism to transmute fresh oxygen within his bubble.

He couldn't count on Xara suffocating herself, even in Hephaestus's deadly atmosphere. She could always use Atomicism to have a fresh supply of air. There was practically nowhere safe for her to go on the surface. Eventually, she *would* expire.

But Lucian didn't want to wait around for days, or even weeks. By then, his friends would be dead. Even now, they were fighting for their lives on Psyche's surface. Without the stasis barrier, it was only a matter of time until sheer numbers overwhelmed them.

He had to believe defeating Xara was possible, otherwise, he never would.

Streaming more power into his shield, he allowed the magic to expand outward into the surrounding magma. The molten rock swirled as his magic gained control of it. He pushed it upward, the Orb of Thermalism pulsing with ether. The magma rose faster and faster, Lucian riding it in his bubble. The power of the Orb kept that magma focused as a single column of fiery devastation, and he pushed it all toward Xara.

Lucian warped himself out of the volcano to an island of rock outside. The volcano rose in the distance, fire and ash pouring from its cone. If Xara was still in there, there was no way she could have survived.

Minutes passed with no sign of her, but Lucian wasn't going to assume anything. The outpouring of lava and smoke became even more pronounced, and molten rock and ash rained from the sky.

That was when the volcano exploded outward at incredible speed. Lucian had half a second to warp himself somewhere else before the mass reached him.

He was now on the salt flats of Hephaestus, and even at this distance, he could feel shaking in the ground beneath him, could see the tinge of gray smoke on the horizon. He quickly realized the explosion had not been his doing, but Xara's. She had blown up the inside by creating *another* fusion reaction.

He reached out for her, feeling her somewhere in the volcano's vicinity. Adding Atomicism to his shield, he warped back.

He was back on the island, and had he not been holding Thermalism, the hot ash falling from the sky would have ignited him instantly. He opened himself to every Aspect, existing in the Ether rather than the Shadow Realm. He flew toward a shining beacon of orange and gray light that had to be Xara. Those colors were a sure sign she was gathering the requisite ether to create *another* fusion reaction.

She turned at the last moment, obviously surprised to see him shooting toward her like a bolt of lightning, Lightspear extended. Just as the fusion reaction unfurled, he used Space-Time Magic to warp them into orbit above the planet itself.

Lucian's air supply remained intact because of his shield, but Xara's fusion reaction still went off. Lucian strengthened his shield with every Aspect, and was blasted away from Xara from the sheer force of the explosion. He created a gravity well, creating a force to act against the incredible power pushing against him. He increased the force until he finally started not only slowing but heading back in Xara's direction.

He saw her floating against the backdrop of the planet, waiting for him to come. When Lucian was close enough, he tethered her and warped them both back to the surface of Isis.

He pushed off her, driving her into the dust. She staggered up, facing him with her spear out. They both faced off, neither going for an obvious attack.

Xara wiped her mouth, where blood had dribbled down, as she panted for breath. "It would seem . . . we are evenly matched."

Lucian noticed splotches on her skin that hadn't been there before. Having two Orbs afforded Xara some measure of protection against fraying, but it wasn't perfect. She had drawn not only on her Orbs but her own ether reserves. And she had overdrawn a countless number of times just to keep up.

And all of that had an effect.

"You're fraying, Xara. Do you want to keep this going?"

She smirked. "What do you want me to do? Give up?"

"That would be nice. Maybe you can fight on for a time, but if you give me your Orbs now, I'll let you live."

That was when Xara's eyes glowed with violet, Psionic light. "Whether I live, or you strike me down, the truth remains. You must face *him*."

"Xara, if you do that, there's no going back. You've lost. If you hand me your Orbs, I'll let you get out of this alive. I'll warp you to someplace on Psyche that's safe enough."

She spat. "I am the Chosen of the Manifold, *not* you! Vera's prophecy was about *me*! The Ancient One chose *me*! I passed Sorcerer Lakhmu's test. *I* received the revelation about the Orb of Atomicism. And you had to come along and ruin everything!"

"You didn't pass the Test, Xara. *I* did. It's time you faced the truth. Vera's fed you lies almost your whole life. I . . . almost went down that path. But maybe you just didn't have a friend to keep you from following her. Maybe that's the only difference between me and you."

Xara looked truly shaken before staring at him hatefully. "You pity me? Do you think the difference between me and you is a *friend*?" She laughed derisively. "I'm strong, Lucian. Stronger than even you know."

"And yet, I've beaten you into a corner."

"That's what you think? This is far from over."

"Xara . . ."

But already, she was throwing her hands in the air. The Shadow coalesced around her, just as it had when she'd absorbed the two mages from the throne room. That Shadow levitated toward Lucian, reaching out with a long, sinuous limb. Despite everything, she was going to absorb his powers.

Xara's body shook as she channeled the phantasm. Lucian held Lightspear in his hand, knowing that it was the only way to destroy this abomination.

The Shadow's voice entered his mind. *Inevitable. We are . . . inevitable . . .*

"Like hell we are." Lucian threw Lightspear, but the Shadow simply eddied around it.

You are mine, Chosen. The Orbs are mine!

Lucian reformed the spear in his hand. *No. You're just dead.*

The Shadow surged forward to consume Lucian, but he warped out of the way and faced it from behind. He drove

Lightspear forward, but the Shadow dissipated like smoke, reforming behind Lucian.

A coldness overwhelmed him, a general draining of all his energy and hope. He was so tired. He just wanted to lie down, fall asleep, even if it meant never waking up again . . .

But he remembered Serah, and he remembered his friends. He leaped into the sky, looking down at the Shadow from above. The Shadow vibrated, as if in anticipation, and floated up after him.

Lucian infused Lightspear with Radiance, shooting a beam of light out from the spear point. The Shadow simply ate that blast, absorbing the energy. It continued its relentless advance.

Lucian recognized the truth. There would be no more running for either him or it.

Either he died, or it did.

The Joining comes . . . the Shadow taunted.

Lucian threw his spear, keeping his tether active on the Shadow to guarantee a hit. But at the last moment, the Shadow dissipated, reappearing again just below Lucian, almost close enough to touch him.

Lucian cried out, surrounding himself in an aura of light, streaming it as bright as he could. Ether roared through him. He directed it all into a Radiant shield. The amount of light outpouring from his body would have made anyone instantly go blind. He was shining like the surface of a star.

But it did not stop the Shadow. It was determined, hungry to absorb his Focus. Lucian thrust his spear. At first, the spear's light eddied around the Shadow, and the Shadow came perilously closer. Lucian could feel its cold overwhelming him. Lucian streamed harder and drew *more* ether. All was white, except the Shadow itself, an island of black in a torrent of resplendence.

The Joining, the Shadow said, exultant. *The Joining!*

Lucian felt despair such as he had never known. Within the Shadow, he could peer into that great darkness. And in that darkness were ghostly, ethereal faces. Xara Mallis. Vera Desai. Others Xara had absorbed, including the two mages from the palace, all trapped within.

Lucian knew he wasn't seeing them, but their Focuses. All of them had Joined with the Ancient One, and if Lucian couldn't defeat him, he would as well.

The portal yawned before him, ravenous and eager to swallow him. Lucian felt himself surrounded by darkness, the light retreating. Even Lightspear seemed to lose its radiance. Such was the dominance of the Shadow that there was no obvious place to attack. The Shadow stretched all around him, out of range of his spear.

Xara watched him balefully from within the darkness, and within her, Lucian could see two lights floating; one was orange and the other was silver.

The Shadow was attempting to draw him in, but it was at that moment that he had a premonition. He could draw Xara *out* of the Shadow.

But she had to be willing.

Xara, he said, his mind connecting with hers. *It's not too late. You can stop this now by giving me the Orbs.*

You are not the Chosen, she spat. *I am!*

You're going to be trapped in there for all eternity. Is that what you want?

I'm already dead, Lucian. It's too late for me. The Ancient One has won.

Vera's ghost simply watched from the side, her gaze hollow.

Evil cannot overcome the resisting soul, Lucian said. *Are you consenting to this, Xara?*

You would spout Lakhmu's prattle at a time like this?

Stop being a fool! It's not too late. Resist it!

The Shadow pushed against him more powerfully. He felt his defenses buckling. The coldness and darkness deepened as the halo of light protecting him retreated. Hope was draining.

But still, Lucian had to try. *Your body is still here on the outside, Xara. Together, we can stop the Ancient One.*

Something seemed to shift in Xara, perhaps the fulcrum that would undo an entire ideology. Vera seemed to sense this because she broke her silence.

Xara, Vera said. *The plan must continue unabated, no matter our own emotions. Remain in place. Our sacrifice will ensure humanity's future.*

Vera is using you, Xara. Just like she tried to use me.

It was all Lucian could do to keep the Shadow from overwhelming him. If it absorbed him, all of his Orbs would join with Xara's Focus. She would be reborn as the Third Immortal, controlled by the Ancient One.

All that would happen unless Xara fought back.

Lucian only had seconds left. *Xara! I'm not trying to trick you. I'm trying to do what's best for you.*

Why? Why not let me die?

Even after everything, you don't deserve to be alone for eternity.

I . . .

Xara? Vera looked at her. *After so long, you would abandon everything? I allowed myself to die for the greater good! Hold on a little longer, and you will be well-rewarded.*

The Ancient One will betray you, Lucian said. *Fight back!*

Xara looked up at him, as if in realization. With a sudden decision, she reached with her hands toward Lucian. Lucian grabbed her, his form pure ether just like hers. The surrounding light expanded.

But Vera grabbed her from behind, catching her in limbo.

I won't let you escape, Vera snarled.

Lucian's vision darkened. He had remained too long in this place. His shield of light was practically gone, having only seconds left.

He had nearly given up hope when Xara's voice entered his mind.

You . . . are right, Lucian.

No! Vera said. *What are you doing?*

The Orbs of Gravitonics and Atomicism shone like twin suns in Xara's ethereal hands. And each of those hands was touching Lucian's own. In Xara's eyes, Lucian saw permission to take them, along with the realization that she had delayed too long and this very action would kill her.

But at least she would be free and atone for some of her past.

Good luck, Lucian. The Chosen . . . will know the way . . .

No! Vera screamed. *All our work, for nothing! For nothing!*

It was too late for Vera's plans because Lucian was absorbing both Orbs. Even as they joined his Focus, Xara's ethereal form dissipated, escaping the chasm within the Shadow, going to the Manifold from which it had originated. The light surrounding Lucian intensified, blasting away at the darkness. As the chasm closed, it silenced Vera's scream of terror, a scream that knew all of her plans had been for nothing, that this was truly the end for her.

And then the Shadow recoiled from Lucian, retracting into a small ball of darkness floating above Isis's surface, just a few meters away from Xara's prone form. The Shadow strengthened with sudden vigor, surging toward Lucian in one last ploy to absorb him. If it succeeded, the Joining would be inevitable.

But without Xara's influence, it was directionless. Lucian drove Lightspear directly into its heart.

An eerie, high-pitched scream pierced Lucian's mind as

Lightspear overpowered the Shadow, shrinking it little by little. Lucian's hand vibrated, and the pain was unreal, like touching the surface of the sun. His entire body shone white, the Orbs thundering within him.

And yet, he held on. He *would* survive this. He *had* to survive this. All he had to do was think of Serah, think of his friends, think of his mother.

They were waiting for him on the other side.

At last, the Shadow shrunk and was vanquished. And silence reigned on the vast plains of Isis.

37

DEEP DOWN, Lucian knew he hadn't defeated the Ancient One, but merely a piece of him, and a small one at that.

The Shadow had overcome Xara just as it had Vera. Their Shadows had joined as one, and the power of Lightspear had vanquished both this day.

However, one Shadow remained. Sharo Khalin was still alive, and his Shadow lived on. He would be a weaker challenge than Xara, but Lucian would not underestimate him.

And there was still the *Alkasen* to consider. Lucian could never forget that. This was not the end of his road, but the beginning of a much harder one.

He'd healed magic itself, repaired by the joined Orbs in his Focus. No longer would mages fray. The Madness would no longer visit them.

The wind swirled around him as his body shone with an ethereal light. Old wounds and hurts were mended, such as he willed it. He became the author of change, the author of reality itself.

He was the Third Immortal. He held not only the Seven

Orbs but the Lost Aspect, and what was more, he had prevented the Shadow from Joining him. The Orbs' power thrummed within his Focus. Anything he wanted to do, he could do it. With the Orbs, he held the keys to the universe, the secrets of creation and destruction.

He found he wanted none of the power. All he wanted was to go back to who he used to be. To be Lucian Abrantes, and nothing more.

But of course, that was impossible. He had to be content with having the power of a god. Or perhaps an Ascended Being. Admittedly, godhood would have its perks. Lucian didn't intend to remain immortal forever. Just long enough to finish the job, to stop the *Alkasen* and save humanity.

He looked at Xara's body. She had not stirred once since defeating the Shadow, proof that she was truly dead. He created a grave and placed her in it. It was strangely fitting to bury her here, the planet she had long been associated with, the planet where she'd found the Orb of Atomicism, where her journey had begun. It was also where her journey had ended, where she had partly atoned for her dark role in the Starsea Cycle. He felt a moment of regret, knowing he could have ended up like her, had it not been for the influence of his friends. Emma, especially, in those early days on the way to Volsung for training. Perhaps that was the role of friends. They kept one from diverging too far from the right path.

Lucian allowed Lightspear to dissipate. There was nothing more to do on this planet.

He warped back to the devastated Summer Palace on Psyche. The action was immediate, no more difficult than blinking. He stood in the ruins of the throne room to find a scene of madness and chaos. Above, the wyverns were swooping down, attempting to kill the mages of Ansaldra's court. He searched for his friends, finding them all thankfully alive.

"Lucian?" Fergus asked. "Rotting hell, you're alive!"

The others gathered, and Serah threw herself at him. He allowed a brief embrace before he considered the sky above. The other mages, those still alive at least, were shooting fireballs and lightning bolts, and attempting tethers against the wyverns, almost to no effect.

"I have to stop the battle," Lucian said. "Xara is dead."

He didn't even get to see them react. Lucian leaped into the air, flying high above the ruins of the city. Xara's troops were in the middle of looting the town, while the dragons were picking at straggling civilians.

The first thing he did was create a Binding barrier over the throne room so that the wyverns couldn't penetrate it.

One wyvern diverted course to attack him. He raised his left hand, grabbing it by the neck with a tether. It screeched as it flapped its wings madly, to no avail. Lucian connected to its mind.

Xara is dead. Tell the others to flee if they want to live.

He drew his arm back and gave the wyvern a telekinetic push, sending it flying into the distance. It shrieked like a banshee.

Slowly, Lucian's message spread. First a few, and then most of the wyverns flew toward the west.

The airships retreated, forming ranks again on the outskirts of town. Even the soldiers below paused their sacking of the city, seeming to sense a difference.

Lucian focused on other things for the moment. He noticed *Blood Wyvern* hovering high above the airships, far out of range of their cannons.

He warped to the bridge, appearing right behind his mother, who was looking down on the devastation of the city.

"Hello there."

Mira jumped out of her seat, placing a hand on her heart. "Holy shit, son, you nearly gave me a heart attack!" Her eyes widened upon seeing his general state. "My God, what's happened to you? You look awful!"

"Thanks, Mom. The battle is over." He nodded toward the city. "They just don't know it yet."

"Yeah, the wyverns are running from *something*, but the soldiers didn't seem to get the memo. Is everyone okay?"

"Yes. Can you touch down in front of the palace there?"

"You mean that giant complex of smoke and rubble?"

"Yes, that's the one."

As she turned the ship downward, she looked over at Lucian, who strapped in beside her.

"Lucian, what the hell happened here? You look strangely peaceful for someone who's just been in a battle. Does that mean you won?"

"Yeah. I . . . defeated Xara Mallis."

"Seriously? She's dead?"

"Yeah. I'll explain it all later. Right now, we just need to make sure our people are safe. After that, we can focus on saving as many lives as we can."

Within minutes, they were touching down in a destroyed courtyard. Once they locked down the ship, Lucian tethered them toward the throne room, which was completely open to the elements after suffering the devastation of the battle. There, everyone was waiting for him.

Ansaldra was the first to approach. Now that the main part of the fight was over, Lucian wasn't sure what to do with her. Justice demanded Lucian exorcise her from Selene's body, and yet, her idea had proven pivotal to holding on long enough to defeat Xara.

He ignored her for now, approaching his friends instead. "Everyone all right?"

"What happened?" Serah asked. "Is she dead?"

Lucian stood and looked at the entire group. Every pair of eyes was on him. "She's dead."

"Are you certain?" Ansaldra asked, her green eyes intent. "Is she truly dead?"

"Yes. What's more, the Shadow that possessed her is gone. I drove Lightspear into its heart."

"And the Orbs?" Fergus asked.

Lucian knew he had them. All the same, he reached for his Focus to feel them. The potential power he felt there was unbelievable.

"Both mine." He looked at the entire group, who stared at him in shock. "Xara's claim to being the Chosen of the Manifold is as dead as she is."

Ansaldra's eyes expressed awe, and perhaps even fear. Perhaps she realized her position was no longer secure.

"If he is the Chosen . . ." one of the Mage-Ladies said, "then wouldn't that make *him* the true leader of Starsea?"

Ansaldra seemed uncomfortable with this notion. "Well, that may be so, according to my prophecies. But he still needs guidance. A person of exceptional abilities and qualities must assist him with the administration of any star empire . . ."

Lucian just watched her, somewhat amused. She had no power over him, and she knew it. Despite that, she was grasping at straws.

Jagar, however, wasn't having it. "You're still possessing Selene's body and mind. That is not yours by right."

Ansaldra rose to the challenge. "Are you daft, my dear husband? If I hadn't done that, none of us would be alive right now. Not even *you*. It wouldn't have given Lucian the power he needed to match Xara. What do you think powered the barrier that protected us? If not for me, *all* of us would be dead!"

"What's your point?" Jagar asked, unimpressed. "We can't allow you to live and breathe in a body that isn't yours. You stole a young woman's life. For that, justice must be served."

"Now hold on a minute," the mustached Mage-Lord said. "Our noble queen has a point. Without her, we would all be dead. Is that so immaterial?"

"Sycophant," Jagar spat. He turned to Lucian. "What do you think, boy?"

The situation was sticky. He knew Jagar was technically right, and yet, if Ansaldra had not possessed Selene during the destruction of the Golden Palace, they probably wouldn't be standing here right now. That didn't make it right, but it was a fact.

He also knew Ansaldra hadn't done it out of the goodness of her heart. She had thrown in her lot with Lucian, knowing there was no future with Xara. At least with Lucian, she might have a chance.

The question was, would Jagar accept anything less than Ansaldra's death? Lucian had the feeling he already knew the answer to that question.

Ansaldra made her play. "By now, they've surely noticed the absence of Xara Mallis. We *must* restore order. I am still the Sorceress-Queen of Psyche. There's no one better for the job than me."

Even as Ansaldra turned, ostensibly to begin this process, Lucian pulled her back with a tether. She was getting a little ahead of herself. The action caused a gasp to escape the surrounding Mage-Lords and Ladies. Even Ansaldra's face was the perfect picture of affront.

"Did I say you could go?" Lucian asked.

Her face flushed crimson, and for once, it seemed she had nothing to say. Even Jagar was nodding approvingly.

She licked her lips. "How might I be of service, Chosen?"

"Jagar is right. You are possessing Selene de Mordred, and in your time as queen, you have committed many crimes."

Ansaldra almost pouted. "Do we *have* to do this now? As you said before, time is of the essence."

Without waiting for her response, he reached for the Orb of Psionics and attacked her Focus, forming a perfect block around it. A visible aura of violet magic surrounded Ansaldra as the brand took hold. It was the same attack as he'd done on her in the Desert Spire almost two years ago, only this time, he did so without effort. Within seconds, Ansaldra was completely neutralized.

And not only did he cut off her magic. He read her mind, down to her very soul, knowing every intention and every lie. With every Orb of Starsea, the action was as simple as a thought.

Lucian then knew his decision.

"What is the meaning of this?" she cried. "What are you hoping to accomplish by turning me into your enemy?"

He delved her Focus, looking for any proof that Selene might be in there. For all Lucian knew, she was gone for good. Lucian drew more power from the Orb of Psionics until he found what he was looking for. Selene *was* there, her personality buried beneath the Queen's dominance. With just a thought, Lucian could undo Ansaldra's hold on Selene for good.

Ansaldra's eyes widened as she recognized her peril. She fell to her knees. "Please, Lucian. Allow me to live, and I will serve you faithfully. My defeat is abject and total. My entire queendom is yours, and all the privileges afforded thereto. As said by Sorcerer Lakhmu, you are the Sorcerer-Ascendant, the

Chosen of the Manifold, the Third Immortal, and the unquestioned Ruler of Starsea! Allow me to live, and I will be your faithful servant, until my final breath. This, I swear!"

Lucian considered. He had to admit having Ansaldra on his side had its uses. But she had already shown her true colors multiple times. He remembered long ago when he had to deliver justice to the Eye that had pursued them in the desert. Though guilty beyond the shadow of a doubt, it had not been easy to execute the man.

But Lucian had grown. Ending Ansaldra, especially in this way, was distasteful. But she had committed crimes beyond count, and if *he* couldn't deliver justice, who would?

And he might have let her live—were it not for Selene. That she would continue to possess another human was inexcusable.

"Queen Ansaldra," Lucian said. "You say you will be faithful. But repeatedly, you have proven your faithlessness. I can't allow you to possess someone, especially someone I consider a friend. And I have read your thoughts, your memories, and your intentions. You lied to me about the cave on Mako."

Ansaldra's eyes narrowed dangerously. But there was nothing she could threaten him with. Not anymore.

"You said you didn't go in. But you did. You met with your Shadow. Your Test was not to defeat it but to resist it. And you didn't. It promised you knowledge and magic beyond your conception. While it did not possess you outright, you took that bargain."

Lucian could feel her struggling against her block, but it was like a fly trying to escape a trap. The more she struggled, the more hopelessly she became ensnared.

Lucian continued. "That sorcery, straight from the mind of the Ancient One, taught you to weave your webs and place an almost unlimited number of brands on anyone you wanted. He also taught you what you're doing now. Complete Focus transferal." He watched her closely as everyone around him listened. "Your journey ends today. If I allowed you to leave, you would still be here a thousand years from now, changing bodies as soon as you used up the last one. And perhaps one day, you might become strong enough to become a living conduit of the Ancient One." Lucian shook his head. "But that will never happen. I will release your Focus, and you will get exactly what you deserve. Nothing."

Ansaldra screamed, and failing to break her block, simply stood and ran toward Lucian, producing a small, curved knife she had hidden in her dress.

The action was as pointless as it was useless. Lucian exorcised Ansaldra's Focus from Selene's mind. And just like that, the Sorceress-Queen of Psyche was no more.

———

Selene blinked for a moment, befuddled. Then she looked around at the dozens of expectant faces, focusing on Fergus, who stood directly in front of her.

"Fergus? Where are we? Is this . . . the Golden Palace?"

Fergus went to her and helped her to stand up. She looked around at the devastation of the Summer Palace, obviously shell-shocked. But Fergus offered a comforting arm, which she took.

"It's a long story," Fergus said. "You've just been under the spell of the Sorceress-Queen."

". . . Where is she?"

"Gone. Her Focus has departed your body, and had nowhere to return to."

"Then . . . she's dead?"

"That's right," Lucian said.

Selene turned, noticing him for the first time.

"Are you feeling okay?" Serah asked.

"A little lightheaded," she said. "How long did she have me under her spell? The last thing I remember was the Golden Palace." With dawning realization, she turned to Lucian. "Did you use the Prophecy of the Seven to find the Orbs, like we talked about?"

He nodded. "It's a long story, but I have them all now. Right now, we're in Malia. The battle should be over, more or less."

"Battle?" Selene asked. She turned, apparently recognizing some of the worn faces around her. "Mage-Lady Miana? Mage-Lord Cantos?"

Both of them looked at the ground, apparently shamed that they had done nothing to protect her from the Queen.

"We shouldn't wait any longer," Jagar said. "I did what I came here to do. Ansaldra is just a memory now. But the clean-up is far from over."

Mira stepped up. "Well, it wasn't just *me* who came here. It was the wyverns, too. Maybe they can enforce the peace."

Indeed, Lucian could see through the broken masonry and into the west that the sky was aswarm with wyverns. But there were far too many to be just those from the Valley. It was *all* the wyverns, including those who had followed Xara Mallis.

"They know," Jagar said, in realization. "They know the Queen is dead."

Lucian looked at the others. "I need to find Akhekh."

Explaining nothing more, he launched himself toward the west, flying so quickly that he reached the wyverns in just a couple of minutes.

Akhekh was easy to pick out. He was the largest wyvern of all, and Xara's wyverns intermingled with the others, their former war was seemingly forgotten. Their screeches filled the air. Lucian couldn't be sure, but they sounded more exultant than warlike.

Lucian connected his mind to Akhekh. *What's going on?*

Ansaldra is dead! We are getting reports from the Western Sands that the Red Eye of Cupid has faded.

The Red Eye? Do you mean the storm on Cupid's surface?

The very one. It is our prophecy that it would end upon Ansaldra's death, just as it was formed by her coming to our world. The wyverns are now at peace. I must ask, though. How did she meet her end?

She was possessing our friend, something I couldn't allow. I looked into her mind and saw her treachery. I ended things there.

It was you, then? The Chosen will be most honored among wyverns indeed.

Akhekh, I have a favor to ask you.

To the one who ended Ansaldra, you can ask anything.

I need you to enforce the peace in Malia. There is still looting and fighting. Don't kill unless it prevents further killing. We must bring the city under control.

For the one who slew Ansaldra, our mortal enemy, we will do this. And we must ask for something in return. We would like to work out a treaty, to be honored until the end of days, that the Riftlands of Psyche and the Mountains of Madness shall be forever ours. We are content to let the humans have the Golden Vale and the deserts beyond. The Pass of Madness can remain as a conduit between both sides.

That sounds good.

Consider the treaty honored. Oh, happy day! Ansaldra is dead, and Psyche will be ours again!

The task complete, Lucian flew at the head of the wyverns. Well over a thousand flew behind him, right for the streets of Malia.

But he could see that the invaders were withdrawing, retreating north up the road along the river.

The battle was over, and all Eight Orbs of Starsea were his. He had defeated the Shadow possessing Xara Mallis. Vera Desai, too, was gone because of its destruction. Even Ansaldra Dara was dead and gone. However, things were far from over.

There was still one sorcerer who had visited the source of power on Mako. Though he had temporarily bested the Shadow possessing Sharo Khalin, Lucian had no doubt that the High Prophet still lived. He would not be as powerful as Xara, not by a long shot. But as long as the Ancient One's influence on this reality existed, Lucian couldn't underestimate him.

More than that, Earth was under threat by the *Alkasen*. The *Alkasen*, who would renew their efforts by attacking it, if only to draw Lucian to them. There was only one person who had the power to stop the *Alkasen*: the Chosen of the Manifold.

He thought it over as he looked down on what was now his domain. Now that he had all the Orbs, the next stage of his journey would begin. It was time to begin the search for the First Gate, which would lead him to the Heart of Creation. He didn't know where to start with that. There were far more immediate concerns, like making sure everyone was safe and provided for.

At least the fraying would no longer be a danger. Perhaps, with magic healed, and the Worlds at his back, it would be enough to stop the *Alkasen* from destroying Earth.

He flew back to the broken throne room. It was time to gather the citizens of this world, along with its mages.

It was the dawn of a new era. The fraying had ended, and the mages would be contained to Psyche no more.

EPILOGUE

"HOW'S THE Mad Moon today, Commander? Even madder?"

Commander Carthen ignored the captain as he looked down on the violet-tinged surface of Psyche's Voidside. The clouds were clearer today, affording a rare view of the Golden Vale. However, Carthen wasn't looking at the moon itself, but the readout on his slate, which he held in both hands.

Carthen wasn't an imposing figure physically, but he more than made up for it with his trim gray Warden uniform, coupled with the golden sun insignia of the commander pinned to his collar. He was the highest-ranking officer stationed on Warden Prime, the largest League defense platform in orbit around Psyche. Even a captain could be safely disregarded, but not for too long.

"Captain Warwick," Commander Carthen said. "Did you come here to give me more of your pithy remarks, or to update me on the status of the prototype starship?"

Warwick's face reddened slightly. "Forgive me, Commander. As you know, it's taken quite some time to retrofit our sensors to detect the quantum engine's drive signature. We have completed the transition."

"And?"

"The starship traveled across Psyche's surface to an area the locals call the Burning Sands. There, it dropped completely off our scopes with no warning."

"I see. What else?"

"We picked it up again above a city on the Southern Sea. Where the battle is taking place. It's still there, to my knowledge."

"I see." Commander Carthen had been keeping himself well up-to-date with that battle. The mages' internal affairs made for superb entertainment, and this war was certainly no exception.

But there was something strange about *this* conflict. It was above and beyond all previous ones. They had even detected the explosion of fusion bombs. Though Carthen was too young to have experienced the Mage War, his training had given him incredibly accurate simulations of it. And with the new technology the Pirates had, that allowed them to jump star systems without using the Gates . . .

Or *was* it a new technology? Somehow, it might all be connected to Lucian Abrantes, the terrorist who had assassinated Hegemon Palmer. Too many of the pieces fit, even if the overall puzzle made no sense.

At last, he responded to Captain Warwick. "It is time for us to intervene."

"We've *already* intervened."

"I'm not talking about a few ripsaws on a desolate part of the moon," Carthen said. "That was . . . ill-advised. I intend to take the prototype intact, of course, but the prototype is no longer the primary aim."

"What is?"

The commander's face grew stony. "Killing Lucian Abrantes."

"The terrorist?" Warwick frowned. "What does *he* have to do with it?"

"Everything, perhaps. There was no other way for that prototype to go from the Zion system to . . . *here*. Its cloaking abilities must have allowed it to slip by our sensors undetected. Lucian Abrantes and the Pirates' incursion into the Alpha Centauri system are connected. He is a powerful mage and a dangerous individual." He paused, considering. "I'm thinking it has less to do with this supposed *new warp drive technology*, as the media are calling it, and more to do with *him*."

"You think *he* can jump star systems?"

"Connect the dots, Captain. Abrantes appears in the Alpha Centauri System with Yang's fleet. Then, he disappears. The prototype ship is now logged to his name, and he is its absolute master."

"It's logged to *his* name?" Warwick asked, in disbelief.

"Indeed. Nothing we can do about that. And now, that same ship finds itself on Psyche. Despite its great speed, there is no way it could have made the journey across eight Gates in so short a time."

"Maybe Abrantes sped it up," Warwick said.

"Perhaps. But that also means Lucian is *on* that ship."

Even Warwick couldn't argue with that. "Well, that begs the question, sir. Why is he on Psyche?"

"Uniting the mages under his banner for one purpose. He is working with Admiral Yang of the Pirates. Together, perhaps using the Swarmers to do their dirty work, they want to bring the League to its knees."

"A bold conclusion."

"The evidence fits. We have witnessed a swift conclusion to the war, coinciding with the appearance of the prototype spaceship. If Abrantes can jump star systems, as I fear, then there is only one plausible conclusion."

"What is that?"

"The mages will no longer be confined to Psyche. If Abrantes can jump star systems, why can't he do it from the surface of a terrestrial object?"

"That would be a disaster."

"Indeed. Just what the League needs, thousands of prisoner mages running amok in the Worlds. Why couldn't he warp a *hundred* of the psychos to every League world, all at once?"

"What is your suggestion then, Commander?"

"There is only one thing we *can* do." He paused, lending gravitas to his point. "We must enact Operation Tabula Rasa."

Captain Warwick's face went white as a sheet. "Commander . . . there are tens of thousands of people on Psyche. Most of them are non-mages. Women. Children. Most of them were born on this world. Yes, it is a prison, but the execution of operation Tabula Rasa requires a mountain of evidence to justify. The Hegemon herself must approve it, barring an active rebellion that poses an imminent danger to the League . . ."

"If this isn't such a rebellion, Captain, nothing is." Carthen gave a small smile. "Unfortunately, the bombardment will destroy the evidence."

"I . . . see." Warwick cleared his throat. "Of course, I swore an oath to uphold the Constitution of the League. I stand ready to enact any orders you have, Commander."

The two men were silent as they looked out the viewports. The station was now over the Mountains of Madness, wrapping around the moon quickly. Cupid was a large presence, but strangely, its red eye had dissipated, leaving only a creamy white surface. It seemed an ominous sign, especially considering everything the commander had stated.

At last, Commander Carthen looked down at his slate,

accessing the code that would send out the order to every tachyon lance platform in orbit around Psyche, about two hundred in all. It was an order the combat crews would obey without question. It was the moment they had all trained for.

Commander Carthen pressed the button and waited.

Within seconds, pillars of blue light rained down on the surface, stream after stream. The unearthly light flashed on the two men's faces, a silent light show of death.

Commander Carthen smiled. He had never seen anything so beautiful.

THE END OF BOOK SEVEN

THE STARSEA CYCLE CONTINUES IN BOOK EIGHT

THE SIEGE OF EARTH

ABOUT THE AUTHOR

Kyle West is the author of a growing number of "science fantasy" series: *The Starsea Cycle, The Wasteland Chronicles,* and *The Xenoworld Saga.*

His goal is to write as many entertaining books as possible, with interesting worlds and characters that hopefully give his readers a break from the mundane.

He lives with his lovely family in the Atlanta area. Be sure to check out his site and sign up for his newsletter for updates.

https://kylewestwriter.com/

ALSO BY KYLE WEST

Prophecy

Bastion

Beacon

Sanctum

Kingdom

Dissolution

Aberration